Praise for

Avenger: The

"I am a huge fan of J.R.R Tolkien and Terry Goodkind and I seriously believe that these books, Defender and Avenger, could be another classic in the fantasy genre."
Reviewer Amy Sanders, Read To My Heart's Content Book Blog

"...I cannot wait for the next book in this series."
Reviewer Mindy Kleinfelter

I liked this one even more than the first...it is a joy to read some of the quips...some of them even made me laugh out loud. The story is filled with elements that a lover of fantasy will adore...I enjoyed the read and highly recommend it. —"
Reviewer Cheryl M.

I enjoyed this second book in the Sanctuary Series even more than the first (the first was good too!)
Reviewer Jen, Goodreads.com

Defender: The Sanctuary Series, Volume One

"This book is full of action, adventure, emotion and anticipation, so much so that I didn't want it to end!"
Reviewer Gina Hurteau-Jackson

"I have always been a fan of fantasy novels and this book rates way up there with "Lord of the Rings" and others...am so excited for the next in the series I can barely contain myself and please give this book a chance because it is really going to be one of the best of our time. Great author and great novel!"
Reviewer Amy Sanders, Read To My Heart's Content Book Blog

"The characters are well written and the dialog can be very witty...will gladly order the next book in the series."
Reviewer Jeremy/Andrea S.

"...despite my early reservations, I found myself wanting the next book in this series and I do recommend it to anyone looking for a fantasy with plenty of action and adventure!"
Reviewer Littleroonkanga2

"Cyrus leads a cast of wonderful characters and the character development is topnotch...I would highly recommend this book to anyone who loves to get "lost" in a fantasy world when they read."

DEFENDER

The Sanctuary Series

Robert J. Crane

DEFENDER
THE SANCTUARY SERIES: VOLUME ONE

2nd Edition

For information regarding permissions, please contact cyrusdavidon@gmail.com.

Find Robert J. Crane online at
http://www.robertjcrane.com

Cover art, line editing, formatting and layout provided by
Everything Indie
http://www.everything-indie.com

Dedicated to the memory of Joe Cook – a true warrior.

Acknowledgments

Writing a novel is a herculean effort, and requires much help. Here are the culprits involved:

Thanks to Diane Talluto and Rebecca Burns, two teachers who encouraged my writing efforts long before any others.

Every book needs a cover, and if you're writing a book on dragons, I think it better have a damned cool cover. Thanks to Daniel Lundkvist, an artist of incredible talent, for the Black Dragon. His work can be found at DLART.SE.

Much thanks to Shannon Campbell, Heather Rodefer, Kari Phillips, Scott Garza and Debra Wesley for all their contributions to this book. The four ladies mentioned, especially, took enormous amounts of time to read through the book multiple times on several revisions and render their opinions and assist me in fixing my (numerous) errors.

Thanks to the GC Alumni, who inspired me to finally work on a story I'd had in mind for years and years, and motivated me through praise and occasional threats to keep working until I finished. They helped me believe I could tell a story people would be interested in reading. I still hope that's true.

Thanks to my mom and dad, and my wife and kids. Your support has been absolutely invaluable. I couldn't have done it without you all.

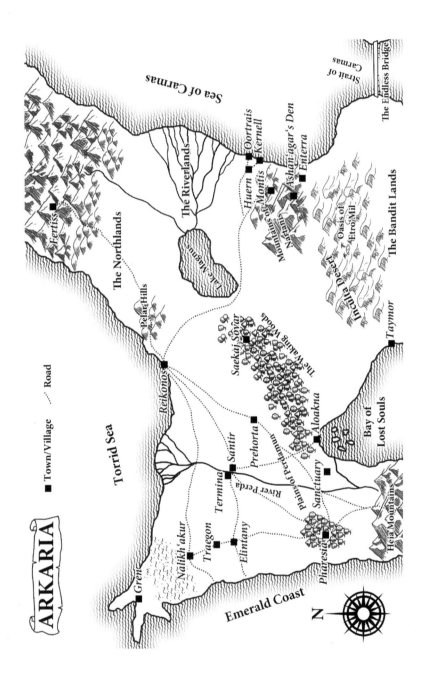

NOW

Prologue

The blood pounded in his ears as he rode his horse into the wind. *We're close to the end now*, he thought. The Plains of Perdamun had been set upon by a blustery autumn wind. It whipped across the front gate of Reikonos, through the crops of the farmers' fields, all the way to the valleys and passes of the Heia Mountains. It was an ill wind, out of the north, from beyond the Torrid Sea, and it smelled of decay.

Nestled at the split of the river Perda at the place where the northern branch flowed to the Torrid Sea and the eastern tributary flowed into the Bay of Lost Souls, there was a crater in the ground. Gaping, enormous, the only signifying mark on it was a simple headstone with an engraving that in beautiful, flowing script explained how the crater came to be in the midst of the smooth, unbroken grounds of the plains.

From across the lonely fields came the black cloaked figure on a white horse, making his way toward the scar in the ground. His traveling cloak revealed boots of metal, and hands that were encased in gauntlets. The hood of the cloak was raised and no helmet could be seen underneath. He rode to the edge of the crater and dismounted. With a gentle stroke across the back of the horse he walked away, a few murmured words in its ear; it whinnied at him in a friendly way.

He stared across the gap for a moment before his eyes came back to rest on the monument. Granite, glorious, a testament to the courage and fortitude of a group of fighters so noble that it took the power of the very gods themselves to wipe them from the lands of Arkaria. A feeling stirred, deep in his soul, one not felt in...years. One of longing, of regret, of the barest, most skeletal sense of fear. The last sensation was the most curious, since the tall, cloaked stranger had not felt afraid for a very, very long time.

He shook it off. He had seen great and terrible things in his time, and this was not nearly the worst of trials he had faced. Tracing his way back to the horse, he reached into a saddle bag and pulled out a leather bound tome. The worn cover indicated that the volume was hundreds, possibly even thousands of years old. A string marked the spot in the book that he was searching for, and once opened, he knelt and began to murmur an incantation. Reaching under his armor, his hand clutched something close to his chest. Invoking powers he had never before called upon, he whispered,

"I invoke thee who hear my plea,
I request thy aid,
For those who are soon to die."

Closing the book, he centered his vision upon the crater. A flash lit his eyes as powerful magics moved before him. Seconds later, another flash. Then another, then lightning, radiating from the crater's center – a shockwave of energy issued forth followed by a loud CRACK! that shook the countryside. The traveler, already kneeling, caught himself with his right hand, moved by the release of power before him.

An ethereal vision confronted him – like wisps of smoke, something began to wave and drift in the crater. Growing more solid, lines took shape and what began as the faintest afterimage became a building. It contained elegant lines and stones, archways and towers, but had a distinctly different appearance than a castle – it was made for a different purpose than housing an army and protecting its subjects – and was fading into view where once there was only the nothingness of the crater.

The traveler rose from the ground, cloak left behind him. His blackened armor glinted in the overcast day. His swords marked him as a warrior. His eyes surveyed the scene before him as though he were seeing a long lost friend.

And for the first time in long memory, the warrior smiled.

8 YEARS EARLIER

Chapter 1

Flames lit every surface in the caves and lava floes burned all around him, like some version of the Realm of Death he had heard tales of in his youth. There were flames leaping out of holes in the walls and floor like fiery stalagmites. Cyrus Davidon stood in the midst of it all, minding his steps very carefully, lest his black armor end up blacker still from an inadvertent scorching.

The sweat rolled off his face as he surveyed the group around him. Over one hundred adventurers, all with common purpose. They had come to this place intending to slay a dragon. There was some nobility in that, Cyrus reflected, but it was diminished by the fact that the dragon was trapped in these depths and not a threat to anyone but those looking for it. Which meant that most of them were here for the dragon's sizeable treasure hoard.

"There's nothing like fighting for your life with a small army of opportunists to watch your back, is there?" Cyrus murmured.

"You're not joking. It makes you wonder if there's even one of this lot we can trust," came the voice of Narstron a dwarf who had traveled with Cyrus for many seasons and had shared a great many adventures with him.

"Trust is earned, not given. This group is so raw they'll be dead before they even prove themselves," came the voice on the other side of Narstron. Andren was an elf by nature and a healer by trade, a spell caster with the ability to bind wounds through magical means. "This lot has seen far too few seasons – and this is likely their last. Dragons aren't to be trifled with." He peered at Cyrus with his eyes narrowed. "You'd better have a damned good reason for accepting the invitation of a stranger in the square to come on this mass suicide."

"I do." Cyrus looked around, body tense, eyes coming to rest on the expedition's leader. She was an elf, her armor was encrusted with rare gemstones.

"I have to believe," Narstron said, "that the placement of those gemstones has to cut down on the effectiveness of her armor by a good margin."

Andren snorted. "If that highborn elitist trash's armor has ever seen combat I'll eat the dragon we're going to face in one bite."

She had approached them in the square of the human capital of

Reikonos, inviting them to join an army she had assembled for the purpose of killing this dragon. "He's a tremendous threat to all life," she'd begun after introducing herself as Angelique. "He was the Dragonlord of the southern lands, King of all the dragons, and intent on leading his people in a march to war against all the northern kingdoms – the elves, the humans, the dwarves, the dark elves, even the gnomes!"

"What's this dragon's name?" Cyrus had asked her, eyes squinting against the midday sun in the square.

"Ashan'agar." Her voice was almost reverent.

Cyrus's pupils dilated. His breath hung in his throat.

Narstron shook his head. "I think we'll pass –"

"We'll go," Cyrus had answered, cutting off Narstron.

"Splendid." The elf clapped, such was her enthusiasm. "The treasure hoard for this dragon is supposed to be quite rich, and of course we'll split it equally, of course, after I take my fee for leading this expedition..."

That had been hours ago. Narstron brought Cyrus back to the present, in the fire light of the cave. "She's abrasive, even for an elf." He turned to Andren. "Why is it elves have no problem condemning other, younger races for their faults but praise is quick to flow and judgment slow to come when it's one of your own?"

"Don't go lumpin' me in with her lot." Andren eyed the dwarf in accusation. "She may be elven royalty. No low-born elf – you know, like me," he said with a touch of pride, "would ever lead the way she's doing it."

Narstron laughed. "How many elven royals are in your kingdom anyway? A hundred thousand?"

"Eh, a little over five thousand members of the royal family – and that's for the whole kingdom," Andren said.

"Makes me wonder how you get anything done."

"Halt!" Angelique held her gem-studded gauntlet aloft in a motion to halt the march. They were in a wide cavern, with considerable webbing in the corners of the room. There was no lava or fire, which was the first room without it that they had seen since entering the caves. "We need to address some basics before we go any further. I know that some of you are new, haven't seen much combat." She sniffed and made a face, as though she was trying to get the stench of something unpleasant out of her nostrils.

She droned for a few minutes about basic matters of combat in confined spaces. Cyrus took the time to look around at their army. It was a distinct mix of different races. He noted that the largest part of it was composed of dwarves, elves and humans. Though he hadn't noticed them earlier, there were three gnomes cloistered nearby. Quite small compared to a human of his stature, gnomes were often skilled in the magical arts. Cyrus also caught sight of two dark elves – blue skinned, a little shorter than humans, with pointed ears and white hair.

Cyrus's exposure to dark elves was limited. Although the city of Reikonos had a healthy dark elf population, they were ostracized, unwelcome in many shops, and forced to live in a specific section of the slums. Conversely, humans and regular elves were killed if they approached dark elven cities.

Most of the army seemed to be listening intently as Angelique walked them through such basics as minding your footing, sticking together as a group during battle and allowing time for the healers to assist the injured. Tuning her out, Cyrus realized that many of these adventurers had joined singly, rather than in groups as he had. Only a very few parties were banded together, seeming like islands in the middle of an ocean of people.

In the closest group to his, only a few feet away his eye caught those of a human man who had a bow slung across his back and two short swords in scabbards hanging from his belt. A slight smile permeated his lips as he met Cyrus's gaze. He touched two fingers to his head in a subtle salute to the warrior. *A ranger*, Cyrus thought; *a wanderer of the wilds.*

The ranger had three companions with him. The first was an elven woman whose sash and robes identified her as a healer, like Andren, tasked with mending wounds. Her face was expressionless.

The elf to her right was also a woman but wore the markings of a druid, a spell caster with the ability to control the power of nature itself. She had flaming red hair, almost the color of the lava and a bright smile that greeted Cyrus as he made eye contact with her.

Their third companion was wearing heavy armor that was molded to her form, but she was obscured by the shadows lingering around her. In the semi-darkness of the cave, Cyrus could see nothing of her face and only her silhouette told him she was female.

"Not bad," Narstron said under his breath, looking into the shadows at the armored figure.

"How can you tell?" Cyrus looked at him in confusion.

Andren and Narstron exchanged a look and chuckled before the dwarf answered. "You humans can't see in the dark for shite."

The ranger stepped forward to introduce himself. "I'm Orion." He was confident and at ease.

"Cyrus Davidon. These are my compatriots." He introduced the ranger to his band. "We're the Kings of Reikonos."

"Kings of Reikonos?" Orion looked at him with uncertainty. "Is that a guild name?"

Cyrus nodded, burying his unease at having such a bold name. "Interesting," Orion said, voice sincere. "I can't say I'm familiar with you. Where's your guildhall?"

Cy held back a slight flinch. Many guilds were bands of adventurers, and had great halls with enormous quarters for each of their members. The Kings of Reikonos had an old horse barn that had been refitted into a military barracks before being abandoned. It was in the slums of Reikonos. "We're not far from the markets and the square."

"Ah, centrally located. We're a bit off the beaten path in the Plains of Perdamun, about five hundred miles south of Reikonos." Favoring Cyrus with a smile, he gestured to the regal looking healer in his party. "This is my wife, Selene."

Turning to indicate the red-haired druid: "And this is Niamh." She flashed a smile at their party. "Hiding in the shadows over there is Vara." The silhouette gestured in what might have been a wave; it was difficult to tell for human eyes in the darkness.

"So," he turned back to face them and lowered his voice, "what do you think of the leadership thus far?"

"I'm still waiting to see some leadership," Andren said. They all got a chuckle out of that.

Finishing his laugh, Orion's face turned serious. "We're in for some rough times very soon. I know these caves and we are walking into great danger. There is a nest of spiders nearby," he indicated the webs on the walls, "that are the size of dwarves. Beyond this room are the dragon's guardians – rock giants that are at least ten feet tall, with a skin so thick it resists fire. This dragon, Ashan'agar, has a powerful hypnotic magic – he controls everything in these caves."

He paused for a moment to let it sink in. "With an

inexperienced group such as this and incompetent leadership it will be a miracle if this assault works. Stick close to us," he said, and the confidence he spoke with made Cyrus think that the army was listening to the wrong leader.

As if to punctuate Orion's observations, the expedition leader's words intruded into his thoughts. "...I don't know exactly what we'll be facing ahead from the dragon, but I predict that as dragons are solitary creatures, we'll have a clear path to the dragon's den."

Cyrus looked at Orion in alarm. "Don't you think you should tell her?"

The ranger looked amused. "I offered to counsel her with experience. She said she had it under control. I've walked in the shadows of these caves and she hasn't," he said with a trace of sarcasm, "but she has it 'under control'." He snorted. "I'm here to help save these people when things go wrong, lest they all die."

Chapter 2

Cyrus felt a twinge of fear at Orion's words. Human warriors were trained by the Society of Arms in Reikonos and didn't feel fear easily, nor often. From the earliest days of youth in the Society, they had a culture based around combat. If you won, you won. If you lost, you fought harder the next time. If you died you went off to the afterlife. Cyrus had feared neither death nor pain for himself since he was six summers old, and still didn't.

He looked at Narstron and Andren. On the outside they looked confident. He knew that inside, each was roiling. Though he never admitted it publicly, Narstron had once confessed that he knew that Cyrus was a better warrior – not because the human was taller or stronger, but because the fearlessness that the Society of Arms had instilled gave him an edge in combat that allowed him to make a commitment to battle that could only come from being willing to die at any moment.

Narstron didn't feel that, nor did Andren. They would fight for their comrades, but to die in a battle for the sake of battle? Only a true warrior – and a devotee of Bellarum, the God of War – could ever feel good about that. Faith in the God of War had been hammered into him in the Society from an early age.

But this fear wasn't fear for self, Cyrus realized. It was fear for those around him. He was their leader, and he brought them to this place. If either of them died, he was responsible. He choked on the bitter aftertaste of that thought.

A commotion broke his reverie. He watched as a spider half the size of a man spun down on a web and pincered one of the gnomes from above. Blood flew in a line, splattering across the floor, searing as it hit the hot rock. Cyrus jumped forward, along with a few others, dismembering the arachnid. Cries from behind him – and then to the side – caused him to look around.

The top of the chamber rose to a peak, and though it was too dark for his eyes to see the detail of the ceiling, he could see movement. The dome of the cavern was covered in the spiders.

Orion was at his side. "There are too many." The ranger's eyes were fixed; staring up at the imminent danger. Warriors and rangers took positions at the edge of the army, protecting the spell casters from the encroaching spiders.

"This way!" Angelique ordered from (far) behind him. Cy caught a glimpse of her in retreat, leading the spell casters toward the dragon's den. Shrugging at Narstron and Orion, they backed in unison out the door and onto a massive bridge that stretched for several hundred feet across a lake of lava.

The spiders halted at the entrance to the bridge. Backing up, Cyrus shot a look behind him and saw two guardians at the other end of the span. Spiders forgotten, Cy fixated on the ten foot tall giants blocking their passage. Seemingly hewn out of living rock, they stood silent guard along the path to the Dragonlord.

"Attack them!" cried a high pitched voice. With some alarm, he realized it was Angelique, and she began to charge across the bridge.

"Wait!" Orion's voice boomed over the army, and some of them actually halted – including, surprisingly, Angelique herself. A few continued to charge – one of the dark elves, a gnome and two human healers.

Approaching the guardians, the dark elf was half the size of his opponent and the two foot tall gnome disappeared under the foot of a rock giant. The dark elf brought his sword against the giant on the left. One of the humans, a healer, whose battle abilities were limited, made the decision to engage in the melee. A giant's arm swept out, knocking the healer off the bridge and into the magma below. With a scream, he dropped into the lava, and his pale skin sank under the fiery surface.

Horrified, they watched as the giants overpowered the dark elf and the other human and sent them both to a similar fate. As they disappeared below the surface of the lake of fire, a hush fell over the ragtag army.

A few screams filled the cave as an air of panic set in on the expedition. Broken bones and gashes could be healed by a mending spell. Powerful healers even possessed the ability to reverse death. Those were rare. Death and pain still held fear for adventurers, who were by nature a blindly optimistic lot. The less veteran among them had not faced this before.

Cyrus could see the panic moving through the crowd. "This is about to get very ugly," he breathed.

"No doubt." Narstron raised his sword. "For a group of people that consider themselves adventurers, I don't think these fresh faced rubes have tasted the downside of 'adventure'."

Looking back Cyrus saw the spiders had formed a wall blocking the chamber they had entered from, pincers jutting hungrily toward them.

"They're servants of Ashan'agar," Orion's voice came from beside him. "You know who he is?"

Cy nodded. "The Dragonlord exiled from the dragon kingdom in the southern lands. He was king of the dragon city Hewat at one point, wasn't he?"

"He was. According to rumor, something happened in their most sacred temple, south of their city in the mountains – something that caused a shakeup in Hewat about fifty years ago. He was exiled by the new Dragonlord and mystically sealed in this cave."

"Any idea what he did?" Narstron's face was screwed in concentration as he asked the question.

"No idea." Orion shook his head. "No one has contact with the dragon kingdom. They are not known for kindness to so-called 'lesser beings', so all we have are rumors and speculation." He focused back on Cyrus. "Everything in these caves is sworn to his service, and they obey his will. And apparently his will is that we go forward." Orion's expression twisted as he looked back at the spiders still advancing slowly toward them.

A call came from across the army, bringing their attention back to the rock giants in front of them. "No need to panic!" called the voice of the oblivious Angelique. "Run through them!"

Narstron rolled his eyes as Andren shrugged and Cyrus's jaw dropped in shock. The panic in the front ranks was evident and the fore of the army began to charge again. Orion's shouted plea for calm was drowned out in the commotion caused by the forward movement of the army-turned-mob.

Taking one last look back at the wall of spiders guarding the entry to the bridge, Cyrus started moving forward. He didn't fight to the front of the battle line, afraid to push any of the combatants off the bridge and to their deaths.

The rock giants were swinging their massive fists, battering their attackers and taking little damage to show for it. Every few seconds, one of their blows would land, flinging some poor soul off the bridge and into fiery death below. A few fortunate members of the force were squeezing between the giants and into the caves beyond.

Cyrus watched, incredulous, as the one of the giants knocked several of their number off the bridge. He was close enough now... and the giant was leaning over, beginning to straighten up after swinging low to send combatants into the lava.

Cyrus charged at the back of the rock giant. Sure that he was invincible, the giant didn't even bother watching his back. Cy hit him full force, slamming his pauldrons into the back of the giant's knees, buckling them. It wasn't a blow that could cause damage to the craggy skin of the giant – in any other circumstances, the rocky creature would have been able to fall to one knee, get up and smite him. Unfortunately for the giant, he was in a position where balance mattered. Arms pinwheeling, the giant plummeted into the lava which he had gloried in sending his foes.

Turning to face the remaining fiend, Cyrus watched as Narstron and Orion plunged blades through both its legs, breaking through the external layer of rock and dropping it to its knees facing the army. He watched as the giant fell amid a bevy of blades.

"Nice work, Cyrus. Never seen anyone take a rock giant solo before." Orion's eyebrows were raised, impressed.

"The rest of our army ran through there," Cy brushed off the praise, focusing on the trouble ahead.

"Guess we better keep moving." Orion was back to business.

They ran to catch up, dodging through the caves. They crossed another bridge to an island in the middle of the lava; a wall surrounded the island, extending hundreds of feet to the ceiling of the chamber. It was not a natural formation and even in the dim light of magma and fire it appeared to be made of a material much stronger than stone or brick.

They crossed under a smaller gate built into the wall and entered an enormous chamber with a circular platform raised in the midst of the magma that encircled the room. Charging through the arched entryway, Cyrus tumbled into the chamber just as somebody was half leaving – half their body flew past him, the other half was still lying on the floor at the dragon's feet, severed by the claws of the beast. The balance of their force was huddled inside the archway, stunned at the sight before them.

Cyrus had never seen a dragon before – not a real one. He had seen a few drakes and wurms; pale shadows, imitations of dragon kind. There were few dragons in the north, preferring to live among their own in the southern lands. Ashan'agar was a dark red color with scales as big as Cyrus's helm, a body fifty feet long with a long neck extending twenty feet from his body and spines that protruded from his back and ran from his neck to the end of his tail.

The Dragonlord's head was focused on two spell casters on the other side of the chamber. The air around its head began to distort, and a gout of flame shot from its mouth toward its prey. The flames consumed the spell casters, immolating them. They dropped to the ground and the fires consumed them within seconds until there was nothing left but a pile of ashes.

"Interlopers!" came a deep roar. It took Cyrus a moment to realize it was coming from inside his own head.

He struck at the belly of Ashan'agar. Narstron followed him, each of them hacking at the thick scales. A roar blasted through the cavern and the dragon began to turn, trying to face the foes plaguing him. He spread his wings, filling the room from end to end and reared up on his hind legs, exposing Cy and Narstron to his piercing glare.

They scrambled for cover, running between the dragon's legs. Cy took a moment to ram his sword between two of the scales of the beast's belly, prompting a scream that shook the cavern.

Tail whipping, the dragon set down from the attack as Cy and Narstron hid behind his ankles and started hacking away. They could see Orion standing in the archway, firing arrows at the dragon. Only about one in four was finding its way between the scales but it was causing enough irritation to split Ashan'agar's attention.

A high-pitched warcry caught Cyrus by surprise. A woman, clad in shining armor, leapt from the archway with a two-handed sword clutched in her hands. The jump she made was, by far, too much for a human to accomplish. Her sword drove into the shoulder of Ashan'agar and her feet found purchase between the scales. Possessed of extreme litheness the elf perched on the dragon's shoulder, driving her sword deeper into the wound she had created.

Cyrus looked over to see Niamh gathering up survivors. He watched a gust of wind surround her and grow to the intensity of a tornado with her at the center. When the winds receded she and the group surrounding her were gone, leaving only a handful of the army's remnants behind.

"Niamh is teleporting the survivors out!" Cy's shout to

Narstron was barely audible over the screeching of the dragon.

"She what?" The dwarf was behind the leg of the dragon.

"Looks like she and the others disappeared!"

"She teleported!" Cyrus shouted back. "She's a druid; they can do that! She's getting the survivors to safety!" The tail of the dragon swept down, narrowly missing the warriors.

"I could use a little safety meself!"

Cyrus looked up at the woman on the dragon's shoulder. It was an elven woman, but not Angelique in her ornate armor. He could see blond hair drawn into a ponytail, waving back and forth with the frenzied movement of the Dragonlord.

Ashan'agar had decided she was the greatest threat facing him and was scrambling to move his head into position to deal with her. As the long neck waved the elf removed her sword and dropped to the ground behind the dragon's front left leg. She rolled perfectly out of the fall and sprang to her feet in a run toward the back of the dragon, where Cyrus and Narstron were both hacking away trying to find weaknesses.

Dodging behind the leg on the same side as Cyrus, he acknowledged her with a shout. "Nice work!" She fixed him with a momentary glare as she passed and turned to bring her sword to bear with an artistry that Cyrus had never seen, even from the instructors at the Society of Arms. Her first three strikes did more damage than all of his and Narstron's efforts combined, biting through the layer of armored scaling and into the flesh beneath it.

"Nice of you to join us, Vara." Narstron buried his sword once more. As the dragon's leg lifted, the dwarf tugged the sword back from the moving limb. "You could have stayed on the shoulder, though; we have things firmly in hand here." Cy realized with a shock that she was the fourth member of Orion's party, the one who had been hidden in the shadows.

"Based on the damage you seem to have inflicted," her voice came, taut and imperious, "it appears that the two of you have only one thing in your hands, and it is most certainly not your swords." The shadow of a smile graced her lips. "Why don't you," she said to Cy with a mocking sweetness, "concentrate your efforts where I just cut that scale off? You'll have better luck with that rusty butcher's knife you're carrying now that I've cleared the way."

"I know that we're facing a dragon here," Narstron said with annoyance. "But you could at least try and buck your nature by not being a pretentious elf."

"I'm sorry," she said without a trace of irony or sincerity. "Should I say 'please' when I direct you to help me kill our large and implacable foe? Would that help assuage that sense of inferiority dwarves carry like a shield anytime someone instructs you toward intelligent action?"

Narstron's reply was swallowed in the next bellow of the dragon. Having shifted his focus to the trio striking at his legs, Ashan'agar began to sidestep, trying to expose the threats beneath him. Unfortunately for the dragon they moved more quickly than he did; although it did prevent them from attacking him further.

As they passed in a circle, Cyrus couldn't help but be reminded of a dog chasing its tail. *A multi-ton, scaly, fire breathing, super-intelligent dog that commands every beast in a several mile radius chasing its tail,* Cyrus corrected. Even facing death he couldn't help but chuckle at what had to look absurd to anyone watching. Vara, only inches away, heard his laugh and cast a look at him that branded him an idiot.

Ashan'agar turned swiftly in the opposite direction. The dragon brought a claw around, felling Narstron; a geyser of blood erupted from the dwarf's abdomen as he fell.

The Dragonlord bellowed in triumph. "Fools! Witness the death of those who oppose me!"

"Go!" Blood spurted from between Narstron's fingers as he tried to sit up and failed. With his free hand, the dwarf waved at Cyrus to keep moving.

Cyrus, shocked, looked to Vara for guidance. "Don't stop running," she said. The ice in her eyes suppressed his concern. An unexpected step by the dragon left them exposed for a moment and Vara's reflexes allowed her to shove Cyrus with a surprising amount of force back under the dragon to continue the pattern.

"The only thing stopping him from finishing your dwarven friend is us," she said as she shoved Cyrus once more, herding him under the dragon's belly.

Cy's gaze flitted to the archway. The bridge into the chamber was packed with spiders and rock giants, clawing to get past Orion and the other defenders. Selene was moving to drag Narstron off the platform while Ashan'agar was distracted by Cyrus and Vara.

Ignoring the shout of protest from Vara ("Stay away from the foot, you fool!"), he jumped on Ashan'agar's left hind leg and jammed his sword as hard as he could into the gap between the center claw and the scales on the middle toe.

He rolled off the foot and looked up to find the guardians on the bridge barely holding. Narstron was assisting them after Selene had healed him but they were outnumbered and had lost several of their number to the lava. Cyrus looked up to see the full anger of Ashan'agar, former king of the dragons.

The Dragonlord's eyes locked onto his, pools of swirling black looking into the depths of him. "I see you, Cyrus Davidon," he said, his harsh voice now melodic. "I can hear your thoughts. Serve me, and I will spare your life."

The face came closer to Cyrus, and he could see every scale. Spikes jutted from the top of the dragon's head as it slithered toward him, snakelike. It moved slowly, eyes fixated on him. It was such a sweet sound, the dragon's voice in his head. "I have many treasures..."

A flash of images forced their way into the warrior's mind. A flaming staff, a glowing sword, gold, coins, and... the Serpent's Bane. "I know what you seek, Cyrus Davidon... I have it, you know... the Serpent's Bane..."

"I do," the warrior said, motionless, eyes focused on the Dragonlord's.

"Tell me you aren't marrying this thing!" Vara struck at Ashan'agar's legs, but the dragon was hindering her efforts with wild swings of his tail.

"Kill her for me, Cyrus Davidon," the Dragonlord's voice boomed. "Kill the others, be my General and lead my armies... serve me... be my emissary and walk where I cannot... do my work..." The face grew closer and closer. "...and I will give you the Serpent's Bane... and all else your heart desires... I will give you purpose..."

Cyrus smiled at the dragon's face, now only a foot from his, luxuriating in the thought of possessing what he came here for. "No," the warrior said, all dreaminess gone from his voice.

The dragon's head recoiled but it was too late. Cyrus plunged forward from his motionless position with reflexes far beyond those of a normal human. His sword was raised and brought down in the blink of an eye – which in the case of Ashan'agar, was the last blink his right eye ever performed. Cyrus's sword ruptured the eyelid and punctured the dragon's eye.

A scream filled the cavern and Cyrus's head, driving the

warrior back. So stunned was he that Cyrus relinquished the grip on his sword's hilt as the dragon's head whipped in agony. In a fit of rage the Dragonlord began to flap his wings and rose from the ground in a shuddering, hovering flight. The force of the air from the wings kept Cyrus on his knees until he felt strong hands reach under his arms and drag him to his feet. "No bowing down to the Dragonlord today, brave warrior," Vara's quiet voice breathed in his ear. He staggered to his feet and braced himself against the wind from the beating wings.

"Fool!" came Ashan'agar's voice once more in his mind. "I would have given you everything you sought!"

"I always wanted to be the slave of an oversized snake," Cyrus tossed back.

"...Impudence..." came the voice in his mind. "I will kill all of you for this insult."

"And I thought we were headed for a nice cup of tea."

"Cyrus! Vara! Over here!" Cy turned back to the bridge just in time to see Niamh running full tilt – on air! – over the heads of the attacking giants and spiders. "Hurry!" The druid landed behind the line of defenders on the bridge. Orion and Narstron were anchoring the ends closest to the edge, taking the greatest personal risk but each successfully trading blows with a giant – the rest of which were bottlenecked by Narstron and Orion's efforts.

Between the two giants in the front of the line, a few spell casters poured magic into the fray and kept the spiders from making headway around the rock giants. The druid began casting her teleport spell again – Cyrus and Vara had seconds to make it to them before they would be gone.

"Hurry!" Vara called above the sounds of battle, wind and raging dragon. Her voice was strained; the urgency unmistakable and a distinct contrast from the calm she had displayed to this point. Cyrus took one last look past the dragon, at the glint that he knew was the treasure horde.

Turning his focus back to the archway, Cyrus realized there was no way he could make it in time. Vara jumped, missing the archway by inches and landing with a sword swipe that cleared the spiders attacking the middle of the defenders line.

He chanced to look back and saw the dragon drawing a deep breath, ready to spew the fire Cyrus was certain would consume him – and watched as Ashan'agar staggered from a blast of ice that hit the dragon in the face, rocking him back just enough in his hovering flight to send him into a spin. The Dragonlord crashed to the ground, struggling to get back to his feet.

Charging forward, Cyrus passed Niamh, who winked at him while brushing the frost from the hand she had cast the spell with. She began to murmur an incantation as Cyrus took his place in the middle of the line and plugged the gap next to Vara. He knew Niamh's teleport spell was coming quickly, and that they only needed to hold for a few seconds…

"Glad you could join us!" Orion yelled. His blades were moving with lightning speed, blocking the giant's fists with each blow, the odd strike catching a spider crawling between the fiend's legs. Cyrus grabbed the sword from the ground and attacked the spiders that were crawling through the gap between the giants that Narstron and Orion were keeping at bay.

Vara was at his shoulder, slicing at the surging arachnids while he cleaved at them with brute force. Cyrus felt a wind whip around him, gentle at first, but then howling with hurricane intensity, his feet left the ground, and the spiders and rock giants, the caves and lava that surrounded him were no more.

Chapter 3

The blast of wind died down around him, and Cyrus found himself in the middle of the central square in Reikonos, the fading light of sundown painting the plaza in a light that didn't look dramatically different from the orange and red of the lava in the fire caves. Some of the other survivors were still clustered around, recovering from wounds and discussing the chaos of the day. He immediately accounted for the Kings of Reikonos... finding them both present he began to relax. Several of the survivors were seriously wounded, and Selene was healing them as she went.

Vara looked irate and locked onto Cyrus immediately. "Was he speaking to you with his mind? Did he try to command you to do his bidding?"

"Yes." Cyrus blinked. "He told me to kill you and the others."

Her eyes narrowed, but she did not say anything further.

"How many made it out?" Cyrus asked.

Niamh grimaced. "Based on the count I did, 32 out of 121 that started this morning."

Cyrus looked around at the remains of the army, fresh-faced rubes no more. "Did the leader at least have the decency to die?"

Vara shook her head. "Unfortunately, no. However..." Her words drifted off and she pointed to where the bejeweled elf was sitting propped against the wall of the fountain in the center of the square. She was trembling and her eyes were wide, staring into the distance. "I don't think she'll be leading any more excursions anytime soon," Vara concluded with a tinge of satisfaction.

"I guess that finishes our business here." Cyrus looked at the kings. "Ready to go?"

Andren was already in motion. "I got a keg waiting on me back at the barn. So long!" He set off at a run down the road to the slums. Narstron said a quick farewell and followed.

Cyrus turned back to Orion, not meeting the ranger's eyes. He stood with them, strangers that had helped save his life, and fumbled for words. "Thanks for your help. If not for you, that would have turned out much worse."

Orion studied him intently. "Cyrus, was that your first

expedition?"

A flush of heat crept up the warrior's cheeks. "I performed that poorly?"

The human ranger shook his head. "No. You handled yourself very well. But am I correct in assuming that now that I've met the three of you I now know every single one of the Kings of Reikonos?"

When Cyrus nodded, the ranger went on. "I thought so. You have a great group for adventuring but unless you're doing things like this," he gestured at the living flotsam around them, "you're not doing much in the way of adventuring. If you're on expeditions of this kind, it's only a matter of time until you die in some hole."

Cyrus met Orion's gaze defiantly. "I learned that lesson well enough today. I don't think I'll be going on any more expeditions with people I don't know and don't trust."

Orion's stare bored into him. "Then unless you want to give up adventuring you'll need a bigger guild to join."

The heat rose up Cyrus's face again. "I know what larger guilds want from adventurers. I promise you I'm not even close to having the type of training they would want me to have. And of course there are sacrifices they'd ask me to make - membership dues, leaving behind my friends - and I would never leave them behind to advance myself -"

Orion cut him off. "Not all guilds are like that. Ours isn't. We don't have any membership dues and we could use more people like the kings. We've got a sizable force, we're going to places where there is an abundance of loot - which can buy a lot of good armor with mystical properties, things that help you to take harder hits as you face worse foes."

He took a step toward Cyrus and reached up to place a hand on the warrior's shoulder. "Niamh, Vara and I are on the Council that runs our guild. We would invite you to join us."

There was a sudden and inexplicable lump in Cyrus's throat. "I'll... have to talk it over with my guildmates. But thank you." The flush in his face began to subside.

"It was an honor to meet you, Cyrus." Niamh reached out and took his hand. Selene echoed the druid. Vara was frozen, blue eyes locked on him, and made no move or gesture to say farewell.

"How will I find you to let you know the answer?" Cyrus asked Orion.

The ranger smiled. "I'll be around. You can find me here or in the markets frequently enough. And if that fails, you could always visit our guildhall in the Plains of Perdamun."

Cyrus thanked them again, and turned to leave. Remembering the question he had forgotten to ask, he turned in time to see the winds beginning to whip up around them, Niamh's spell already in motion. "What's the name of your guild?" he asked, taking a last look at all of them. His eyes came to rest on Vara, who was looking back at him, eyes drilling into his, burning the memory of the look on her face into his mind.

As the blast of wind encircled the party and carried them away, Cyrus heard Orion's answer carried on the dying breeze.

"Sanctuary…"

Chapter 4

Cyrus approached the Kings of Reikonos guildhall, its rectangular shape standing out in the small dwellings of the slums. The faint, almost otherworldly glow from the last vestiges of sunlight added to the torchlight in the thoroughfares. The torches were lit all the time because the slums' location in a valley sandwiched between the taller buildings of the commerce district and the markets never exposed the streets to direct sunlight but by the light of midday. The slums were darker than the square by far; almost darker than the lava-lit cavern.

So here I am, Cyrus thought, *living in the slums of Reikonos.* He looked around at the decrepit town of shanties and lean-tos that filled the streets around him, choking out the real structures and dwellings.

The City of Reikonos was built on the coast of the Torrid Sea, but even after living in the city his entire life, he had only seen the sea twice – once on a visit to the docks and the second time from the top of the Citadel, the massive tower that was the seat of Reikonosian government. The nicest houses in Reikonos were on bluffs, directly overlooking the ocean. The slums were far from the water.

The refurbished barn that served as the Kings' guildhall had always been embarrassing, since the day he'd paid every last gold piece he possessed to buy it. But it had never felt so confining before. Taking a deep breath, he opened the door and stepped inside. There was a conversation going on when Cyrus walked in. It died as he entered. Andren and Narstron turned to face him expectantly.

"What?" He looked at them with absolute nonchalance.

"Two questions," Andren began, tall mug of ale already in his hand. "What was the name of their guild and did they ask us to join them?"

Cyrus took his time answering, eyes downcast. "The name of their guild was Sanctuary." Cyrus began to unstrap his plate mail at a leisurely pace.

"Quit stallin' and get on with it!" Narstron's leg twitched with excitement as he sat on his bunk.

"The answer to your second question," Cyrus let a smile play across his lips, "is yes, they did."

Andren upturned his glass, downing it in a single pull. Narstron looked insufferably pleased as he pumped his fist and yelled, "Yes!"

"What about our meager means?" Andren asked as he refilled his glass from the keg. Fueled by alcohol, he brought forth a topic that he might not otherwise have broached.

"No membership dues and they're training as they go." Cyrus paused. "We still have to discuss this. I'd like us to be unanimous in our decision. Just to be clear – we are talking about folding the Kings. Shutting it down and walking away –"

Andren broke in. "Because this place is the sort of home we all dreamed of. We're broke! We're barely scraping a living with what we get from the places we can go with the abilities we have. Isn't anybody else sick of sleeping in bunk beds like we're children?"

He pounded his chest. "I'm well nigh tired of it. I'd be better off if I'd stayed in the Healer's Halls than living this adventurer's life! You know we're better than this. We are being handed a golden opportunity to move up in the world. As long as we stick together, we can make this work for us. And if Sanctuary doesn't feel like the right place we can always fill our pockets and keep moving up, right?"

Face impassive, Cyrus looked at him. "I know it's hard to believe, considering how… unpleasant things are for us, but we've scraped enough together to get this far. We know next to nothing about this Sanctuary group and joining them is a big commitment."

Narstron made his mind known. "We know that four of their people risked their lives in a dragon expedition they knew was doomed from the start to try and save lives. We might have died had they not been there." He folded his arms across his barrel chest. "That tells me everything I need to know about them, right there. I think we can trust them."

Cyrus laughed. "It wasn't but an hour ago you were wondering if there was one person in that expedition we could trust. Now you're ready to trust four of them with your future."

He held up his hands in surrender. "I'm not saying we don't do this but I need at least a night to think over the possibilities."

He smiled at what he saw in their eyes – hope, something that had been gone for far too long. They had joked and had fellowship here and built a bond that would endure. But it was a bond born of common suffering: bunk beds, secondhand mattresses, equipment and furniture that were falling apart.

"I'm as excited as you," Cyrus added. "To have performed admirably enough that we're invited to join them is an honor and we should be proud." He paused. "I just need to be sure this is the right decision." With the last word, he strode past them to his bunk and lay down, drawing the curtains. It didn't do much to help the sound, but they'd all gotten used to living in close quarters. They kept their voices down, but Cyrus heard the possibilities in every word, as well as a few other things.

"What about that Vara?" Andren murmured. "She is really something. Her armor must be powerfully enchanted to let her leap like that. And did you see how fast she swung that sword?" He chortled, a low sound filled with unmistakable lust. "I wouldn't mind helping her take down that ponytail."

"I doubt you'd survive the attempt, old friend," Narstron said. "I suspect there's nary a man she's met that she hasn't employed that armor and sword on – the armor to keep them at bay, and the sword to put them out of their misery when they least expect it. You're right, though: to move that fast and hit that hard, a little girl like that has to have some powerful friends. That armor is worth a fortune, I'm sure."

Andren guffawed. "If ever someone got her out of the armor, he would behold the sweetest sight ever known to man." The healer paused. "Actually, two of the sweetest sights, I suspect," he said, laughing, the alcohol having overtaken all good sense.

Narstron laughed along with him. "Too true, but I think your error was in assuming it'd ever be a man that would witness. Maybe a woman?" A chuckle came from the dwarf. "She's royalty, right?"

"Have to be. Unless..." Andren's voice drifted for a moment. "Vara... unless she's..." His voice drifted off and he said something that sounded to Cyrus's ears like 'shell massacre'. Andren was quiet for several moments after that.

The discussion continued but Cyrus tuned it out. *What am I doing here?* The thought made its way to the surface of his mind again, unbidden.

Tired as he was, the talking didn't keep him awake, and soon he'd entered a fitful sleep, filled with visions of dragons, gold, battle, guildhalls... and a ponytailed elf, in shining silver armor, looking at him with an expression that was a cross between loathing and something very different.

Chapter 5

Cyrus awoke in the middle of the night. Silence surrounded him, broken only by the faint snores of Narstron in the bunk to his left. Rubbing his eyes, he rolled over and let his feet touch the floor. Strapping on his armor (he never left the hall without it, lest he be caught unprepared), he strolled through the streets of Reikonos. His feet carried him through the commercial district, where the shopkeepers had closed for the night.

His eyes came to rest on the storefront of a jeweler; a glass window with the name of the establishment emblazoned across it. In the bottom corner of the window was a sign big enough to be seen from some distance: 'No Dark Elves'. A common sight in the commercial district, where shops were affluent and catered to different clientele than in the slums or the markets. Posters were nailed to the left of the door, a few of which screamed 'WANTED' and 'HERETIC' in bold letters and carried artists' renditions of the faces of the accused.

A life in the slums was not what Cy had planned when he'd taken over leadership of the Kings of Reikonos from the previous leader. Gunter had been a human wizard, a great thinker who had passed the mantle of leadership so he could quest for knowledge in the elven capital of Pharesia. He had left a depleted guild bank, an untenable morale situation, and no guildhall.

The only three people in the guild at the time were Cyrus, Narstron and Andren. Talk of disbanding and joining another guild had given way to talk of expansion when no suitable options had been found, and Cy had been naïve enough to believe that he could lead them to glory. Efforts had yielded a few recruits here and there, but without a guildhall they were left meeting in wayside inns – a blow to their credibility when they proclaimed themselves 'a guild on the move'.

Scorned by any reputable recruit, Cyrus had used his entire savings to clear up that nagging image problem, not considering the consequences of having their guildhall in a barn. Most of their potential recruits lasted less than a full night. *Who can blame them?* Cyrus thought. *I don't even want to live there, and it's my guildhall!*

His feet carried him down the street to the Reikonos market, the center of all commerce in the land of Arkaria. Almost every race was welcome in Reikonos (though not always heartily accepted, like the dark elves). Even a handful of the savage trolls bartered in Reikonos, and they had been at war with nearly every power in Arkaria less than twenty years earlier.

As he walked from stall to stall, he watched as vendors plied their wares, even now, in the wee hours of the morning. The rest of Reikonos might yet be asleep, but the market had a pleasant hum. He saw things that he wanted, that could help him; armors and potions, swords and helmets, things that could bear an attack by titans. And, he reflected, seemed less likely to be his as the gods coming down and smiting him.

His path carried him past a line of merchants and when he looked up he found himself face to face with Orion, who had finished bartering with a trader. "Fancy meeting you here, Cyrus. Having trouble sleeping?"

Cyrus blinked. Realizing the fruitlessness of arguing an obvious point, he decided to switch to the offensive instead. "Do you always do your shopping at 3 o'clock in the morning?"

"I usually don't, but I've got a busy day tomorrow and I wanted a new pair of chainmail pants." Reaching out, he took them from the trader. "What do you think?" he asked as the small, flawlessly crafted chain links rolled down.

Though Cyrus was by far too big for them, he recognized the exquisite craftsmanship and material of the chainmail. They would easily have cost double what he had spent on the guildhall. "Those must cost a fortune – they're very impressive."

Nodding in thanks, Orion switched subjects as deftly as Cyrus had deflected his earlier inquiry. "What's on your mind at this hour? Could it be the invitation I proffered?" He began to walk toward the Square.

Cyrus fell into step beside him. "Yes, I am wrestling with that decision."

"What exactly are you wrestling with? Are your guildmates not interested?"

Cyrus laughed. "No, they're definitely interested. In fact, were it up to them, we'd have been suppering at your guildhall last evening. No, it's me you have to convince." Looking around to make sure no one could overhear them, Cyrus took a step closer to Orion and lowered his voice.

"These are my people. I've shepherded them through good times and bad. I have their best interests at heart. They're good people, a bit rough around the edges, but honorable." He paused, considering his next words. "There are guilds that would use us for our talents, and discard us as easily – or leave us to die when it became convenient."

Orion's eyebrow rose. "Do you believe Sanctuary is that type of guild?"

Cyrus deflated. "No, I don't. Everything I've seen indicates you'd go out of the way to help a stranger avoid death; I can't imagine you'd abandon your own."

Orion smiled. "You take so much responsibility for your people's lives that you want to make certain that we would do the same."

"If Sanctuary holds up to the same code of honor I've seen from you, Niamh, Selene and," Cyrus drew a sharp intake of breath, "Vara, I have no doubt we'd be in good hands. I have a hard time entrusting my guild to yours without seeing more than I have." He settled on what he really wanted to convey. "I just want to make sure that you're the rule, not the exception."

Orion nodded agreement. "I understand. I have a proposition for you."

"The sleeplessness from your last proposition has yet to fade."

The ranger laughed. "Hopefully this will ease your sleeplessness. I propose you join our army in battle so you can meet the rest of the guild and see what we're all about."

"You'd permit that? I would accept."

"Great! When and where are we going?" A voice from behind startled them both. Narstron stood behind them, rubbing his hands together.

"Kortran, the City of the Titans – tomorrow evening. We'll meet you inside the gates. It's in the southern lands, in the valley at the south end of the Gradsden Savanna." Orion walked up the raised steps to the fountain in the square. Another spell caster, an elven woman in red robes sat on the edge of the fountain, awaiting him. She stood up and joined him as Orion smiled down at them. "You won't regret this."

Watching the ranger vanish in a burst of blue light as the magics engulfed him, Cyrus could only hope he was right.

Chapter 6

It was hot on the savanna. Even with the sun setting it was much warmer than the slums in Reikonos that they had left hours earlier. Cyrus and Narstron had crept away from the guildhall at the noon hour while Andren was still passed out. He had handed a wizard in the square fourteen bronze pieces to teleport them to the Gradsden Savanna. They had walked through the tall grass all afternoon, working their way toward Kortran, which was nestled in a valley where the savanna gave way to impassable mountains.

Narstron did a surprisingly good job of cutting through the grass that barely stretched above Cyrus's navel. Though he would never admit it, he was pacing himself so he didn't leave Narstron behind. After a few more minutes they reached a large rock and crouched behind it. Before them, a mammoth stone arch stood as a protective gate in front of a pass leading down into the valley.

"Gods, it is massive," Cyrus breathed. "It's the height of forty humans – or fifty elves – or eight hundred and seventy three dwarves."

Narstron let the remark pass. "It's not the height of the arches that has me concerned – it's the size of the titans guarding them."

Cy's eyes moved down from the top of the archway to the bottom and found two titans, at least twenty feet tall, stationed as sentries. He and Narstron crept forward, coming to rest and hiding behind the last clump of bushes between them and the titans.

"And in terms of a plan?" Cyrus looked at Narstron.

Taken aback, Narstron pondered before his reply. "Charge?"

A flash of irritation crossed Cyrus's brow. "No healer. Brilliant thinking; typical of you."

"Got a better idea?"

"Where are we meeting them again?"

"Inside the gates."

"Damn."

"Indeed." Shaking his craggy head, a shout echoed forth from him. "'Lo, Sanctuary, where are ye?!"

Cy's stomach dropped – a sick feeling, made worse by the sight of two titans turning their heads to fix upon them. Their eyes burned with the fire of a killer about to destroy a helpless victim. Cyrus followed his stomach immediately, dropping to both knees behind the bushes. Narstron lingered, head sticking out of cover. "No need to hide; they've seen us."

A roll of the eyes, a breath of exasperation, and the sound of his sword being drawn – steel on scabbard, instinctively in his hand – all these sensations passed in a moment. A moment which was cut short by the war cry of the sentries charging toward them. "Bugger." Cy tensed. Not one to run from a fight, he prepared himself mentally for the impending possibility of death. Leaping from behind the cover of the bushes, he followed Narstron, already a half dozen steps ahead of him, moving toward the titans.

Roots suddenly sprung from beneath the earth, as though the grass had grown rapidly around them, entangling the feet of both titans, holding them in place. Arrows rained upon them and a bolt of lightning struck both of them from out of the clear sky. They were easy prey for the warriors when they reached them.

When both were on the ground, dead, Cyrus looked up to find Selene, Orion and Niamh standing behind the stone archway. "That's the problem with warriors," Orion chuckled. "No subtlety. Haven't you boys ever heard of an invisibility spell?"

"I can't cast spells." Cyrus looked up as he closed the distance between them, Narstron in tow.

"You're injured, Cy." Selene looked on with concern when they had reached the archway. A faint trickle of blood ran down the armor on his wrist where one of the titans had grazed him.

"Flesh wound."

She tut-tutted at him in a very matronly way, and murmured an incantation under her breath. He felt a healing wind cross his arm, and the blood stopped, flesh bound and made whole.

"Good timing." Niamh's red hair blew in the hot wind. "What was your plan if we hadn't been here to save your sorry asses?"

"I don't think you just saved our asses on that one, Niamh." Cy blinked. "I'm pretty sure they would have chopped up the whole of us."

"Yeah, but you're all ass, all over, so..." She smirked.

They chuckled. "Come on," Orion called out, "we heard you shout from the meeting point. The rest of the guild is waiting."

They hurried under the archway down the path to the valley beyond.

Cyrus breathed deeply as he trotted along; the air was slightly cooler as they began their descent into the valley. Boulders obscured the road ahead until they came to a point where the path widened. Adventurers were assembled throughout the area.

Almost eight feet tall, a troll stood in the midst of a group of elves, dwarves and humans. Cyrus's sword was immediately unsheathed and in his hands, watching. Clad in a black tunic that clashed with his green skin and carrying a staff that glowed with mystical power, the troll was lounging against a rock. Cyrus forced a steely calm over himself.

Orion, sensing a tense moment, placed a hand on Cyrus's shoulder. "It's okay: he's one of us."

Cyrus's jaw unclenched. "Do you regularly associate with trolls?"

"Vaste is different." Orion paused for a minute. "You were too young to be in the war."

Cyrus's eyes were cold. "You're right; the war with the trolls was going on when I was a child. But my father died in the Dismal Swamp campaign. I don't even remember him. My mother raised me on tales of what the trolls did until she died."

"I assure you that Vaste was not in the war; he's younger than you are. Nor is he your typical troll; he's a healer.

"I thought trolls were too stupid to use magic."

"A common misperception. That's a rumor that spread during the war. Most trolls don't know how to use magic because it's a lost art among their people." Orion looked at the black clad troll. "In fact, Vaste is considered an outcast among his people. They don't much like the ways of outsiders – the trolls that survived the war are a tightly cloistered community."

A long pause filled the air between them. "That's all right," Cyrus said. "Us 'outsiders' don't care for their ways either – slaving and banditry."

Orion raised his hands in a gesture of surrender. "I'm not going to try and convince you that the empire of the trolls hasn't done those things. All I'm telling you is that Vaste is different."

Cyrus resheathed his sword. "We'll see."

"Most gracious of you," came a familiar voice from behind him. "I can only hope you are as kind toward others – say, orphans and stray dogs." Vara brushed past him to stand next to

Orion. "If not, I fear you'll be devoured by a puppy while trying
to figure out which end of your sword is to be used for best
results." Her gaze was cold and her voice reflected it. The armor
still shone, but today her long blond hair was worn in a severe
bun atop her head.

"So nice to see you again, m'lady," Narstron said with sarcasm.

"I'm sorry," Vara said, looking from left to right with
exaggerated emphasis. "I hear someone talking, but I can't see
them." She looked down and her face registered faked shock, lips
forming a perfect o. "Oh, look, a street urchin." She reached down
to pat him on the head. "Well, it looks as though you're getting
plenty to eat."

Narstron scowled at her.

Vara turned back to Orion. "Now that the stragglers are here,"
she looked pointedly at Narstron but did not acknowledge Cyrus,
"we're quite ready, whenever you are."

Cyrus's eyes looked around the adventurers. He studied the
troll named Vaste, watching his posture, seeing how he interacted
with the elves around him. Most trolls, even the half dozen or so
that were permitted in Reikonos, looked hostile, tense and barely
restrained. This one did not. He was calm and even laughed at a
joke that one of the elves had made. Cyrus watched as Vaste
threw in a witticism of his own and the group roared with
laughter.

Cyrus's gaze turned to another small cluster of Sanctuary's
adventurers. In the group was a dark elf, his hair black and skin a
deep navy. He wore armor that while not as blackened as Cyrus's,
had seen fair use. A battle axe was slung across his back, and he
sported a half-serious look. He stood next to an elven man who
could be described in no other way but radiant – his platinum hair
was cropped short and he had the markings of a healer.

On the elf's right was a much younger looking elven woman,
who wore robes of deepest crimson. Her laugh was airy and loud.
The last hole in their circle was filled by someone too short for
Cyrus to see at first. As he strained his neck to look around the
red-robed elven woman, he caught sight of a gnome, with a dark
blue robe that hung perfectly on his tiny frame.

Orion broke Cyrus's preoccupation. "Why don't you introduce
yourselves around? We'll be moving in a few minutes, but we've
got things to plan first."

"Yes," Vara added, "do hurry along, and we'll let you know

when we're ready for you to poke at something with those dull and rusty farm implements." She waved her hand at their swords.

Orion shook his head. "Can't you be nice to anyone?"

She pursed her lips as Cyrus turned from her and walked toward the group he had been observing. "I'm nice enough to you, aren't I?" Orion cleared his throat. "Well," Vara said, "I haven't impaled you yet, so count your blessings."

"Just once," Narstron muttered, "I'd like to meet a paladin that's not so self-righteous and full of themselves, so focused on their 'holy crusade' – whatever that may be – that they'd ignore someone dying in the street as they passed."

Cyrus was befuddled. "Paladin?"

"Tell me you're joking. Paladin? White knight? Holy crusader?"

Cyrus shrugged. "If they didn't teach it at the Society of Arms, I didn't learn it."

"They're like you. They use one sword – but unlike you, they can also use magic. They can heal a little bit, mend some wounds; not as well or quickly as a healer, mind you, but well enough to get themselves out of a scrape."

"So what? They can use a sword and a little bit of magic."

"It's a lethal combination." Narstron locked his eyes on Cyrus. "You land a deadly sword thrust, impaling your foe. What happens if they're a warrior like us?"

"They're dead unless a healer is backing them up."

"Exactly. But a paladin," Narstron's eyes glinted, "they take a couple steps back, cast a spell and knit the wound up, and they're back at it a moment later, until they run you through." He gestured pointedly, miming the motion of stabbing Cyrus.

Cyrus's eyes narrowed. "What made them so damned special to be able to use magic?"

The dwarf shrugged. "What makes anyone able to use magic? You've either got it or you don't. And if you do, they send you the Leagues."

"What are the Leagues?" Cyrus frowned.

"Like ours is the Society of Arms, the organization that teaches adventurers their trades. Theirs is called the Holy Brethren. Paladins use their magic and swordplay for their cause, which is personal to each of them – like saving the poor, or protecting the downtrodden or freeing the slaves."

"Sounds kind of silly."

"Yeah. And they always worship one of the 'good' gods, like the Goddess of Love, or the Goddess of Life. They have a code of honor. For example, your foe turns his back to you – do you strike?"

"Damned right you do." Cyrus nodded. "It's the best time; they can't hit you back."

Narstron shook his head. "See, a paladin won't do that. It's not 'honorable'."

Cyrus nodded his understanding. As he and Narstron approached the group of adventurers, the radiant elven man turned to face them and beamed at them with a dazzling smile. "I can't tell you what a pleasure it is to welcome you to our band today," he said in a tone that indicated he wholeheartedly meant it. He took Cyrus's hand in a firm but warm handshake.

"My name," the elf began, "is Curatio Soulmender, and I am the chief healer of Sanctuary, and one of the guild's officers." He favored them with a look that was as close to opposite of Vara's normal expression as could be found. "Let me introduce you to some of our compatriots."

He turned first to the dark elf with a sweeping gesture. "This is Terian Lepos. He is Sanctuary's sole dark knight."

"A dark knight?" Cyrus said with a start. "Kind of the opposite of a paladin?" He looked to Narstron for guidance.

"Quite right. Dark knights use treachery, black magics and serve 'evil' gods." Narstron looked at Lepos almost apologetically. "Sanctuary seems like a rather noble outfit to employ a dark knight."

"We may serve 'evil' gods, by your definition," Terian said with dark eyes fixed on Narstron. "But I try to restrict my activities to conform to Sanctuary's code of honor."

"Really?" The dwarf's eyes widened. "I thought dark knights were into soul draining, life sucking and backstabbing."

"I haven't done any of those things... today." Terian smiled.

"I faced a dark knight once," Cyrus said with sudden realization.

Lepos raised an eyebrow. "You're still alive, so I presume you either had help in the battle or you met a very poor dark knight."

Red flushed the warrior's cheeks. "I did have help and you're right," he acknowledged with only a trace of shame. "If I hadn't been with a healer, the dark knight I ran across – a bandit – would have killed me." Cyrus's eyes narrowed at the memory. "He cast a spell while we were fighting and it literally tore the breath out of me. I nearly passed out from the pain."

Another slight smile appeared on Terian's face. "He used an incantation that stole a bit of your vitality – your life or your soul, depending on how you view it. It's a useful spell; it's kept me alive a time or two."

Narstron nodded. "I need something like that."

Terian threw his head back and cackled before replying. "Do you need it badly enough that you're ready to initiate a soul sacrifice with Mortus, the God of Death, or Yartraak, the God of Darkness?"

The dwarf's eyes widened. "Perhaps not that badly."

Lepos had a smile of mirth on his face but said nothing as the lady elf in the crimson robes spoke up. "Don't mind Terian. He's a bit... prideful. My name is Nyad Spiritcaster."

Cyrus took her hand and alternated between looking at her and Curatio. "I had always heard that elves don't have surnames."

Nyad laughed. "That's the effects of humans on us. We don't have surnames – not in proper elvish society. However," she explained, "I left Pharesia, the elven capital, when I first struck out on my own as a young elven woman of one hundred and eight –"

"One hundred and eight?" Cyrus echoed in astonishment. "I'd heard elves were long-lived, but I didn't really know how long-lived."

"Most elves live several millenia." Nyad continued, "I left Pharesia, a place where elven culture is very strict and where there isn't much influence from the outside world. No elf in Pharesia would even think of having a last name!" she said with a conspiratorial chuckle. "However, have you heard of Termina?"

Cyrus nodded. "Andren told me about it. It's a massive elven city on the river Perda southwest of Reikonos."

"It's at the very edge of the Elven Kingdom, and while our capital is still very much in line with our caste system, Termina is a place where elven norms become a bit murkier. It was there I picked up my surname. Most elves who have lived in Termina have done the same. It's quite trendy, and it makes it easier to relate to offlanders..." She coughed. "Excuse me, non-elves."

"I've heard stories about Termina." Cyrus chose his words carefully. "I've heard that in the kingdom an elven woman would never look at an outsider or a member of a lower caste for fear that she would lose status." He thought about it for a moment. "Which would actually explain Vara. But in Termina it's supposed to be different..."

"It is," Nyad nodded. "The kingdom is very caste driven. Marrying or bedding an outsider would drop your status in the eyes of everyone. If a high-born elf and a low-born elf were to become involved, the high-born would lose significant face. In Termina, however, anything can happen. And does."

"But," Narstron asked, "isn't Termina part of the Elven Kingdom? Ruled by that massive royal family of yours?"

Nyad blushed deeply, the color of her robes. "Of mine?" she asked in a pitch above her normal conversational tone. "I don't know what you mean," she stammered.

Narstron studied her with a raised eyebrow, aware that he had touched a nerve. "Of your kingdom," he clarified. Cyrus looked at Curatio to gauge his reaction, but the healer's expression was guarded. Terian, on the other hand, looked highly amused.

"Yes, the royal family rules Termina." She paused for a moment and composed herself. "Pharesia has been the capital of the Elven Kingdom since its founding, long before humankind was around. Since the rise of Reikonos, and the growing trade with offlanders, that commerce has become vital to our economy. Without Termina, the Elven Kingdom would fall within a year."

"How is that possible?" Cyrus looked at her in disbelief.

She shrugged. "Commerce is a dirty practice in Pharesia and that attitude radiates to the towns and villages of the kingdom. Only a lower-born would be a merchant while being high born or royalty is exalted above all else." She looked Cyrus in the eyes. "When you demonize the merchants that bring your society prosperity and consider those who engage in it to be sneaky or criminal, you create a society where people want to be royalty and nobody wants to do the uncouth work that allow the royalty to survive."

Cyrus exchanged a look with Narstron. "They actually consider merchant work to be dirty in the Elven Kingdom?"

"Low status work," Nyad corrected. "Merchants are like kings in Termina because there is no status barrier, money is exalted. Everything is for sale in Termina, and royalty and merchant are equal, and the same goes for offlanders. As long as you have money, anything is negotiable."

"It sounds dramatically different from Pharesia," Cyrus said.

"It is. About a tenth of the population of Termina is non-elves, and their," she coughed again, seemingly her way of covering a somewhat embarrassing statement, "foreign ways have tremendous influence on the mostly younger and impressionable elven population of Termina."

A roar sounded as two titans charged into the clearing and looked upon the party with outrage. "More intruders!" one of them bellowed.

Niamh was hovering (*How does she do that?* Cyrus wondered) overhead and suddenly dark bolts were flying from her hands, lightning coursing through the titans.

Cyrus darted into the battle. The titan before him was within his reach when it veered toward its comrade. The second titan assumed a defensive posture and blocked a sword-swipe, barely keeping it from removing his arm. A burst of fire bowled him over and consumed him. Cy started to alter course toward the one that had attacked his fellow but it was strangely still. The titan's eyes were fixed and unmoving, staring straight ahead.

"Whaddya think, Curatio?" piped the gnome standing in the group with him. "Can I keep him?"

The elf smiled, and again it put Cyrus oddly at ease. It took him a moment to realize why. Stern was an attribute that could be assigned to most elves. They weren't much for friendliness with outsiders. "Sure thing, J'anda."

The army resumed a relaxed state. Cyrus could not shake a feeling of discomfort with a titan now standing in their midst. The gnome in the circle made his way past Curatio and looked up at Cyrus expectantly. "I am J'anda Aimant."

Cyrus leaned down. "Forgive me; I haven't had much contact with gnomes."

J'anda chortled. "What makes you think I'm a gnome?" Cyrus looked at him curiously, not sure that he'd heard J'anda correctly. Cyrus blinked and the gnome was gone, replaced by a dwarf, still wearing the same blue robe, but resized to fit the much bulkier and taller frame.

"Uh... I can't say I've ever seen anything quite like this before..." Cyrus said.

"Ah," J'anda replied. "Then you'll really be impressed with this." This time, Cyrus didn't even blink – but the dwarf was gone and replaced with a human. Fine, delicate features graced his face. He smiled at Cyrus, and before the warrior had a chance to reply, J'anda's ears grew and he had become an elf.

"Now that's impressive," Narstron said. "I can't say I've ever seen an enchanter go through that many illusions."

Cyrus relaxed a little. "An enchanter. That explains your ability to control the titan."

J'anda gave him another dazzling smile. "One of my many talents, I assure you."

Cyrus regarded the enchanter carefully. "What else can you do besides change your form and charm a titan to do your bidding?"

J'anda's same charming smile made its way across his face, "An excellent question, and one you will surely learn the answer to should you join Sanctuary. I'm not charming this titan – I'm completely bending his will to mine. I could tell him to walk down there and attack the rest of the titan guards," J'anda indicated the path ahead, "and he would do it cheerfully. And he will," an air of impatience filled the enchanter's voice, "as soon as we get moving."

"I've had some experience with that recently." Cyrus's eyes focused on the titan captive's. They were blank, unfocused.

"Oh?" J'anda smiled. "Were you witnessing it or did you get your will bent?"

"No, I didn't get my will bent." Cyrus remained expressionless. "But it was attempted."

The elf's eyebrow went up. "You resisted?"

Cyrus honed in on the enchanter. "Yes. Ashan'agar, the Dragonlord, tried to get me to do his bidding."

Both of J'anda's eyebrows retreated upward. "My goodness. How did you escape his power?"

A shrug. "I don't know."

Whatever response J'anda might have offered was cut off by the sudden arrival of Vara. "When these giants came around the corner, they said something about 'More intruders'. Can you find out what that means?"

"Certainly." J'anda nodded in accommodation. The enchanter's eyes looked up at the titan, gazing deeply. J'anda did not move or speak for several moments, and when he broke his gaze from the titan, he was unsmiling. "Someone attacked their city last night from the southern entrance. Something was stolen. Something valuable."

"Any idea what?" Vara blew air impatiently out of her lips.

"He doesn't know," came the enchanter's reply. "Whatever it was, they're not making it common knowledge."

"We're ready to move," Orion commanded the attention of the entire group. "Let's get this excursion underway. Security is bound to be tighter than we expected if they just got hit last night, so be on guard." He began walking backward down the path to Kortran. "Move out, Sanctuary!"

Chapter 7

As the group began to move Cyrus tried to stick close to Orion. A flash of red made him start as a familiar figure emerged from the shadows.

"Niamh!" Orion seemed pleased to see her. "What news from the city?"

The elf smiled. "No more guards in the road ahead. Which is fortunate," she raised her voice, "because this lot has all the stealth capability of a bar full of drunken trolls! We're clear all the way to our objective," she told the ranger with a smile. With a spell she faded back into the shadows.

Cyrus turned his attention to Orion. "What is our objective?"

Orion looked back at him. "How much do you know about the southern lands?"

Cyrus shrugged as they walked forward. "I know that we're in them, it's damned hot, and there are riches in here somewhere."

Orion smirked before replying. "All true. There are three factions in the southern regions: the elves of Amti, a colony that is mostly independent of the Elven Kingdom somewhere east of the Savanna, in the Jungle of Vidara. Then there are the dragons of Hewat - you recall their former king?" The smirk grew wider. "The dragons are far south of here; the only way to get to them would be having a wizard open a portal to the wastelands, or to go through Kortran. Which brings us to the titans. Three factions, all fighting for the southern lands. The elves' and dragons' territory is separated by the territory of the titans, so they rarely engage in battle."

"Why don't they ally?"

The ranger shuddered. "Dragons don't have much in the way of allies: just people they're not at war with. Titans and dragons are a pretty good match, but the elves of Amti? They're outnumbered and small compared to a titan or a dragon."

Cyrus looked around. "Pretend you're a titan." Orion nodded. "You had intruders last night, they steal something valuable and secret enough that your guards don't even know what it is, but you don't increase your security?" Cyrus looked at the ranger with disbelief on his face. "This doesn't look like a city at war. We're heading in and I've yet to see more than token resistance."

"They are at war. The problem is the war doesn't come to Kortran. I've heard of outposts getting attacked on all sides. But taking it to the heart of their capital? The dragons aren't threatened enough and the giants aren't ready for that sort of strike.

"Hewat is south of here through fifty miles of mountain passes. Most of the titan forces are guarding those rather than worrying about attacks from the elves to the north." The ranger wore a pitying expression. "I doubt Amti has made an offensive move against the titans in years. Their city is only standing for one reason: the titans haven't found it yet."

"How do you miss an entire city of elves?" Cyrus boggled.

Orion shrugged. "The location's secret. You have to have an elven escort lead you there blindfolded. Back to your original question: the elves have done the only thing they can do without attacking directly. They've placed a bounty on the heads of the titans." His eyes lit up. "The elves really don't have an army, but they have money.

"Money buys armor, weapons, things with mystical power that can bear and deal damage better." He held up his hand to halt the army as they crested a rise. "We're here for those bounties. We need better equipment. Mystical equipment increases the power of our spell casters magic in addition to giving more resistance to hostile spells to our fighters."

It had gotten so dark that Cyrus could no longer see more than a few paces in front of him. Faint lights in the distance indicated there was a city not far away. He had been following Orion, not worried about where he was going.

He felt a hand gently grasp his arm and looked over to see J'anda, who smiled as he placed something cold in the warrior's palm.

Cyrus tried to bring the object closer so he could see it, but J'anda closed Cyrus's palm firmly. A glow of blue exploded in his hand soundlessly and the sparkles of light shot up his arm to his neck. A flash of light lit the warrior's eyes. Blinking it away he could see; the darkness had faded. "It's an orb of lucense," J'anda whispered. "Magical spell that conveys night vision. Thought you might like to see where you're going," he said with amusement.

"Another of your mysterious powers?"

The enchanter shrugged with a whimsical smile. "There are so many."

Cyrus looked back down the path and his breath caught in his throat. The city of Kortran was stretched out before him. The path diverged into an ovoid ring road that looped around both sides of the valley and rejoined at the far southern end opposite them. A path led down from the split into the city proper like a ramp into the bowl of the valley.

The buildings were intricately carved. In fact, much of the city was carved out of the rock itself on the ground level as well as along one side of the outer ring road. The other side – what Cyrus believed was the eastern facing – had only two enormous arches that led into the mountainside, each seemingly going in different directions. Both of them had very intricate facades, carved with ornate statuary and more sophisticated in their appearance than the city's other buildings.

In the center of the valley, larger stone buildings dotted the cityscape sprinkled between the more common stone and mortar dwellings, most of which carried intricate woodwork.

Niamh breathed from somewhere to his left, "I never get tired of seeing this." Looking around, Cyrus realized that she had not faded into the shadows – her voice seemed to be coming out of thin air.

"I'll never get used to that," he muttered as he shook his head.

Niamh appeared next to him, caught his attention and smiled. "What, magic?"

He shook his head. "Yeah. It's not like we saw a lot of it in the Society of Arms, where I was raised." Cyrus turned to her. "You're a druid?"

"That's right."

"I've only known one druid. This is going to sound a little stupid," Cyrus began. He looked around to see if anyone was looking at him. "What exactly does a druid do? I know you have power over nature..."

"Yes, we deeply appreciate nature. The spells I cast," she licked her lips, "tend to center on control of nature and the elements. I can cast fire or ice spells – not as powerfully as a wizard, but well enough – command water, plant life, even animals to some extent. I can summon a mystical wind that can teleport us from place to place... and a few other things."

Cyrus's eyebrow shot up. "I've seen some of that. Useful magic, that's for sure."

Niamh nodded. "The good news is you don't have to worry about spell casters facing you in Kortran. Titans don't have healers, or wizards or druids. They favor martial strength to the exclusion of intellectual pursuits like magic. Just like all followers of the God of War." Scorn dripped from her words.

Cyrus flushed. "Bellarum, the Lord of War? What's wrong with worshiping him?"

"Not you too?" She shivered as though something dirty had crawled on her. "I don't exactly shy away from battle, but I'll never understand those who worship warfare and consider it some sort of 'spiritual experience'."

Cy raised an eyebrow. "Most don't. It's okay – I don't understand your magic."

"Maybe I'll explain more about it sometime."

Cyrus nodded and then realized they had been halted for nearing five minutes. He looked around for Orion, and found him whispering with Vara and Curatio. After a pause Orion signaled the army to move down the path into the city. They moved slowly, but Cyrus could see no activity in the city itself. He looked down at his feet as the texture of the path changed when they crossed onto the ring road – it was made entirely of a rich, dark wood.

Orion beckoned them down the ramp. J'anda's titan still walked with them, casting shadows in the light of Kortran's lamps. The enchanter paused with his titan, holding position in the middle of the road. "Shall I guard here?" he whispered to Orion.

"Not a bad idea in case we have to retreat," the ranger said, turning forward again to lead the army into the heart of the city.

They left the ring road behind them as they descended, the large buildings surrounding them. Once they reached the bottom of the ramp, they crept into the darkness of a nearby alley, sticking close to the wall for cover. They followed back alleys for a few blocks to one of the larger buildings on the outskirts.

"Armory, maybe?" Narstron wondered, having reappeared at Cyrus's side, startling the human.

"Whatever it is, I guess this is where Amti's most wanted villains hide out." Cyrus took in the scale of the building with some surprise. They were truly enormous up close.

It took three people to open the door. Cyrus peered into the darkness within, and felt a not-so-gentle shove. He looked over his shoulder to see Vara smiling at him mirthlessly. "After you," she said with a bow and hand outstretched toward the door.

Without another word, Cyrus ran into the building.

Chapter 8

Cy took a sharp breath as he realized there was a titan in the room. It was sleeping on an oversized wooden chair in the corner. Letting out a sigh of relief, Cyrus watched it as they crept past.

They filed into the next room. Cy caught a flicker of motion behind a chair leg, and bolted forward. He ate up the distance to the chair quickly, cutting around the edge as something burst out and slammed into his chestplate, knocking him back a step.

Whatever had hit him dropped and rolled back, coming to rest a few paces away. When Cyrus's gaze locked onto it, he saw it was a swarthy elf, moaning in pain and rubbing his shoulder. Orion, Vara and Narstron had been only paces behind him, and now surrounded the elf, weapons drawn.

Holding his hands up, the elf twitched before speaking, which he did in a low, hissing voice. "Friends, I can't thank you enough for coming for me!" Something about the elf seemed oily to Cyrus. "My name is Erart, and I have been a prisoner here for far too long."

Orion looked at him with undisguised skepticism. "I doubt that. Any elf in Kortran would either be dead or a traitor."

A sign of panic entered the elf's eyes. "No! No, I swear I am a prisoner, trapped here in the city! I was scared to leave!"

"You're a liar." Cyrus looked him in the eyes. He could see it, the subtle evasion as the elf avoided his stare, then relaxed before tensing every muscle in his body.

"HELP!"

The elf's call caught them off guard. The next sound they heard was the tearing of cloth. Cyrus turned to see a tapestry pulled to the side, and three titans stepped out of the passage behind it. He looked back to see the door they had come through open to admit the sleeping titan plus another. Terian swept toward the titans behind them, sword already in motion.

Orion unstrapped his bow in a split second, arrow nocked and flying a moment later. Cy had turned and charged to close the distance between himself and the titans before him. He could hear Vara and Narstron behind him as Sanctuary's army engaged the titans to the rear. Orion's first shot was perfect: he caught the leading titan in the eye, causing him to let out an agonized yell.

As he dodged past the first foe, Cyrus raked his sword across the achilles tendon, causing it to topple and knock his closest following comrade backward. Dodging the two falling titans, Cyrus leapt upon them and quickly slit the second titan's throat before he could free a hand to stop the warrior.

The third titan emitted a roar at the death of his comrade. Glancing back, Cy saw Narstron give the half-blind titan the same treatment Cyrus had given the first. It looked like a geyser of red when he ripped out its throat. Vara looked annoyed but followed Cyrus to the third titan.

The titan took a swipe at him designed almost as much to keep him back as to do him any harm. He feinted at the titan's right leg, then pulled away. It fixated on him, ignoring Vara. She gracefully sidestepped and slammed her sword down on her enemy's foot. He let out a howl of pained outrage, but before he could take a swipe at her, three things happened very quickly.

First, an arrow sailed into the titan's upper lip, causing him to emit another startled yelp. Orion followed his arrow with a second that caught the titan squarely in the shoulder and caused him to drop his sword.

Second, Narstron jumped onto the last survivor's leg, and drove both his blades into the side of its knee, slipping them under the kneecap and causing the leg to buckle and to drop the titan to the ground. Vara added a powerful sword-swipe to the afflicted area.

Finally, Cyrus charged into the opening created by their attack and jumped up to bury his sword into the side of the titan's neck. With a wretched sound the titan fell to his hands and knees, then lay down and died. Cyrus looked around. *The four of us just took out three titans with no healer! Not bad.*

"My goodness, that took forever thanks to the two of you," Vara grumbled. Cyrus rolled his eyes while Narstron clenched his teeth.

"I thought it went rather smoothly." Orion favored the two warriors with a smile. Vara exhaled impatiently as she turned back to the Sanctuary army.

Cyrus turned to find the Sanctuary army running out the door in a mass, one titan dead on the ground, the other missing. He took off at a run, Orion a few steps ahead of him. The elf, Erart, was nowhere to be seen, Cyrus noticed as he flew through the door. *Where is the other titan?*

He and Orion pushed their way through the army, accidentally stepping on a gnome. He saw Niamh wielding twin bursts of fire from each hand, blasting the retreating titan's leg, bringing it down. Terian was striking it with his sword. Vara jumped from behind Cyrus to land on the it's back, delivering an impaling strike with her sword as the wounded titan let loose a cry.

Vara cut it short by stabbing into the titan's lungs, but it was too late. The silence created by the titan's death was filled with the sound of doors opening, bells ringing and shouts filling the air.

"RAIDERS AT MAJANI MANOR HOUSE!"

Other voices took up the call as titans poured into the streets of Kortran. Above the shouting, a fell voice cut through all others. "DESTROY THE INTRUDERS! TALIKARTIN, CLAIM THEIR SKULLS!"

Two titans stood above the rest. "That's Emperor Razeel and Talikartin the Guardian. We cannot defeat either of them," Orion breathed. "RETREAT!"

"I hate retreating!" Cyrus shouted – but didn't argue.

The rangers' bows hummed with arrows as they fell back, dashing past the titans that were swarming from every house into the narrow alleys and avenues. Cyrus stayed with the rear guard, but no titans had caught up to them yet - the arrows were proving a discouragement. Nyad let loose a spell that rained fire upon any who crossed beneath it. While it didn't stop the titans, it certainly slowed them, as they stopped to put out the flames upon emerging from it.

Cyrus charged up the ramp, one of the last to go, the closest titan only fifty feet behind him. Narstron was moving fast enough that Cyrus was having trouble keeping up. The titans had a stride five times that of a human and near ten times that of a gnome. *There is no way we can all make it*, Cyrus thought as he watched the fastest of their pursuers close the distance.

Cyrus passed Niamh, who had stopped to cast a spell. Cutting his momentum for a beat to aid her if needed, she completed her incantation and blazed past him. He watched as roots burst from the ground, breaking through the wooden road in front of them, wrapping around their enemies' feet and then ankles, dragging them down. As the roots reached their legs and pulled them to their knees, more burst forth and wrapped around arms of the titans, yanking them to the earth in a firm embrace.

Faces askew with anger, the trapped titans screamed in outrage, vines and roots clawing at them, grasping for purchase. Behind them, those that were free of the roots were attempting to climb over their trapped brethren.

Cyrus's attention turned in the direction they had been retreating: a lone giant stepped over him and rushed into the ranks of his ensnared comrades, killing a few of the surprised titans before they reacted and brought down their traitor. Cyrus looked back to see J'anda salute his enslaved titan as it was killed by three of its own.

Orion's voice rang over them, just behind him now. "Spell casters, fall back to the entrance – warriors, paladins, hold the line as the rear guard!" Orion caught an irritable look from Terian Lepos before adding, "Yes, you too."

A few of the more enterprising titans used their trapped fellows as stepping stones. One front runner was ahead of the rest. *Fresh meat*, Cy thought.

The warrior feinted to his left as if to slip past the titan but instead dodged to the right at the last second and plunged both swords into the titan's foot. Shocked and in pain, he screamed and plunged face first into the ground.

Cyrus scrambled up his fallen adversary to the back of its neck. He drove his sword blade into the base of the titan's skull. He looked up to see Narstron, already covered in the blood of the next titan. They locked eyes for a moment and he could hear Narstron utter the warrior's cry of exultation: "Ye gods, the battle!" Cyrus shot him a smile. *This is what warriors live for*, he thought with great satisfaction.

"Uh, boys?" Niamh's voice rang out. "Care to join us in the retreat?" She gestured at the Sanctuary army, almost back to the ring road. Vines sprung up from Niamh's spell, covering their escape as the three of them retreated up the ramp. A roar behind them startled Cyrus. He looked back to see the one called Talikartin the Guardian, his helm a shining silver to match his armor. Black sleeves flowed from beneath his chest plate and rough skin, scarred all over, covered the titan.

Beyond Talikartin, Cyrus caught sight of Emperor Razeel. He had a crown of gold shaped like the skull of a dragon and a green dragonskin cloak wrapped around him, buttoned at the collar. When he spoke, a terrible, cruel voice echoed through the caverns.

"Intruders! I am Emperor Razeel of Kortran, the City of Titans."

"Thank the gods he spelled that out for me," Narstron quipped from behind Cyrus. "I was certain I'd stumbled into a troll brothel purely by mistake."

"You would know from experience what those are like," Vara's voice came from behind them.

"You may win this day – as you did yesterday," Razeel continued, "and some of you may escape like the cowards you are – but your transgressions will neither be forgotten nor forgiven by the citizens of Kortran." The Emperor clenched his fist. "Talikartin the Guardian, make them pay with blood for the citizens they've killed and the priceless treasure they have stolen from us."

Talikartin was a titan among titans. Massive, his muscled frame bespoke of a power both physical and mystical. He broke free of the vines that clawed at his feet with ease. With a swing of his arms the titan swept his own people from his path, scrambling to get to the rear guard.

Niamh whispered behind him, "We are not going to get away on foot – not from him."

Cyrus looked back at her, a question on his lips. "Can you cast a teleport spell like you did in Ashan'agar's den? Get some people out of here?"

She shook her head. "Too many people; they're too scattered and far from me – one of the wizards needs to –" She stopped. "Nyad! We need an area teleportation spell!"

The blond elf looked stunned for a moment. She stopped and concentrated, whispering to herself. A bluish burst of fire engulfed her from toe to head – shocking Cyrus, who wondered for a moment if she'd accidentally scorched herself by mistake. He turned back to brace himself for Talikartin's assault. Out of the corner of his eye, he saw Narstron doing the same. A burst of blue fire shot past Cyrus's eyes and hovered in front of him, a little ball of cerulean flame. Looking back, Cyrus saw the Sanctuary army, one by one, disappearing into the bursts of blue fire.

"Grab the orb!" Niamh shrieked. Talikartin was only thirty paces away now. The Sanctuary army was gone. Narstron grabbed the orb hovering in front of him and disappeared into blue flames. A whirlwind engulfed Niamh and she too was gone.

Alone, in the city of Kortran, Cyrus looked for a moment across the mass of titans, ensnared, and caught sight of the Emperor Razeel again, whose eyes were afire in outrage.

Talikartin was close now, reaching back, intent on raining a crippling blow on the lone warrior in black, a blow he could not stop or avoid. "Return Ferocis to us and I will make your death painless."

"Ferocis?" Cyrus's hand remained at his side. *Twenty paces.* "Do not be coy! Return Ferocis – the Warblade of Bellarum – that you took from us, and I will make this fast. Otherwise, your death will not be swift."

Cyrus's eyebrow raised. *Ten paces.* "Tempting. But I didn't steal it." His eyes moved from Razeel to Talikartin, locking on the shocking blue pupils of this titan among titans. *Five.* And the warrior smiled. "So long, Tali," he mocked, scorn dripping from his words. "I'll be back for you – and your Emperor."

His hands reached out and grasped the orb as Talikartin's hand arced forward. Blue fire exploded, encompassing his vision and Talikartin the Guardian's killing strike vanished before him.

Chapter 9

The magics of teleportation faded from his eyes. He had arrived at Reikonos Square and no one from Sanctuary was anywhere in sight. Just another day: no dragons, no titans – just people going about their business. Most were headed to the markets or the commercial district, a few perhaps to the slums and the illicit trade within, others heading toward the Citadel or the city gates. Unsure what to do next, he turned to head back to the guildhall.

"Hey." The voice startled him. Floating a few feet above, smiling from ear to ear, was Niamh.

He returned her smile. "Glad to see you. Everyone made it out okay?"

She scowled. "Everyone but you, we thought. Another five minutes and I was going to assemble a search party." Her smile returned. "Glad I didn't have to. Ready to check out Sanctuary?" She cocked her head.

He hesitated. "I can't go without Andren. I give my blessing to join Sanctuary without reservations. But we have to get Andren first." He gestured in the direction of the slums. "Our guildhall is just through there; I'll go and be right back."

She floated down and grabbed him by the shoulder as he was turning to leave. "Hold it right there, hotshot. Nyad caught up with Narstron here at the same time I did. They're probably already at Sanctuary right now; Nyad has a teleport spell that can bring them right to the foyer." Her grin was now from ear to ear. "You and me? We got a ways to run. Hope you're not too tired..."

A few moments later Cyrus felt his feet touch the ground as the teleport spell died away and found himself in the long, wild grass of the Plains of Perdamun. Finding Niamh next to him, still floating, he finally found the moment to ask the question that had been on his mind. "How do you do that?"

She grinned again. "How do I do what?" She flipped her flaming red hair over her shoulder. "You mean, how do I fly? Walk on air?" She laughed, a sound that harmonized with the breeze rustling in the grasses of the plains. "It's magic, silly ass."

"I figured that much out for myself."

She paused, murmuring under her breath. Cyrus felt the light touch of magic, flowing from his feet up to his head. He looked down... and he was floating. "Because I'm a druid, a servant of nature, most of my spells are based on using nature's power. For example, the roots of the trees of Arkaria? I can command them, like I did in Kortran. I also have a spell that imbues you with the essence of a falcon – which means you can fly."

Without warning, she took off running north at top speed. With only a moment of delay Cyrus's reflexes kicked in and he followed her. *Not bad*, he thought, wind rushing in his face. They flew across the plains, the tall grass swaying in their wake. The grass here was much less dry than that of the Gradsden Savanna. It was lush and green, and swayed in the autumnal wind.

Niamh had been exaggerating the length of the run. After only five minutes, enormous stone gates appeared before them, parting a very tall wall. Over the top of it he could see a large building peeking out. As they ran through the gates, he was momentarily breathless.

It was a building unlike any he had seen; towers were topped by spires at the four corners of the building. The front had multiple archways leading from the towers to the center of the structure; an arch larger than the rest peaked at the roof. An enormous, circular stained glass window placed roughly twenty feet above the largest doors Cyrus had seen other than in Kortran. The tallest spire of all was a tower in the center of the building leading several hundred feet above the rest of the structure.

Niamh stopped at his side. "Welcome to Sanctuary."

Looking around he found the grounds were impressive as well. To his right were stables, and beyond them he could see an archery range. On the other side of the main building was a smaller stone building with a wooden roof that belched smoke from three different chimneys.

"Oy!" Narstron called out, coming from the stables with Andren and Nyad in tow. "Thought you might not have made it out."

Cy looked at him, eyebrow raised. "Yeah, I can see you were torn up about it, too."

He looked at Andren warily; the elf looked sober, for once, and a bit put out. "Thanks for bringing me along." His expression was sour.

"Sorry." Cyrus shrugged.

Changing his focus to Nyad, he bowed slightly. "Thanks for saving us all in there, Nyad. How long does the orb from that teleportation spell last before it disappears?"

Looking slightly baffled, she answered, "I think a minute or two? I've never stuck around long enough to find out. I do know," she said, "that it will follow you around 'til it goes out."

Niamh surveyed them anxiously. "So, are you gonna apply to join us or what?"

Cyrus looked at her, then looked at the expectant eyes of Andren and Narstron. "After consideration, I think Sanctuary is the kind of people we can rely on. So, yes." Nods of approval from Andren and Narstron followed.

Niamh beamed at them. "Well, all right. Ready for the grand tour?"

After they nodded, she led them through the entryway and into an enormous foyer. Hallways exited from all sides, but ahead of them was another, slightly less massive set of doors that were open wide and led into a great hall – complete with dining tables. "Great hall," Narstron mused aloud. "'Tis truly great. Is this where the meals are served?"

Niamh looked down at him. "Sure is. Three squares a day, plus there's always food available. There's a pretty extensive kitchen. Most of the cooking is done by Larana Stillhet. She's the handiest person around. She can cook, sew – almost any skill you'd need, she has. That's her workshop out back."

"The one with the three chimneys?" Cyrus asked.

Niamh nodded. "She tends to the domestic side of Sanctuary."

"What about ale?" Andren asked before Cyrus could follow up on his question.

"Larana is a master brewer, too."

"I can't tell you how excited I am to be here," Andren said.

After seeing the empty great hall, they went back to the foyer in time to see Vara crossing the room from the nearby lounge. She made no move to stop and talk to them, but Cyrus caught a glance from her that she averted after she noticed him looking.

"Vara!" Niamh called out, halting the paladin's progress. "Don't be rude to our guests."

The elf stopped, her armor heaving from the exertion of her pace across the floor. She faced away from them for a moment, seeming to compose herself before turning back with a wide smile that was disingenuous. "So pleased to see you all." Her voice was honey-sweet. "I do hope you find your way around well enough, and if you need any assistance in finding the exit, by all means, let me know." Her expression reverted back to disdain.

"You know," Narstron said, outraged, "I have no idea where your attitude comes from. You don't even know us!"

Her eyebrow raised but the rest of her face stayed in the same unpleasant expression. "And you think that would improve your case?" Without waiting for a response, she turned on her heel and left, striding up the staircase across the foyer.

Niamh had a pinched expression. "Don't worry about it. Vara is really... prickly. But she'll warm up to you all; it just takes time."

"How many centuries, approximately?" Andren said.

"Vara is who Vara is," came a deep voice from behind them. "Asking her to change would be like commanding the Torrid Sea to be still." Cyrus tensed as he realized who was speaking. Vaste the troll joined them. Looking down at Cyrus, he graced the warrior with a smile that carried a surprising warmth.

Cy looked evenly at him. "So you're Vaste."

"And though we haven't been introduced, I know your name to be Cyrus Davidon." Vaste's enormous hand came up to his mouth in a motion that made the green troll look reflective. "But what's in a name? Is it a name that's more important... or the content of one's character, would you say?" He paused, regarding the warrior, waiting for an answer.

Cyrus looked at the troll suspiciously, pondering the question, trying to look beyond the obvious answer. "Of course the content of someone's character would be more important than their name," he answered finally.

"Well said," the troll said with a nod. "So even if someone, say a gnome, had a suspicious name, something that sounded like it might make them goblin-born, would you look to the content of their character before you judged them?"

Cyrus raised an eyebrow. "Well, yes."

"Very decent of you. That's a wise sentiment indeed. How would you judge the content of that person's character? Through their deeds? Actions? Words?" The troll's stare once more locked on to the warrior, brown and black eyes shining down at Cyrus.

Cyrus could feel himself being verbally backed into a corner. "I suppose... that would be the usual way you would divine someone's character. See if their deeds matched their words."

"So logically speaking," the troll finished, with no trace of a smile, "you'd have to wait and see what words and deeds came from a person before you could really tell anything about them, wouldn't you?"

The rest of the group looked on. Nyad looked confused while Andren seemed annoyed. Narstron attempted to engage Niamh in a quiet conversation and ignore the exchange between Vaste and Cyrus.

Cyrus knew when he was beaten. "Point taken." The warrior took a deep breath. "I am pleased to make your acquaintance, Vaste. I'll be looking forward," he continued with only a trace of irony, "to getting to know you."

The troll bowed his head, smile fully returned. "And I you, Cyrus Davidon." Vaste bowed at the midsection, looking for a moment like a tower falling down, and walked away.

"Cyrus!" He heard his name called across the foyer. He turned to see Orion. "Glad to see you made it back safely." Orion's grin matched his own.

"Hell, I'm glad I made it back safely. I just... had to deliver a message before I left."

Though he didn't ask, the curious expression on his face indicated the ranger caught what Cyrus had said. "How are you feeling?"

"Frankly, I'm getting a little tired of cutting and running," Cyrus replied without expression.

Orion chuckled. "Get used to it in adventuring. Don't get me wrong, we usually win. But when you're that outnumbered, it makes it tough to do anything but live to fight another day." He paused, and clapped his hand onto Cyrus's shoulder. "I have no doubt that we'll be seeing a string of victories that you'll be a big part of." Walking over to Niamh, he murmured something to her. "I'll see you at dinner. There's a Council meeting about to start; we have to go." He headed up a nearby staircase, Niamh in tow, in the same direction Vara had gone.

A disturbing thought occurred to Cyrus. "Is Vara on the Council?"

Nyad smiled. "You mean is she an officer of the guild? Yes, she is. Now, would you like to finish the tour?"

As she led the way to a chamber in the back of the building, Cyrus walked beside her. "How long have you been with Sanctuary?" he asked, making conversation.

Nyad looked sidelong at him. "I've been here for a few years so I've had an opportunity to get to know the members of Sanctuary well. They're a great bunch of people."

They reached a door and Nyad paused to look directly into Cyrus's eyes. "This guild is a brotherhood, dedicated to the ideal of service. They will go to their deaths for you, if you're with us. But if we have an enemy, the converse applies – we'll go to our deaths to pursue them, especially if they've harmed a guildmate."

She did not break eye contact with Cyrus, and in that moment he saw the wisdom of a being much older than himself, something he had not noticed in her frivolity and cheeriness.

She opened the door before Cyrus had a chance to reply, and he took it to be her signal to close that subject of conversation. She continued by showing them through the armory. Inside stood an aged human with a craggy face. His armor looked even more battered than Cyrus's. "This is Belkan, our armorer," Nyad said as she gestured to the old man.

The man she called Belkan grunted at them and nodded. She introduced them.

"Davidon?" Belkan's furry white eyebrow raised when she mentioned Cyrus's name. A neutral expression forced its way onto the armorer's face as he looked the warrior over. "Pleased to meet you." His eyes fell to Cyrus's sword. "I suspect we can find better than that."

Cyrus looked around and nearly drooled at the selection of weapons and armor on the walls. "I lost my sword fighting a dragon. I just picked this up off the ground."

The bushy eyebrow raised again. "A dragon?" Belkan shook his head and muttered something unintelligible. "Stop by in the next couple days and we'll find you something. Now get going," the old man waved them off. "I have things to do."

The next stop was the Halls of Healing. As Cyrus walked through the door, he found Curatio sitting in front of a table with a gnome atop it. As they walked in, the gnome pointed at Cyrus. "That's him! He's the one who stepped on me: I remember the black armor!" His entire arm was no longer than Cyrus's forearm, and his voice had an almost comical pitch

Remembering that he had accidentally trod on someone in Kortran, Cyrus said. "I'm sorry! I was trying to get to the titan before it sounded the alarm. I didn't even see you there!"

The gnome nodded, perturbed. "Typical of tall folk; feet too far from your eyes to see where you're going."

Curatio smiled. "You're going to be just fine, Brevis."

Without a word of thanks, the gnome jumped down from the table and skittered out the door. Shaking his head, Curatio turned to the group. "Nice to see you all here! You seem like you've got the attitude we're looking for. If you need anything, just ask. If you'll excuse me, I have a meeting to get to. Nice to see you."

They left the Halls of Healing, and after seeing the lounge they made their way to the applicant quarters. Their chambers were a series of dormitory-style rooms, each applicant having their own, with a common bath for all the applicants. Nyad left them to get settled after letting them know when dinner would be served.

After spending a few minutes in his room – a desk, bed, mirror and a comfortable chair for sitting - Cyrus left to explore. Pausing to consider the wisdom of prowling around where he had not been invited, he shrugged inwardly. *What are they going to do?* he thought. *Kick me out?* With a chuckle, he left the applicant quarters and went up the nearest staircase.

At the top of the staircase Cyrus found himself in a room that housed a set of ornately carved double doors. From behind them he could hear voices – then the sound of a woman laughing – Niamh, he believed. *This must be the Council's Chambers.* Looking beyond the door he saw a staircase that lead up to the floor above the Council Chamber. Curious, he began walking toward it.

A sudden hissing sound made him freeze as he realized he was no longer alone. Descending the staircase was a paladin, which Cyrus knew from the regal bearing of the knight. His armor was scuffed but undamaged; he had clearly seen many battles and the wisdom that radiated from him showed it. He stopped before Cyrus, who was transfixed. His helm covered only a bit of his face, but he could see one of the eyeholes was covered in the helm.

Looking at Cyrus through the other with a stare that seemed to pierce directly into the warrior's heart, the knight spoke. "Greetings, Cyrus Davidon. Do not be afraid, for I would not harm you. I am Alaric Garaunt." A glimpse of humor flickered into his eye, the look of a man who was equal parts tired and wise. "I am the Ghost of Sanctuary."

Chapter 10

Cyrus stared at the vision before him. The paladin stared back. "Nice to meet you," Cyrus said. "How do you know who I am?"

A smile creased Alaric's mouth. "I know all that happens within these walls." He gestured vaguely. "I don't mean to be mysterious... at least not at this moment," the paladin said with an enigmatic smile. "You have heard of the Sanctuary Council?" When Cyrus nodded affirmation, he continued. "The Council is six officers sworn to the good of Sanctuary with a leader and an elder to assist. I am the leader."

"Ah, so that's why you're the 'Ghost of Sanctuary'," Cyrus said with a nod. "It's an honorary title for the leader."

Alaric shook his head gently. "No, I am the Ghost of Sanctuary because..." he paused, "...that is who I am. I am also the Guildmaster," he added. Catching the look of confusion on Cy's face, he smiled again. "In the matter of position, I want you to be clear on the role I occupy. In the matter of my title, I was aiming for mysterious." He chuckled. "I see it worked."

Clearing the confusion in his mind, Cyrus asked, "So, how long have you been with Sanctuary and how long have you been the leader?"

Instead of answering immediately, Alaric began to walk in a slow circle around the warrior, forcing Cyrus to turn to follow him with his eyes. "The answers to your questions are one and the same. I have been here since the day Raifa Herde, Erkhardt the Mighty, Cora, Pradhar and I gathered here and formed this guild."

Cyrus's mind raced. "What happened to the others?"

A flicker of sadness crossed Alaric's face. "A story for another time, perhaps. I, and the others of the Council, are pleased that you have joined us." He looked Cyrus in the eye. "I have no doubt you will become a great servant of Sanctuary."

He noted Cyrus bristle at the mention of the word servant. "Don't misunderstand me. When I say serve, I mean that true leadership is service. In other guilds, the leader is dictator, especially in the high powered armies. Their General's word is law, their bonds of fellowship non-existent. The members serve the ambitions of the leader, whatever they may be – hunger for power, desire for riches."

The paladin's eyes penetrated into Cyrus's. "Though we all desire material success, great leaders derive their accomplishment from a life of service to their people's ambitions. A feeling of purpose and significance rather than having the best armor and weapons in Arkaria." His words hit a chord within Cyrus, who had to look away from the paladin's gaze. *How did he know?* Cyrus wondered.

"That is not to suggest you cannot have both the bonds of fellowship and riches." A twinkle lit Alaric's eye. "Though perhaps you do not understand, someday you will see what I mean. For now, I must go to the Council." He stopped, surveying the warrior before him. "We will speak again soon," he said with absolute assurance. He turned and slid through the door of the chamber, opening it so thinly that Cyrus could not see anything within. Cyrus went back to his quarters, urge to explore oddly sated.

The appointed hour came for dinner and Cyrus made his way to the Great Hall, Andren and Narstron in tow. They found themselves in a group of over a hundred people, all as hungry as they. Many tables with benches were set up with a head table for the Council members at the back of the room, nearest the entrance to the kitchen.

A human woman worked behind the counter in the kitchen, bustling around with a few other servers as a line formed. As Cyrus made his way through, selecting from a wide variety of different dishes, he was pleasantly surprised: one of them was a meat pie. "This is my favorite!" he said.

The tanned woman in the kitchen smiled and blushed, not meeting Cyrus's gaze. "You're welcome," she mumbled.

The three of them quickly found a table. "Very friendly lot," Narstron commented. "I've gotten a good half-dozen offers to explore different places since I got here."

"Do you mind if we join you?" An elven healer made her way over with a dwarf in tow. Cyrus couldn't help but gawk – not only was she two feet taller than her companion, but he was wearing the most bizarre helmet Cyrus had ever seen. It came to a point on the top and two prongs on the sides swept forward. *If I lose my sword in battle again,* Cyrus reflected, *swinging this dwarf by his feet would give me an adequate cudgel as replacement.*

"I'm Celia," the elf introduced herself. "This is my husband, Uruk." They enjoyed a conversation with the two of them throughout dinner. Cyrus noticed that the Council went through the serving line last, in what he assumed was a reflection of Alaric's leadership philosophy.

As the meal concluded, Alaric stood. The genial conversation and idle boasting in the hall died down quickly, a mark of respect for their leader. "I have a few announcements to make. First, for those who wish to attend, there will be a Sanctuary-sponsored Alliance invasion of Enterra, capital of the Goblin Imperium, tomorrow night." Cy caught a glimpse of Vara out of the corner of his eye, feigning vomiting under her table. "Orion has asked," Alaric continued, "to say a few words about this invasion, which he will be leading."

Orion stood and placed his hands on his hips. "Tomorrow night we'll be meeting the Alliance guilds at Enterra. For those of you who may not be familiar with the Alliance or Enterra –" Cy knew he was talking about himself, Narstron and Andren, even though he didn't look at any of them specifically – "we are part of a three guild alliance composed of Goliath, the Daring and ourselves. Our targets are the Emperor and Empress of Enterra – as is their treasure trove."

Orion took his hands off his hips. "We've received word that the Emperor Y'rakh," the ranger stumbled over the goblin emperor's name, "has begun preparations to build their army for a march toward the Gnomish Dominions." Orion paced the forward length of the table. "Our goal is simple: to make our way into the depths of Enterra, kill the royal family and sack their treasury."

Orion stopped and pounded his left fist into his right hand. "If we kill the royal family it should defray any plans for conquest they have. The goblins of Enterra are also the keepers of the Earth Hammer, one of the mystical weapons supposedly imbued with the power of the gods; in this case, that of Rotan, God of Earth.

"Our biggest challenge," he said as he resumed pacing, "will be keeping quiet. This will not be a full scale invasion as we lack the numbers to defeat the goblins by brute force. We will take only our most experienced people. About a hundred of us from Sanctuary and roughly one hundred each from the remaining two guilds gives us a force of approximately three hundred." There was a sound of awe from the crowd. Orion dismissed it. "The goblins have an army of over ten thousand in Enterra. We are bringing enough force to fight our way in and decapitate the Royal family." His words were greeted with great approbation.

The applause continued until he was seated once more and Alaric had stood. "Dinner is adjourned," he proclaimed with mock seriousness. "Good luck to the invaders tomorrow. Those of you chosen to participate will receive notice. Goodnight." The great hall emptied quickly, as members of the guild filed out, many heading upstairs but more heading to the lounge.

Cyrus found himself in a corner of the lounge, a sprawling room with multiple tables and a variety of ways to entertain oneself. He was in a conversation area with comfortable seating. Andren was enjoying the fruits of Larana's brewing abilities while Narstron looked pensive.

"Fine ale," Andren said.

"All the finer for being free." Cy gave a sly look to Andren, who did not respond.

Narstron was almost bouncing in his chair, barely containing his enthusiasm. "I wonder when they'll announce who gets to go to Enterra?"

"I'm assuming you'll want to go, then?" Andren said, sarcasm in his voice.

The lightness of his tone was lost on Narstron. "I've always wanted to see Enterra. When I was a lad, growing up in the caves of the dwarven capital of Fertiss, a scouting party captured a goblin and brought it back to the Society of Arms." He paused. "Sometimes villages in the south would get sacked and they'd say it was goblins that done it. When they attack, they leave no sign – nothing that would tell you that they were the ones that did it. They even cover up their footprints.

"Anyway, they found one wounded in a destroyed dwarven settlement." Narstron's eyes narrowed. "We couldn't understand him at first, but after a while, he learned our language." His eyes grew intense at the memory. "Goblins are brutal creatures, absolutely nasty killers. They would have no hesitation about gutting you.

"But this one," he hesitated, "he told stories of Enterra sometimes." The dwarf looked embarrassed for a moment. "You know we dwarves like to be underground; it's just how Rotan made us –"

"Filthy mud diggers, yes," Andren said.

Ignoring Andren, Narstron continued. "This goblin told the stories... of how the stones of the city shone in the torchlight." His voice took on a daydreamy quality. "I've always wanted to see it since then." He straightened up. "I just hope I get chosen." Narstron turned to Cyrus. "Whaddya reckon the odds are?"

"I'd say your odds are good." Cyrus looked around and caught sight of the gnome, Brevis, holding court in front of a group. Whatever he was saying had them enthralled, but he had the look of a man discontented about something.

Cyrus shunted his attention back to Andren. "By the way, you never told me that elves live thousands of years."

"Not exactly a cheery subject, is it?" Andren tipped his ale back. "I don't enjoy reminding you that I'll be here long after you're dust."

"So you'll live longer than a human?"

"Already have," he answered. "I'm two thousand years old, well into middle age. Most elves could make it to five thousand – maybe six if they're really long lived."

"What about the 'Old Ones' you told me about – the first elves, the ones that were immortal?" Narstron asked.

Andren frowned. "Legends and bullshit, that is." He looked evenly at Cy, catching his gaze over his glass of ale. "Don't you have a bit of your own business in Enterra?" When Cy didn't answer, the elf pressed him. "Same business you had with Ashan'agar?"

Cy silenced him off with a look. Checking to make sure no one had overheard them, he turned back to the circle and lowered his voice somewhat. "Yes, I do." Reaching beneath his chestplate, his hand emerged with a small, tattered piece of parchment that he carefully handed to Andren.

The elf looked at it without saying anything for a beat. "This looks impossible." He threw it back and it drifted in the air for a moment before the warrior caught it. "Good luck."

Narstron shrugged. "A lot of work, but not impossible."

Cyrus eyed the piece of parchment. "When I assemble this sword, it will be worth it." He had read it enough times to have memorized it, but his eyes caressed the list on the paper once more before he folded it up and put it away.

Serpent's Bane – the guard and grip are in possession of Ashan'agar, the Dragonlord.

Death's Head – the pommel is held by Mortus, God of Death.

Edge of Repose – the Gatekeeper of Purgatory holds the blade as a prize for one who knows to ask for it.

Avenger's Rest – G'koal, Empress of Enterra has the Scabbard.

Quartal – the ore needed to smith the sword together is found only in the Realm of Yartraak, God of Darkness.

Brought together by one who is worthy, they shall form Praelior, the Champion's Sword.

Vara was seated by herself in a corner, quartered away, allowing Cyrus to study her unobserved. Her nose came to a point, accenting the regal bearing of her face. Her pointed elven ears were behind her blond hair, which was hanging free for the first time since he'd met her. Instead of her armor, she wore a cloth shirt and pants that, while seated, clung tightly to her. She was very fit; Cyrus could tell.

Andren leaned over to Cyrus. "Taking a closer look at our resident ice princess?" Cyrus didn't look away from Vara. He whispered, "If you keep staring at her like that, she's likely to feel the heat of your intentions and burst into flames – round about her groin." Cy averted his eyes and turned back to the group. Narstron was laughing quietly.

Andren looked at him with pity. "You have something for elven women? Was your wife an elf?"

Cyrus blushed. "No, she was human."

"Wouldn't have surprised me if she was an elf." Andren sighed. "More elven women marrying human men these days than elven ones." His eyes cast downward. "Makes it a bit difficult on the rest of us." He refocused on Cyrus. "Why didn't we ever meet your wife? I know you saw her not that long ago. Afraid to bring her to our old digs?"

A flash of memory hit Cyrus, and the words his former wife had spoken drifted to his mind unbidden. *"You cling to your friends because you have nowhere else to go and nothing to do with your life."* His teeth gritted at the memory. "Showing her our guildhall was not going to impress her," he said, controlling his emotions.

"See? That's why you should date a dwarven woman, if you could find one not taken by a dwarven man," Narstron shot at Andren, who looked away. "Dwarven women found our old guildhall quite homey. It's so dark in the slums that it's like being underground." The dwarf smiled at the memory.

"Oh please," Andren dismissed him. "Are you going to talk about that wench from the slums bar again? She had a bit more flesh than it took to cover her bones, if you take my meaning."

"Aye, that's how I like them," Narstron said. "Anyway, she didn't mind being in there, even with you lot snoring away."

"Oy, that explains certain night noises." Andren grimaced. "I'm going to meet some new people," the healer said as he stood up and walked away.

"I have to go sit in my quarters and clean my brain out with my sword," Cyrus excused himself. He took one last sidelong glance at the table where Vara sat reading and reflected that he had no interest in meeting new people but wanted to understand one he'd already met.

When he returned to his room he found an envelope on the bed. It said, in very simple lettering:

You are chosen to go to Enterra. – Orion

Chapter 11

The next day dawned bright and sunny, but by midday the promise of its glory was cut short by rain that had by dinner turned into a thunderstorm.

"Fortunately, we don't have to travel in that." Narstron laughed with relief. He and Andren had gotten the same invitation as Cyrus. If not for teleportation spells, Enterra was several months journey. Instead, a druid would transport them directly to the southern edge of the Mountains of Nartanis, only a few hours hike from Enterra's entrance.

Cyrus looked across the crowd and found Brevis and his cronies laughing about something. Orion was talking quietly to Selene, who was unable to conceal a smile. Curatio, J'anda, Nyad, Vaste, and Niamh were scattered throughout the crowd but Cyrus found more curious those who were absent. Alaric was nowhere to be seen, nor was Terian or Larana. Vara was also missing, he thought, but then caught sight of her entering from a nearby doorway.

"Vara!" Brevis called out to her. "You should come with me."

She continued walking. "No, I don't think so."

"What does it take," he sauntered up to her, looking her straight in the knees, "to get some time together, just you and me?"

She halted forward progress, turning back with a frown. "I have no interest in one-on-one time with you, gnome, and I have told you this many, many times. Should you continue to persist in your incessant innuendo, I will personally kill you and have Larana turn your corpse into a weapons rack for my quarters. That way, every day, I can draw my sword from one of your orifices," she concluded as the gnome blanched. "Would that qualify as some 'time together'?"

Laughter echoed through the hall as Vara turned on her heel and resumed her course out the door.

Niamh materialized next to them. "Hi, guys," she greeted them. "Everybody stick close: we're going to be taking off in just a second. Squeeze in; druid teleportation spells don't reach out nearly as far as a wizard's," she said.

She murmured a few words under her breath and the winds picked up, just as they had in Ashan'agar's den, and soon Cyrus felt his feet touch the ground again. The strong smell of sulphur wrinkled his nose and he looked down to the ash and black dirt then raised his gaze up to the horizon. Volcanic rock was everywhere – streams of lava poured forth from volcanoes, pooling in lakes of magma. Drakes flew across the sky in the distance. Cy looked around him as whirlwind after whirlwind deposited Sanctuary's army upon the volcanic soil of the Mountains of Nartanis.

Cyrus found it hard to believe that days before he had been standing in the same place, on the way to Ashan'agar's den. Looking to the east, he knew the entrance to that cavern was in the distance and shuddered at the thought of what might have happened had Sanctuary not been there.

Once the army was assembled they began their trek. The gnomes and dwarves scrambled to keep up while the humans and elves had to put forth very little effort to keep pace. No one had brought horses, knowing that they would be venturing underground.

After a few hours they left the volcanic foothills and found themselves navigating around the edge of a crater. They approached a keep built into the side of a gargantuan mountain, gates built over a cave entrance with goblins walking the walls and manning the entrances. Cyrus had not seen goblins before. Between three to five feet in height, they were a sort of gaunt, squat, green and scaly creature with fearsome teeth. Their large ears drooped over their skulls.

They halted at the cover of the crater's edge. Orion addressed the groups quietly. "We meet the Alliance inside the gates. Remember, stealth is our primary concern. There is an area inside the entrance where we'll be forming up. Our spell casters will cast invisibility spells on the warriors and rangers, then on themselves and we will move to the rendezvous point. Remember, invisibility can be an unstable spell, so move through the gates quickly."

"Why always *inside* the gates?" Cyrus muttered.

Orion signaled and Cy watched as one by one the army disappeared. He muted his own cry of shock as Niamh cast a spell on him and his hand and sword vanished. "It's okay, Cy, hold on." Her next spell made it seem as though a veil had been lifted from his eyes – everyone reappeared, although they looked faded, as though they were in a heavy mist.

Orion signaled the move after everyone had been made invisible and they walked through the gates, prompting a puzzled look from a nearby goblin who heard something but trusted his eyes. Cy continued to walk even after he had lost sight of where he was going in the dark, and he suddenly felt one of his feet meet empty air where he had thought there would be rock.

He fell forward, arms rushing out to cushion his fall, trying to roll out of it. He hit the ground a few feet later with a crash of armor on stone. He heard laughter all around him, and felt a hand reach into his and pull him to his feet. The hand was soft, gentle, but not without calluses. A lightness crept through his eyes akin to the sensation J'anda had created when he helped Cyrus see in Kortran.

An elven woman had helped him up. She was pretty and short, with a bow slung across her back, tangled in her long brown hair. He could now see in the darkness of the cave around them. Dirt walls led off into the distance, and a few people sat around waiting.

"Are you okay?" she asked.

"Yes." *What is it with all these pretty elves?* "Nothing bruised but my massive arse and my bigger ego." He blinked. "Who cast the spell on me? I can see now."

"It was me," Vaste said from behind him. "I was afraid you'd fall into me, and frankly I'm not sure I could support your 'massive ego' since I'm too busy carrying your arse."

She laughed, a lovely sound, like a wind chime. "I'm Elisabeth, from the Daring." She looked past him. "Hi, Vaste." The troll nodded as he passed them.

"Pleased to meet you. I'm Cyrus Davidon, with Sanctuary."

She laughed again. "Nice to meet you. Hi, Curatio!" She waved past him. Curatio made his way over and they hugged. "Good to see you again!"

Cyrus looked around. The Sanctuary force had settled in for a break after their long hike. Curatio and Orion exchanged greetings with Elisabeth as others trickled over and joined them. Doing a quick head count, he only saw about two dozen people waiting.

"Cyrus, this is Cass Ward from the Daring." Cyrus smirked at the warrior that joined them, a hulking human with armor painted grey. Catching the look exchanged between the two of them,

Orion remarked, "Do you know each other?"

Cass answered first. "I would never claim to know this disgusting and uncivilized barbarian, who gives warriors of the Reikonos Society of Arms a bad name," his voice dripping with a sort of mocking sarcasm.

"Nor would I ever claim to be affiliated with this boasting heap of horse dung." Cyrus's repartee was just a bit slower getting out. "Yes, we know each other – no we don't hate each other. Cass and I were friendly rivals. We started at the Society of Arms at the same time, went through warrior training together." Looking sidelong for a reaction, he continued, "He's just never gotten over the fact that I am, in fact, a much better warrior – and much better looking – than he could ever claim to be –"

"Hardly!" Cass cut him off. Dropping the mocking tone, he finished Cyrus's thought. "We've always had a grudging respect for each other." A pause. "Well, he's always had a grudging respect for me… I always thought he was as useless as an empty keg of ale…" His reply left Cyrus shaking his head but smiling back slyly.

Cass turned his attention to Orion. "We have about thirty here tonight. It was the best we could field at this point."

Orion chewed his lip. "I appreciate your help, Cass. Goliath should be able to compensate for that."

A voice broke in, feminine, abrasive, and straight to the point. "Goliath will not be attending tonight." Cyrus caught sight of the owner of the voice as she edged closer. It was a female dark elf wearing the light robes and lettered shawl given to healers by the Healer's Union when they finished their training.

Curatio smiled, ignoring the poor tidings. "As always, it's a pleasure to see you, Erith Frostmoor."

The dark elf acknowledged Curatio's greeting. "Sorry to be the bearer of bad news, Orion." Her face wore a distasteful expression, as though the words she was speaking had soured within her lips.

Orion's jaw dropped. His head swiveled between Elisabeth, Cass and Erith. "Where's your Guildmaster, Partus?"

Erith exchanged a quick glance with Cass and Elisabeth. "Partus and most of our more experienced adventurers decided to part ways with those of us who wanted to make the Daring a great guild. They took about seventy-five percent of our number and left to join Goliath."

Orion looked stunned. "They have the largest force in this Alliance... and they aren't coming?"

Erith shook her head at Orion's last inquiry. "The forces of Goliath are fully occupied in a march through the Ashen Wastelands."

Curatio's low whistle broke the group out of a moment's silence. "They would dare to march through the dragon homeland?"

Erith nodded. "They've made the decision to kill dragonkin in order to ally themselves with the titans of Kortran."

Cyrus shook his head in amazement. *Why would anyone ever voluntarily align themselves with the titans of Kortran? Madness*, he thought.

"They have some considerable wealth – perhaps unique armors and weapons as well." Curatio shrugged, but his voice sounded hollow.

Erith shook her head in annoyance. "If that's your price for being a servant of Emperor Razeel, then start begging now." A pause emphasized her point. "Goliath will be killing dragonkin for the next three months before they'll even be allowed into the city of Kortran to begin talking peace with the titan envoys."

During this exchange, Orion was feverishly plotting, strain visible on his face. "We can still do this. We were planning to rely on stealth – now it's just more urgent than ever with less than half the force we planned."

"Why don't we just cast invisibility on our entire force and sneak down?" Cyrus asked.

"The goblins will have guard checkpoints set up – they'll have the ability to see through invisibility spells, so it won't matter," Curatio said. "Invisibility is only for short distances."

Orion nodded. "We'll need a screening force to take down sentries, and we'll focus our attacks on the guard points." He nodded, almost to himself in affirmation. "This will still work; we'll just need to keep a tight formation. And, J'anda," he shouted, turned to the enchanter, who appeared from out of the crowd, looking very human today. "You'll need to be especially on guard. We'll put the warriors out front to occupy the goblins and give each a dedicated healer and support force." He nodded to himself again. "This will work."

"I can certainly keep quite a few of them contained," J'anda said, "but I am uncertain about the abilities of the other enchanters to ensnare more than one mind at a time. It is..." he paused, looking for a diplomatic way to state his point, "...complex, keeping more than one enemy confounded at a time."

If Cass was skeptical he kept it to himself. "I have full faith in your plans, Orion. I only wish we had more support to offer you, but the full might of the Daring stands ready. Which warriors will you choose for this excursion?" He gestured to himself in what Cyrus thought to be an overly dramatic fashion.

"You will be one of the three." Cyrus caught a tone of appeasement in Orion's voice. He was a little too enthusiastic in agreement with his ally. "Narstron and Cyrus from Sanctuary can be the other two, unless anyone else has a candidate to put forward?"

Cyrus was surprised. He knew there were other warriors in Sanctuary with longer tenure than he and Narstron. He looked at Orion and nodded with a confidence he didn't feel. "We won't let you down."

Over the next few minutes they broke the force into support groups, centered on the warriors. Cy found himself in a group with Elisabeth, J'anda, Niamh and with Erith as his healer. "Nice to meet you, Erith. I'm Cyrus Davidon."

She smiled humorlessly. "You've healed one warrior, you've healed them all. Try not to make my job hard by doing anything stupid – like, say, getting yourself killed."

"Well, ma'am, I can promise you I'm going to try not to die."

"Try very hard." She stopped smiling. "I don't know the resurrection spell, so if you die, you're not coming back." She reared her hand back and slapped him on the backside. "Now get in there and fight."

He looked in disbelief at the healer, but she didn't crack a smile. Almost positive that she wasn't serious, but not eager to test the theory, he walked forward with the lead element of the army as they began their descent into the caves.

"I need a ranger out front," Orion called out. "One who's good at stealth."

Elisabeth raised her hand, slight smile on her face. "I've never been accused of being sneaky, but I have been known to disappear stealthily from time to time."

Orion did not return her smile, clearly frazzled. "I need you to sneak down the tunnel and scout the goblin defensive positions. Get their attention, bring them to us one at a time if possible, or in small groups." Elisabeth nodded with some enthusiasm. "If you run across a checkpoint, leave it be; we'll attack it as a group."

Elisabeth melted into the shadows of the cave, and even with his improved vision, Cyrus could not see her. She soon returned with three goblins – Cyrus attacked the first, slashing his sword into the scaled flesh. His group jumped into the action a moment later and the beast was hit with fire, ice, a small bolt of lightning that seemed to originate from midair, and a great many blades. It died within seconds, having never had a chance to do anything but stab at Cyrus once with its claws, drawing blood through a gap in his armor.

He heard Erith's voice behind him. "You're only getting three mending spells for the entire invasion, so you'd better pace yourself." He looked back as he felt a healing wind on his arm as the spell took hold and saw her holding up her finger. "That's one!" Irritated, he held up a finger of his own, and she was beset by a case of the giggles. "That's two! I'd be careful, if I were you!"

They proceeded down the tunnel, Elisabeth bringing goblins to them a few at a time. They ignored side tunnels as Orion guided them down following a very worn map. They passed through areas of dirt and rock tunnels, and into areas of carved and intricate stonework, clearly built with incredible engineering skill. They alternated between action and boredom; long minutes would pass with no sign of the ranger, and then she would appear bringing groups of goblins in quick succession. None of their foes had a chance to run and their shouts did not attract others.

As they descended, a far-off chatter filled the air.

"It's the city," Narstron said. "Goblins are awfully loud, aren't they?"

"Sounds like your snores," Andren said under his breath.

Upon reaching a checkpoint, they halted, hiding in the shadows of the tunnel. About ten goblins were visible either in the entryway or atop a battlement built into the cave. They had a clear view for a long distance; there was no safe approach.

Orion looked ahead, face inscrutable. "This will be tough. It's the entrance to the royal chambers. We need to be careful."

Narstron looked under the ranger's shoulder. "Why don't we just charge the gate?"

Orion took on a pained expression. "There's a garrison of at least five hundred goblins inside the walls of their complex, not to mention considerably more a few minutes away in the city."

Narstron's eyes went wide. "Good enough reason, I suppose."

Orion waved for J'anda to join him. He discussed something at length with the enchanter while they waited.

"So where is the Daring's guildhall, Elisabeth?" Cyrus said, attempting to make conversation.

She looked at him before answering, favoring him with a smile. "We're in Reikonos, not far from the bank, in the guildhall quarter."

Erith cut in and gave Cyrus an amused look. "You're a pretty lousy flirt, even for a meat-head warrior."

He sent her a glare before he could stop himself but when he saw the ear to ear grin of triumph on her face, he held his tongue. Niamh pretended not to hear her and changed topics. "Erith, when did the Daring start having the problems you were describing?"

Her smile turned back to the sour look she'd worn since they met. It gave him a warm, happy feeling to see her like this. "It's been a problem for years. We've been allied with Goliath since before Sanctuary came along, and with their fortunes on the rise and ours falling, it was only a matter of time before some rats decided to jump ship." She grimaced. "Of course, I don't think we'd anticipated that the rats in question would be almost the entire officer corps..."

"I had no idea that the Daring were having that much trouble." Niamh's voice was sympathetic.

"It's not something we're publishing on our recruitment materials." Erith's voice turned hard. "We'll build back; we just need some time. Unfortunately, without the Alliance we don't stand much chance of being able to offer experienced adventurers what they want, which is a chance to get more powerful weapons, armor and gold."

Niamh nodded. "I agree, but this turnout doesn't bode well for the future of the Alliance. It just doesn't seem like Goliath cares for supporting their allies. We all know this isn't the first event they've failed to attend. I remember when we thought of this Alliance as one guild."

"Many still do, Niamh." A malicious grin split Erith's lips. "It's just that some of them think that instead of Alliance, it says 'Goliath' on our crest."

Three goblins burst from the gates – the others looked strangely dazed. The first three were dispensed with in moments.

Cyrus caught his with a slash of the blade across its skinny neck before the rest of his group could engage it. The goblin's head floated through the air and came to rest in front of Erith, splattering her with blood.

She was irate. "You did that on purpose!"

Cyrus didn't attempt to hold back his grin. "Did not."

"Did too!"

"Children, please," Cass said, smile bleeding through into his voice. "Nice work, Cy. If I didn't know how truly wretched you were with a sword, I'd swear you aimed that shot right at your healer."

Cy snorted. "If you know what a princess my healer is, you should know why she needed to play catch with a goblin skull."

"Who are you calling princess?" Erith sputtered, all trace of humor gone.

Orion called for more incoming goblins but instead of three, six charged forth. Cyrus stepped forward, nicking the side of the first goblin but failing to penetrate the scaly hide. He swung his sword at the second target, and connected with its forearm, drawing blood. Both goblins screeched and clawed at him.

He managed to dodge the first one's slashes, but in avoiding it he moved too close to the second and it managed to stab between the joining point of his arm and his chest plate. He felt the claw pierce him, and bit back the pain as he aimed a riposte across its eye socket. His slice took the goblin's eye, causing a howl of pain. The rest of his party descended upon it, cutting it to ribbons as he turned to deal with the first.

He found it turning on its heel to flee, but before it had a chance he swiped with his sword, giving it a firm cut across its back. As it staggered, off balance, Cyrus watched a shape detach from the shadows – Elisabeth plunged two swords into its lower back, prompting a scream of pain that cut off as it fell backward and she slit its throat. She looked back to see Cyrus watching her, as she wiped her daggers off on the tunic of the goblin. "Not very pretty when you look at them up close, are they?"

"No," Cyrus said, "They're not."

The last sentry at the entrance to the castle needed to be dealt with, Cy reflected –

He looked up the see it dead, riddled with arrows. Orion and a few other rangers were replacing their bows on their backs. "Mesmerize is an impressive spell, isn't it?" Orion chuckled. "It left them dazed to the attack going on."

A piece of the puzzle clicked for Cyrus. A powerful enchanter could control the mind of their enemies, and J'anda had lulled the goblins into a virtual coma to get them to come in small numbers. Now he wondered if perhaps some enchanter's spell had kept them from running when they realized they had waltzed into a trap.

He had no time to further reflect on this possibility, as Orion called them to action again and they swept through the undefended gates, finding themselves out of the darkened caves and into hallways of stone.

Chapter 12

Cyrus scanned the room as they entered a large chamber that could have come from any castle he'd ever seen. There were no patrols within the halls. "Easy so far, isn't it?" he said to Cass, who was walking alongside him.

Cass chuckled before answering. "We're moving fast and we've been hiding the bodies of the sentries we've killed. It'll get tough; just wait. I expect one hell of a fight in the throne room. Many, many guards there in addition to the royal family, who are not weaklings – they're chosen from the finest fighters in the empire. It takes over a year of contests and battles to the death to determine the Emperor after one dies."

"That process has to whittle down their numbers," Cyrus realized.

"Weakening their military by killing a great many of their veteran fighters," Cass finished for him. "You've got it. That's why Orion's plan is ingenious." The warrior smiled. "We let them destroy themselves as a fighting force and we seize their treasury."

Cyrus looked at him, surprised. "You didn't learn about goblin culture at the Society of Arms."

Cass laughed. "Hell no. They don't teach you anything beyond what to do with a sword. I read a lot about the world after I left." He slapped Cyrus on the shoulder. "You should try it."

They crept down the hallways, which were wide enough for them to walk four at a time. Orion stopped them outside a large door. They had passed a great many doors as they went, but this was the most baroque and impressive thus far, with carvings that covered it from floor to ceiling. "Behind this door are the Emperor and Empress of Enterra. J'anda, prepare the enchanters." Cyrus saw Narstron at the head of his group, eagerly anticipating the battle. Andren was assigned to his team, as was Vaste. "When the door opens, we storm the room. Everyone ready?" Orion held up three fingers and began to count down... three... two... one...

He threw open the door and the three warriors stormed past the ranger, picking their targets. Narstron was on the right flank and he engaged three guards on the right side of the room. Cass charged forward to the throne and caught the Emperor Y'rakh with a strike of his sword. It bounced off the Emperor's thick skin, and Y'rakh flung out a hand, hitting Cass with a blow that propelled him backwards into a wall. He recovered quickly, but it put him out of the fight for precious seconds as his group moved to engage the Emperor.

Meanwhile, Cyrus caught sight of his target, G'koal, the Empress of Enterra. She stood slightly shorter than he but well over the height of the average goblin. He leapt forward, sword raised, and swung it at her. She met him with a perfectly timed backhand that sent him flying across the room the same way he'd seen Cass go sailing.

He hit the wall and bounced up to see four Goblins blocking his path to the Empress. He watched as blue lights surrounded two of them, enchanters working to mesmerize them while he dealt with the other two. Empress G'koal was leering at him from the throne platform, across the room, silently daring him to come back for her. She had a sword drawn, holding it her side. The scabbard caught his gaze – it was red, with patterns running the length of it.

His group was behind him at the door, moving through warily after seeing him flung across the room. A mending spell ran across his body and he cast a quick look at Erith, whose face was edged with concern. "That's four!" he said in mild surprise.

Her eyes found his, and all trace of sarcasm was gone. "Be careful," she mouthed, too quietly for him to hear but plain enough to see.

His group joined him in attacking the two goblins keeping him from re-engaging the Empress. His head was ringing from the hit he'd taken, but he killed one of them while his party killed the other. He saw Narstron and his group in the midst of at least ten goblins. Several had the dazed expression of mesmerization, but a few members of the dwarf's party had fallen; there were bodies scattered around him. To his left, Cass waded into combat with the Emperor, his force behind him. Goblins were trickling out of a door in the wall behind Cass.

"Orion!" Cyrus shouted. "We've got goblins coming through that door!" He gestured in Cass's direction.

Orion had a look of sudden panic. "It's the door to the barracks! Elisabeth, keep it shut!" The ranger nodded and charged into the breach, knocking over three more goblins as she slammed the door shut. "Keep an eye out for any that make it past her!" A few grunts of acknowledgment met his order.

A look at Narstron's part of the battle told him that things were not going well on the right flank. More dead bodies, but what seemed to be the same number of goblins. Cyrus changed direction and led his group into the fray with Narstron. They killed four goblins with no appreciable decrease in the numbers of the enemy.

As Cyrus looked up from the battle he noticed two more goblins slip into the fight. His eyes followed their path back to the door where Elisabeth had stood moments before, which now was only slightly obstructed by the corpse of an elf – goblins were pouring through in waves. He watched them hit the rear flank of Cass's group at the door. Selene and Vaste were cut to ribbons by ten of the beasts. Another three pounced on J'anda, who was casting spell after spell, trying to stem the tide of foes. He crumpled and Cyrus realized for the first time, as the enchanter's illusion dropped, that J'anda was a dark elf.

The moment the enchanter died, the noise level in the room exploded as every one of the goblins J'anda had mesmerized – almost thirty by that point – woke from their trances. Cass's group, focused on the Emperor, was hit by a wave of goblins. Cyrus watched Niamh barely escape in a gust of wind too small to take anyone else with her. Nyad was killed as four Goblins impaled her with their claws from three different directions. Eyes rolling back in her head, she dropped to the ground.

Cyrus redoubled his efforts, swinging his sword as hard as he could. He was rewarded with three kills in three seconds – two decapitations and he pierced the last goblin cleanly through the heart. Even as the last goblin dropped, four more swarmed to replace it. Blocking their strikes as he retreated toward the wall, he heard Erith's scream behind him, and watched as two goblins finished her off. Behind her he watched Orion melt into the shadows unseen.

Time slowed down for Cyrus. He saw Curatio, of all people, swinging a mace, crushing the skulls of three enemies with one swipe. He watched as five goblins swarmed the healer, pulling him to the ground. Cass died, the last of his force, as the Emperor let out a screeching cry of victory.

His own party decimated, Cyrus moved closer to Narstron,

who was now cutting through a pile of goblins attacking him with great intensity. The dwarf's blows were so strong that they were severing limbs and heads with every slash. Andren was buried under the dead, he was certain. Cyrus had his back against the wall, swinging like mad, and could see Narstron doing the same, using his lack of height to evade the enraged goblins that came after him in a swarm.

Cy risked a quick look at the Empress. His eyes froze as a human-sized figure emerged from behind one of the thrones, gliding toward the Emperor, completely covered in a long black cloak, head obscured by the cowl.

Cyrus felt a sudden, sharp pain in his shoulder. One of the scaly creatures clamoring over him had found purchase in his armor and fully exploited it. He felt the hot blood running down his side, felt his right arm cease working abruptly, and he had one arm left to swing his sword with.

A strangled victory cry rose from the throng to his right and he caught sight of Narstron lifted aloft on the shoulders of a crowd of goblins. A strange chant rang out over the room, something that sounded to Cyrus's ears like, "Gezhvet! Gezhvet!" He twisted back to deal a killing blow to a goblin in front of him and saw the black cloaked figure reaching a hand out to the Emperor, who pulled a large warhammer from his belt and hand it to the figure somewhat reluctantly.

Cyrus's senses were flooded with the beasts as his focus shifted to the growing number of goblins attacking him. The strange, pungent smell of them filled his nostrils. It was suddenly hot in the depths of Enterra, and there were more goblins than he could count. He felt another sharp pain, this one in his leg, and it brought him to his knees. As he looked up into the black eyes of Empress G'koal, standing over him triumphant, he tried to swing his sword at her. She swung her blade across his neck, hard, as he watched it, eyes transfixed on her elaborate scabbard. He felt a draining sensation, then lightheadedness, and his last vision was of the goblin Empress, somehow, impossibly, smiling in victory.

Chapter 13

Cyrus awakened, light bleeding into his vision. He saw Selene, badly wounded, shaking and crying, standing above him. He recognized where he was, as he looked up – it was the entrance to Enterra, where he'd fallen over and been helped up by Elisabeth.

"Selene!" he cried out. "What happened?" He caught sight of Curatio and Vaste moving among bodies, lined up in rows. The invading army, Cyrus realized.

The elf did not respond at first. "Niamh fetched help," she said, struggling with every word.

Sounds of battle from down the corridor drew his attention. A goblin corpse flew through the air and landed at the edge of the rows of bodies. Alaric Garaunt followed it, anger radiating from the paladin even though his mouth was the only part of his face that was visible through his helm. The knight was flanked on either side by Terian Lepos and Vara, who each wore a neutral expression.

"The corridors in front of us," Alaric said, voice taut with rage, "are quite clear now." The Ghost calmed. "We won't be seeing any more goblins in this segment of the caves for some time, I suspect. The rangers are bringing the dead out as quickly as safety permits."

Cyrus looked to find Curatio nodding quietly. The healer turned away to another body, channeling powerful magics that lit up the inside of the cave. "If you can bring them to me, I'll resurrect them as quickly as possible." The healer tensed for a moment. "This would go much faster if not for the fact that Vaste, Selene and myself are the only healers that know the resurrection spell." Curatio paused for a moment, looking almost reluctant. "Is there no other...aid...for us?"

Alaric's face was hidden behind his helmet, masking most of his expression, but his mouth was drawn tightly in a line. "It would appear you have things under control. If the situation becomes dire, we will do..." the knight paused, searching for words, "...whatever it takes... to resurrect them all before time runs out."

Vara made her way forward. "I can help. Though my mending spells don't have the power of a healer's, they can at least help relieve the pain." Curatio nodded and Vara began to move among the wounded, starting as far from him as possible, breathing a few words here and there. Cyrus could hear thanks being murmured to her.

Brevis stood up to catch Vara's attention. "My boot is missing."

Vara looked at him, calm, cool, uncaring. "This affects me how?"

Brevis looked back at her, expression dull. "Did you take it?"

She blinked three times in rapid succession. "I didn't touch your corpse except to drag it out of the way to make room for more bodies," she said in a tone of near disbelief. "Besides," she told him. "You're far too ugly to molest when you're dead."

A familiar glint found its way into Brevis's eye. "What about when I'm alive?"

A roll of the eyes. "When you're alive, you smell too poorly." Vara continued to work her way through the ranks of the freshly risen, casting healing spells.

Cyrus sat up, gingerly at first, and looked around. He saw Orion talking to Cass and Erith. None of them had been healed yet, and each was clutching painful-looking wounds. He suddenly understood why he was in such pain. No healer had the magical energy to spare for mending spells when there were so many dead to be brought back. He caught Andren's eye in the corner and hobbled his way over to him, nearly falling over and catching himself on a cave wall for support.

Andren handed him a flask. "You look worse than I do," he said as Cyrus took a drink. "But not as bad as Orion." The ranger, though uninjured, had a haunted look in his eyes as he and Cass exchanged words with Erith, whose normally dark blue skin was much paler. "Or Curatio, come to that." Curatio was working feverishly with the other two healers, casting resurrection spells as quickly as they could. "You only have so much time to cast before someone is dead for good."

Cyrus broke his silence as he took another drink from the flask. It tasted like rum from the islands in the Bay of Lost Souls. Something stirred in the back of his head, making its way through the fog of discomfort from his broken ribs and countless bleeding wounds. *At least none of them is gushing blood,* he conceded. "Wait," Cyrus realized, "why aren't you healing the wounded?"

Andren's cheeks reddened. "I'm drained. I tried to cast a heal on myself four times and it sparked out." The healer took another swig. "I'm surprised that Curatio and the others can manage a resurrection spell – they're supposed to be really draining, and if they just got resurrected themselves..." Andren shuddered. "They're burning their own life energy if they're out of magic."

"How does that work?" Cyrus was curious.

"Only so much magical energy at a time," Andren said. "Just like your arms get tired from swinging that meathook of yours, cast enough spells and you run out of magical energy. Resurrection spell brings you back near dead, low on every type of energy – magical, physical, emotional, mental. You need rest." Another swig as a haunted look crossed Andren face. "They don't have time for rest, though."

Cyrus looked at him in accusation. "About your healing spells. You gonna try again?"

Andren glared at him. "Give me a minute, will ya? I dunno about you, but I just died, and frankly it was an unsettling experience for me!" The healer took another deep swig from the flask. "I'm trying to get back on an even plane here."

Orion was picking his way through the wounded. The healers looked as though they had completed their work, and all the bodies were moving, moaning, some even crying out. Druids and paladins were healing the worst afflicted first, as they regained their strength. The healers looked exhausted; Curatio was bleeding profusely from a gash on his forehead that hadn't healed. Niamh walked up to him and cast a spell to seal the wound. She gently wiped the blood from his face as she smiled down at him.

"Cyrus." Orion approached, looking stricken. "We have a problem."

"Oh?" Cy looked at the ranger, and awareness crept back to him. He realized what had been stirring in his mind earlier, a curious absence. "Where's Narstron?"

Orion looked away. "We don't know."

Andren was on his feet in an instant, all other concerns forgotten. "What do you mean you don't know? Where the hell is he?"

Orion shrugged helplessly before answering. "We don't know. We've been looking for him –"

Cyrus almost bowled Orion over moving past him toward the tunnel down into the goblin city. "Then we go back after him."

"Cyrus," Orion said, "I've been into the throne room three times. I sorted through a pile of goblin dead, but I couldn't find any sign of him. Elisabeth is down there right now, left just before Selene resurrected you." Orion shook his head sadly. "We don't have much more time."

Cyrus and Andren sat there, stone-faced, peering down the tunnel. Long minutes passed as they waited, willing a small figure to come trudging up from the depths. The minutes turned into an hour. Then two. The entire force, still recovering from their grievous wounding, waited, murmuring respectably behind them. Niamh had cast a night vision spell on Cyrus again and he stirred as a small shape made its way out of the darkness. A figure, but who...?

It was both of them. Elisabeth moved quietly along the tunnel, dragging Narstron's body behind her as quickly as she could manage. Her breaths came in ragged gasps and she was bleeding from her side. "Ran into a sentry that didn't take kindly to me bringing him back."

Curatio stepped forward, already casting the resurrection spell. Cyrus held his breath as the magical forces he summoned crackled with energy into Narstron –

And did nothing.

Curatio began chanting under his breath again, the same effect – nothing happened. He did it again, and again, until finally the elf fell over, completely spent, face blank.

Andren dropped to his knees over the dwarven body. He was weeping softly. Cyrus saw Niamh gasp and turn away, while Terian, Alaric and Vara stood expressionless. Cyrus bit back the emotion he felt, a deep, burning sensation that grabbed him in the chest. He wanted to take his sword and run through Enterra, killing everything he found. He wanted to take hold of a goblin, and beat it until its bones were no more. He wanted –

He wanted Narstron to be back. He half expected him to open his eyes, to make a joke about how he had killed more goblins than Cyrus or Cass or anybody.

But it didn't happen. Cy looked down into the dwarf's features. He'd been pierced at least a dozen times in the torso. "I found him dragged into one of their sacred places – near their treasure trove. There were hundreds of goblins on the other side of that door," Elisabeth told Orion. "It's like they were expecting us. There's something else I need to tell you, but more important things come first: the army of the goblins is on the move, Orion – they are assembling and we need to get out of here."

Orion was speechless; it was Alaric that spoke first. "Get your groups together!"

A clattering came from down the tunnel – the sound of an army on the march. Cyrus's scowl deepened, as he stepped over the body of his friend. Alaric, recognizing his intent, didn't fight him, just gestured to Niamh – and the whirlwind of her spell swept him out of Enterra, away from the army, and when the howl of the winds died down...

...his howl could be heard through the Plains of Perdamun. A cry of grief, of rage, of loss and sorrow. It took Alaric, Terian, Vara and three others to haul him back to Sanctuary. By the time they reached the front gates, he was unconscious, still bleeding from the wounds he'd suffered in Enterra's throne room. Some of them would never truly heal.

Chapter 14

Cyrus looked out his window over the grounds of Sanctuary. He could see the gates, and watched as small figures rode through the entrance. It had been three days since Enterra. He had slept in the Halls of Healing the first night and had not regained consciousness until noon the next day. The rest of the first day and second night he had been restless, not talking to anyone. He had spent most of his time down by the river Perda. No matter what had happened, the river still ran. The world had collapsed around him, but it still ran. Looking from his window across the plains he couldn't believe it had been three days. Today was the funeral.

At the appointed hour, he put on his armor, freshly cleaned but still black, and headed downstairs. Walking through the doors and outside, he followed the crowd across the grounds to the graveyard. A raised dais was set up at the far end of the cemetery, with chairs and a podium. In the center of it all was a small casket – the sight of which nearly dropped Cyrus to his knees.

He took his place to the right of the coffin and Andren sat beside him. Alaric and Curatio sat on the left side of the dais, along with a dwarven priest: a follower of Rotan, the God of Earth. The priest stood first, and delivered his message, followed by a few kind words from Alaric and Curatio and a rambling remembrance from Andren, who was quite drunk. No one stopped the healer, who went on for some time before ushering himself off the dais, sobbing.

Cyrus didn't hear a word, lost in his own thoughts. He could tell from Alaric's motions to him when it was his turn to speak. He walked to the podium, still numb. Scanning the crowd, he saw the entirety of Sanctuary was there, even Vara. Erith, Cass and Elisabeth were there from the Daring. There was a mix of emotions on the faces before him.

He cleared his throat. "When I was a young warrior, fresh out of the Society of Arms in Reikonos, I was at a bandit camp in the Pelar foothills. I was facing some very poorly trained enemies, some bandits armed with small maces and rusty swords; inadequate weaponry, little strength and no chance against a fighter with any real experience. Unfortunately, I was a fighter with no real experience. I had been cornered by three of the bandits, and my sword broke against one of their blades. I was about to be killed.

"A dwarf came screaming out of nowhere, and distracted them long enough for me to stab one of them with the remains of my blade. I took his weapon, and the dwarf and I killed the other two. We've been together ever since." The sting of the memory halted him in his recollection. "We were inseparable. Along the way, we found another adventurer," he swept his arm to indicate Andren, who was still weeping, "who shared our vision of exploration, and battle, and the idea of striving to better ourselves.

"We knew, as warriors, the dangers in the world and we faced it every day. A warrior's purpose is to take the punishment so a healer, a wizard, a ranger doesn't have to. Narstron lived that mission, every day." His eyes came to Vara and he stopped for a moment. There was a single tear drifting down the elf's cheek.

"He served his god, he served his guild, his family, and he fought to his last on a battlefield of his choosing, taking every enemy with him that he could."

Cyrus turned to face the casket, strode over to it and placed both hands on it. He lowered his voice. "You were my oldest friend in the world, and I will miss you. I don't believe in what you believed in, and I don't serve Rotan – but a follower of Bellarum believes in vengeance. I swear, by the God of War, you will be avenged." He leaned down and touched his forehead to the casket in the deepest bow he could, then turned on his heel and marched back to his chair, stiffly and formally so that he could focus on something other than the pain.

They lowered the casket into the ground and the first shovels of dirt were thrown upon it. As the funeral ended, many people tendered their regrets. He took them politely, but his eyes were elsewhere. Vara walked slowly through the graveyard to the far corner, and knelt on a grave. She sat there quietly for a few moments before she stood, dusted herself off and walked back to Sanctuary's entrance.

After taking the last of the condolences from the Allied envoys he found himself wandering past the rows of tombstones to the grave that Vara had stopped at. Standing over it he found a simple marker.

Raifa Herde
Beloved Healer
and Wife

He looked around, startled, seeing a few other names he recognized – Pradhar, Erkhardt the Mighty on nearby tombstones. Each one of them, the names Alaric had mentioned –

"I see you've found the answer to your earlier question." Alaric Garaunt appeared at his shoulder. "Here lie three of the founders of Sanctuary."

Curiosity overpowered Cyrus's weariness. "How did they die?"

Alaric hesitated. "Let us walk. The druids have a garden that you must see to believe."

Cyrus thought for a moment of protesting but instead fell into step beside Alaric as the paladin walked. Neither made any attempt to speak until they crossed a small bridge over a flowing stream running into a small pond a few feet away. When Cyrus thought he could endure no further silence, Alaric spoke. "I come here, sometimes, when issues weigh upon me." He paused. "A plant cannot grow without rain – and rain does not come but through a storm - the mildest shower to the most tempestuous thunderstorm. And so it is with us. We grow in times of trial, in storm and rain. I do not think anyone loves the storms of life." The paladin's face grew serious. "They sweep us to and fro – off the course we had planned for ourselves."

He focused on the warrior's eyes. "I have no words to make your grief go away. I would not deny you that pain, as it may define you and make you stronger. In the early days of Sanctuary, the titans were a strong presence in this part of the Plains. They attacked once when we were weak. Since that day, the day we laid Raifa to rest, I have seen thirty-two funerals for our own. I would bring every one of them back were it within my power. But it is not."

The paladin looked weary. "I have learned more about what it takes to be a leader in these times than I ever did when things are going well. I do not wish you suffering, but I wish you to learn all the lessons that are only available to those who navigate through the heart of the storm." He paused for a long time. "Tomorrow will be easier," Alaric said with great certainty. With a final hand on the shoulder of the warrior, he left Cyrus staring out over pond with much to consider.

Later that night, Cyrus found himself alone in his quarters. Looking around, he couldn't help but remember the warmth and chatter of the Kings of Reikonos guildhall fondly. *If we were still there*, Cyrus thought, *Narstron would still be alive.* Clutching his pillow tighter, he prayed for tomorrow to come, so he could see the easier day that Alaric had mentioned. When he was still awake at dawn, he realized that while the Ghost had said it would be easier, he didn't say it would ever be easy.

Chapter 15

A few days after the funeral there was a knock on Cyrus's door in the early hours of the morning. He looked around, startled. The knock came again, more insistent this time. Feigning sleep, he answered the door to find Terian Lepos standing in the hall. "Yes?" the warrior asked, befuddled.

"Let's go," Terian said with a directness Cyrus might have found refreshing under other circumstances. After several days with no sleep, Cyrus didn't find anything refreshing.

"Go where?"

"Who cares?" the dark elf said, already turning to leave. "Anywhere and anything is better than the sleep you're not getting right now."

Cyrus didn't argue. After arming himself, he followed Terian down the stairs and out the front gates of Sanctuary. They walked in silence to a path that lead into the Waking Woods, an enormous forest that stretched north almost halfway to Reikonos. They walked for over an hour into the woods, not saying anything. The warrior finally stopped at a disturbing sound in the distance – ghouls howled in the darkness.

"What the hell are we doing here?" Cyrus asked the dark elf.

"Like I said, anything and anywhere is better than your nightly routine, isn't it?" He uncapped a flask and handed it to Cyrus. A strong odor of alcohol permeated from it. Cy made a mental note to introduce Terian to Andren later, and took a long slug of the liquor. "We're going to run around in the woods with the dead for a while, I think." A long, languid scream tore through the night – ghoulish and inhuman. Terian pocketed the flask and took off at a run along the path through the woods.

"Wait!" Cyrus said. Pondering his options he decided the best course of action was to turn back, walk through the front gate of Sanctuary, go back to bed and forget any of this had ever happened. He quickly discarded that idea, remembering that while he might have been in bed, sleep wasn't on the agenda. "Great," he muttered to no one in particular. "A haunted forest." He took off after Terian, catching glimpses of the dark knight's armor in the moonlight.

Howls of outrage came from his left, then his right, as the undead of Waking Woods came after them. Not stopping, he ran behind the elf, who Cyrus could swear was giggling in front of him. "You know why it's called Waking Woods?" Terian shouted over his shoulder.

"I don't know, but you're attracting the attention of every undead creature in the area with this shouting!" Cyrus was so irritated he couldn't keep his voice down.

"This part of the woods used to be a place where the followers of Yartraak, God of Darkness, and Mortus, God of Death would sacrifice their victims." Terian slowed down to let him catch up. "See, right there." Terian came to a stop and pointed to the shape of a pyramid towering above the trees.

"I've heard the legends, and I've been told since I was young that you do not stop in Waking Woods at night, because there are sections that are incredibly dangerous... yet here we go stopping in one of those sections." Cyrus was a step below panic.

Terian put both hands on his knees, bending over, winded. "It's a funny thing, that legend about not stopping. I heard it too. You were raised in Reikonos?" When Cyrus nodded, he continued, the screaming of the ghouls very near now. "I'm from Saekaj Sovar, the dark elf capital on the north end of Waking Woods. Funny we'd have heard the same legend, since there isn't that much contact between Saekaj and Reikonos."

Cy was looking over his shoulder now. He could see nothing in the darkness. "Wouldn't that mean that there might be some credence to it?"

"You were told to run like hell, right?" Terian asked him, voice calm. "You were young, and new, inexperienced... and they told you to run through Waking Woods, every part of it, even the supposedly safe ones, without stopping, right?"

"Yes," Cyrus told him, "but in fairness, they didn't just warn us about the undead: they also warned us about bandits and belligerent dark elves – not necessarily in that order."

Terian chuckled. "Have you ever stopped and faced the ghouls here?" His axe was drawn.

Cyrus paused. He resisted the ingrained urge to run, and drew his sword. He was a warrior. Fear was something he conquered, not vice versa. He assumed a defensive position, closing his eyes, and listened to the death rattle making its way through the trees to them. He opened his eyes as the ghoul burst into the open. It was a roughly human figure, with only patches of skin and clothing covering its bones. It looked at the two of them, and let out a scream of otherworldly fury.

"Be careful," Terian called out from slightly behind him. "I'm not a healer, so try not to get hurt too bad."

A sick feeling of doom crawled up Cyrus's stomach. "What am I supposed to do if I get injured?"

Terian shrugged in a very casual manner. "Don't worry; I'm pretty good at bandaging wounds." He thought about it for a beat. "Of course, that's not gonna help you much in battle, but afterward I'll be able to patch you up real good."

Burying Terian's last statement, Cyrus let out a howl of outrage, and putting forth all the fury he'd liked to have directed at the goblins over the last few days, he tore into the ghoul with his sword. It withered under his assault, falling back, blocking halfheartedly. He slashed at it, over and over, pieces of bone chipping off as it weathered his strikes. He cleaved the bone at the wrist cleanly in two, and it lost its weapon.

Letting out a cry of its own, it made to stab him with its wrist bone, and he knocked it aside so brusquely that it broke the whole arm off at the shoulder socket. Forcing the sword across its jaw, he severed the maxilla from the mandible. The screaming stopped. He moved his right foot between its legs, forcing it to take a step back.

He brought his hands around and crushed the ghoul's skull with the hilt of his sword and brought the other arm around its neck, pinning it against his leg. He brought his hands up above his head and hammered them down, shattering the skeleton into pieces, scattering them over the forest's floor. The bones clattered against each other as they rolled across the wet grass.

The sound of slow clapping of armored gauntlets broke him out of his stunned silence. "Isn't facing your childish fears much more fun than staring at the walls all night?"

His heavy breathing subsided, Cyrus turned to face the dark knight. "How did you know I could best this fiend?"

Terian shrugged again, a noncommittal movement of his shoulders. "I assumed you could because I can. And since it was easy for me, I figured you could at least kill it without dying." More howls issued through the forest. "If you'd like, we can draw in some more."

Cyrus thought about it for a minute. He drew his sword to a fighting position. "I'd like that very much." Seeing the look of hungry anticipation in the dark elf's eyes, he knew that Terian understood the call to war better than anyone else in Sanctuary.

They slayed ghouls until daybreak. Making their way back to Sanctuary by the dawn's light, Cyrus's heart felt somewhat lightened. He made his way back to his quarters in a veritable fog, and dropped into bed without taking off his armor. He fell into a deep, restful sleep, and did not wake until the next morning.

Chapter 16

Cyrus couldn't believe how fast the last six months had gone. He had settled into a routine with Sanctuary – every day he spent adventuring in different areas of Arkaria, participating in the occasional Alliance expeditions and even more occasional (lately) Sanctuary expeditions to break up the regularity of his small group adventures. He was home almost every night at Sanctuary, save for once when he stayed at the old Kings guildhall after a long excursion to the Inculta desert in the far south-east, and with no druid or wizard available to bring him home afterward. That had been a long night, filled with unpleasant memories.

He, Niamh, Curatio, J'anda and Terian walked across the Mountains of Nartanis, on their way to an outlying goblin outpost on a nearby peak. His most frequent adventures seemed to be with officers of Sanctuary – and he'd enjoyed every minute of it. Curatio had proven himself the most skilled and reliable healer Cyrus had ever worked with, effortlessly casting mending spells that seemed to have more power than those of other healers. Andren had proved less reliable of late, spending the months since Narstron's death in even more of an alcohol-fueled haze than before.

Coming over a hill, Terian, who was leading the party, indicated for them to halt. He was crouching behind a rock and gesturing for the rest of them to do the same. For Cyrus it wasn't even a question – he grabbed Niamh and J'anda and moved them bodily to the nearest cover. Curatio was already diving behind a boulder. They made it just in time.

Sweeping above them, scales as black as obsidian, was a dragon. It was at least as large as Ashan'agar, Cy reflected. It swept over them in a lazy flight, flapping its wings and landing just beyond them, close to the edge of a lake of lava.

Terian leaned against the rock, facing them. "It's Kalam. Sighting him here is an incredible find." The dark knight was pensive for a moment. "I bet he has a lair close by."

"How did you know his name?" Cyrus hissed. "Terian's Dragon Compendium?"

The dark knight shrugged, and Cyrus watched as Kalam lay down less than one hundred feet from the lake of lava. A series of boulders had been pushed into a circle that was almost nest-like. Even at this distance, Cyrus could see the glint of objects in a corner of it, and he knew that Kalam was a hoarder of treasures, just like every other dragon.

"What the hell is this beast doing out of the southern lands?" Cyrus wondered.

"And so close to the lair of our friend Ashan'agar?" Niamh said with a smile.

"I would be willing to bet," Terian changed the subject, "that a great many guilds would love to get a shot at a black dragon." He looked around nervously. "Only the secluded location is keeping him alive right now. If any of the biggest guilds like Amarath's Raiders, Endeavor, or Burnt Offerings knew where he was, he'd be dead and they'd be picking that nest clean." He paused. "We can have a hundred people from Sanctuary out here in half an hour."

Cyrus shook his head. "No," he said slowly, chewing his lip, "that's not going to cut it with a dragon like this. Trust me. We need aid from the Alliance if we want a chance of taking him down without losing a lot of people."

Terian looked at him, nostrils flaring. "We have a shot to take him for Sanctuary, and your first instinct is to turn him over to Goliath?"

"I doubt they're that dishonorable, Terian," Cyrus said. "If we call for aid, the Alliance rules will bind them; we'll end up splitting the loot, but it's better than –" he raised a hand to cut off Terian's already forthcoming reply – "it's better than losing guildmates trying to bring this bastard down or having to retreat and leaving bodies on the ground. We need to be careful, and we need more people to succeed."

Shrugging his shoulders, Terian relented. "Fine, but don't say I didn't warn you if Goliath ends up stealing everything."

Cyrus turned to Niamh. "We need a Sanctuary officer to get the Alliance involved. Will you get word to the other guilds?"

Niamh nodded. "The Daring and Goliath are both located in Reikonos. I'll take Curatio and we'll go now." She and Curatio were whisked away on the wind of her spell, leaving Cyrus, J'anda and Terian watching the nest of the dragon.

"At some point," Cyrus said with a curious look at Terian,

"maybe you can share with me why you despise the Alliance."

Terian was watching Kalam from behind a boulder. The dark elf stiffened at Cyrus's inquiry, but did not turn back to answer him at first.

Cyrus exchanged a look with J'anda, who shrugged, wearing the illusion of a dwarf. "Just because I'm a dark elf," the enchanter said, "don't expect me to understand him."

"Why do you hide that you're a dark elf?" Cyrus asked J'anda.

"Meh." The enchanter looked away. "It's not that I'm ashamed, by any means, but let's face it: dark elves are not appreciated in the world outside Saekaj Sovar. After I got beaten in Reikonos twice I decided that my dark elven pride was best displayed elsewhere."

Terian snorted. "So much for being yourself."

J'anda smiled. "Why would you ever want to be yourself, when there are so many more interesting people to be?" With a flick of his fingers, the dwarven illusion disappeared and J'anda had become a mirror image of Terian himself.

The dark knight shook his head in annoyance. "Although your looks have improved in the last thirty seconds, I have no patience for people who are not what they appear to be." The dark elf looked back at Cyrus. "Which is, by the way, the answer to your question about why I despise the Alliance."

Cyrus looked at Terian, befuddled. "Huh?"

There was a long silence. Terian seemed to be pondering the black dragon, but then turned to face Cyrus. "I was there when the Alliance was formed. It was created with the best intentions. Three guilds, all of whom wanted to grow and be of assistance to each other, the heads of which were longtime friends, decided to become formal allies. Sanctuary, the Daring and Goliath each brought something different to the table, but it was a partnership. If one was in need, the others were there. It started nobly," Terian continued, far off look in his eyes. "Unfortunately, that was a long time ago."

"I still don't understand," Cyrus interrupted, "What you mean when you say they're not who they say they are?"

"He's just jealous," J'anda said, dispersing his Terian illusion in favor of an elven appearance.

"I have no problem with the Daring or even most of the rank and file of Goliath." The dark knight's eyes grew intense. "But Goliath's officers... they may appear to be allies, but I assure you they are not. Somewhere along the way the ideals of friendship and mutual assistance that was the core of the Alliance at its founding got perverted by their greed and lust for power." Terian looked back down the slope to check on the sleeping dragon. "Now we're allies in name only." The dark elf looked back to fix his gaze on Cyrus's eyes. "Or did you think that the lack of attendance at Enterra was a one time occurrence?"

"I have tried not to think about that night," Cyrus answered, face frozen.

"Well," Terian said, "try not to think about this, then. Before Alaric and the rest of us came charging to the rescue that night, he sent a messenger to Goliath asking for assistance. Their whole complement was at their guildhall; one of their officers, Tolada, sent his apologies – he said they were unable to help."

"Wait a minute," Cyrus said, jaw tensing. "To opt out of the invasion was one thing. But you're telling me they knew we were in dire need, and chose not to come to our aid?"

Terian's smirk stretched across his face. "Doesn't it feel good to know that you have allies that will be there for you no matter what?" he asked, voice dripping with sarcasm. He straightened. "I believe our first wave of reinforcements just landed."

Looking up the hill behind them, Cyrus saw Curatio leading the way through the rocky terrain above the dragon's nest. The elf made his way down the hill, minding his footing. Cyrus could see Vaste standing head and shoulders above the rest of the reinforcements. A blinding flash of light shone off the armor of a female elf, and Cyrus knew by the blond hair that Vara was among them. Andren also made his way down, in the company of Nyad and below her, Brevis. Cyrus felt a tap on his shoulder.

"Orion!" He turned with a start. "Glad you're here. Look what we found – or should I say what almost found us."

"I see." Orion squinted against the sunlight. "Looks like we're perfectly positioned. He won't see us forming up from back here." He turned to Cyrus. "Pretty exciting, isn't it, leading your first attack?"

Cyrus's jaw dropped. "What are you talking about? I'm not leading this."

Orion turned serious. "Of course you are. Niamh issued the call for aid you sent out."

Cy was shocked. "I just thought we should get an army here, fast. I didn't plan to lead the attack. He looked at Orion. "Look, you're Sanctuary's General, why don't you take over?"

Orion froze. The ranger had been absent from Sanctuary frequently over the last six months and had led only one expedition, a boring and overpowered sweep through the pass of the Heia Mountains to the southern lands. With the exception of a few bandit camps and three titans, there had been no resistance at all during their two day march through the pass.

"I don't think so," Orion said, shaking his head. "You called us together, it seems only right that you get the glory. I'm sure you'll do fine," he finished as he faded into the burgeoning crowd, which had filled out with the arrival of the Daring.

"Cyrus," Erith greeted him. "How are you?" she asked, dropping her voice so low that no one around them could hear her.

"I'm better," he answered.

"Good," she said, voice loud again. "Now try not to die, will you? I'm in the middle of a good book," she waved a volume that she held in her hand, "and if I have to heal you mid-battle, I might lose my place." She paused for a moment. "Or forget to heal you." A grin split her face. "Either one of those would be bad, but one would be worse for me, I promise you that!" She cackled as she wandered off.

A dwarf and a dark elf walked side by side with a few others in tow. The dwarf squinted against the sunlight, looking around until his eyes found Curatio. Tapping the dark elf next to him, whose face was hidden in the folds of his brown cloak, the dwarf altered the course of the group toward Curatio.

"We are here, as called for by the dictates of the Alliance," the dwarf said, a note of impatience in his voice. "Are you going to organize, Curatio, or are we simply going to sit around and stare at the dragon all day?"

Curatio smiled at him. "Tolada, it's always a pleasure to see you." Try as he might, Cyrus could not detect insincerity in the elf's greeting.

The cloaked dark elf reached out with a skeletal hand and laid it upon Tolada's shoulder. "Now, now," came the dark elf's voice, "let us not be hasty or uncivil." Throwing back the cowl of his cloak, the dark elf revealed a visage that was as skeletal as his hand. His face was old, desiccated, and thin. His cheeks were sunken, eyes almost like slits. When the dark elf smiled, it gave the appearance of a snake that was ready to coil around its prey.

Curatio nodded. "Pleased to see you as well, Malpravus. Thank you for bringing Goliath along today."

The dark elf named Malpravus bowed. "We are pleased to stand with our old allies in so noble an endeavor as striking down one of the dragons. Tell me, Curatio, who among you leads this assault? We should begin as quickly as possible."

Curatio looked around before his gaze landed on Cyrus, who felt his blood freeze. "This is one of our newest warriors, Cyrus Davidon." Curatio looked back to Malpravus. "He's the one who called us here."

"Excellent, excellent," Malpravus said, almost too quietly for Cyrus to hear. The dark elf's eyes rested on him and a great rush of discomfort filled Cy as he realized everyone around them was staring at him, waiting.

Curatio waved for him to join them. Shuffling, Cyrus entered the forming circle of Alliance officers. Elisabeth greeted him with a smile from her place next to Tolada. Cass beamed in support, as did Erith when she was certain no one was looking. Malpravus studied him carefully, still wearing the frozen smile. "So, my boy, do you have a plan?"

"Ah..." Cyrus looked to find Curatio, Niamh, Terian and Vara all standing behind him. Vara rolled her eyes and looked away, but the others looked at him with encouragement. "I have a few ideas," Cyrus said, uncertainty causing his voice to quaver. He blushed.

"I see," Malpravus said, unconvinced. "Well, having had some experience in facing dragons, perhaps it would be best if I were to... assist you..."

Cyrus heard perfectly timed twin coughing fits from behind him originating from Terian and Vara. They were silenced quickly by what Cyrus assumed was a glare from Curatio. "No," Cyrus said with a confidence he didn't quite feel, "I think I've got it well in hand." This prompted a raised eyebrow from Malpravus, who bowed in acknowledgment.

Cyrus looked around the circle, taking a deep breath before speaking. "The biggest danger we face in using traditional assault tactics is the dragon's fire-breathing capability. In order to counteract that –"

"Wait," Cass said. "Not all dragons breathe fire. Are we sure this one does?"

Terian spoke up from behind Cyrus. "This is Kalam, one of

Ashan'agar's former ministers. He is definitely a fire-breather."

Cyrus looked back at the dark knight. "Some time you'll have to explain to me your intimate knowledge of the Dragon Kingdom." The dark elf shrugged and smiled before Cyrus turned back to face the Alliance Council.

"Since he does breathe fire," Cyrus said, "to approach him with standard tactics would be dangerous." Looking down the hill to where the black dragon lay, Cyrus thought for a moment. "I believe we can nullify that danger with a little advance action."

"Excellent." Malpravus's voice was smooth and hissing. "Then of course you'll be willing to be the warrior in front of the dragon, keeping his attention while the rest of our force engages from behind?"

"And spare one of your better armed and equipped warriors from having to face this foe?" Vara shot from behind Cyrus before he could respond.

Cyrus answered before Malpravus could respond. "I'll stand before the dragon and keep his attention. It's my responsibility."

Malpravus looked at him with an expression of undisguised pleasure. "My, my, you are quite brave, aren't you?"

"In Sanctuary," Cyrus said, "we accept only the brave. Gather your spell casters and place them behind the rocks surrounding the nest. Once I have the dragon's attention, engage with all your forces." As the group began to disperse, Cyrus gestured for Elisabeth to join him.

Before the ranger reached him, Cyrus felt a strong hand on his shoulder, hauling him around. He faced Vara, whose normally pale complexion was mottled with rage. "He wants you in front of that dragon," she said without preamble, "because he knows that whoever is in front is most likely to die and he's trying to spare any of his warriors that fate." She thrust a finger into his face. "And you," she said, "were stupid enough to play right into his hand with your stubborn nobility!"

He blinked at the elf before replying. She had said not a word to him in the last six months. "It's my first time being lectured by a paladin about not being stubbornly noble. I assumed Malpravus was trying to do something of the sort. But it is my responsibility: I am the leader." He studied her, seeing the bottled irritation threatening to boil over.

"I know you called the attack, you troll-brained sack of meat!" She looked at him with incredulity. "That doesn't mean you have to be the head warrior! Goliath warriors always handle the head warrior duties, because they're the best equipped to take the hits!" She glared at him. "Now, go to Malpravus and tell him you were wrong, that you want him to do what he's damned well supposed to do and put his best equipped warrior in front of that bloody dragon!"

He met her gaze but did not answer for a long moment. "I won't," he finally answered. "They may be better equipped, but they won't know how to pull off what I'm going to do."

She looked at him, eyes narrow, visible skin along her thin neck an angry red shade all the way up her cheeks. "Malpravus has warriors armored well enough to take a blast of fire. What if your plan fails and that dragon sends a jet of flame your way?"

"Then the temperature in my armor will rise rather severely in a short period of time, and you'll be free of one annoying warrior." She blanched, but his face remained expressionless. "Honestly, why do you even care?"

"Of all the people I've known that have died while battling dragons," she spat back at him after a moment, "you're the first I've met that fully deserves the fate that awaits him." She turned on her heel and disappeared into the crowd, ponytail dancing behind her as she stormed away.

Chapter 17

After a brief conversation with Elisabeth, Cyrus set everything in motion. The Alliance army crept down the hill toward the nest. Kalam had begun to snore loudly from within the rocky enclosure. Cyrus waited, staring at the dragon's closed eyes while he waited for the signal. Cass waited with him.

"Are you sure you want to do this?" Cass said. "I've never heard of anyone using this strategy to take out a dragon before."

Cyrus nodded. "That's because I came up with it myself and it's unproven." He saw Terian wave from where the melee fighters were stationed. "What I'm most concerned about is making sure no one gets fried while our army is doing their job." Catching sight of Elisabeth, waving from the side of the nest, he slapped Cass on the shoulder. "Just be ready to jump in if I die." Favoring the warrior with a wicked grin as Cass paled, Cyrus left the cover of the last boulder between him and the black dragon.

His boots crackled in the magmatic rocks as he crossed the ground to Kalam. Cyrus smiled as he saw Elisabeth approaching much more stealthily than he was, and also more quickly. In her hand was an old spear. She approached Kalam's left nostril as Cyrus reached his position in front of the sleeping dragon. *What was that old proverb about letting sleeping dragons lie?* Cyrus watched as Elisabeth raised the spear and stabbed it into Kalam's exposed and snoring nose, puncturing into the nostril on the other side of the dragon's face.

The reaction was immediate. A screech of outrage and pain rose forth from Kalam as he screamed awake and scrambled to his feet, spear hanging like a tribal nose piercing in the cartilage that separated the dragon's nostrils. Raring back onto his haunches, smaller front legs attempting to grasp the source of the pain, Kalam finally got a glimpse of Cyrus, standing before him.

"Good morning!" he said as the dragon settled its angry eyes upon him. "Sorry to wake you so unpleasantly, but I needed to get your attention. Do I have it now?"

The dragon didn't respond verbally, though Terian had mentioned that Kalam, like Ashan'agar, was capable of speech. Cyrus could see the smoke rising from the dragon's mouth, as he prepared to send down a flame that would destroy the warrior. He began to draw in a breath...

...and stopped suddenly, screeching in pain, unable to breathe through his nose. He coughed a small burst of flame that didn't reach even halfway to Cyrus. The warrior grinned. *Now all I have to worry about is a dragon that's fifty feet long and thirty feet tall,* Cyrus thought. *With claws the size of a dwarf.*

Letting loose a fearsome bellow, Cyrus charged forward at the same time as the Alliance forces began to attack from behind. Spells hit the aggravated and injured beast, but he ignored them in favor of the scornful, agitating human that was taunting him after causing grievous bodily harm. The dragon lunged for Cyrus, and the warrior felt the claws of the beast hit him, too fast for him to dodge. He slammed into the ground, hard at the same time Erith's mending spell was cast upon him, curing him of all wounds. He staggered to his feet, glaring at Kalam.

By this time the rangers, warriors and knights were attacking Kalam's flank, carving through his scales bit by bit. Cyrus saw Vara, her sword a blur, opening wounds for the other battlers to exploit. The dragon's neck extended and the head lanced out toward Cyrus, eager to finish his foe so he could deal with the other injuries he was sustaining from the army behind him.

Cyrus was able to barely dodge but managed to bring his sword around for a glancing blow against Kalam's face as it shot by. The cut continued down some of the more sensitive tissue on the dragon's neck. Cyrus could hear an indignant scream from the dragon as it brought its head up; whether from his wound, the frustration of missing Cy, from the fighters tearing into his flanks or the spell casters that were hitting him with damaging magics, the warrior could not tell.

Spots of dragon blood were hitting the ground all around them now, and every place they fell let out a puff of black smoke as the heat of it burned the ground. "Stay away from the blood!" Cyrus shouted. He knew he was late as someone behind the dragon screamed.

Kalam twisted again, repositioning himself to get a better angle of attack on Cyrus. This time, the warrior was prepared. The dragon's head dived at him with full force; Kalam had fully committed to this attack. Cyrus thrust his sword skyward and prayed to Bellarum that Erith was feeling charitable. The dragon hit him with the top of its skull, crushing him against the ground.

Cy felt bones break, organs mashed to a pulp...and then a cool breeze of another mending spell, this one from Curatio, and the wounds faded and his bones knit back together.

Kalam's head rolled to the side, and another small burst of flame issued from his mouth making it look as though his head was on fire. Cyrus rolled to his feet, sword still lodged in the dragon's head. Before Kalam could finish shrugging off the effects of the impact, Cyrus grabbed the hilt and brought the sword downward, lengthening the wound into a gash before pulling the blade out.

At the rear, the fighters had hacked away at Kalam's haunches enough to allow them to cleave his back legs off while the head was stunned, immobilizing the dragon. With a final roar, Kalam rolled over on his side. Vara soared from the back of the dragon to land a dramatic sword thrust between the scales and into the dragon's heart. With a scream and a burst of smoke, Kalam, the black dragon breathed his last.

Cyrus looked at the body. Tongue hanging out his mouth, the dragon's face was wrecked: Cyrus's slashes had opened up the dragon's face and the vein down his neck, where hot blood oozed and dripped, searing the ground. Spell damage checkered Kalam's torso, with scales ripped off sporadically from the blasts of spell casters. Rejoining the fighters at the back of the dragon, he saw the rear legs cut off with messy sword strokes, and not a single scale left anywhere on the back of the beast, nor any meat left on its bones in the rear.

"All right!" Tolada's shout echoed through the Mountains of Nartanis. The dwarf's daggers were clean; by comparison, Elisabeth's dripped with steaming dragon blood.

Cyrus turned to the crowd grouped around the rear of the dragon. "Everyone okay back there?" he asked.

Terian broke his way to the front of the crowd. "Everyone's fine. A couple of people suffered burns from the dragon's blood, but other than that, things went smoothly."

Niamh and Andren came running up from the spell casters' group. "That was amazing!" she exulted. "We're all fine; he never got anywhere near us."

Erith, Curatio and Cass trotted up from behind, catching the last bit of Niamh's statement. "Looks like no fatalities and only a couple minor injuries, already healed," Erith said. She looked around and nodded, impressed. "When I heard you had an idea for taking the dragon out, I thought for sure that because you were a human and a warrior, it would be a stupid idea. But," she grudgingly admitted, "that worked well."

Malpravus approached, entourage in tow. "That was impressively led," the dark elf said with the same leathery smile. "I've never heard of a tactic to hamstring a dragon like that. We'll be adapting it for use the next time we go to the Ashen Wastelands," the Goliath leader said.

Elisabeth smiled. "Making it so painful he couldn't breathe through his nose really did kill his ability to project his fire breath."

"Couldn't have done it without your help," Cyrus said.

Elisabeth blushed. "Any ranger could have done that."

"Would you mind," Cyrus asked her, "helping to divide the spoils between the guilds?"

"An excellent idea," Malpravus said. "In fact, we should go now and see what sort of hoard this dragon has left behind for us."

Dividing the dragon's hoard took less than an hour. The gold and other assorted treasures were split equally. The dragon had gold and baubles, armors and a variety of other items. *How did he carry this?* Cyrus thought.

Cy had found a small rock and was sitting on it, watching all the goings-on. Terian approached him from behind and clapped him on the back with a low whistle. "You enriched Sanctuary's guild bank by a considerable amount today."

Cyrus smiled but didn't move or turn his gaze. "Goliath didn't take everything?"

Terian's smile faded, replaced by a dark expression. "No, they didn't, but not for lack of trying. There were a few treasures that became points of contention. Malpravus tried to claim that a solid gold statuette was worth only a few coins." The dark elf shook his head in annoyance. "Even Tolada couldn't find it in his black little dwarven heart to agree with his Guildmaster on that."

"I thought we were already wealthy as a guild."

"No." Terian snorted. "You've seen the little stipend we pay to our members on a monthly basis, maybe a little extra if we have a windfall month – like this month, thanks to you – but we haven't had a month like that in the last few years."

Various tradespeople from the Alliance were disassembling the dragon's corpse, taking the usable scales, draining the blood for potion ingredients, and taking the meat for cooking. He saw Brevis squabbling with an elf over a vial of dragon blood and some steaming dragon meat. The dragon was skinless and stripped of all its musculature by this point – which was not a trivial undertaking with a creature so large. Cyrus watched as Brevis and the elf parted ways, the gnome now working on getting a piece of the dragon's entrails. Shaking his head at the morbidity of picking the corpse clean, Cyrus turned back to the body of the army, talking among themselves in fellowship.

Orion sidled up to him. "That was an impressive victory," he said, smiling at Cyrus. "You're a natural leader."

Cyrus chuckled. "I had a pretty good example to learn from."

"You mean Angelique?" The ranger's eye glinted and he grinned.

"Yeah," Cy laughed. "A fine example of what *not* to do." His expression turned serious. "You should lead again."

Orion nodded, but his smile had frozen, stuck in place and clearly fake. He turned his attention back to the crowd, as Elisabeth had stepped onto a rock and was trying to get everyone's attention. When she had silenced the crowd, she began. "Let's all take a moment to thank Cyrus Davidon from Sanctuary for today's victory."

Enthusiastic applause greeted her statement, and he was forced to stand up and take a bow as the army turned toward him in acknowledgment. Elisabeth waited until the applause had died down. "I have an announcement to make. The Daring have received word through sources that in two days Mortus, the God of Death, will be leaving his Realm for a week to meet with other gods. We will be sponsoring an invasion to enter Death's Realm, defeat the forces guarding it and escape with whatever spoils we can long before Mortus returns.

"The higher powered guilds do these sort of incursions every chance they get. We will begin in the evening hour, the day after tomorrow." She looked around, expression tentative. "Can I have a show of hands to see who would be interested in attending?"

Almost every hand was in the air, some waving around like children in class, waiting to be called on. A smile broke across Elisabeth's face. "The meeting point will be the Gates of Death, on Mortus Island in the Bay of Lost Souls. We will assemble at dusk. I look forward to seeing you there." There was an excited buzz about the crowd as she finished.

Looking back, Cyrus saw the corpse of the dragon was almost entirely picked clean, with nothing left but a pile of bones. He watched with curiosity as Terian directed Vaste and J'anda, and the three of them worked to pull some of the bones off to the side, including the skull, now stripped of flesh and scale. Niamh and Nyad worked their way over to the others, each carrying armfuls of smaller bones.

Mentally shrugging it off, he turned to find Elisabeth had broken through the crowd of well wishers and curious raiders and was only steps away. "Congratulations!" She hugged him. "That was amazing; even Endeavor couldn't have pulled this off without a fatality." She smiled as he blushed.

"Glad I could be useful." He brushed aside her compliment. "Death's Realm? That should be a challenge."

She nodded. "I'm looking forward to it. The 'big three' guilds run these incursions every chance they get – whether it's the Realm of Darkness, or Death, even the Trials of Purgatory." She could not hide her glee. "If we do this right, we'll be announcing to Arkaria that the Alliance is a force to be reckoned with. We'll be able to attract more powerful adventurers from other guilds that aren't happy where they are but don't want to take a step down. It's a great growth opportunity for the Alliance."

Cyrus nodded, but had paid particular attention to a few of her comments. "Do you think we'll be going to the Realm of Darkness anytime soon? Or Purgatory?"

She looked a little puzzled but answered anyway. "Well, Purgatory is godless; just a number of different mystical creatures spread out as you descend through the five trials. The rewards for completing it are amazing, which is why the big three guilds – Amarath's Raiders, Endeavor and Burnt Offerings – share it among themselves and don't allow anyone else in."

Cy frowned. "What?"

She nodded. "Those three guilds treat Purgatory like farmers harvesting their fields." She smiled. "The Trials restart when a new group goes through, and all the enemies you face are reborn from the last time someone went through. The entity that runs it gives new rewards every time the trials are successfully completed."

Cy shook his head. "But how do the big three guilds keep out others?"

Elisabeth blinked. "The only way to exit the Trials is through portals. And the exit portal after you complete the trials sends you into the middle of the Reikonos guildhall quarter, so everyone knows what you've done. A guild called Retrion's Honor finished the Trials successfully three years ago, and when they exited through the portal, the 'big three' slaughtered them in the streets of Reikonos."

Cyrus's jaw dropped. "I heard about that! The Reikonos guards didn't even try to stop them."

Elisabeth shook her head. "The Reikonos guards couldn't beat any one of them alone: together they're far too powerful. The Council of Twelve was furious, threatened to expel them all from the city, until the three guild leaders came to the Citadel and made 'restitution' with ten million gold pieces. Since then, no one's had the courage to try Purgatory."

She took a breath. "You asked about the Realm of Darkness? I'd love to go there, but we don't have any way of knowing whether Yartraak will be there or not, and the God of Darkness is really powerful; not someone we'd like to tangle with."

Cyrus raised an eyebrow. "I don't think I'd like to face any of the gods any more than I'd like the three most powerful guilds in Arkaria attacking me."

Elisabeth laughed. "You'd stand a better chance against the three guilds. They don't even challenge a plane when the god is actually there; gods can smash mortals into such a pulp that a resurrection spell has no effect. Taking on a god is suicide."

Cy nodded. "So you've heard the tales of the mortals that faced the gods?"

A little sadness glimmering in her eyes, Elisabeth nodded in answer. "I think everyone has. The legend of Requiem, the guild from ten thousand years ago, is the most familiar cautionary tale about tempting the wrath of the gods." She smiled. "You should probably rejoin your guild; it looks like everyone is about to leave."

After exchanging goodbyes, Cyrus walked back to the Sanctuary group, trying to find Niamh. Instead he found Andren. "I found out a little bit more about the Realms. Elisabeth doesn't think we'll be able to go to Purgatory or the Realm of Darkness anytime soon. But if I can find what I need from Death, I'll be making progress."

Andren grunted. "This sword of yours had better be worth it, for all the trouble it'll take to get it."

Cyrus brushed him off. "Where's Niamh? I need to get teleported out of here."

"Niamh left a few minutes ago with J'anda, Vaste, Terian, and a hell of a lot of that dragon's skeleton. I think you're gonna need to find alternate transport."

Cy looked at Andren. "Can I come with you when you cast your return spell?"

The elf raised an eyebrow. Every spell caster could use the 'return' spell to take them back to a point that they had chosen to attach themselves to. It was a personal teleportation spell; not nearly as wide reaching as a druid or wizard's spells. Catching a ride with a spell caster that used the return spell meant getting intimately close with them. "No. If you were a pretty woman, it might be a different story," Andren said, fidgeting. "Or a woman at all. No. Find another way." Before Cyrus could argue, Andren murmured an incantation and vanished in a twinkle of light.

"You bastard," Cyrus said, watching other spell casters teleported back to their respective guildhalls. He caught a glimpse of Nyad disappearing in the burst of magic accompanying her teleportation spell. With her went a group of fighters bound for Sanctuary.

Getting frantic at the thought of being left behind, Cyrus scrambled to find a druid. He saw Brevis, with Gertan and Aina – two of the gnome's allies – and hurried over to them. "Aina, will you teleport me to the druid portal near Sanctuary?" he asked the elf.

Aina was a stately woman, tanned in a way that suggested she spent more time outdoors than inside. She wore a shawl that covered her auburn hair, and a cuirass that didn't quite cover all her abdomen, revealing a flat and muscular stomach. She rarely showed emotion, making it difficult for Cy to get a sense of her.

Before she had a chance to answer, Brevis leapt in and answered for her. "Of course she'd be glad to teleport you! The hero of the day, the first person to lead a decent adventure in six months? We'd be honored to have you accompany us back to Sanctuary!" Something in the way he said it, the self-serving sneer in his voice, triggered a warning in Cyrus's head. Aina nodded, affirming Brevis's answer and allowing Cy to relax about finding his way home. Within moments, the winds were gusting around him; with a blast of air, they left the Mountains of Nartanis behind them.

Chapter 18

As the winds of the teleport faded, Aina was already casting another spell. The power of the Falcon's Essence moved through Cyrus and his feet lifted from the ground once more, floating delicately over the grasses of the Plains of Perdamun. Brevis smiled at him, a snaggle-toothed smile that had no warmth. "Why don't we run with you to keep you company?"

Cyrus hesitated. "That's kind of you, but it's only five minutes back to Sanctuary and you can all cast return and save yourselves some time."

"Nonsense," he said. "We would consider it a great pleasure to keep you company. I've been meaning to talk with you, anyway, so this is a perfect chance." Cy kept silent, knowing that whatever kindness the gnome had offered had been with this in mind; the chance to bend the warrior's ear.

"Oh, really?" Cyrus nodded, trying to pay as little attention possible to the scheming gnome running alongside him. Aina and Gertan followed a few steps back.

"Indeed, indeed," he continued. "It has not escaped our notice that you are involved in helping this guild." Cy raised an eyebrow. "I believe," heavy emphasis was placed on the I, "that we have lagged far behind Goliath because we lack in a critical area."

"What's that?" Cy said, keeping his voice neutral.

"Why, leadership, of course!" the gnome said, as though it were obvious. "We have experienced adventurers, have grown considerably in recent months in capabilities, equipment and experience, but we don't have expeditions! Our General is scared to attack so much as a bandit camp!"

"In fairness to Orion, I have heard that bandits in the Plains are much stronger now than they used to be."

Brevis waved away Cyrus's statement. "Even that abominable assault on the Heia Pass was at least doing something! It added riches to the guild bank. We have a General, and the Council sees fit to have him do nothing. He's gone more of the time than he's here!" Brevis concluded with a flourish. "And his wife is worse still. Mark my words. I'm certain she had nothing else going on today but failed to show up nonetheless. Support the guild? Ha!" His laugh sounded like a bark. "She's a selfish one." His face turned serious. "Someone needs to say something."

Cyrus could see Sanctuary as they crested a hill. "Orion is scared. He led an excursion that ended in disaster and someone lost their life, which he didn't anticipate. He blames himself, and he won't let it go." Cyrus blew the air through his lips noiselessly. "That's not something you get over immediately." He took a breath. "I think, based on my experience today, I'm going to start leading expeditions. Maybe if I do it, and Orion sees how well it's going, he'll get his confidence back."

Brevis missed the point entirely. "See?" He gestured to Gertan and Aina. "This is exactly what I'm talking about! This is the sort of leadership we need: someone who's willing to get things done. We need to be rid of Orion – you should take his place as Sanctuary's General, command our army."

Cyrus felt his brow furrow. "I will not support removing Orion as General. I'm happy to help the guild, but I'm not going to depose the man."

"You're missing the point," Brevis sai. "When you've got someone who has such an attitude of entitlement you have to cut that out of your guild!" The little gnome made an almost absurd chopping gesture that looked as though it would be ineffective on anything, a ridiculous counterpoint to what he was proposing.

Cyrus studied Brevis with barely disguised annoyance. "Don't you think Alaric knows what he's doing by keeping Orion in place?"

"No! And don't get me started on what I think should be done with Alaric. He's never once led a battle that I've seen; rarely does anything. I've never seen a Guildmaster gone as much as he is. Almost as if he vanishes into thin air..." Brevis's words trailed off as they approached the gates of Sanctuary. "Give everything I've said some thought, I'm sure you'll come to the same conclusions I have."

"I'm sure I won't." Cyrus didn't even try to lie, but Brevis seemed not to notice.

"Of course, we'll talk again in a day or two." He scrambled off as though late for an appointment, Gertan and Aina trailing behind, but not before she had dispelled the Falcon's Essence, returning him to the ground.

Shaking his head at the absurdity of the gnome plotting a coup, Cyrus breezed through the doors to Sanctuary. He watched Brevis walk up to a group in the foyer, greeted with great fanfare. Cyrus knew that Brevis had some influence in Sanctuary, though it was hard to imagine the odd, antisocial gnome having much support. From the staircase on the other side of the foyer, Selene entered with an entourage of her own, Celia and Uruk behind her. Cyrus saw it only a moment before it occurred; Brevis and his group casting mutinous looks at Selene, and her completely oblivious expression as she crossed close to them, not noticing the gnome or his circle until he stepped into her path, halting her advance.

"So, I noticed you weren't with us when we fought the dragon," Brevis said.

"No, Brevis, I wasn't. So nice of you to notice."

"I'm sorry you weren't feeling well," he said, voice dripping with insincerity that was lost on Selene.

"What do you mean?" She looked confused. "I feel fine."

"Oh, then you must have been gone when they called for help."

"No." She still had a befuddled look. "Celia, Uruk and I were talking and planning a trip to the Emerald Coast with Orion. They have a little village on the edge of the ocean; it's supposed to be quite marvelous." Cyrus desperately wanted to intervene, to tell her to shut up, but he could not find words that wouldn't cause a scene.

"Oh, I see." Brevis seemed to relent for a moment. "It must be an important trip."

"Yes; we're planning to go there to relax, just the two of us couples."

A glint of victory shone in the enchanter's eye. "So, planning a vacation is more important to you than helping guildmates who are going into danger – what kind of person are you?!" The last part of his statement was blurted: it came out as a sort of crazed scream, an indignant accusation that caught the attention of everyone in the foyer.

Selene's jaw dropped, skin flushed in horror at his bluntness. "I-I don't see how it's any of your business what I –"

Brevis didn't wait for her to finish. "You're a member of this guild who doesn't seem to want to help anybody in this guild."

Selene was staggered. "That's not true!"

Undeterred, Brevis went on. "Why did you miss the event

today? Don't you care when your guildmates face mortal danger?"

Selene had fallen into the trap. "Of course I care, but –"

"Actions speak louder than words." The self-satisfied smile on Brevis's face indicated he thought he had made a profound point. There were enough nods around the foyer that Cyrus knew others felt the same.

Vara, Curatio and Alaric entered the foyer from the great hall at that moment. "What is going on here?" the voice of the Ghost silenced the proceedings. Selene, on the verge of tears, looked askance at Alaric, who was moving toward her.

Brevis did not meet Alaric's eyes as he approached. The paladin's gaze bored in on the gnome, who suddenly found an excuse to leave. With Gertan, Aina, and a few others in tow, he headed upstairs. Selene looked at Alaric as he approached, eyes brimming with tears, and the Ghost said to her, "I believe Orion was looking for you, m'lady, after we adjourned from the Council a few moments ago." She nodded, wiped her eyes with her sleeve, and led Celia and Uruk upstairs as well, using a different route than Brevis had taken.

Cyrus watched them go, and felt Alaric's attention turn his way. "I hear congratulations are in order. Vara told me you unleashed a very successful strategy on the dragon, something that no one had seen before." The elven paladin blinked twice and then glared at Alaric, but bit back whatever reply she might have made.

Cyrus blushed. "I suspect Vara would not be so generous in her praise." He paused for a moment. "Or that she would give praise at all."

Vara shifted her glare to Cyrus, but it was more annoyed than dangerous. "In point of fact, you chattering pincushion, I did tell Alaric that you were quite brave in your action today, and that the strategy you employed was surprisingly brilliant." She tossed her ponytail off her shoulder. "I did not, however, expect him to share that assessment with you."

Cyrus looked at the elf in surprise. "Why not?"

The annoyance on her face compounded. "Because human warriors, you who have all the magical ability of a head of lettuce and the aggregate brainpower of a cabbage – which your skull mightily resembles – in my opinion, should not be in front of any monster, demon or beast we ever face in any adventure, anywhere, at any time. Since your kind seems to be not only front and center but the ecstatic choice of our leaders, I at least do my part to make certain that you lot – the few, proud, the idiotic – don't walk into said battles with an overinflated sense of your own infallibility." She crossed her arms.

"So," Cyrus said, keeping his expression as straight faced as possible, "you're concerned about the possibility of warriors getting killed?" He smiled. "How sweet."

Vara's nostrils flared. "I am more concerned with you, you tuber-headed narcissist, getting me and mine killed with your human arrogance."

Alaric looked on with amusement at their exchange while Curatio wore an uncertain expression. "I trust," Garaunt said, "that you are not concerned about human arrogance from all of us?"

Vara's expression of indignant annoyance calmed at Alaric's words. "No, I've never known you to be arrogant," she said in a hushed tone. Turning her eyes back to Cyrus, fury burning in them, "But this one, since the day I have met him, has consistently tried to overreach his potential."

"Yes, but that's because you view my potential as being capped at using a knife and fork."

"I've seen you eat in the Great Hall," the elf shot back. "Perhaps you should find a more thoughtfully chosen argument to refute with next time."

"If we may come back to my original point," Alaric said. "Cyrus has done a masterful job of leading the assault using innovative tactics that saved lives." The paladin surveyed Cyrus carefully through his helmet, one eye looking directly into the warrior's.

"Anyone else would have done the same," Cyrus mumbled.

"Nonsense!" Curatio interrupted him. "We took on a very powerful dragon without a single death." His eyes grew intense. "I've faced many dragons and seen them cause numerous deaths." He turned back to Alaric. "I would echo Vara," he said, causing her to cringe behind him. "It was a very unique stratagem, and it paid off beautifully."

"I agree, Curatio. It seems the warrior is being modest." He regarded Cyrus with some interest. "Walk with us: we have matters to discuss." Alaric, Curatio and Vara turned toward the door to the grounds, Cyrus following behind them. As they descended the front steps to the lawn below, Alaric began to speak. "It has been a while since last we talked, Cyrus. How are things going for you in Sanctuary?"

Cyrus thought for a long moment. Always on the move, or in Council chambers, no one could fully account for Alaric's time. On the few occasions Cyrus had seen him at dinner, he tended to greet the warrior with enthusiasm, ask him how things were going, and then proceed to the next person he had to converse with. But occasionally the Ghost of Sanctuary sought him out, taking him on a walk and talking with him, like this.

Shaking off his thoughts, he focused on Alaric's question. "It's been good."

"Good enough that you'd consider running for officer?" The paladin looked at him with a guarded expression.

Cyrus felt the heat in his cheeks again. "I don't know that I have that much to offer Sanctuary."

"Nonsense!" Curatio dismissed his modesty again. "You've shown yourself to be a capable leader. With the growth of the guild, we're considering expanding the officers' Council. We believe you to be the best candidate for that post."

Cyrus demurred as the quartet turned the corner to the side yard of Sanctuary. "What about Brevis?"

"What of him?"

Cyrus looked at Alaric quizzically. "He's quite popular. What you walked into earlier was him, taking Selene to task for not coming to our aid."

Alaric was slow to respond. "Neither was I at the battle. Should I be 'taken to task' as well?"

Vara looked mutinous and Curatio remained silent as Cyrus answered. "In Brevis' eyes, all of us should probably be slapped around for some offense or another." Two of them laughed at his statement while Vara continued to keep her peace, irritation etched on her face. "I'm serious, Alaric," Cyrus said. "Brevis is dangerous for Sanctuary right now. He's aggravated and he's got several targets for his resentment – Selene, Orion and – you."

The Ghost removed his helmet, placing it into the crook of his elbow. Alaric Garaunt was not a young man by any means. His face was stern, but handsome; his brown hair, streaked with grey, was long enough to reach the top of his neck. His left eye was covered by an eyepatch that wrapped around his head. A thin beard and mustache covered the face of the Ghost. Leveling his gaze on the warrior, Alaric looked at Cyrus with his good eye, and the warrior would have given one of his own to be elsewhere. "Me?"

Cyrus nodded. "He feels that Orion is wasting the General post since he's not leading anything, that Selene is too selfish to help anybody but herself, and that you're allowing them to do whatever they want because Orion is an officer."

Alaric stopped walking as they reached the archery range. "And what do you believe?" His eye bored into the warrior, and Cyrus could feel a ghostly chill in his stomach that might have been the basis of Alaric's nickname.

It came out in a rush. "I think Orion feels so guilty about Enterra that it'll be years before he willingly leads another expedition on his own. I think Selene has been acting selfishly, as people are wont to do, and I think you'd back them both to your death, because they're members of Sanctuary. You've got the kind of loyalty that means more to you than your very life." He stopped, breathless. "And while we're being honest – Curatio, I thought all elves other than low-born were a bunch of uptight, arrogant tightasses like Vara until I met you."

The healer barely suppressed a laugh. Alaric was not so able, and he let out a roar so deep and loud that it startled Cyrus. Vara, for her part, glared at him but did not argue.

Alaric's laughter died down, and Curatio's smile was diminishing when the Ghost next spoke. "Well, you certainly didn't hold back your opinions." His joviality began to evaporate. "You are correct, I believe, in your assessment." Alaric cast a knowing eye to Vara. "Not about you." Returning his gaze to Cyrus, he continued, "Orion is somewhat damaged in terms of his confidence, and Selene has become wrapped up in herself." Alaric tapped his fingers on his armored greaves, drumming them several times, creating a deep rattling noise of metal on metal as Vara ground her teeth in irritation. "This brings us to an interesting conundrum.

"Although I have had very little use for expeditions, they are an activity that many adventurers wish to participate in. This is good: it certainly prospers the guild bank, and is no more dangerous than any other adventure one might pursue. Our problem is, how do we continue to offer these benefits to our members when our General doesn't want to schedule or run any expeditions?"

Cyrus shrugged. "It's quite a challenge."

"Indeed, it is, but I believe you hold the solution." The oblique smile on his face hinted that Alaric had an agenda.

"What did you have in mind?" Cyrus asked, caution infusing his tone.

"I told you before: I think you should run for officer," Alaric replied.

"Won't Orion get upset you're stripping him of the title of General?"

Alaric shook his head. "You're getting the wrong idea, perhaps because the guild seems to misperceive this. There is no formal 'General' title. Every officer picks duties that they feel best fit their strengths. Whether it be dealing with applicants or running the Halls of Healing," he nodded at Curatio, "Orion felt his abilities lay in the direction of leading expeditions." He frowned. "His change of heart does leave us with a rather sizable hole in our Council." Alaric cast a sidelong glance at Vara. "And since my most knowledgeable leader won't lead any excursions and Orion is scared to..."

Vara bristled. "I didn't say I won't lead any." She smoldered for a moment. "But people don't respond well to my leadership style."

"Hard to imagine, that," Cyrus quipped. "I can see it now: 'You! I hate you, go over there and die, okay?'"

Vara looked daggers at the warrior but when she spoke it was with an icy calm. "After all my searching, you've found the exact sentiments I've been wanting to express to you since the day we met."

Brushing off the paladin's repartee, Cyrus asked, "How long do you have to be in Sanctuary before you can become an officer?"

Curatio and Alaric exchanged a confused glance, while Vara looked annoyed. Curatio answered, "According to the charter, one year."

"Then this is a moot point. I am ineligible to be an officer of Sanctuary." Cyrus tried to put on a disappointed look, but honestly felt a bit relieved at not having to go through a popularity contest that he wasn't sure he'd be able to pass. Vara, surprisingly enough, did not look any happier at the revelation.

Alaric nodded. "Time loses its meaning for me. It feels like you have been here longer." Not sure his meaning was taken, the Ghost corrected, "I hope you realize I mean that in the best

possible way: that your loyalty seems like that of someone who
has been here since the beginning."

"I appreciate the sentiment. But I don't think even having a
new General that leads excursions every night of the week to the
most interesting locations in Arkaria would satisfy Brevis. He's
got a burr under his saddle and I don't think it's going to be
settled until someone is gone. Whether it's him or Orion and
Selene, mark my words," he said, "Sanctuary isn't big enough for
all of them. At least not in Brevis' eyes."

"We'll have to discuss this in Council." Alaric surveyed the
grounds before him. "Though I wish we could fix Orion's broken
spirit, I cannot – at least not immediately." He turned back to
Cyrus. "But I intend to have your word on something before we
part. Our Council needs leadership. You are a leader."

Cyrus shook his head. "I was only leader in my last guild
because no one else wanted the job. I'm not a leader."

Alaric nodded over Cyrus's shaking of his head. "Yes, you are.
Curatio, Vara, can either of you see any reasons, anything in this
warrior's character, that would prevent him from being an
honorable and useful addition to the Council of Sanctuary?"

Curatio answered immediately. "Absolutely not. I believe
Cyrus to be a guildmate of the highest caliber and that he would
be an excellent officer."

Cyrus looked at Vara expectantly, waiting for her to add a
negative critique, to say something that would reflect her disdain
for him, his skills, his abilities, his character or even his personal
hygiene. None was forthcoming. After a long moment's pause,
Vara turned her gaze back to Alaric. As her eyes passed over him,
Cyrus saw something nearly indefinable in her expression, that
same something that he had noticed the first day they met. "No,"
she said without emotion. "I can't see any reason he shouldn't run
for officer."

Alaric nodded. "Then it is settled." The paladin turned back to
Cyrus. "I want your word that in six months, when you are
eligible, you will submit your name for candidacy and do your
duty to Sanctuary by becoming an officer." He held up his hand to
forestall protest. "I will not allow any argument. I want your
word."

Though Alaric's voice and manner had issued a command,
Cyrus knew in his heart that he could tell the paladin no, if he
really wanted to. He shifted his gaze from Alaric to Curatio, who

was hopeful; a warm and encouraging smile upon the elf's face. Cyrus desperately wanted to say yes... to be an officer, right now. Protests aside, he wondered what happened in Council meetings, wondered how he could help, *if* he could help. Long minutes passed, none of them speaking, all waiting for his answer.

Vara would not meet his eyes, and her gaze was fixed in the distance, giving him a look at her profile. Her mouth was set in a hard line, keeping whatever emotions she had tightly bottled. The hair stretched in a ponytail over her shoulder, the sun shining on her spotless armor. He looked at her for a few minutes, silence still hanging in the air. She never turned to him.

As all these thoughts were bubbling in Cyrus's head, one solitary phrase slipped through his lips, a whisper, barely audible: "You have my word."

Chapter 19

It was not yet four o'clock when the crowd began to gather at the portal to the Realm of Death. Cyrus came with the bulk of the Sanctuary army, who had hiked to the edge of the Bay of Lost Souls, only a few hours southeast of Sanctuary's gates. Nyad and a team of wizards had conjured a boat that they sailed on across the bay to the Island of Mortus.

Cyrus could tell the island was small: he could see the entirety of it from where they had landed. In the middle of it all was a gateway that looked like a portal – a stone arch that crackled with black energy. No light escaped from it and the area around seemed dim even in the late afternoon sun. Alliance members were gathered about it in very casual groups.

The Daring were already waiting when they arrived. Erith was seated atop a little black and white pony, and when she saw Cyrus she giggled. "What's going on, meat head?" she shouted.

"How the hell did you get a horse over here?" Cyrus asked her, bewildered. The dark elf shrugged and smiled at him.

A few of Goliath's members flew to the island on winged mounts. Cyrus fixated on a warrior riding a griffon, a creature with the beaked head of a bird of prey and heavy, matted fur with a four-legged body. Claws jutted from its paws, digging into the ground as the creature landed and the warrior dismounted. *I'd like one of those*, Cy thought.

Cyrus waved at Elisabeth when she arrived. Any thought of striking up a conversation with her was forestalled: she was swamped with well-wishers and people seeking instruction. Cyrus knew how she felt: leading an invasion of this magnitude couldn't be easy – at least not based on his experience. She went to work with a scroll, studying plans carefully.

She was all smiles as she stepped onto a rock in front of the army. "We have quite the assemblage tonight," she announced with great pleasure. "I'm going to be reorganizing you into different elements in order to form a cohesive fighting force. We expect guardians by the entrance to the Realm and additional forces at certain key points which we're going to be hitting.

"Opposition will be tough," she continued, "but we have very good numbers on our side. Our main warrior for tonight will be Kilgar from Goliath," she announced, making a sweeping gesture toward a hulking human as Cyrus rolled his eyes, "but we'll also need some backups to ensure that if an enchanter can't control an enemy, it doesn't wreak havoc by killing our spell casters." Lack of armor made spell casters easy prey for strong enemies. Even with a quick resurrection spell, it could take thirty minutes to an hour for them to regenerate enough magical energy and shake off the sickening effects of death to effectively cast spells again.

"Cyrus from Sanctuary, Cass from the Daring and Yei from Goliath will be our secondary warriors." Cyrus blinked in surprise. He cast a sidelong look at Cass and then Yei. The Goliath warrior was a massive troll, bigger than Vaste. Yei had recently painted his armor into a bizarre, multicolored scheme involving deep purple, bright red and some strain of yellow. Terian had remarked during the assault on Kalam that it "defiled his eyes" to even look at the warrior.

"We'll need our enchanters focused on occupying additional monsters, beguiling them by use of your charms or simply mesmerizing them." Her voice turned serious. "We are outnumbered here, and we will be facing wave after wave of foes." She proceeded to break the force into elements assigned to support each warrior.

"By the time we get this entire force facing the right direction, I'll be older than Curatio," Andren said under his breath. Niamh overheard him and giggled. Cyrus said nothing, but privately he agreed; leading this force of several hundred was going to be like trying to lead a herd of cats from the front.

When they had organized, the combined army lined up in formation before the portal. It was wide enough for only a few people to enter at a time. They lined up in order as best they could; the space around the portal was completely packed – as was the island itself.

"On my mark, I want a full charge into the portal and out of the way, as quickly as possible – without trampling any gnomes," Elisabeth added. Cyrus heard a squeak of appreciation from somewhere in the crowd in front of him.

It was a tense moment. The portal glared at them, almost defying them to enter. Cyrus could hear the heavy breathing of Vaste next to him, and caught sight of J'anda ahead, his now elven features fixed in a look of intense concentration. Yei was scratching himself.

The seconds ticked away, and nerves were chewing at Cyrus. He could hear his heart pounding; he'd never before set foot in the domain of any god. *At least I'm not challenging Bellarum,* Cyrus thought. The God of War had to be at least as intimidating as the God of Death, he conceded, missing the irony of that thought in the intensity of the moment.

Looking sideways in the moments before the order was given, Cyrus's gaze fixed on the smiling visage of Malpravus. The cowl of the Goliath Guildmaster's cloak was once again covering his head, leaving the dark elf's face shadowed but for the dim sunlight playing on it. His expression was bizarre, triumphant. His eyes flicked to the side and saw Cyrus looking at him. With a nod, Malpravus bowed toward the warrior.

"GO!" Elisabeth's shout boomed across the island and in a blink, Kilgar and his group were in the portal and fading, the second group charging in behind them. Cyrus thundered forward, felt a twisting sensation in his stomach as he stepped into the darkness and his vision distorted like he was underwater; all trace of the world he had left behind on the island had disappeared.

When Cyrus's feet hit the ground he was already moving forward, sword in hand. The sky was blood red, like a sunset that had never quite finished. Spread out before him were rolling fields, as far as the eye could discern, spreading out in every direction but one. His eyes alighted on an enormous structure in the distance. It had a gigantic base, miles wide, and gradually drew to a point on top. It was the single biggest tower he had ever seen.

Cy felt a thump as someone ran into him from behind. He realized he had stopped along with everyone else and turned his head to see Cass peering around him. "Frankly," the Daring's chief warrior said with a slightly disgruntled expression, "I was hoping for a little more combat on this side of the portal."

Cyrus snorted. "I hope Mortus isn't lingering to give you your fondest wish."

Elisabeth made her way to the front of the army. "I was told to anticipate more resistance at the entryway." Lines knit across her face as she scanned the area around them.

"More resistance?" Andren said from just behind Cyrus. "How about any resistance?"

Cyrus did not stop scanning the horizon, even as the rest of the Alliance force began to relax. "These must be the Fields of Paxis," Cyrus said under his breath.

"Indeed they are," came the reply from Vaste, startling Cyrus. "The Realm of Death is broken into many parts to reflect the fate awaiting the worst of us." The troll smiled. "Did you know that Mortus, even as God of Death, doesn't get all the dead?"

"I'd heard that," Cyrus said, still looking for trouble.

"He only gets the really bad eggs; those who have done horrific things." The troll shuddered all the way to the top of his enormous frame. "The Fields of Paxis are the entry point or sorting area for the newly arrived. The least of the offenders are sentenced to wander these fields eternally without guidance or hope of escape. The worst are judged here and sent elsewhere." The troll gestured into the distance to the tower.

"The Eusian Tower," Cyrus said without inflection.

"You got it," Vaste confirmed. "Three main areas within, places of torment for the dishonored dead..." The troll's voice drifted off.

"I hate waiting." The warrior turned his eyes back to the horizon. "I hate waiting for possible death even more."

"You should never go on a date with Vara then," the troll said. "Not only does she take forever to get ready, she is the very definition of 'possible death'."

Cyrus laughed. "I don't think there's much danger of that."

"Her killing you or you going on a date?"

Cy raised an eyebrow. "The latter. I'd actually lay odds on the former."

The troll looked at him, face unreadable. "More than you probably realize."

"Hah!" Cyrus laughed out loud. "The woman can't stand me."

"An all-too-familiar experience in your dating life, I'm sure." Ignoring Cyrus's rude gesture, the troll pressed on. "But in Vara's case, you have to understand her."

"Do I really want to?"

"Can't answer that for you," Vaste replied. "But I can tell you that Vara was nearly married once – to a human warrior, of all things." The troll looked around before finishing his statement. "I heard it ended badly."

Cyrus raised an eyebrow. "The fact that she'd ever consider marrying a human is laughable. The idea that she'd have any involvement with a warrior puts your story well into the realm of fiction. She hates –"

"Yes, yes," Vaste cut him off. "Haven't you ever wondered why she can get along with me or Nyad, or Curatio – any one of a number of other guildmates – but not you?"

"I'm gonna go with... because she's a heinous bitch."

Ignoring him, Vaste went on. "I'd have thought you, genius of the umpteenth order, Mr. Strategy and Tactics and 'Assessing the Battlefield', would have figured it out. She doesn't like you because you remind her of someone."

"I don't buy it."

"Very well then," Vaste said, still inscrutable. "Far be it for me to disagree with the mighty Cyrus Davidon, who knows the hearts of all whom he meets."

"Not all of them," the warrior said. "But there's no room in that heart for love; past, present or future."

"Perhaps not," Vaste said and let the matter drop.

At the front of the army, Elisabeth had been consulting with Malpravus and a few others. Shaking her head, she turned from the Goliath Guildmaster to address the army. "We're going to move to the Eusian Tower now. I expect whatever enemies that aren't here but usually would be are in the tower."

The army of the Alliance moved forward through the tall grass of the fields. The journey to the Eusian Tower took a little over an hour, during which time the color of the sky changed not at all. As they approached, Cyrus felt several times that they had to be close to the entrance, such was the size of the tower. When they finally reached the entry, he had to admit that even the Citadel in Reikonos, the tallest building he had ever seen, would easily fit into the shadow of the Eusian Tower. They marched through the doorway, and Cyrus once again found himself in near-complete darkness.

Chapter 20

Upon entering the Eusian Tower, the Alliance force paused. Vaste cast a spell next to him, and a veil lifted from Cyrus's eyes, allowing him to see in the darkness. They were in the middle of the largest open indoor space Cyrus had ever seen. It seemed to stretch for miles up and down. They crossed a massive bridge to a central platform that had three additional bridges spanning out in each direction of the compass.

As no foes were in sight, Elisabeth addressed them. "There are three wings to the Eusian Tower: one is the personal chambers of Mortus and his guards." She looked up and gestured straight ahead from the direction they had entered, indicating a mammoth door made of solid metal, large enough that it would not have looked out of place in Kortran. "It is also where his treasure trove is. In order to gain access, we'll have to go through the other two wings of the tower," she said, brimming with confidence. "Defeating the guards in both wings will draw out the reserve in his private chambers. We'll start with this direction." She pointed to their right.

"How does Mortus have any treasure left if guilds are constantly stealing from his Realm and killing his guards every time he leaves?" Cy frowned.

Vaste shrugged. "If you're a god, I guess you can make more treasure."

"His followers pay him tribute in their temples," Cass said from behind them. "And he can recreate his guards with ease."

"Yeah, but if someone stole all your possessions every time you left your house, wouldn't you stop leaving?" Cyrus asked.

"They don't get all of Mortus's possessions," Cass said. "He keeps the best of them sealed under magical barriers that only the power of a god could breach."

They stopped talking as they crossed the bridge and entered an archway. As they progressed down a dark corridor, Cyrus felt a deep-seated chill run through him. It took him a moment to realize that it was not internal; the temperature had dropped significantly as they continued along the corridor, which had also begun to slope downward.

They emerged into a cavernous area – not nearly as tall as the entryway but which extended so far into the distance that Cyrus could not see the opposite wall. Stretching down the middle of the cavern was a frozen lake, with blocks of ice stacked around the sides.

Cyrus said with surprise, "I expected to see more dead people in the Realm of Death, y'know?"

"I know what you mean," Vaste said. "Where's the fire and brimstone? Where's the damnation?" The troll looked at the frozen lake and shook his head in disappointment. "I was expecting more damnation."

"Damnation is here," a rattling voice breathed next to them. Cyrus jumped in surprise before he realized that the words issued from Malpravus, who was at his elbow. "The damned are all around you," the dark elf said with barely contained glee. "You cannot see them." Malpravus inhaled deeply, as though he was enjoying a particularly pleasant scent. "There is a great deal of torment present here – many, many damned souls, enslaved in the ice."

Cyrus looked at the Goliath Guildmaster, eyes wary. "Why can you see the dead when we can't?"

Malpravus looked into Cyrus's eyes and the warrior could see a hollow blackness in the dark elf's sunken sockets that reminded him of the portal leading into Death's Realm. "I am a very powerful necromancer, boy. The dead are mine to wield; it is only natural I would be able to see them."

"I don't think there's anything 'natural' about what you just described," Vaste said.

A smile lit the features of the necromancer as he steepled his fingers. "Those of us who study the nearly lost art of necromancy are very misunderstood."

"I could stand for your 'art' to get a bit more lost." Vaste bristled. "Manipulating the bodies and souls of the dead and deriving power from them is a far beyond morbid practice."

Malpravus remained calm in the face of Vaste's criticism. "Someday you will understand that however you must acquire it, power is the most important thing in this world." The necromancer held a bony hand up to stay Vaste's reply.

Malpravus fixed his gaze on Cyrus, giving the warrior sudden cause to squirm internally. "I see great potential in your leadership, lad. I expect to see great things from you after the battle yesterday." Without another word, the necromancer glided away, his cloak sweeping against the ground.

Vaste and Cyrus exchanged a look. "That was... disconcerting," the troll said, perfectly capturing Cyrus's sentiments.

"I get the feeling that he's even creepier among his own guild."

Whatever reply Vaste might have made was cut off by an inhuman wailing. Seeking out the source of the cacophony, Cyrus's eyes were drawn to figures moving in their direction across the frozen lake. The first of them was barely visible; a thin figure, emaciated, with skin of the grayest pallor and sunken eyes. Bloody, cracked lips uncovered sharp teeth and a nasty, nausea-inducing smell of decay preceded the shadowy beasts. The first of the rotting creatures leapt into their midst, reminding Cyrus of the first time he had met Vara.

He jumped into action, pushing through the crowd to engage the creature. "Wendigo!" he heard someone cry out. Cyrus brought his sword to bear as the wendigo's claws swiped into the crowd and sent three spell casters flying, dead.

Horrified, Cyrus struck with his sword into the grey flesh, leaving the wendigo with an enormous gash from shoulder to waist. Seeming not to notice, it lunged at him, teeth exposed, missing him by mere inches as the warrior dodged. He aimed a counter blow at the wendigo as it passed, but missed. The wendigo sliced him three times in rapid succession. Two glanced off his armor but the third landed perfectly between the joints on his left arm, digging into the muscle of his forearm.

Cyrus grimaced and dropped his left hand from his sword, holding it in his right to fend off the wendigo's advances. The point faced directly into the heart of the creature, which was keeping its distance, circling to his left to evade the tip of his blade. Cyrus pulled his injured arm against himself until he felt a spell mend the wound; he looked down to see the gash healed, but blood still trickled from beneath his armor and the painful sensation did not immediately cease.

Cyrus feinted at the wendigo, not returning his left hand to the hilt. The beast overreacted to the warrior's bluff and dodged to the side, running into three rangers who stabbed the exposed back of the creature. Cyrus smiled as the wendigo turned to face the new threat and he drove his sword with both hands into the back of its head. A piercing scream filled the air and the wendigo went limp.

"No time for a victory dance!" Andren said from behind him. Cyrus scowled and turned to face the healer. Numerous wendigos were making their way through the ranks of the army. Cyrus saw J'anda's arms sweeping about, casting spell after spell. The wendigos were halting, sunken eyes rolling back in their heads, mesmerized.

An attack from behind caught him off guard and knocked Cyrus to his knees. He felt claws grasping at him, digging into his sides just below his armpits in the vulnerable seam of his breastplate and back plate, penetrating the chain mail beneath his plate armor. The stabbing sensation increased as the wendigo that had grabbed him dug its claws in further. He reversed the grip on his sword and stabbed backward at the creature, gagging at the sickening stench of decay that filled his nose. A howl of pain told him he had not missed, and Cyrus stumbled forward, feeling the claws withdraw from his flesh.

He turned back to engage the wendigo, fighting past the agony in his side, and lunged forward, catching it on the arm with a sword thrust. A yelp filled his ears and forced a grin to the warrior's lips, even as he ignored the pain. Other fighters – rangers, paladins, dark knights – were attacking the wendigo that was focused on him.

Every time the creature started to turn, changing its attention to the others behind it, Cyrus would bellow a warcry and leap forward, hacking and stabbing, turning its attention back to him. The first three times he scored gashing blows, leaving jagged cuts in the flesh of the undead-looking beast. The fourth, as soon as he yelled at it, the wendigo immediately refocused on him, not allowing him to get a strike in.

Elisabeth brought her daggers to bear in a powerful backstabbing blow that brought the wendigo to its knees. Cyrus swept forward with all his speed and decapitated it. When it dropped, Cyrus appraised the area around him for the next fight.

J'anda stood only a few feet away, the enchanter's face a mask of concentration. "If you're looking for something to do," the dark elf said, eyes closed and illusionless for only the second time since Cyrus had met him, "you could try killing that one before my spell breaks." His finger rose to point at one of the gray fiends that was standing close to the ice.

"How many of these do you have mesmerized right now?" Cyrus asked him, incredulous. There were at least forty wendigos standing completely still throughout the army, as if the cold had frozen them.

"Well," J'anda said, voice straining, "we have eight enchanters and each of the other seven has one wendigo mesmerized. So if you subtract seven from however many there are, that would be the number that I have under control." A tight smile made its way across J'anda's blue lips. "It takes quite a bit of concentration and magical energy to create the illusion that mesmerizes these fiends, so forgive me if I stop speaking now."

Cyrus shook his head and trotted with the rest of his element to the wendigo that J'anda had indicated. Positioning his group around it he struck with an impaling attack at the same time that his other fighters did, making short work of the wendigo, which died with a feral scream.

A quick look at J'anda showed the enchanter pointing in the direction of another of the frozen beasts. He and his group moved through the wendigos one at a time, along with the other elements of the army, until all the gray-skinned fiends had been killed. Kilgar drove his sword through the last as a sigh of relief ran through the cavern. From behind them came the sound of very slow clapping.

Cyrus turned to see J'anda Aimant, eyes half-lidded, bringing his hands together in applause. "Well done. Perhaps someday soon we can find an enchanter with enough talent to take at least two foes at any give time?" J'anda ignored the glares of the enchanters surrounding him and snapped his fingers to become a gnome.

They stood by the edge of the frozen lake while Elisabeth again consulted with Malpravus, Tolada and a few of the other Alliance officers. Cyrus stood with Andren and Vaste, looking across the ice into the darkness. "Andren," he asked the elf, "Malpravus told us that the dead are all around us, and being tormented. Do you suppose that's true?"

Andren did not respond at first. "Yep. There are tormented souls all around us right now."

"Why can't we see them?" Cyrus asked, puzzled.

Andren looked at the ice at his feet and pointed down. "Do you see anything at all? A shape, a specter, anything?"

The warrior peered at the ice. "It looks a little darker, like smoke or something."

Andren nodded. "That is one of the dead. A necromancer can

see them as easily as I can tell the difference between an ale and mulled mead. Which is no great difficulty for me, but most can't. The training one goes through for his branch of magic makes him more sensitive to the spirit emanations that you can barely perceive. What looks like a faded specter to you appears to me as an old elf, buried to his face in the ice, screaming in agony and unable to see anyone around him."

Cyrus looked at Andren, eyes wide. "That's what you see? And it looks as clear as if he were alive?"

"I can see a bit better than you can but that has more to do with my age and magical training. I would imagine it would be clear to a powerful necromancer. What I see is a bit of a distorted image – as though smoke is obscuring the lines of their faces, and their words were being spoken through a waterfall."

Any further questions were drowned out by Elisabeth's order to move the invasion force back into the center of the Eusian Tower. As they walked back up the tunnel the temperature returned to a bearable level. The chill, however, failed to leave them.

Chapter 21

As they mulled around the center of the tower, Cyrus passed Erith, still riding on her horse, as he strode to the front of the army. Catching his eye, she spoke. "I miss healing you today. Any other day, I wouldn't, but today I'm healing a dark knight, and he takes two hits and crumples like a ranger in a windstorm."

"Hey!" the dark knight and ranger in Erith's group chorused in unison, outraged.

"What?" she snapped back over her shoulder. "It's not my fault that the two of you can't get hit without dying." She turned back to Cyrus. "I'd have better luck keeping an ant alive while a child stomped on its anthill." Rolling her eyes at the dissenting opinions behind her, she tossed another insult over her shoulder. "The ant would probably be more grateful, too," she grumbled. "Your fighter dies one or three times…"

Elisabeth rallied their army into the tunnel opposite the one they had just left. As they descended, there was another dramatic temperature change – this one turning the air brutally hot.

"It's like an oven-heated punch to the face," Andren said.

"Feels kinda like home," Vaste said. The tunnel opened to another large cavern, this one again having a deep gash in the middle of it – but instead of containing ice, there was a lake of bubbling, boiling oil stretching into the distance.

"You think there are more lost souls in there?" Cyrus asked.

Vaste nodded. "Mortus is not a benevolent god. Those worthy of torment in the afterlife are subject to him, and remain with him for eternity."

Andren took a swig of liquor from his flask. "Any guesses as to what it takes to land yourself here for eternity?"

Vaste's eyes narrowed. "It's all speculative, but there is the traditional range of sins – murder, thievery, intemperance…" The troll looked at Andren.

"Intemperance?" Andren asked, eyes wide. "You mean drinking?" An almost imperceptible nod from Vaste sent a visible shudder through Andren. "I reckon I'll be quitting drinking, then." Cyrus raised an eyebrow at the healer, who looked offended. "I can quit any time, you know." Cyrus held his hands up in a gesture of surrender, at which point Andren began to nervously eye the boiling oil again.

A few of the adventurers wandered closer to the edge of the bubbling lake; Cyrus remained leery and kept his distance. In an instant the surface of the oil erupted in several places around the bank of the pool as something shot out of it. *Whatever it is*, Cy reflected, *looks a hell of a lot like snakes held by their tails out of the oil.*

With a reptilian head atop a long, twisting segment of scaled neck, seven of the creatures burst forth and attacked those that had wandered too close to the shore. Cyrus watched as several adventurers were grasped between the jaws of the snake heads – or in the case of one of Goliath's rangers, grasped by the ankle and flung into the oil. Cyrus caught a glimpse of Malpravus, among those standing close to the shore, calm in the midst of the storm of action.

Cyrus rushed toward the shore, but before he could get there, he heard an elven voice behind him proclaim, "I can handle this." Something in the way it was said caused him to turn around. Nyad was already casting a spell, flames forming around her hands.

"No!" he shouted, but to no avail – the fire spell burst from her fingertips and blasted past the snake heads to hit the oil behind it. Flames began to spread across the surface of the lake.

"Oops!" Nyad said. "I'll fix it!" Once more, she began to cast a spell, this time with a whiff of what looked like smoke as a warning, something flew from her hand to the edge of the pool of now flaming oil, expanding into a cloud and raining on it.

Cyrus did not even have time to react. An explosion rocked the cavern, sending a burst of fire surging in all directions. The warrior dropped to his knees and covered his face as a wall of flame washed over the Alliance army. It dissipated quickly, but not before catching a few people on fire, including Nyad herself. He tackled the wizard, rolling on the ground to suffocate the flames.

Turning his attention back to the lake, the seven heads remained above the thick, flaming liquid, unaffected by the fires around them. Smaller pools had also caught on fire, making the cavern look like the den of Ashan'agar.

"Ah," Vaste said from the ground next to Cyrus, "there's the fire and brimstone I was looking for and... damnation."

"I think," Cyrus said, running his fingertips over the scorch marks on his already blackened armor, "I'm going to have to cut the heads off some snakes now."

"Do run along then," Vaste said from a prone position. "I'll be here, watching in case you get hurt."

"Much appreciated," Cyrus grunted as he lifted himself to his feet.

"Thank you," Nyad said in a muffled voice, face in the dirt as the warrior ran past her to the edge of the pool.

He looked to the lake of fire, seven snake heads still dancing back and forth within it, trying to grasp at any poor soul close to the edge. Malpravus stood by the shores, ignored by the waving heads. Cy dived to avoid two of them as they swept toward him. They missed him narrowly and with such force that one of them drove into the ground and did not move after the impact.

Rolling to his feet, Cyrus grasped the hilt of his sword in both hands, and swung it from over his shoulder into the unmoving neck. The beast screamed and flailed, but could not muster enough strength to break free. The warrior stomped on the hilt of his sword with a plated boot, driving the blade the rest of the way through the neck. The head screamed and the neck retracted into the pool of fire. As it entered the flames, the severed head screamed and stopped moving.

Two more heads swept in with a violent attack on the warrior, who dodged one of them but was caught flat-footed by the second, knocking him into the dirt. A healing wind ran through him, repairing the arm he knew had been broken. Rolling from his back to his hands and knees, he stood and charged past Vaste ("You're welcome!" the troll shouted, still laying on the ground) to be greeted by the same two snake heads, writhing at the end of their reach, snapping their teeth at him.

"It's a hydra," came the calm voice of Malpravus, who was gently stroking the neck of one of the snakes. "The heads are all part of the same beast."

Cyrus stayed out of the reach of the hydra heads, thrusting forward with his sword to strike a stinging blow to one of the heads, which hissed and withdrew. "Two questions come to mind – one, why isn't it attacking you, and two – could you help me out?"

A wide, almost malevolent grin split the necromancer's face. "Yes, I can help you, I suppose." Reaching into his robes, the dark elf pulled a long dagger from a scabbard on his belt. Whispering something too low to be heard over the fire and screaming in the cave, Malpravus drew the dagger back and thrust it into the neck of the hydra that he had been stroking only moments before. The neck stiffened and dropped to the ground, great tongue lolling out of its scaly mouth. Malpravus cackled and brought the dagger to his lips.

"That is *not* normal," Cyrus said before he lunged to strike at the remaining head. Malpravus made another bow to the warrior, arms extended out from his body, wide smile still fixed on his face. Then the dark elf turned on his heel, and swept away from the lake of fire, gliding back to where most of the Allied army was recovering from the explosion and avoiding the heads of the hydra.

Cyrus lunged once more, committing all his weight to the attack, and caught the hydra head off guard; he rammed his sword into the mouth of the creature. It screamed and tried to flee, but to no avail – close enough now to engage the beast physically, Cyrus threw his legs around the hydra's neck and jammed the sword further into the mouth, pushing it until it burst through the top of the hydra's head. The neck went limp, and the snake head dropped, pinning Cyrus to the ground.

"Yes!" exulted Tolada, who rushed up with a hammer and began to pound on the head that lay across Cyrus.

"Hey!" the warrior shouted, unpleasant impacts to the head reverberating through him. "It's dead already! Why don't you either pick a live one to attack or help get it off me?"

"It's all the same beast!" Tolada said, face alight with glee. "It can still feel this!"

"Tell you what," Cyrus said, eyes narrowed in irritation. "I'm gonna stab you through the hand until you can't move it anymore. Then I'm going to pound what's left of it with a hammer, and you let me know if you can feel it!"

Muttering something about a lack of allied cooperation, the dwarf put aside his hammer to help roll the hydra head off of Cyrus. By the time the warrior got to his feet, the Alliance force had engaged the other heads. Spells were flying through the air, bringing the waving heads to the ground one at a time, where they were greeted by vicious attacks from the melee combatants. Within a few minutes, the hydra was defeated.

"All right," Elisabeth said, "let's drag it on shore."

"Drag it out?" Cyrus sputtered. "I vote we toss it back into the flaming oil."

She smiled at him in understanding. "Do you know how valuable the bodies of the creatures we kill are? That's some of the real wealth of these Realms – the same as it is with dragons. Sure, there's a hoard of treasures around here somewhere, but there's gold in selling the skins, the scales, things that yield high prices. That's the reason why guilds like Amarath's Raiders, Endeavor and Burnt Offerings are wealthy. They have access to materials no one else does and trade agreements with shops and companies that make them more money."

"I don't care if his left buttcheek is worth a million gold; let's toss this thing back in and be done with it."

Elisabeth frowned. "His butt isn't worth anything. Hydra testicles, however, are worth a few hundred thousand gold each." She brightened. "Let's hope this one is a boy!"

Once they had finished extracting the most valuable of the materials from the corpse of the hydra (including three testicles, to the delight of Elisabeth and Malpravus), and those that had been tossed into the flaming oil had been recovered and revived, the Alliance army moved back up the long tunnel and into the platform of the entryway once more. Casting a sidelong look at the door to Mortus's chambers, Cyrus saw they were still sealed.

"I'm not sure what's going on here," Elisabeth said. "I was told that defeating the enemies within both caves would get the attention of Mortus's guards..."

A loud noise filled the entryway and the enormous doors split and began to open, sweeping wide to reveal an army within. A moment of panic set in among the allies. "We need to face them outside!" Elisabeth shouted. "Retreat to the Fields of Paxis!"

The Allied army broke and ran, retreating over the entry bridge and down the steps. Once outside, Elisabeth commanded once more, "Stop! Hold position here!" For the most part, her command was obeyed and they reformed at the bottom of the hill outside the Eusian Tower. A few adventurers continued beyond the rally point and up the hill, stopping once they reached the top.

The first rank of the army of Mortus appeared in the doorway to the Eusian Tower; four rows of the horrific wendigos, followed by demons with red skin, bulging muscles and fearsome teeth. Pointed ears stood atop their heads, giving them all the appearance of a devil. There were fewer of them than there were wendigos, but each of the devils stood one and a half times the height of a human and was armed with a weapon.

"The hell of it is," Cyrus heard Andren say from somewhere behind him. "There are actually more of us than them." He paused. "But I suspect they might pack a slightly nastier punch than most of us."

J'anda called out, "Those demon knights – I cannot mesmerize them; their will is too strong."

A few of the gray-skinned fiends halted their advance, bedazzled by the enchanters' spells. The remaining wendigos broke ranks and charged, demon knights following behind.

The first wave of foes hit their front line warriors hard. The sheer numbers forced every Alliance fighter and some of the spell casters into one-on-one combat. The wendigos were strong and vicious, creating a poor match for most of the allied combatants. Cyrus swung his sword with all his strength, dispatching two of the bloody creatures in a row. By the time he had killed the second wendigo, the battle had turned into a complete melee. A demon knight waded toward him, accidentally killing a wendigo on its way.

Cyrus brought his sword up in time to block the first blow from the demon knight, which wielded a blade that looked like a massive meat cleaver. The strength of the demon knight's strike chipped some of the steel from his sword where the blow impacted. *Guess I'll be needing a new sword soon,* Cyrus thought. *I'm sure Belkan will be pleased.*

He successfully dodged the next attack and drove his sword into the leg of the demon knight which elicited a grunt and a backhand slap that sent Cyrus reeling, dragging his sword out of the wound. A small geyser of blood shot from the hole in the demon knight's leg, but the grotesque face of the creature displayed no reaction beyond a strange slurping sound as its tongue danced outside its lips.

The demon knight jumped forward with no warning, knocking aside Cyrus's sword and burying its teeth into the veins of his neck. Cy brought his sword down, burying it through the eye of the demon knight, which relinquished its biting grasp and fell over, dead.

Cyrus felt himself fall, warm blood rushing through his fingers as he tried to staunch the bleeding. He looked up to see Niamh, fingers glowing with a small healing spell, and he felt a swell of vitality as she kept him alive until he felt the spell from a healer that completely mended his wound.

Pushing back to his feet again, Cyrus ignored the agony from the now-healed wound as all battle around him stopped. A commotion came from atop the hill behind them. Something was thundering on the other side, and when it crested the ridge, Cyrus's jaw dropped in shock.

It was the bones of a dragon, but not just any dragon. The crests and gnarls of the skeleton, the jutting spikes and fearsome teeth, left no doubt which dragon the skeleton belonged to. *Kalam,* Cy thought in astonishment. *Shit.* Shooting a searing glare at those around him, he yelled, "Who helped Terian resurrect that thing?"

Vaste shouted over the crowd. "It's not resurrected. Kalam must be on his merry way to the afterlife or else he got co-opted by Mortus to defend this Realm. It's probably his penance."

A rumbling came from the skeletal jaw of the dragon's bones. A hot rush shot through Cyrus, flushing his face and spurring him into action. A demon knight in front of him had turned its back to see the events unfolding on the hilltop. Behind the demon knight, Tolada stooped down to pick up the hammer that he had dropped in shock at the sight of Kalam.

With two long strides, Cyrus used the dwarf as a step to launch himself through the air and bury his sword in the neck of the unsuspecting demon knight. As it fell, Cy pulled the sword as roughly as he could, decapitating the demon, and dropping the head to the ground. He reached down to retrieve it and ran toward the base of the hill.

The battle had resumed, wendigos and demon knights hacking at the allied army. Shuffling his way through the fight, stabbing wendigos and knights as he passed, Cyrus finally broke through the battle and climbed to an elevated position on the hill. From the height it afforded him, the warrior could see J'anda working to mesmerize the wendigos. "J'anda!" Cyrus yelled. "Can you charm the wendigos and use them to battle for us?"

The dark elf did not respond for a moment, eyes closed, but then nodded.

"Do it!" Cyrus shouted. The dragon corpse lingered at the top of the hill, cutting off any chance of retreat for the Alliance army. Cy let loose a bellowing warcry that caught the attention of everyone, even the fiends. Thrusting the head of the demon knight into the air above him, Cyrus taunted them. "You over-bulked, under-brained servants of Mortus don't even have the stones to take on a real threat – you're content to wade in among spell casters and rangers who can't give you a taste of real combat – COWARDS!"

Without waiting for reply, Cyrus threw the head at the nearest demon knight, only a few paces away. It caught the head and stared at it for a brief moment, shocked. Cyrus slammed into the demon full force on a downhill charge – his sword pierced it and he jammed the edge of his right vambrace into the mouth of the knight, breaking its lower teeth and cutting open its lip. A squeal of outrage filled the air as it attempted to push the warrior away. Cyrus gripped tighter, bringing his sword down again and again. His final blow penetrated the heart of the demon knight, ending its resistance.

Howls of outrage came from the forces of Death's Realm. Cy ran back up the hill. His speed and quick action by two of J'anda's charmed wendigos were the only thing that saved the warrior from being hauled down by the entire army of Mortus, now solely focused on him and following him up the hill.

Cyrus could see a faint light in the bone-dragon's eye sockets as it thundered down the hill toward him. *How the hell do I fight a pile of bones?* he wondered. *And a battalion of these damned demon knights at the same time? The dragon's enchanted... and even if it's a magical creature, it can take damage...*

The dragon's skeleton let out a hiss as he approached. Its head swung down, jaws open and extended. A rattling voice could be heard: "I am Kalam, defender of Mortus, the God of Death."

Cyrus grunted as he ducked the dragon's first attack. "I am Cyrus, warrior of Sanctuary. I piss on you and your god!" Bringing his sword around, he struck as hard as he could at the bone of the dragon's front right ankle. A small crack appeared in the bone. He ran under the dragon, beneath where the belly would have been, and rattled his sword along every rib until he reached the tail, laughing all the way.

Dodging from behind the back leg he turned, and with a savage grin raised his hands above his head for a double-handed swing of his sword. He landed the strikes on the cartilage midway down the skeleton's tail, and severed it at the halfway point. "I killed you yesterday," he smirked at Kalam. "Today I'm going to dismember you."

Five demon knights crested the hill, a small cluster of

wendigos close behind. Somewhere down the hill was the Allied army. The dragon's skeletal remains now had no tail – but it still moved around to face him. Cy didn't wait to be within biting distance – he charged back under the dragon, and took aim at the same ankle he'd already cracked, landing another crushing blow in the same spot, widening the crack, then moved as the dragon repositioned and landed another and another until the crack was large enough that he could jam his sword into it.

There was no howl, no outrage, no sign that the dragon's remains even felt the damage. Rather than chase the bone dragon, he grasped at the knee joint and held on while the undead monster thrashed about. Using the blade of his sword as a pry bar, he wedged it into the fracture he'd made in the ankle and applied all his weight to the hilt until –

CRACK!

Kalam's foot broke loose and the bucking, heaving skeleton wobbled as it landed on its shin bone, losing its balance and toppling down the hill toward the tower. Cyrus rolled clear as it came crashing down, tons of bones onto the ascending demon knights – at least eight of which were smashed immediately, along with more than a few wendigos. He saw a gray-skinned torso fly through the air and land in the bony debris. With only a few exceptions, the allies escaped harm.

Wasting no time, Cyrus charged into the wreckage, ignoring his arriving Allies and hacking at the rear knee joint of Kalam, who was attempting to rise. He was joined by Orion and Tolada, surprisingly, and they snapped the leg free and moved on to the next. The third was removed with a bit more effort, leaving the skeleton of Kalam thrashing.

Cyrus scaled the dragon rib by rib as it jerked to get upright but couldn't. Moving with care in case it began to roll over and turn him into mush, he reached the neck, flailing in the air. He wrapped his legs around the base of the neck, and brought his sword down again and again on the vertebrae until finally it gave a sickening crack and splintered. One more massive blow broke it into slivers and dust, and sent him, along with the dragon's neck and skull, crashing to the ground below, where he heard a great many cracking bones, a few of which were his own.

Cyrus jumped to his feet as soon as the healer's spell hit him and charged at the nearest demon knight, which was already on its knees, and finished it. The wendigos that weren't charmed were now falling, one by one to mesmerize and to death at the hands of the allies. The last demon knight was brought down by a stunning blow from Cass that cut it in half at the waist. They finished killing the wendigos and within an hour the Realm of Death was silent but for the cheers of the Alliance army.

Chapter 22

The Alliance members waited in the Fields of Paxis while the officers of the Alliance split the treasures in Mortus's chambers among themselves. After a half hour, Elisabeth stormed down the steps with something in her hand. Her eyes were narrowed and every step exuded irritation. She stopped in front of Cyrus and paused for a moment before she spoke, composing herself. "You must have really wanted this pommel," she said. "I've never seen you ask for anything from an excursion before."

She opened her hand to reveal a circular piece of metal with the carving of a skull at its center. "I do," he said, voice desirous.

She handed it to him with care, then crossed her arms. "I didn't expect us to have to kill the same dragon two days in a row. You really saved things from getting ugly." She paused. "Uglier than they're getting among the Alliance officers right now, anyway."

He pulled his gaze away from the Death's Head. "Doesn't look like you had much fun in there."

She sighed. "We're not. When I planned this, there were a few things that we swore we weren't going to do. Foremost among them was not stealing Letum."

Cyrus looked at her with a blank expression. "Letum?"

She stared past him, her mind on something else. "Mortus's Staff of Death. It's supposed to be on a pedestal in there, protected by enchantments, but it's not." She shifted her gaze to him. "I guess it's lucky that it's not, because your pommel would have been under the protection of the enchantments as well."

"Lucky for me, I guess." He shrugged. "Never heard of this Letum. Maybe Mortus took it with him when he left?"

She waved her hand. "You think he dissolved the barrier he set up to protect his most treasured possessions before he left, when he knows that every time he leaves his Realm gets ransacked? I doubt it, but it doesn't matter. It's causing quite a stir among the other officers, though; quite a few accusations flying around –"

"Elisabeth!" Cass's voice drifted down to them as he descended the steps, Erith beside him. "We're leaving."

"Did you get everything resolved?" She looked up at the

warrior in grey, face expectant.

"I've resolved not to punch Tolada in his aggravating face, but that's about it." Cass pointed back up the steps. "We can argue until Mortus comes back, no one's going to confess to taking Letum and we're not going to search everyone here to figure out if they've got it. Especially," he gritted his teeth, "since there are no protective barriers around the pedestal."

"Couldn't someone have broken through the barrier?" Cy looked at them, face blank.

Erith laughed. "Through a barrier erected by a god? Unlikely."

Whatever else might have been said was halted by Malpravus, gliding down the steps with the officers of Goliath and Sanctuary trailing behind. Niamh's face was suffused with rage, Curatio's eyebrows were arched in irritation, and Orion looked annoyed.

"I would call that a successful endeavor," Malpravus said, coming to a halt beside Cyrus. "Once again, your bravery has been instrumental in our victory." The necromancer's eyes drifted to Cy's sword and armor. "I can only imagine what you'd be capable of if you were wearing the armor and wielding a sword of the power Goliath provides to our warriors." He leaned in close to Cyrus's ear. "You should imagine that as well." Leaning back, he grinned at the warrior. "Let us away, my friends." He and his entourage swept down the stairs.

The entire Alliance army teleported out of the Realm of Death moments later, each to their respective guildhalls. Cyrus found himself back in the lounge at Sanctuary, sitting alone, mulling over what he'd heard.

An armored figure eased into the chair across from him, jolting him out of his reverie. "I heard there was a ruckus in Death's Realm today," Terian said.

"You mean among the officers?" Cyrus looked at him.

"No, I mean with the remains of a dragon that we killed yesterday coming back to take another swipe at you." Terian's eyebrow raised. "How did you hear about the Alliance officers getting into an argument?"

"Gossip."

"Ah." The dark elf nodded. "So, you got your pommel?"

Cyrus's jaw dropped. "How did you know about my sword? Andren was the only one I told!"

Terian shrugged. "When he drinks too much, he talks too much." The dark knight paused. "Which is pretty constant, come to think of it." He smiled. "Don't be paranoid. You can tell your guildmates about things you're working on. This is an honorable group; they're not going to steal something from you. They might even help."

Cy stroked his chin. "I'll need their help as I get closer to putting it together." He paused for a moment. "Terian, have you heard of Ferocis?" Terian shrugged. "You know, the Warblade of Bellarum?"

Terian frowned. "How did you know about it? Did Alaric tell you?"

Cyrus looked at him in confusion, but before he could ask another question, shouts interrupted them from behind them. They sprang to their feet and entered the foyer to find a crowd gathered; raised voices reached their ears as they made their way toward the center of the disturbance. Cyrus bumped into Nyad, and when she turned to him there were tears streaking down her face.

"What's happening?" Cy asked her, Terian at his shoulder.

She blinked as she looked past Cyrus to Terian. "Brevis ambushed Selene again. He called her selfish and when Orion stepped up to defend her he told him the only thing more useless than a selfish healer is a General that won't lead. Please, stop it!" She focused on Terian. "You're an officer. Please, you have to stop this!" Her face was flushed, and the tears were flowing freely.

"You didn't even take command when the invasion force was ambushed in Death's Realm! Cyrus had to win the battle because you don't even have the guts to marshal us in an emergency –" Brevis ranted, but was suddenly cut off.

"SHUT UP! JUST SHUT UP!" Orion exploded. "What do you even *know* about leadership, you pointless hole?"

Cy turned to Terian, "You have to stop them."

Terian folded his arms. "I don't think I do."

Cyrus was stunned, blinking at him in disbelief. "Are you kidding me? You're an officer. You have to intervene in this: it's a dispute between guildmates!" He kept his voice low enough so that Terian was the only one that could hear.

"No, Cy." Terian shook his head. "He's not saying anything that's untrue. He's not saying it in a nice way, but I don't think I should stop the truth from being spoken."

Brevis's voice drowned out any further comment at that point. "– know more about leadership than you do at this point, I'd wager. Not that it would take much. Larana would make a better officer at this point than you do, and she never says a word!"

Larana squeaked loudly in muffled outrage from somewhere in the crowd, but did not say anything.

The argument stopped for a moment before it started again, full force, with both sides yelling at each other. "Don't you call her that –"

"Afraid to tell it like it is, typical of a coward –"

"DON'T YOU CALL ME A COWARD, YOU KNEE-HIGH PILE OF SHIT!"

"WHAT IS GOING ON HERE?!" A voice like thunder rocked the room, overriding any other sound. Alaric strode down the stairs, commanding the attention of both parties. The crowd parted for him to make his way through. When he reached them, they launched into their stories at the same time.

"– attacked Selene and myself –"

"– said nothing but the truth, one hundred percent –"

"SILENCE!" Alaric commanded. "Are there no officers present besides Orion?"

The crowd moved aside as Terian approached. "I saw the last few minutes of it. Sounds like a dispute between the two of them. Maybe we should send them outside and let them duel."

Alaric held his tongue, and his enormous helm contained most of his expression, but his mouth was etched into a thin line. "Did you not intervene, Terian?"

The dark elf shook his head. "I did not."

Cyrus could see the narrowing of the Ghost's eye, the clenching in his jaw, but he breathed not a word of critique on the dark knight's handling of the matter. He turned back to Brevis and Orion. Selene stood behind her husband, shoulders shaking as she cried quietly. "What prompted this, Orion?"

Orion looked shocked. "Terian, you were here and you didn't step in on our behalf?" He looked at the dark elf in amazement. "You left me twisting in the wind?" The ranger's brow furled. "I'm a fellow officer!"

Alaric clapped his gauntlets together, catching everyone's attention. "Orion, I asked you what happened."

Orion blinked and his attention shifted back to Alaric. "We were coming into the foyer and Brevis just started attacking us – telling us we're awful guildmates –"

"Because you are –" the gnome said.

"SHUT UP!" Orion cut him off again. Alaric raised his hands to restore order, and Orion continued. "He verbally attacked us – insulted us – called me worthless as an officer and a General."

Alaric turned to Brevis. "What caused you to verbally assault your guildmates?"

"I have seen them continue to slide, month after month, into a spiral of selfishness," the enchanter began, chin high, eyes defiant. "I have seen them turn their backs on guildmates that are going into mortal harm and do things for their own self-aggrandizement that risk lives, like that Enterra incursion. Narstron died, and for what reason?" He sneered. "I haven't heard of the goblins marching on the warpath! It was a smokescreen, an attempt to get us to go somewhere that was pointless and unprofitable for us."

A few nods and words of agreement answered him over the crowd. Orion looked around, stunned by the condemnation, while Selene put her face in her hands, sobbing.

Brevis turned back to Alaric. "I said nothing that others weren't thinking. I just had the courage to speak up. Neither will I apologize; someone needed to say it."

Alaric Garaunt shook his head. "Brevis, this is not the way. In Sanctuary we treat each other with courtesy and respect. While you may have a disagreement or a conflict with Selene and Orion, you should have addressed it behind closed doors, or to the Council." He continued to shake his head. "This ambush is unworthy of you and your guildmates and will not be tolerated. You will apologize to Orion and Selene," Brevis looked as though he'd swallowed something particularly bitter, "if not for the content of your message then for the method of delivery."

"That's not enough, Alaric," Orion said. "He should be cast out for what he did."

Alaric was still for a long moment. "That is a matter for the Council to decide. With Vara on leave of absence attending to family matters," Cyrus blinked in surprise, having not heard this, "Niamh and Curatio away for the day and yourself involved in the dispute, it leaves only Terian and I capable of rendering a decision." He straightened. "That is not enough for a disciplinary matter. I will not settle this without more of the Council involved. All I will do for now is demand Brevis apologize. Any consequences will wait until we have a quorum –"

"I will *not* apologize." Brevis's comment was lost in the shuffle of what happened next.

"– until the Council rules on the matter," Alaric finished.

Orion looked evenly at Alaric. "And what of Terian, who stood by and let this happen? You are the leader of this guild, and you don't seem concerned at all that one of your officers committed a total dereliction of his duty." Terian was silent, but his eyes burned into Orion's until the ranger was forced to look away first. "What are you going to do about him?"

Alaric watched the ranger, eyes betraying no emotion. "We will discuss it in the fullness of time."

Orion shook his head, lower lip jutting out. "That's not good enough." He looked around the foyer. "All this time, all this effort, and this is how you would treat us? We're leaving." He took Selene's arm and led her to one of the staircases.

Alaric moved closer to Brevis, and the two of them began a discussion in hushed tones. The hall was silent, the crowd still present, waiting to see what happened. A few minutes later, Orion and Selene emerged from the stairway again, laden with bags, a host of large trunks hovering behind them.

"This is your last chance, Brevis," Alaric said to the gnome, low enough that only Cyrus and a few others could hear him. The enchanter shook his head like a child refusing to eat his vegetables.

Orion and Selene reached the entryway and he looked back, across the crowd one last time, seeming to take in the whole view of the scene assembled, turned on his heel and walked out, Selene at his side.

Alaric waited until they had descended the steps, then took a step back from Brevis as though he were a plague victim. "Brevis, you have failed to keep a civil interaction with your guildmates, and now you have refused to apologize. We will debate this disciplinary matter in Council, and decide on the consequences."

"No need," Brevis replied. "I said what no one else had the courage to say, and I won't be hung out to dry for it." The little gnome set his chin high. "I will leave as well." Gertan and Aina behind him, he walked toward the stairway and out of sight.

On their way up, they passed Celia and Uruk coming down, laden similarly to Selene and Orion, everything they owned on their backs or magically following them. Nyad let out a great sob at the sight. They made their way through the crowd, exchanging hugs and saying a few farewells, but avoiding Alaric, whose gaze watched them from the center of the foyer.

For the next thirty minutes, a steady flow of guildmates in ones and twos came down the stairs, carrying with them all their worldly possessions, saying goodbye and walking out of the enormous doors of Sanctuary. One by one, Alaric watched them all go, strangely silent the entire time. When nightfall had come, and the outpouring had stopped, they had lost nearly a hundred members of Sanctuary.

"Terian," Alaric spoke, breaking his silent vigil. "We must confer." He turned, heels clicking on the stone floor and walked toward the stairway. Terian followed behind him, a little slower.

Cyrus looked at the faces of those around him – J'anda, Vaste and Andren. In them he could see indifference and determination. Nyad and Larana were crying, clinging to each other for comfort. But in other faces, he saw a different sort of determination, another decision being made, and he knew that those who left today would not, by any means, be the last.

Chapter 23

It had been only a few days since the 'explosion in Sanctuary' as Alaric had taken to calling the exodus, and Cyrus's instincts had proven correct. There had been a steady flow of exits in the days following the departure of Selene, Orion and Brevis. When the final tally had been done, they'd lost one hundred and thirteen guildmates, two of them officers.

One of those departures had been particularly painful. Cyrus had come back from a walk around Sanctuary's grounds to find Terian on his way out the door, a knapsack on his shoulder, axe slung behind him. "Terian!" he'd shouted. "Where are you going?"

The dark elf had looked up at him and waited before replying. "I'm going to roam the world for a while."

"What does that mean?"

Only the trace of a smile showed on Terian's lips as he answered. "It means I'm going to roam the world for a while. Wander." He gestured over his shoulder. "I left a note for you, with a gift. It's in your quarters."

Cyrus had run up the stairs and into his room, only to come to a sudden stop. His leg hit the side of the bed – not his old, regular sized one; it was gone, replaced by another made from the bones of Kalam, the ones he'd seen Terian and the others carrying away on the day of the Alliance call to arms. It had been framed with four enormous elephant tusks as the posts, and took up most of the quarters. It was big enough that three trolls could comfortably lie in it, and had been crafted beautifully. There was a small note lying on the sheets, which he picked up and read.

Cy,

You should always celebrate your triumphs and keep something around to remind you that when things are bad, they weren't always bad. I'd feed you a line about how although I'm gone, I'll always be in your heart, but we both know that's all a bunch of crap that girly elves and pansy-ass dwarves would say to each other to keep from crying. Here's a bed: use it a lot, and not just for sleeping if you can find a woman who won't run screaming from you – gold might need to be involved. You're a hell of a warrior, but I'm a way better fighter. I'll see you around the world.

– Terian

In spite of himself, Cyrus couldn't help but laugh at the words his friend had left behind. Though not filled with profundity or a sorrowful farewell, they were the ones Terian Lepos would have wanted said to him if Cyrus had been leaving. Looking around, he realized that with the bed in the room, there was no floor space. "What the hell am I going to do about this?" he murmured. Looking back at the parchment, he saw a small postscript.

By the way, if you're worried about having this bed in your quarters, I wouldn't sweat it. I doubt you'll be in them much longer.

Raising an eyebrow, Cyrus turned in the doorway and bumped into the Ghost of Sanctuary. Although Alaric Garaunt was half a foot shorter than him, it mattered little to none. He was still intimidated by the man, though not in a physical sense. The Ghost did a double take upon seeing the bed, and looked at the warrior. "How many women sleep in there with you?" A slight frown creased his face. "Where do you change out of your armor?" He paused. "*Do* you change out of your armor?"

Cyrus looked back into the room, and closed the door behind him. Alaric seemed to regain his concentration. "Odd to see you down here, Alaric. Did you need something?"

The paladin refocused on Cyrus. "Yes, I need to speak with you in the Council Chambers." The Ghost turned and extended his hand toward the staircase, indicating that Cyrus should go first. They walked in silence up to the Council Chamber. Cyrus had not been to this floor since the day he had met Alaric.

The Ghost opened the door to the Chamber, and inside was a massive round table with eight seats. A stack of parchment waited at a chair in front of set of double doors that led to a balcony, framed by windows on either side. Alaric marched to the chair and sat down, gesturing for Cyrus to join him.

The Ghost studied him for a moment before he began to speak. "Though it has taken many days, and many conversations, I think we have turned the corner on this dramatic explosion within our guild."

Cyrus sat back in the chair, thinking before answering. "I hope this exodus is winding down."

Alaric nodded his agreement. "I believe the worst losses have been our officers. Here is my conundrum. I've sent a few druids and wizards looking for Niamh and Curatio, but in all likelihood they are fine and decided to spend a few days out of contact, in some elven village or another looking for some obscure artifact. Under normal conditions, that would be fine." Alaric ran his hands over his helmet before resting them on the back of his head. "Unfortunately, we are by no means operating under normal conditions. Although I am confident they will return soon, Vara could be gone for an indeterminate length of time. We have things to accomplish in the interim."

Cyrus blinked. "That is a problem."

"It was." Alaric smiled. "I believe I have it solved. Are you still willing to serve Sanctuary?"

"I am, but –"

"Then I hereby promote you to Officer of Sanctuary."

Cyrus was stunned. "According to the charter, don't I have to go through an election? And be in the guild for a year?"

Alaric exhaled heavily. "Under normal conditions, yes, but frankly I have no time for this. We have work that needs to be done. You will not be the only one dragooned into service. I will also be placing Vaste and J'anda into the service of the Council."

Cyrus looked over the parchment at him, which were summons to each of the individuals he had just named. "You said there's work to be done. What do you mean?"

Alaric broke into a smile. "We have to rebuild."

Cyrus felt the excitement from Alaric's words, and leaned forward in anticipation. "What do you need me to do first?"

Chapter 24

Vara returned from her mysterious leave that night in a bad temper, speaking to no one. The next day they were arrayed around the Council table for his first meeting. Alaric headed the table, with Cyrus sitting next to Vaste, and on the other side of the table, J'anda, wearing no illusion today. A soft cough brought their attention to the Ghost and he began to speak.

"I hereby convene the new Council. We are here on urgent business, but the two of us in the 'old guard' would like to welcome the new officers –"

"Ahem," Vara interrupted him. "I would prefer not to welcome the new officers. I am still wishing the old officers were here, along with the other guildmates we lost." The paladin folded her arms. "I can't leave for a week without everything going to hell."

Cyrus smirked at the elf. "You think your diplomatic skills would have mitigated our losses? I suspect that your absence was fortuitous in aiding our retention."

Alaric wiped the grin off his face and moved on before Vara could respond to the warrior's jibe. "Our first order of business is our wayward officers. We haven't sent a full search party yet –"

The door to the Council chamber opened, interrupting him. As Niamh and Curatio walked in, he finished his thought. "– and apparently we won't have to." Without his helm, Alaric's emotions were much easier to discern: he glared at them like an angry mother. "Where have you been?"

Niamh's face was suffused with excitement and even Curatio looked more lively than usual. "You would not believe what's happened!" Niamh began, ignoring the new faces around the table.

"I have a feeling they'll say that about what happened here, too," J'anda said under his breath.

"They've discovered the entrance to the realms of the gods – they're open to mortals!"

A moment of silence greeted this pronouncement. Cyrus looked left, then right, to see if anyone else was going to say it.

They didn't. "Uh, Niamh... we were just in the Realm of Death last week..."

Her eyes flared and her red hair swished back over her shoulder. "Yes, I know that. But before we only had access to Death, Darkness and Purgatory. There's a new gateway opened and it leads to all the others: Love, Wilderness, Storms, and the Realm of War..."

Cyrus's spine straightened. Alaric looked around the table before focusing again on Curatio and Niamh. "What effect do you think this will have immediately on Sanctuary?"

Curatio scrunched his face in consideration. "Every major top-tier guild is scrambling to explore the new realms. They've abandoned their excursions to Purgatory and other locations so they can focus on these new realms because they believe the legend – that there's a path to the upper realms: fire, air, water, earth, good and evil."

Alaric shifted his gaze to Cyrus. "Can we hit some of those realms?"

Cyrus looked down in contemplation for a moment. "With the forces we have? I doubt it."

Curatio looked around the table at the new faces. "Not that I'm sorry to see you all in here, but where are Terian and Orion?"

The story was told as the two of them took their seats. Niamh's face became a horror-struck mask. Curatio took it better, reserving comment until the end. "We've spent the better part of two years building to have more than half our number blown out the door because of this sort of stupid, petty squabble."

"Agreed, it is unfortunate," Alaric said. "However –"

"Unfortunate?!" Niamh shrieked. "Unfortunate is when you go to bed with an elf after a night of drinking and wake up with a troll. This is a disaster, Alaric! Two years of effort lost in one day!"

Vaste leaned close to Cyrus and murmured, "I want to know where she's been drinking." Cyrus looked at the troll and nodded in understanding.

"As I was saying," Alaric began again, "this is an unfortunate setback." He pointed to Cyrus. "We have an officer capable of leading excursions, which is the most attractive factor in growing a guild."

"You had an officer capable of that before," Vara said with only a trace of annoyance.

"Yes, but willingness is key," Alaric said, causing Vara to

narrow her eyes. "Now we merely require a larger army. Our first priority is recruitment." He looked around the table. "Ideas?"

J'anda raised his hand, causing Alaric to look at him pityingly. "You're an officer now, J'anda. You may freely speak."

A look of embarrassment crossed the face of the dark elf. "We should do a recruitment drive like we did in the past when numbers were low. Send officers to the major cities of Arkaria and hold a series of meetings to get across to anyone interested what we're looking for in guildmates. We talk to members of the city's armies, we talk to other adventurers, to anyone who's had any experience." He leaned back in his chair.

"An excellent point," Alaric said. "We have stopped those because we felt fairly 'on-target' for growth. We will need to re-institute those recruiting practices to grow. I recommend we send delegations immediately so we can find candidates to begin the process."

Cy raised his hand. "What exactly goes into the application process?"

Alaric looked sideways at Curatio, who fielded the question. "Officers engage with applicants, adventuring with them in smaller groups, trying to get a sense of who they are, what they stand for, and what type of guildmate they're going to be when their back is against the wall. The officers have final say and vote either yea or nay once per month on the applicants."

Cyrus frowned. "That seems labor intensive for the officers."

Curatio nodded. "That was the reason we suspended those type of recruiting events. Our members were bringing in people they'd met while adventuring and we had no time to evaluate the ones that we were bringing in through other means."

Cyrus leaned forward with a frown. "We'll run into the problem again within six months if we don't change that practice."

Alaric raised an eyebrow. "You have a suggestion?"

Cy thought for a moment. "Instead of relying on officer feedback to make the decision, we give our guildmates a say in who is Sanctuary material."

"We need to be careful about who we let in here," Vara said, voice filled with disdain. "We prize honor above all."

Cyrus fired back at her, "Do you have such a low opinion of your guildmates that you don't think they can determine for themselves if a potential member is dishonorable or not? Do we officers possess some special skill I'm unaware of?"

"In the order of your questions," Vara snapped back, "I have a low opinion of only one of my guildmates, and as he's the walking cesspool that made the suggestion, it makes the entire idea suspect." Leaning back in her chair with a smug look on her face, she continued, "As for special skills, yes, I possess a few that you're unaware of but that doesn't say much; I'm sure you could fill many volumes with things you're unaware of."

"Yeah," Cyrus said, cheeks flushed, "and the title of those volumes is 'How to Be a Pretentious, Arrogant Elf With a Huge Chip on Her Shoulder for No Apparent Reason, Part One through Four Hundred' by Vara."

"Cyrus, that is unnecessary," Alaric said, ending the verbal sparring match before the elf could riposte. "Old friend," he said to Vara, who was glaring at Cy, "this idea has merit. We, the Council, serve our members, but that doesn't mean they are stupid or easily fooled. Taking advantage of their insights means we can grow faster."

Somewhat placated, Vara stopped speaking. When put to a vote, after a moment of delay, she voted in favor.

"So that's settled." Alaric cleared his throat. "Next, we have an Alliance officer's meeting tomorrow, and we'll need to send representation." He coughed. "Naturally, I will be attending, simply because I have no choice in the matter." The sour look on his face was evidence enough for Cyrus that he cared little for that idea. "Curatio, I trust you will be there?" A nod of affirmation came from Curatio. "Very well, and as senior officer remaining, Vara, you as well?"

Vara's mercurial temperament showed again. "I am not going to deal with those vultures."

Cyrus raised his hand. "I volunteer."

Alaric looked around. "Very well. Cyrus, Curatio and I will attend the Alliance summit at Reikonos Coliseum. Other business?"

Vaste leaned in and looked around the table. "Who should we send on the recruiting mission?"

Curatio spoke up, "We should send a mix – dark elves can cover some areas the rest of us can't reach without getting attacked, whereas elves, dwarves, gnomes and humans can cover other ground." He paused for thought. "Obviously, no one who isn't gnomish should go to their domain..."

J'anda furrowed his brow. "So even you supposedly 'good' races aren't welcome in the gnomish city?"

Curatio laughed. "No, their city is built so small, we shouldn't send anyone taller than a dwarf." Assorted laughter greeted that remark, and even prompted a smile from the Ghost of Sanctuary. "They have a city where they handle their commerce with outside races, and that's built large enough for others, but there are two other major cities and countless villages in the Gnomish Dominions that are built to gnome's scale."

"Very well," Alaric said. "When next we meet, we'll lay out specifics for this 'recruitment drive.'" With that, the paladin called the Council meeting to a close. As they filed out one by one through the main door, Cyrus took a few minutes to look around the Council Chambers and noticed a door he hadn't paid any attention to before.

Alaric was the last one still in the room, and caught his eye. "It's the Council Archives. All the records of our decisions, meetings, and history are kept in there along with some tomes and spells that are very dangerous, as well as some records of incidents best forgotten." He paused, giving it a moment of thought. "Rather like recent events we've experienced, I suppose." Shifting his focus back to Cyrus, he started to speak again after a moment of consideration. "I'm glad you stayed after the meeting – I have something I want to talk to you about."

Cyrus regarded him with a perplexed expression. "What?"

Alaric finished shuffling the parchment he'd used during the meeting into a manageable stack and favored Cyrus with a penetrating look. "I want to talk about your purpose."

"I thought you wanted me to recruit for the guild and lead them into adventure?" Cy asked, puzzled.

"Not what I meant," Alaric waved him off. "What I mean is what you hope to achieve being a member and officer of Sanctuary."

After a moment of thought, Cyrus answered. "I'd like to recruit a bunch of people, attack tougher enemies and increase the wealth of our guild."

Alaric looked at Cyrus, expression neutral. "Assuming we were able to create an enormous army and explore increasingly challenging places, would that make you happy?"

Confused and looking at Alaric with a slightly incredulous expression, he nodded. "Yes, I believe it would."

"So all you want out of life is wealth and battle?" Alaric raised an eyebrow. "You don't need Sanctuary for that; you could find all that with Endeavor or any of the high level guilds..." His voice trailed off.

Cy felt his cheeks burn with shame. "Well I don't want to forsake all the bonds of friendship to get to the top."

Alaric walked around the table. Cyrus suddenly felt smaller than the paladin. "If all you believe in are the things you can achieve by battle alone, you will do anything to anyone in order to get what you want. There are many who feel that way. There are those in this world that would kill anyone who got in their way, would destroy any who opposed them to advance their own ambitions."

The stare continued. "I know that is not who you are. Your ambition is checked by your beliefs. So I ask you again: what is your purpose? Because you can achieve those aims, but doing them the Sanctuary way, with honor, your goal becomes a pure aim, to advance yourself and your fellows, but with respect for others instead of desire for self alone."

The shame consumed Cyrus. "I've always wanted to be more, to do more, to have more than I had before, Alaric. I was raised in the Society of Arms in Reikonos, and I've never had much to call my own." He felt the warmth reach his eyes. "I gave everything I had to the Kings of Reikonos, to keep them in the best guildhall I could afford, to keep us fed and together. I held us together with the promise that someday we'd have more, that someday I could go for greatness."

Looking out the window, Alaric crossed his arms. "What is greatness to you?"

Confused, agitated, impatient and almost wishing that this man he respected more than any he'd ever met would simply give him the right answer, he blurted out, "I don't know. I always assumed it was being the best – having the best."

Lowering his head and sighing, Alaric still did not look at him. "Are those two things one and the same?"

Cyrus shrugged his shoulders in exasperation. "I don't know. I always assumed they were. In order to face the greatest threats of Arkaria, you need to be powerful."

"We come to it at last. Power." Alaric, turned, arms still crossed, and faced the warrior again. "There are two uses for power. You may use it to fulfill your ambitions and whims, both gross and tame – or you may use it for the good of others. Your purpose directs how you gain power and what you do with it."

Alaric became lost in his thoughts for a moment. "A true officer of Sanctuary is driven by honor and self-sacrifice, knowing that service is its own reward." The Ghost's focus shifted back to the warrior. "Of this I can assure you – if you do not decide now what you believe in, what you stand for, and what you will do with the power and influence you acquire, then you will eventually leave Sanctuary just as Orion, Brevis, or any of the countless others that came before have." Alaric moved his hand as if to forestall any response. "Think about it for a time."

Cyrus thought about it intently for a moment. "What's your purpose?"

A smile cracked the knight's lips. "My purpose is what I have assembled Sanctuary for – to create a force capable of defending against threats to Arkaria."

Cyrus's brow furrowed. "Then why all this interest in excursions? In adventures?"

The Ghost sighed. "Armies do not function well in idleness – they need challenge and things to accomplish. Great threats do not present themselves every day. People as individuals also do not function well in poverty – with the exception of a paladin, of course. A constant series of explorations keeps our fighters sharp, lets us earn money and better positions us to fulfill my primary purpose."

"I admit," Cyrus said with a nod, "while honor has been emphasized since day one here, this is the first I've heard of a greater mission of Sanctuary."

"That would be the result of Orion's singular focus on expeditions at the time you were recruited. We help those who need it and protect against grave dangers to Arkaria." Alaric sighed deeply. "Although I cannot prove it, I suspect one of those dangers is on the horizon at this moment."

"What is it?" Cyrus asked with concern.

"I cannot say for certain; I have only suspicions based on fragments of information." Alaric cast his eyes downward. "And now," he turned back to the window, "I sense I must take my leave of you." There was a hissing and Alaric was covered in a mist, which faded, leaving nothing behind.

Cyrus looked at the spot where Alaric had been, alarmed. "That was... ominous." Cyrus looked around the room. *That did not look like any teleport spell I've ever seen – and paladins can't teleport anyway!*

"He faded into the ether, didn't he?"

Curatio's voice startled Cyrus, who was already on edge, realizing that the 'Ghost of Sanctuary' might not be a nickname.

"Into the what?" Cyrus asked the elf, still astonished.

"The ether," Curatio said. "When he appears, it's like mist taking shape. Same thing when he disappears."

Cyrus's mouth was suddenly very dry. "How does he do that?"

Curatio shrugged. "I'm not certain," he said, expression neutral. "He'll be back in time for the Alliance meeting." Changing the subject, he moved on. "Now that you're an officer, have you moved into your new quarters yet?"

"No. I haven't been an officer very long, after all."

"Let's get you set up, then."

Cyrus followed Curatio up to the next floor and waited as he unlocked a room. Stepping inside, Cyrus was impressed. The officer's quarters were easily four times the size of his previous quarters – and as if that weren't enough, there was a door on the far end of the room to his own private bathroom, complete with running water – something that many cities in Arkaria didn't have.

Looking around, he tried to imagine the placement of his new bed, but dismissed it as Curatio spoke to him again. "We'll have your possessions brought up from your quarters, unless you're dying to do it yourself. The Alliance Officers' meeting will be taking place tomorrow afternoon at the Coliseum in Reikonos. We'll set off after breakfast. A wizard will transport us to Reikonos Square. We'll go on horseback from there."

Cyrus looked at him skeptically. "And Alaric will be back by the time we leave?"

Curatio smiled. "Trust me."

Chapter 25

Alaric appeared for breakfast the next day, looking the same as he always did. "What happened yesterday?" Cy asked.

"We will discuss it in great detail... someday," Alaric said under his breath and returned to greeting other guild members.

When they departed, Cyrus was paired with a white horse named Windrider, who responded to him affectionately. Nyad brought them to the portal in Reikonos Square. Cyrus looked at the portal, an ovoid ring of rock that looked like a door.

They crossed under the shadow of the Reikonos Citadel, ignoring the hot, stuffy air that did not seem to be moving at all. They passed most of the journey conversing about a myriad of topics.

"Do you know how Lake Magnus was formed?" Curatio looked at the warrior as he asked the question, assuring Cyrus that he was not talking to Alaric.

Cyrus shook his head. "I've only been there once."

Curatio nodded. "Most people don't. Long ago, there was a war..."

It dawned on Cyrus that he knew what Curatio was talking about. "Yes, I've heard this. The gods were meddling in the affairs of mortals, pitting them against each other in wars, basically along classic good and evil lines – the titans, goblins and trolls against an alliance of dwarves, gnomes and elves. As the war spread all over the world, it also crossed into the Realms of the gods, as lesser gods tried to eliminate each other – the only stability in the pantheon was the six highest gods. The Elementals – Fire, Earth, Air, Water – and Good and Evil."

Curatio smiled, pleased to have such an engaged pupil. "The names for the gods of Good and Evil have long been lost to the winds of time, but we know the lesser and elemental gods because some still interfere in the affairs of mortals. Sometimes literally," Curatio said with a knowing look.

Cyrus snickered. "You're referring to Yartraak's dark elven harem in Saekaj Sovar, or perhaps the myth that Vidara, Goddess of Life, had a child with a human?"

The healer blushed. "Those are two of countless rumors spread through the ages. I was speaking of interference in mortal events – and of the war that consumed the world and spread to the Realms in ancient times. Bellarum, your god, gathered his mortal armies and sent them into the Realms of his enemies, causing all sorts of havoc."

"Until one day," Cyrus interrupted, "his army killed Eruditia, the Goddess of Learning, with Ferocis, his Warblade, and he was set upon by all the gods, even his allies, and he was punished."

"Quite so," Curatio said, clearly impressed. "The God of War's reputation suffers to this day because of that. You probably know that, if you tell people you're a follower of Bellarum."

"Once or twice, it nearly got me killed," Cyrus said, voice tight.

"Anyway," Curatio went on, "Lake Magnus was a crater that filled with water after Ashea, Goddess of Water, sent down Amnis, the Spear of Water, for her truest follower to use during the war. Like all godly weapons, it was imbued with a portion of Ashea's godhood, making it more powerful than mortal magics."

"I've heard legends of godly weapons," Cyrus said. "I wasn't sure they existed outside the drooling stories of legend told by covetous warriors in the Society of Arms."

"Oh, they exist," Alaric said. "Reikonos has one, though it is not widely known. They have the aforementioned Amnis under heavy guard in the Citadel."

"The Elven Kingdom is in possession of the Ventus, the Scimitar of Air," Curatio said. "It rests in Pharesia and has been there for thousands of years."

"How many are there?" Cyrus pulled the reigns of Windrider to keep pace.

Curatio shrugged. "Each god has at least one, but there are only five on Arkaria that we know of. The four elemental weapons are the most well-known. Amnis, Ventus, Terrenus, the Hammer of Earth – the Goblins in Enterra have that one – and Torris, the Scepter of Fire."

"And Ferocis, the Warblade of Bellarum?" Cyrus asked.

"Yes, and that one," Curatio nodded.

"I forgot to mention at the time," Cyrus said, "but after everyone left Kortran, I was alone for a few minutes taunting Talikartin and Razeel, and they mentioned that Ferocis was stolen the night before we got there."

"What?" Alaric stopped his horse suddenly, eye wide through

the slit of his helm.

Curatio stopped his horse as well. "Are you certain?"

"Fairly certain," Cyrus said. "Talikartin offered me a painless death if I returned it."

"And you are certain," Alaric enunciated every word, "he said it was the Warblade of Bellarum?"

"Oh yes." Cyrus nodded heartily. "I wouldn't forget. I do worship Bellarum, after all – I had heard of the Warblade... I was wishing I had it." Cyrus looked more carefully at Alaric, whose mouth had drawn into a tight line. The rest of the Ghost's emotions were carefully hidden by his helmet. Curatio, on the other hand, had downturned lips and his eyes were wide and haunted.

Cyrus thought for a moment. "I might have seen Terrenus as well, now that I think about it... I saw a cloaked figure receive a hammer from the Emperor of Enterra the night we were there, just before I died."

"Did you see who the figure was that took the hammer?" Curatio and Alaric shared a look of great significance.

Cyrus shook his head. "It was dark and their cowl was down; it could have been anyone."

Alaric frowned. "I cannot imagine the circumstances under which the Emperor of Enterra would freely part with a weapon created by their god."

Cyrus shrugged. "I only know what I saw."

"We should continue." Alaric spurred his horse forward. "I appreciate your bringing this to our attention. It is cause for great concern when coupled with certain... other information."

"Care to share?" Cyrus asked.

"Soon," Alaric said.

They came through the city gates, and Cyrus's eyes fell upon a coliseum constructed some distance from the city proper. An enormous entrance with post and lintel architecture, it was large enough for the biggest troll to walk through on a horse without difficulty. As they brought their steeds through the gates, Cyrus saw an expansive dirt floor, ideal for large battles. A group of people were at the entrance to the arena floor, sitting and standing around. As they rode closer, he started to recognize some of the figures, partitioned into two groups.

On his left side stood the officers of Goliath. Elisabeth was talking with Tolada and Malpravus as well as one of the other officers of Goliath that Cyrus had never learned the name of. Standing almost opposite of them was Erith with Cass. They seemed to be in good spirits, though somewhat sterner than in the past.

Greetings were exchanged after the trio had dismounted. Tolada began to speak. "Welcome, Alliance officers. As always, it is a great pleasure. We have several items on the agenda today, and we'd like to cover them quickly, so as not to delay our passage home to our guilds." He launched into the first item on his agenda. "Last meeting, we entertained a proposal which I feel has merit: the idea of a regular sequence of expeditions with mandatory attendance for all Allied guild members –"

The dwarf didn't get any farther than that before Alaric was standing. Rather than wait to be addressed, he butted in, talking over Tolada. "Sanctuary vetoed that idea and will continue to veto it every time it is brought up." Unlike at Sanctuary Council, Alaric had his helmet on. Cyrus could see his mouth curled in irritation. "It is not our policy to compel people to go to places they have no interest in going." He looked around the assemblage. "That is something best left to the guilds like Endeavor, Amarath's Raiders or Burnt Offerings. It is unworthy of those of us who profess to believe in the bonds of fellowship more than conquest."

Tolada looked ready to rebut when Erith intervened. "The Daring also veto. Since any proposed changes require unanimous agreement before passage," she began to smirk at Tolada, "I'd say you got your wish: three minutes into the meeting and we've already scratched one dumb idea off the list of crap we have to go through."

If the nettle bothered him, Tolada shrugged it off. "Very well. Malpravus has an interesting proposal. We have all heard the news that there are new Realms open to mortals. We have also seen a great departure by the guilds that Alaric mentioned – and it brings us an opportunity to follow them into these new Realms and see what awaits us there." He nodded self-importantly and continued, "We do, however, need a structured force. To that end, Goliath would like to bring forth a proposal to make us more powerful. Malpravus?"

Tolada led the meeting in a smattering of lukewarm applause. Casting a glance, Cy found Curatio clapping politely while Alaric abstained, arms folded. Erith looked mutinous. Elisabeth applauded while Cass did not.

The Goliath Guildmaster seemed not to notice any of this as he glided into position to speak. "We will have a manpower problem going into these new Realms," he pronounced. "Early rumors circulating from the contacts we have in the higher guilds all say the same thing. These excursions require either enormous groups of people, trained reasonably, or a smaller, elite group equipped with the best training, weapons and armor." The dark elf stopped to favor them all with a snake-like smile. "Either path requires a different organizational structure than we have now. We miss opportunities on a consistent basis because scheduling excursions or attacks is of such great difficulty that none but the exceptionally experienced," his hand waved toward Elisabeth, "or the naïve would do it." His hand gestured toward Cyrus.

"In order to form a more consolidated command structure, I propose we combine into one guild." The necromancer paused, looking around for reactions. Stunned shock filled Cyrus's mind. Curatio's lips were pursed. Erith had rolled her eyes again and Cass was stone-faced.

Cyrus heard a faint sound he couldn't quite place; looking down he saw Alaric's hand rattling in his gauntlet, shaking. Cy could see the paladin's jaw was clenched and the muscles on his neck stood out, giving his skin a stretched appearance. "Just where," he asked in a tone that belied his true emotions, "would you anticipate headquartering this new guild you'd like to form?" The question was directed at Malpravus, who was looking befuddled at Alaric's odd posture while asking it.

"Excellent question," Malpravus began smoothly. "Of course, accommodations large enough to house such a... Goliath," he said with a grin, "are difficult to come by. However, I do recognize that one guild present possesses quarters large enough to handle our... modest needs." Every word that came from the dark elf's mouth positively dripped with oil as Cyrus heard them. "Naturally, I speak of Sanctuary's guildhall... oddly placed, true, but large enough..."

"He's been after our guildhall since before we joined the Alliance," Curatio breathed, so low only Cyrus could hear him.

"Veto." Alaric's voice was strained; it sounded as though every muscle in his body was exerted. Cyrus raised an eyebrow at him, wondering if that much pressure could result in all of the Ghost's innards exploding out his back. He furrowed his brow, a question occurring to him after seeing Alaric's disappearing act the day before: did the paladin have innards? Or was he a legitimate ghost?

Erith interjected again. "Yeah, I veto too." Her eyes went back to Tolada. "This might be our quickest meeting ever if the topics keep coming like this."

The dwarf took over for an emotionless Malpravus as the Goliath Guildmaster resumed his seat. "Those were the two topics I had in mind. Does anyone else have anything to cover?"

Erith raised her hand. "I have a proposal for a new Alliance rule."

Tolada looked down at her. "Very well, you may present your suggestion."

Erith walked to the place where the speakers had stood. "I propose that any member of an Alliance guild who leaves that guild must wait at least three months before applying and being accepted at another Alliance guild."

Silence greeted this proposal. Tolada began to shift his weight from foot to foot, studying his boots. Malpravus had the cowl of his cloak back up to obscure his face.

Curatio whispered to Cyrus and Alaric, "We're missing something here." Cy was about to ask him to clarify when Erith continued.

"As we all know, Goliath greatly profited in the last few months from the Daring's struggles. Now, with recent Sanctuary departures going to Goliath, I feel we need something to curb this tendency –"

She said more, after that, but Cyrus didn't hear a word of it for several seconds. His vision blurred, so stunned was he by that admission. His hand went up, completely dumbstruck, and he asked his question before Alaric or Curatio could stop him, assuming that they would have if they could. "I'm sorry, who from Sanctuary went to Goliath?"

Erith was clearly not someone used to being cut off in mid-sentence. "Orion and Selene joined Goliath along with a few others," she told him. Looking her in the eyes he saw a glimmer of empathy.

Cyrus heard a snap next to him, and he was certain that Alaric had just broken at least one bone in his hand, which also answered Cyrus's earlier concern about innards. While Cy focused on the Ghost, he missed Goliath vetoing the proposal.

Tolada took the speaking position once more, with less

enthusiasm than before. "Does anyone else have any other business to bring forward?" He hesitated, waiting for anyone to say anything, looking around for comment.

Erith piped up, "No other business. Let's call this meeting quits and get out of here." She turned to Cass. "Wasn't that the best Alliance officer meeting ever? Not to mention the shortest. I wonder," she said with her trademark sarcasm, "if those two factors are in any way linked?" A glare from Tolada did not seem to faze the dark elf.

Alaric grasped the harness of his horse, and started toward the gates of the coliseum. He did not mount the horse, instead walking slowly as the other delegations saddled up and rode away after saying their goodbyes. Cyrus waved to Elisabeth, Cass and Erith before following his Guildmaster. The other delegations had outpaced them by the time they reached the gates, and Curatio had walked beside Alaric, with Cyrus following close behind until finally the Ghost exploded in a tirade unlike anything Cyrus had seen from him before.

"It is absolutely unfathomable to me that these people can even consider us allies, then profit from our troubles. Vara was correct in her assessment: they are vultures!" He almost screamed the last word in frustration. "We put everything we have into growing and they act as though we're a sick relative; instead of them wishing us well they sneak into our bedroom and choke the life out of us so they can get their inheritance!"

He paused for only a second before heading in another direction. "And did you hear Malpravus's proposition? Yes, we can all become one guild, when the guild's name is Sanctuary, and yes we can all use our guildhall, when you all fill out applications and I kick into the gutter the ones of you I can't stand!" He calmed after the last words flew out.

Curatio, sensing that the worst was over, chimed in. "At least none of those measures passed. And in fairness, if Orion and the rest hadn't gone to an Alliance guild, they would have gone somewhere else; somewhere that they would be of no benefit to anyone in the Alliance."

Alaric shook his head. "We need to be independent. No more Goliath, no more treachery, and no more diplomacy with people who are constantly making your blood boil. I have weathered this so-called Alliance," he said, looking directly at Cyrus, "in order to provide opportunities to those in our guild that desire a challenge without leaving the home that we've built. Now," he continued, almost snarling, "the allies that are supposed to share our best interests are compromising ours to advance their own agendas."

His gaze was powerful, and his words sent a rush of motivation through the warrior that would keep him moving for the next six months. "We face a grave threat, from a source unknown. Build our strength, get us powerful enough so that I can get us free of this wretched Alliance and convince our guildmates that we don't need these vultures any longer."

Chapter 26

"Burnt Offerings has inducted 1,152 people in the last month," Niamh told the Council, reading from a roll of parchment. "Amarath's Raiders have 911 new members; Endeavor has added another 783." The elf looked around the shocked faces at the table, biting her lip.

"Holy Bellarum," Cyrus breathed. "Where did they find that many people?"

"The armies of the major cities and empires, from other guilds a step below them on the food chain, from mercenary companies – from anywhere they could. The short answer," Niamh said with a look of grave disappointment, "is they did everything we were intending to do. I heard they even sent envoys to the troll homeland."

"This does not bode well for our impending recruitment drive," Curatio said, eyes downcast.

Vaste spoke up. "This changes nothing."

"I don't know about that," Niamh said. "They've put out feelers in every major city in Arkaria, letting everyone know that they're looking for new members, that they're not necessarily worried about how well equipped these people are, and they've temporarily suspended their membership dues. They've captured a lot of potential candidates that might have been looking."

"True," the troll said. "But we have something that they don't."

Alaric raised an eyebrow. "And what might that be?"

Vaste leaned forward, eyes burning. "We only care about the content of their character, not how experienced or equipped they are. In short, when it comes to their effectiveness as a fighter, we have no minimum standard. They do." He looked around the table. "Right?"

Cyrus leaned forward. "It's true. They might have dropped equipment requirements, but they will still require at least two years of combat experience, whether in an army, in a guild, or somewhere else."

"Let me see if I understand this correctly," Vara said. "You want to solve our strength problem – the problem we have with a lack of experienced candidates for our army – by recruiting inexperienced candidates for our army?" She rolled her eyes. "Brilliant. In fact, so brilliant I wonder how he," she said, nodding in Cyrus's direction, "didn't come up with it first."

Cyrus let the remark pass. "I think Vaste might have a good idea here."

Vara froze. "Not that I think this will ever be a problem in your case, but I must insist that you don't breed," she said to Cyrus.

"Are you sure?" he replied, burying his annoyance in an ingratiating smile. "I think a few practice attempts at breeding would solve a great many of your attitude problems."

"Oh," Vara said, "I think I'm going to be quite ill."

"If we could focus on the problem at hand?" Alaric appealed to them. "Cyrus, you were saying?"

"Right," the warrior said, "what Vaste says has merit for two reasons: first, we can train rookies. Second, Niamh said that those guilds – and I'm sure countless other guilds a step or two down the food chain from the big three – have been recruiting in every major city." The warrior's eyes were alight. "But most of the people in Arkaria don't live in a major city."

Curatio nodded. "Most of the populace lives in towns, in the villages, on farms, and so on – which are usually not very close to a portal."

"Which means it takes longer to get to them," Cyrus said. "We can go to them, to every village in the countryside and seek out people that might be looking for adventure, young and old – and we can train them ourselves. We won't get many magic users because of how the Leagues scoop them up to train them from childhood, but we can train anybody to use a sword or a bow or a dagger."

"We could build an effective army with warriors and rangers at the core," Vaste said.

"So, again," Vara said, "your plan is to drag in any seamstress or pig farmer with visions of adventure and delusions of grandeur, give them a sword, and place them in the front lines of our continuing battle with the forces of evil and... what? Use their corpses as shields for those of us that can actually fight?"

"Anyone can learn to fight if they want to learn badly enough," Vaste said. "I say we give them a chance and see who among them wants to."

"It won't be easy," Cyrus said. "But if we focus on finding

people who do have, as Vara so eloquently put it," he shot her a dazzling but fake smile, "'visions of adventure,' and show them some success, we'll find new recruits that we can grow with –"

Niamh jumped in. "And we have enough equipment; the Armory is full. We could give them swords and armor without any difficulty; we have plenty of spares lying around that we aren't even using."

"These potential recruits," Cyrus said, "get a shot at adventure, something everyone dreams about, and we get new soldiers for our army."

"You mean a barely-trained rabble," Vara said.

"I'm impressed at your ability to constantly come up with creative insults and ways to criticize but never an idea to fix the problems we're dealing with," Cyrus said. "Tell me, does your myopia extend to all areas of your life, or just your duties as Council member? Because that would explain why you're unable to see why no one likes you."

"Myopia? I see quite clearly, thank you," Vara returned as the color left her face.

"Please. You're so narrow-minded you could wear the finger of my gauntlet as a helm."

"That's no difficulty; your fingers are the size of sausages," she stammered.

"The better to... never mind." Her eyes narrowed, as though she could sense the reply he'd discarded. "My point is, do you have anything to contribute that would help us or are you just here to piss on every idea we come up with?"

The elf said nothing for a long moment. Her eyes remained narrowed, but she did not meet Cy's gaze.

"As long as we emphasize," Curatio spoke up, breaking the tension of the moment, "that honor is of paramount importance to us." The elf looked around the table. "So long as we remember that, we'll be fine – forget it, and we are lost."

"I agree, Curatio," Alaric said. "I would rather have ten honorable comrades at my side that don't know which direction to point their blade than a thousand skilled mercenaries that I can't trust to turn my back on."

A small sound followed as Vara cleared her throat. She had grown paler still since Cyrus's last insult, and when everyone turned to her at the sound, she nodded without meeting anyone's eyes. "Agreed. Honor above all else," she said, her voice breaking ever so slightly.

"Very well," Alaric said. "We have an agreement about what must be done. Let us adjourn."

Alaric halted Cyrus as he began to head toward the door, and waited until the rest of the Council filed out. Vara was the last to leave, and cast a stricken look at the Ghost before she exited. She was still pale as she shut the door. Alaric Garaunt turned his full attention to Cyrus, who was waiting nervously for the Guildmaster's rebuke.

"As the presumptive General you will need to spearhead this recruiting effort," Alaric began without preamble. The knight looked up at the warrior, meeting his gaze with his one good eye. "I doubt you will be back for several months, if you're to go to all the far off places that other guilds won't."

Cyrus blinked. "Are you sending me because I'm the best person for the task at hand or are you trying to put some distance between myself and Vara?"

Alaric leaned back in his chair, studying the warrior. "Your internecine squabbles do not concern me – at least not at their current level of intensity." The paladin smiled ruefully. "Should they grow to be much more tempestuous, I may become concerned, but we are not quite at that juncture yet. No," he finished, "I believe that when it comes to communicating the vision of the road we have ahead, both pitfalls and possibilities, you will be best for the job."

"Very well," Cyrus nodded. After a moment's pause, he asked, "Has she always been this... difficult?"

Alaric thought carefully for a moment before he answered. "Her skill with a sword is almost equal to her skill with her tongue – but the latter is sharper, I fear," said Alaric. "In you she has finally found someone who will neither be intimidated by her forceful personality nor wear down from the constant sustained attack that she can muster."

The paladin cast a sidelong glance out the window, gazing at passing clouds. "Vara," he said without expression, "is the closest I've seen to somebody embodying the essence of a storm." The paladin held up his hands. "Do not read more into that than what I have said. She is very much like a daughter to me since the day I found her, wounded and on the verge of death."

"So that's why she dislikes me so much? Because I'm not intimidated by her and because I won't back down?" Cyrus chuckled.

"No," Alaric said with a smile. "You assume too much. I never said she disliked you."

"If that's what she does to people she likes," Cyrus said, brow furrowed, "I don't want to know how she treats her enemies."

"Nor did I say she likes you," the paladin continued. "Let us focus on the task at hand. It would be best for you to travel with another guild member and leave tonight."

"Here's your helm, what's your hurry?" Cyrus said with a touch of sarcasm. "Who should I take with me and where should I begin?"

"For the next thirty days you should head north, stopping at every village along the way. I will send druids and wizards in advance of you, to give word that you will be coming, and to set up times that you will be there to meet with interested parties. In a little over a month you will be in Reikonos. From there I want you to head east to the dwarven capital of Fertiss, then south into the Gnomish Dominions. Go through the Mountains of Nartanis and along the northern edge of the Inculta Desert, seeing the people of the villages along that line."

The paladin stopped for a moment, considering. "That will take a further three months. Once you reach the village of Taymor, at the far western edge of the desert, on the shores of the Bay of Lost Souls, you will teleport to the oasis in the middle of the desert and you can visit the settlements of the tribes there before teleporting to the Elven Kingdom in the west. It will take you a month to make your way through the Kingdom properly."

"That..." Cyrus said without emotion, "...is an aggressive schedule."

"I will send aid to you throughout but it needs to be done and I know of no one better than you to carry out this mission," the Ghost said. "As you leave these villages we will set up times for a druid or wizard to pick up potential candidates and bring them back to Sanctuary, where we will work with them in your absence on basic training and getting to know them and their character."

Cyrus frowned. "What's the hurry?"

Alaric brought his hands together and steepled his fingers. "The news that Ferocis has been stolen from the titans, by itself, would be of no great concern. People steal things of value on a regular basis. However when two godly weapons are stolen and a third changes hands mysteriously in a short window of time I become concerned."

Cyrus's brow furrowed in concentration. "Let's say someone was stealing these weapons. What would they use them for?"

Alaric was lost in thought for a moment. "They are weapons that bear immense power. The fraction of godhood that imbues each weapon would bring the wielder greater strength, speed, dexterity – mystical shielding to absorb damage they would take." Alaric sighed. "In short, a fighter equipped with one of these weapons would be able to take on an army and emerge victorious if they were skilled in battle. If it were possible, I should like to put one of these weapons in your hands and turn you loose on the Goblin Imperium."

"If these weapons are that powerful, why didn't the titans or the goblins have their most skilled warriors wielding them?"

"It is a double-edged sword, if you'll forgive the metaphor." Alaric pulled his hands apart. "Yes, it increases the strength of the fighter using it, but should that person fall, the weapon can be lost and you would face a much worse foe." Alaric sighed. "The fear that it would be used against them has kept the Scimitar of Air and the Spear of Water under very close guard by their respective kingdoms for a long time." He shuddered. "I do not care to consider the consequences should someone retrieve all of these weapons."

"Why does it matter?" Cy asked, confused. "They've got one god's weapon; didn't you say that's enough to defeat an army?"

"Yes," Alaric said. "So far they have acquired three of six. Can you imagine they will stop halfway to getting them all?"

"How many do you really need?"

"It would depend on your ultimate goal. One would suffice for a loner; someone only looking out for him or herself. They would be able to win any duel they fought, commit any crime, escape from any lawful authority that decided to pursue them. But consider what you would be able to achieve with six superior fighters, each holding one of these weapons. If they fought together, as comrades, it is possible they could even conquer the world."

Cyrus shuddered at the thought of facing six skilled and nearly invincible combatants. "Where is the Scepter of Fire – Torris, I think it's called?"

Alaric nodded. "That was last said to be possessed by the dragons in Hewat." The Ghost smiled. "Any fool that would steal from a city of dragons is unlikely to survive the attempt." Alaric turned his gaze to the window. "But not knowing the foe that we face makes that assumption rather foolish, doesn't it?"

"What should we do?" A steely determination filled the warrior.

Alaric turned back to Cyrus. "Our purpose remains unchanged. We are in no position to fight even a group of six that possess these weapons. They are imbued with the magic of the gods, and in order to face an enemy of this magnitude, we will need a true army. Your mission must begin as quickly as possible."

Cyrus nodded. As he turned to leave, he looked back. "You still didn't answer about who I should take with me."

The Guildmaster looked at him, face inscrutable. "I think it would be best to have different people with you throughout the journey. For the first leg, between here and Reikonos, I would suggest J'anda. It will make things go smoother in your efforts to recruit dark elves."

Cyrus nodded. "Then I will take J'anda, so long as he's willing."

"Before you go," Alaric stopped him as he turned to leave, "I am certain you are fully capable of doing this. Are you certain you are willing? Because this will not be easy; it will tax you and only one who fully believes in the purpose of this mission will succeed in swaying others to our cause."

Cyrus looked at the Ghost, eyes burning. "I'm willing to do whatever it takes to get the job done."

A smile creased the knight's worn features. "Then go, my friend, and let us make Sanctuary strong once more." The Ghost took a deep breath. "Because if we are right, I suspect that soon we will need that strength.

Chapter 27

Cyrus set off the next morning on horseback with J'anda as his travel companion on the road toward Reikonos. Every day, they would stop in at least one village, following a plan drawn out by Alaric. They had large meetings to drum up interest and then follow-up talks with a number of locals throughout their journey, and as soon as they were done, they would leave.

The meetings always seemed to take longer than the time Alaric had allotted for them, and by the second week they were exhausted, having traveled through the night regularly to make their next destination on time.

One night, they had found themselves about to be attacked by a group of highwaymen outside of a village called Prehorta, between Sanctuary and Reikonos. The enchanter had caught the bandits with his mesmerization spell and they stood motionless as Cyrus killed them one by one.

"How does that spell work?" Cyrus asked, curiosity overcoming his fatigue. They had moved down the road and set up camp for the night. They sat around the fire, and he looked at the dark elf, who merely smiled back.

"Would you like to see?" J'anda said.

"Yes, I would."

Before J'anda could raise his hand, there was a cracking of twigs in the underbrush behind them. The warrior leapt to his feet, sword in hand. Cyrus could feel his pulse racing, all trace of tiredness gone as he peered into the darkness, trying to see what was coming their way. The sounds grew louder and closer, soft footsteps walking through the wet grass – whoever it was drew near.

With a start, Cyrus lowered his sword. "You," he said, irritated at being startled, words almost an accusation.

"Me," Vara said, striding slowly out of the darkness, armor glinting in the light of the campfire.

Cyrus regarded her with suspicion. "How did you find us?"

She pointed at the campfire. "It's not difficult when you set out a beacon that says, 'Here I am! Come slit my throat and steal my belongings!'" Instead of favoring him with a look of usual disdain, it was a bit more impish. "It's a bit of a mystery to me how you've survived to the ripe old age you have."

He snorted. "Says the she-elf. What are you, a thousand years old?"

"Hardly." She took a step closer to him. "If I were human, how old would you guess I am?"

"I would assume you were a teenager," he shot back. "And that's based on maturity."

"What makes you think," she said, voice soft, "I'm not?"

"I'm waiting for the insult," he said. Where had J'anda gone?

"I've grown tired of insulting you. It's far too easy." She walked past him, and he felt her hand land on his side, putting a gentle pressure on it, even through the layers of armor.

A chill ran down his spine at her touch. "What are you doing?" he said, alarmed, fighting his instinct to take a step back.

"Shhh," she told him, and he felt her other hand land on his side, undoing the strap of his armor and reaching under the chain mail beneath, finding his flesh and caressing it. "Aren't you tired of fighting? It's all just masquerade." She slid around to his front as his breastplate and backplate hit the ground. Her fingers found their way into his hair, running through it as she brought his mouth to hers.

Cyrus put aside his shock, completely wrapped up in her kiss. She was soft and it had been... over a year, at least. Another surprise hit him: he found he wanted her desperately. He returned her kiss with a passion he could not have imagined, and he felt her other hand working, heard pieces of armor hit the ground and then he felt her pull away from him. Cyrus opened his eyes to see her standing before him, expression filled with the same almost indescribable look he had glimpsed on the day they met.

He drank in the sight of her, eyes dancing, hair gleaming in the firelight. Her hand came to rest on his chest and he felt a rush as she leaned into him. Their kisses were hungry and she continued to undress him, helping him slide the chain mail over his head and then he felt his skin against hers. He pulled back from her embrace, reflecting that Andren had been right in what he'd said so long ago; that what he saw now might be the sweetest sight known to man. Her arms wrapped around him and pulled him close once more; now there was nothing between them but the cool night air as they sank onto his bedroll.

A sudden shock ran through Cyrus, and a feeling that he was spinning, then he was sitting upright once more, next to the campfire, J'anda looking at him with pity. "Sorry," the enchanter said with a little embarrassment. "I apologize for bringing you out of the trance at such a moment, but you were resisting the spell."

Cyrus's breath was ragged, coming in gasps. "That... was what being mesmerized is like?"

"Yes," the dark elf said. "It shows you the deepest desires of your heart and brings them to you in a way that seems plausible to your mind. The spell keeps your mind trapped in your dream so you are unaware of the world outside. The stronger the enchanter," he said with a smile, "the stronger the effect of the illusion."

"Does it feel different than when you are charmed?"

"Much," J'anda said with a smile. "It takes a much stronger will to resist mesmerization. You broke out of it, which is... unusual."

The warrior had caught his breath. "Can you see what is happening in the mind of the person you've mesmerized?"

"Yes," J'anda said with reluctance after a moment's pause. "I don't create the illusion but I help give it form. The magic exposes their heart's desire, and I help craft the illusion to give it to them."

Cyrus stared straight ahead, stunned. "So the deepest desire of my heart is..." His words trailed off and they sat without speaking. Cyrus finally looked up after being lost in thought. "Did you know?" he asked J'anda. The enchanter raised an eyebrow. "What I would see? Did you know before you cast the spell, before it told you my 'heart's desire'?"

The enchanter smiled. "As they say in Saekaj, where there is heat, there is fire, no?"

"We've certainly had a fair exchange of heat."

"You maintain your free will during the course of the enchantment. Your reaction was genuinely yours." The dark elf shrugged. "If you'd like, you could simply say to yourself that you are a man who has been without the company of a woman for far too long, and she was likely the first woman on your mind."

Cyrus's hands covered his face. "This must happen often if you're that skilled at coming up with a lie people can tell themselves to feel better after they find out..." Cyrus's words drifted off as he pondered the implications of what came next, "...what they truly want."

J'anda laughed, cutting himself off abruptly after Cyrus sent him a pitiable look. "Ah," the enchanter said, coughing, and turned serious. "It happens more than you think. The greater danger is that there are people in Sanctuary that ask me to mesmerize them so that they can have that moment of bliss, and they don't want to leave the illusion." The dark elf looked a bit downtrodden for a moment. "I've had to tell someone before that I cannot do this for them, ever again. It was... heartbreaking," the enchanter said in a tone that left no doubt that it was just as he had described. "If you want my advice about Vara..."

"I don't think that would be wise," Cyrus said. "Vara and I are not a healthy match for each other. It would be best if I just buried it."

"You never know," J'anda said. "Perhaps her ire for you is cover?"

"I doubt it," Cyrus said with certainty.

"As you say."

They did not speak of it again until the night J'anda returned to Sanctuary. They were in the Great Square of Reikonos, and had said their farewells. "Tell whoever is coming to join me that I'll meet them here at midday. If they come before that, tell them to come to the old Kings of Reikonos guildhall in the slums."

"The slums?" The enchanter raised an eyebrow, one of his favored expressions. "Hardly the place for so skilled an envoy to spend his night."

Cyrus smiled at the enchanter. "Couldn't have done it without you. Your illusions give you great adaptability when it comes to finding common ground with whoever you're talking to."

"Ah, but you see," J'anda said with a glint in his eyes, "that is not the illusion; that is simply me."

"I believe that," Cyrus said with sincerity. "Take care, my friend. I know you'll do your best to take the people we've recruited and help turn them into a capable force by the time I get back."

"You take care as well," J'anda said. "If Alaric is correct, we shall need all the help we can get to deal with whatever danger awaits from these weapons." After a moment's thought, he said to the human, "About your illusion, your 'heart's desire'..."

Cyrus shook his head impatiently. "I won't dwell on it. It will never happen."

"I see," J'anda said, with sad eyes. "You should always be

careful when saying the word 'never.' Such an ugly word; a killer of all possibilities. In the dark elven tongue, 'never' is a word that doesn't exist – we would say, 'It's an unlikely thing,' or 'It seems improbable,' but there is no word for 'impossible' or 'never', because the things you decide are never going to happen," the enchanter said with an undisguised smile, "have a way of happening when you least expect them to."

With a flourish, J'anda cast the return spell and vanished in a burst of light. While the light of the spell receded from his eyes, the enigmatic smile that the enchanter had flashed him as he left and the words that he said echoed in the warrior's mind for the rest of the night.

Chapter 28

Cyrus blinked the sleep out of his eyes as he fought his way to consciousness. For a moment he was confused, awakening in the Kings of Reikonos guildhall. The sun was barely showing through the wood panels that made up the building. Due to the canyon-like nature of the slums, the appearance of sunlight meant that it was close to midday. Cyrus fought the urge to return to sleep and strapped on his armor and scabbard before bolting out the door.

The clock in the square showed 11 o'clock when he arrived, and Cyrus settled himself by the fountain after filling his cup from it twice. It tasted much, much different from the water he had been drinking from the rivers and springs of Arkaria over the last month, he reflected as his horse, Windrider, came up and dipped his face into the water for a drink. Cyrus shrugged and turned to scan the square, blinked and did a double take.

"Hello old friend," Orion said from a few paces away.

Cyrus nodded. "Hello, Orion. How goes it?"

The ranger smiled. "Quite well. What brings you to Reikonos on this beautiful day?"

"I'm just passing through, but I'm waiting to meet another Sanctuary officer here."

Orion couldn't hide his pleasure. "So the rumors are true: you're an officer now. Good for you."

Cyrus returned the ranger's smile, a bit more guarded. "Yeah. Doing our best to rebuild after the debacle."

Orion's eyes fell and his face turned grave. "Rebuilding is going to be a long road for you, brother. I'm sure you've heard: the big guilds of Arkaria have gotten most of the talent and everyone else has been scrambling to get their hands on as many new recruits as they can. There's not much left at this point."

Cyrus smiled. "We'll see."

Orion walked closer, sitting himself beside the warrior on the fountain. "Listen, when I brought you to Sanctuary, it was because you're a great warrior with the potential to be one of the best – if not *the* best – in Arkaria." Orion smiled again, but with a hint of insincerity. "But that was when Sanctuary was rising, when they were a force to be reckoned with. Because of – all that," the ranger said, glossing over his defection, "Sanctuary is going to struggle as a fighting force for some time."

"You're a great leader," Orion coaxed him. "Goliath could use your talents." Orion looked around the square. "Your only hope of successful expeditions with Sanctuary in the near future is going to be small actions, little invasions. With what you've got left you won't be seeing any of the realms without the Alliance."

"So what you're saying," Cyrus's eyes focused on the dirt at his feet, "is I should leave Sanctuary behind, like you did, so I can move up to Goliath?"

"Right," Orion said. "Isn't your purpose to be the best? Don't you want more?"

"I do."

"Then follow me," Orion's eyes were alight with possibilities, "instead of wandering to the four corners of Arkaria in search of a farmer whose skill with a rusty pitchfork translates into swordsmanship." The ranger smiled at him. "You'll spend the next four or five months in the countryside, working your ass off so you can find a few good people, and the rest will be chaff that gets blown away by the next strong wind."

Orion's hand landed on the warrior's shoulder, reason filling his soothing voice. "Come with us. No need to rebuild, and with your skill and with the equipment we would give you, you could step into the role of Goliath's number one warrior, and be an officer candidate in no time. Malpravus likes you; he says you have great potential."

"Oh my," Cyrus breathed.

Orion did not hear him. "Bypass the next few months or years of hell you're gonna put yourself through to build an effective fighting force – your odds of success are very low. You'll end up frustrated and Sanctuary will still be in the same spot in a year." Excitement filled the ranger's voice. "This is not a time for building strength. You can't compete with Endeavor or the others; they've got a lock on recruiting. You need a guild that's already got strength, that can step up and take you where you want to go."

"Well," Cyrus said, voice flat. "You certainly paint a grim picture."

The ranger shrugged. "It's reality. What do you say?"

"To your proposition?" Cyrus asked, voice again devoid of

emotion. "Thanks, but no thanks. I haven't forgotten what Goliath did at Enterra, even if you have. If I'm to fight to the top, it should be in a place where I can trust my guildmates."

"So you've fallen into the trap of Alaric's 'noble purpose'." Orion shook his head. "Instead of wanting to be the aggressor, the victor, you want to be a defender? Spend your time helping the helpless instead of getting more powerful? You're going to be sorry a year from now, when Goliath is exploring the realms of the gods and you're still struggling to fight off bandits in the Plains of Perdamun." Acid dripped from the ranger's words.

"Perhaps," Cyrus said. "But at least I'll know that if I have a guildmate at my back, I need not fear they'll put a knife in it."

With a tight smile, Orion offered his hand to Cyrus once more, who shook it. "Best of luck, Orion," Cyrus said.

"To you as well," Orion said, but the words echoed with a certain hollow quality.

Curatio had shown up in the square a few minutes later, all smiles. "Good to see you, brother! Let's see if we can make the next leg of this journey as productive as the first."

They headed out the eastern gate of Reikonos and followed the road past the coliseum on a frantic schedule much like he had followed with J'anda, with too little time between meetings and times to talk with candidates on a one-on-one basis. Once again he found himself traveling late into the night, he and Curatio shorting themselves on sleep to meet Alaric's schedule.

"When you get back to Sanctuary," Cyrus had quipped one day as they were leaving a village, "please do give Alaric my thanks for his attempts to kill us."

"Aye," Curatio said with a smile. "I don't think he believed J'anda when the enchanter told him that you were run ragged on the first leg, but I'll make sure he knows it when I return."

"Assuming that by the time we get done there's anything left of you to return. Any news on the weapons?"

Curatio shook his head. "Nyad and I went to Pharesia to warn them and Alaric personally went to Reikonos to speak with the Council of Twelve that rules the Human Confederation. We were informed that both weapons are still there, and safe as they can make them."

"Did they take you seriously or brush you off?"

Curatio raised an eyebrow. "I know we were taken seriously in Pharesia. I suspect Alaric has enough credibility to get his message across in Reikonos as well. How many people do you know who go before the ruling Council of Twelve?"

Cyrus thought about it for a moment. "That would be the first. Not many people get an audience in the Citadel."

Over the next days they found the ground and the air around them getting colder, snow beginning to pile up as they trudged from the summery beauty of the Pelar Hills into the frozen tundra of the north that surrounded the mountains of the Dwarven Alliance that was north and east of Reikonos. Their destination was Fertiss, the dwarven capital, but they made stop after stop at human and dwarven villages along the way.

The humans of the northern clans were dramatically different than the dwarves that populated the frigid lands. Somewhat furtive and suspicious, the dwarves largely kept to themselves. The men of the north, on the other hands, welcomed them with open arms and Cyrus and Curatio had far too much ale in the days that followed.

"Next time we come this way I'm sending Andren in my stead. I cannot recall a time when I've had that much to drink," Cy said one morning after a long, boisterous night at the inn with several potential recruits. His head was still swimming.

"There's a reason for that," Curatio said, looking a bit green. "You're yet young enough to make these sort of mistakes. I'm old enough that I should know better."

In village after village Cyrus made his plea for people to join them, always closing his argument with the same words: "Some of you have wanted adventure from a young age, have wanted to live life on your terms and not reliant on what the soils would give you or the nobles would hand you or what money would come in. Many of us believed that that life was not possible, that we had not the skill nor the ability to live in such a way."

His eyes scoured the crowd, trying to make contact with every person in whatever place they were meeting. "I know this because I have felt the same – that perhaps life had passed me by, that I was always destined to be poor and stuck in a life I cared nothing for. I tell you now," he said, fire in his eyes, trying to pass it on to the others in the crowd, "that this is lies. Adventure still awaits!

"You can have whatever it is you desire, but we must fight for that life. I can train anyone who wishes to learn to be an adventurer, who wants to learn to live for themselves instead of their lords, their masters. I can train them to live a life of adventure, with a purpose greater than living just for themselves."

By the time he got to that point, he had already talked for several minutes about Sanctuary – who they were and what they did, where they wanted to go. His call to action got responses from his audiences. By the time he and Curatio reached Fertiss, they had actually outdone what he and J'anda had achieved in the first thirty days.

Cyrus and Curatio said their farewells in the halls of Fertiss, a city built into the mountains, combining dwarven love of cave architecture with the tacit acknowledgment that many outsiders did business in the dwarven city, and as such, half the town was located outside.

As Curatio disappeared in the light of his return spell, Cyrus reflected that although a genuinely decent elf, the healer was not much for conversation. Cyrus had only successfully engaged the healer about Sanctuary and their efforts. Whenever asked a personal question, Curatio would simply smile, shrug, and move on to another topic; usually an evaluation of one of their potential recruits, leaving the warrior frustrated. Curatio also refused to discuss members of Sanctuary, greatly curtailing their ability to find common ground. "It's not my place to say," was the elf's response when asked about anyone, from Vara (most commonly) to Alaric.

Cyrus settled down for the night in an inn nestled in Fertiss's foreign quarter, where the next person from Sanctuary to accompany him was to meet him on the morrow. He enjoyed a long soak in the inn's hot springs, and it was five o'clock in the evening when he fell asleep in the extra large (to dwarves) bed. He did not wake up until he felt a gentle caress on his cheek at ten o'clock the next morning.

Chapter 29

Cyrus awoke to find Nyad smiling down at him from the edge of his bed, hand gently stroking his face. He blinked three times in surprise before he sat up. "How did you get in here?" he asked in shock. "I locked the door!"

The elf smiled back. "Locks are no great difficulty for a wizard."

"Especially when the innkeeper opens it for you," said a dwarf from the door. "You know this elf? She said she was to meet you."

Cyrus looked down at the dwarf. "Yes, thank you." The innkeeper nodded and shut the door behind him. Cyrus turned back to Nyad in surprise. "I thought they were sending an officer?"

She shook her head. "There are only so many of you to go around, you know. They sent me instead; the Council is busy making preparations for war and training the candidates you've sent."

He yawned. "Sorry, I'm a bit tired; was just trying to catch up on my sleep."

"You'll need it. Alaric has set an aggressive schedule for us," she said, handing him a piece of parchment with dates and times written on it.

Cyrus studied the parchment with a frown. "This is worse than the last two parts of the journey." He looked up at Nyad. "Curatio told me he was going to get Alaric to loosen up the schedule."

Nyad looked back at him. "Yes, Alaric said you might demur. He said to remind you that time is not our ally."

"I suppose," the warrior said. The sleep he had gotten had not cured his chronic sense of fatigue and malaise, but it had helped somewhat.

"Very well then," Nyad said, jumping to her feet. "Let's make a start on our mission." She clapped her hands together like a child and looked at him expectantly, still wrapped up in the covers.

He looked back at her. "I'll be needing to get dressed before we can go."

"All right then," she said, still staring at him. "Get to it! We have not a moment to waste!"

He blinked at her. "Nyad, I'm not wearing anything under the covers. I'd like you to leave so that I can dress."

"Feh!" She brushed him off. "I'm two hundred and eighty-five years old, and spent more than fifty years of my life in Termina. I promise you," she said with a smile, "there's nothing you have that I haven't seen before, many, many, many times."

"You haven't seen mine," he said and refused to move.

Calling him a prude, Nyad finally acceded to his wishes and left, slamming the door behind her. Once he was dressed, they mounted their horses and rode out the front gate of Fertiss, making their way down the mountain paths.

"So you were... uh... *with* humans in Termina?" Cyrus said, uncertain how to broach the subject.

"With? You mean in bed with?" she said with a cackle. "Oh, certainly. Humans, dwarves," she said, voice turned wistful. "A gnome one time – that was very unsatisfying. Even a dark elf or possibly five – that was a strange night," the wizard said, lost in thought. "Termina is a very different place from – well, from where I was raised, which was in Pharesia, of course, but... even more so from the environment in which I was raised."

"How so?" Cy's grip tightened on Windrider's reigns.

"Not that people don't have sex in Pharesia, they do – what's the point of living for thousands of years if you can't enjoy yourself, right?" she said with a sly grin that made him remember that she was older than any human woman he'd ever met by almost two centuries. "In the Elven Kingdom relations are governed by caste. There are promiscuous elves in Pharesia, but if you wish to retain face, you must stay within the boundaries of the proper social behavior and not associate with someone in a lower caste than yourself. In Termina," she smiled at the memory, "anything goes."

Cyrus's eyes were wide, having learned more in the last few minutes about elves than he had ever really wanted to know. Nyad, catching sight of the look on his face, cackled. "Prude," she called out again, louder this time, echoing across the snowy road and through the mountain peaks beyond, mocking him.

"I am... not," he said without feeling.

"You are," she said with another laugh. "Your whole society is." She turned her clear blue eyes on him. "It's not as though everyone doesn't do it. But humans get so caught up in talking about it, as though there's some righteousness to ignoring such a fun practice. And when you do talk about it, it's gossip. So-and-so slept with such-and-such." She snorted. "And don't get me started on the delicate practice of saying 'slept with' instead of –"

"That's enough," Cyrus interrupted, uncomfortable. "I get the point."

She laughed again. "I doubt it, but we've reached the edge of your comfort zone." She looked back at him, eyes dancing. "We'll keep working on that. I've got thirty days to despoil you."

They followed the mountains south to the river Mussa, leaving the frozen tundra and turning inland to follow the river southwest, stopping in the fishing villages by its edge. It was a wet country, with many streams feeding into the river, and a near-constant rain. They met with a succession of farmers and fishermen until they reached the shores of Lake Magnus, the largest lake in Arkaria. Taking a ferry across at the mouth of the river, they headed southeast into the Gnomish Dominions.

Along the way, Nyad would chatter for hours about a variety of topics, most of which seemed to lead back to sexual matters. He could safely say that compared to her, he was a prude. She spoke at great length of her 'conquests' and would not hesitate to throw aside her robes at a moment's notice with nary a consideration to propriety, fording streams in the nude with her robes carried safe and dry above her head.

The third time in a morning that it had happened, Cyrus was fighting against the current in his heavy armor, teeth chattering from the cold, and the elf shook her head like a mother, already on the other side of the stream, redressed and mounting her horse. "Now your prudishness is going to cause you to catch a chill," she clucked at him. Fortunately he did not catch a chill, but when they reached the fourth stream, he at least removed his armor before they crossed.

"Better," she said as he strapped the metal coverings on his wet body. "But you're still going to be cold for a while."

His eyes lingered on her body when she undressed at the next crossing. As a human, she would have looked to be no more than thirty years old, and pretty enough, he thought. He reflected a bit too long, and she caught him looking. With another loud laugh, she pronounced with undisguised pleasure that he was beginning to come around to her way of thinking. Cy blushed but did not argue with her assessment.

He stripped his armor off, and his underthings as well, and crossed in the same manner as she. Upon reaching the other side of the stream, he did not shy away from her eyes as she looked him up and down in appraisal. She moved closer, still in the nude, rain falling down, and wrapped her arms around him, pulling him close in a strangely comfortable manner, and put her hands on his face, drawing it to hers.

She met the heat of his gaze, and did not break off. Her look was sly, though, and there was something else to it. "Let's be completely open with each other before I completely open to you," she said, pressing her naked flesh against him. "If I were to give you the relief you seek..." her eyes studied him, "would you be thinking of me? Or of another blond-haired elf of our mutual acquaintance?" He looked away and her face fell. "I feared as much," she said as she pulled away from him and began to redress.

His cheeks burned with embarrassment and he began to dress, slowly, frustrated. He heard Nyad's voice behind him, formal in spite of the fact that they had just been pressed naked against one another. "You were married, yes?"

"Yes," he said, voice hollow.

"But it didn't go well."

"No," he said without further explanation.

"How long ago?" she asked, now fully clad in her robes, standing behind him.

He struggled as he pulled the wet chainmail over his head. "She and I parted ways over two years ago." He did not meet the elf's eyes.

She whistled, a low tone that seemed completely out of place coming from her. "So now I know from whence your desperation is born." She knelt beside him, carefully adjusting her robes to avoid the mud. "I suppose I would not be wrong in suspecting you have not felt the touch of a woman since then?" She kept her hands away from him, folded in her lap.

All trace of shyness removed, he shook his head. "I see," she said, eyes downcast. "I fear that I may have provoked you to action without knowing the facts."

He turned his head toward her sullenly. "It seems like you knew all the facts already; perhaps someone told you; perhaps you're just exceptionally discerning. No matter what, you've guessed accurately."

The elf looked embarrassed for a change. "I did not know or suspect any of those things until the last few minutes; the only thing I guessed at before was your desire for Vara, but that was obvious to anyone who had watched the two of you for more than a few moments. I did not see the depth of it before I read it in your eyes just now; I thought it might have been a passing fancy."

She blushed. "I am a relentless tease, of course I joke, and as you are a handsome man – yes, I said it – with all the desire inherent, I thought it would be fun to enjoy ourselves to the fullest in our time together. But I cannot," she said, crestfallen, "now that I know about your feelings for Vara." She held up a hand to forestall his protest. "I do apologize, especially in light of the facts of your case. Two years is a long term to serve, but I would be doing you no favors if I were to 'give in' to your desires."

She stood up and looked down at him and he could see wisdom in her expression; it permeated her being. "You are in love with Vara," she said. Though there was no accusation in her tone, it felt like it to Cyrus, who had thought of almost nothing else since his night by the campfire with J'anda.

"Yes," he whispered, hoping for it not to be heard.

"It wasn't a question," she said. "You must resolve these feelings, one way or another – it is unhealthy to be in such a state as they would demand."

He looked down, still seated on the muddy ground. "Can't you just... I think it would be better if we..."

She shook her head. "That way lies madness." She extended her hand and with a surprising amount of strength helped draw him to his feet, armor and all. "You think," she said, looking at him with intensity, "that in all my years I have not tried that? Burying myself in the arms of another willing partner to avoid feelings I prayed to Vidara would pass?"

She shook her head again. "No, I'm afraid until you resolve this one way or another, my answer will remain 'no'." Her hand found his cheek, and brought his mind back to the day, two weeks earlier, when she had awakened him at the inn. She favored him with a sad smile and after he helped her back up on her horse, they rode on in a silence that did not lift until the next day.

Chapter 30

In the days after, the rain stopped as they entered the Gnomish Dominions and Nyad was much more restrained in her topics of conversation. Any time Cyrus steered their talk in a direction that could potentially lead to anything sexual, Nyad would change the subject to another matter. Toward the end of their journey, Cyrus finally brought up the one subject that he knew would be of interest to her. "Fine," he said in response to a diverted inquiry into her time in Termina. "Why don't we talk about Vara?"

Riding ahead of him, he could see Nyad smile. "You know I'm not at all reluctant to talk about others," she laughed. "Although I have to confess, I don't know Vara terribly well; we aren't the closest of confidantes – not that anyone is with her," she added with another laugh.

"What do you know about her?" he asked. "Why does she have such an attitude?"

"Well," Nyad began, "I think that comes from her age."

"Her age?" the warrior said with a furrowed brow. "Do you know how old she is?"

"Everyone – at least every elf – knows Vara's birthday and age," Nyad said. "She's only twenty-eight."

"Twenty-eight?" Cyrus said in shock. "I thought maybe you'd say one hundred and twenty-eight." He paused in thought. "Why would every elf know Vara's birthday and age?" The warrior looked alarmed. "Is she royalty?"

Nyad's face turned dark. "No," she answered in a voice that did not invite further inquiry, something uncharacteristic of the usually bright and cheerful wizard.

They did not speak about Vara again for the rest of the day. Sunset found them south of the Gnomish Dominions, which they had fully explored, stopping at a great many villages. Without sufficient-sized places to meet, Cyrus had taken to addressing their crowds in the streets of the gnomish towns, which got him yelled at on more than a few occasions for disturbing the peace and he had been kicked out of one village.

"Ornery enclave of necromancers in that village, if you ask

me," Nyad had said, rather nonplussed.

On the last day of their journey they climbed into the foothills of the Mountains of Nartanis, stopping in a human settlement called Montis along the northern edge of the mountain range. After meeting with people throughout the day, Nyad followed him to the inn that night. "Successful endeavor all the way around, wouldn't you say?"

"Yeah, that was pretty successful," Cyrus said, yawning. "It would appear we're going to swell the gnomish population of Sanctuary by a considerable margin."

"That's good," Nyad said. "Gnomes don't get a great deal of respect in the world at large; if you picked any race that's likely to be a slave, it'd be gnomes. There are as many gnomish slaves as there are free gnomes."

"I've heard that somewhere before," Cyrus said without much enthusiasm. He looked around the inn. "I suppose this is where we say our farewells."

Her face was locked a grimace. "No hard feelings." Her eyes widened in alarm as she realized what she had said. "I mean..." she paused, calming herself. "You know what I mean."

He grinned. "I know what you mean." He waited a beat. "And for what it's worth, thank you. For... almost everything."

She smiled, and once more her wisdom shone through. "I suspect," she said with a mysterious smile, "that at some point you'll be glad that things did not play out here as they could have. I suspect I'll be sorry that they didn't." Without another word, she summoned the energies of teleportation and vanished in a burst of green energy.

A moment after she vanished, the inn door swung open and a red-haired elf strode in. A flash of recognition crossed her face and Cyrus smiled at her. "Hello, Niamh. You just missed Nyad."

"I wouldn't say I missed her," the druid said. "Ready to go?"

"Not really," Cyrus replied. "I usually get at least one night to recover before the next leg of our mission. Which is fortuitous, because I haven't had more than three hours of sleep per night in a month."

"I'm sure you haven't," she said, "But tonight is not your night. We're assembling an army, remember? Grave threat hanging over our head and all that?"

"It is uppermost on my mind, when I'm not too tired to think." He shrugged. "Any news?"

"No news is good news," Niamh said with a smile. "The weapons are still in place in Reikonos and Pharesia, and we've sent a detachment of our people to both cities to keep an eye on things. Now." She clapped. "We've got a lot of ground to cover, and the terrain between here and Taymor is very rugged; lots of mountain paths and then hundreds of miles of near-desert." Niamh brightened. "Which is actually why they sent me to you now – my spell to imbue you with the essence of the falcon should come in handy."

Cyrus nodded. "That is fortunate, but I'm still concerned about falling asleep and falling down a mountain."

"No need to worry about that, silly ass, I'll guide you. Come on," she said. "We're already running behind."

Grumbling, Cyrus climbed back into the saddle of his horse and tried to keep his eyes open as the lulling of the spell that allowed them to float rocked him to sleep. Niamh had the reins of his horse gripped in her hand as she led the way out of town down a rocky path. So tired was he that Cyrus did not remember arriving at the next village, but was awakened by a shock of cold water on his face and sat up to realize he was laying on a bed of straw.

"You're really heavy," Niamh said in annoyance, standing at his feet with an empty bucket.

"What?" he spluttered.

"You fell asleep on your horse and I couldn't get you in to the inn we were staying at so I just let you drift to the ground in the barn."

"Couldn't you have found some... more pleasant way to wake me up?" he asked, wiping the water from his face.

"Bah," she said. "This was much more amusing. Besides," she blinked her eyes innocently. "I tried shaking you, but like I said, you're heavy, and I couldn't get you to move much with all that armor."

He pulled himself to his feet. "What's on the agenda for today?"

"Well," she said, unfolding a piece of parchment and handing it to him, "we've got early meetings in this town, and then around midday we'll be out of here and into the next town by evening for another meeting."

"If I survive the next two months," Cyrus said, "I will not leave Sanctuary again for a very, very long time."

"Right," Niamh said. "Well, let's get on that surviving business."

The next few days passed in a blur. They crossed the mountainous terrain for a day or two at a time, then spent a half day in a small village or town, Cyrus speaking as usual, and then left as quickly as they had arrived, with a time and a list of names of people who would meet their druid or wizard later for passage to Sanctuary.

At some point, after about two weeks of travel, Cyrus and Niamh had entered into an easy rapport. Back and forth, and able to venture into the realm of personal inquiries.

"You're in love with Alaric?" Cyrus said with just a hint of skepticism after the druid's admission.

"Yeah," Niamh said after a moment. "I don't really know what to do about it, though."

Cyrus blinked in confusion. "I thought you and Curatio were together?"

"Oh, heavens no. He's a lot older than me. And an elf."

Cy's eyes narrowed. "You're an elf." She sputtered for a moment, unable to respond. "If it makes you feel any better," he said with a sigh, "I found out a few months ago that I'm in love with Vara."

"Wow," Niamh said with a laugh. "You might be the only person in Sanctuary with less of a chance at love than me."

"I'm glad you find this so amusing," he said in a sour tone.

"Misery loves company. Or at least a sympathetic ear."

"I've got a question for you. Are you older or younger than Nyad - if you don't mind my asking."

"I don't mind. I'm six hundred and twenty-three. So, yes," she said with a smile, "I'm older than Nyad by a bit."

"Nyad said that every elf knows Vara's age and birthday, and when I asked her if Vara was royalty, she said no but got tense and wouldn't speak any more."

"Vara's not royalty," Niamh said. "Nyad, on the other hand, is - which might be why she got so testy about it. She's a princess of the royal family; the King's youngest daughter. Not only a part of the massive royal family, but a Princess, no less - one of fifty or so, and being the youngest, she's more honored than the older ones."

"They respect youth more than age in the Elven Kingdom? Interesting," Cyrus said with surprise. "Never heard of a race that does that before. But that also leads me to the next question I have

– which is, if Vara isn't royalty, why does everyone know her birthday and age? Nyad made it seem like she was famous throughout the elven world."

"She is," Niamh said. "But... I can't really talk about it, I'm sorry," she said. "Vara's history is tied up in a pretty sensitive topic to elves, one we don't discuss with outsiders."

"Not at all?"

"No," she said, red hair whipping in the wind.

The next two weeks passed more quickly than the first, and Cyrus felt progressively worse as they went. This was compounded by Niamh's steadfast refusal to discuss the topic of Vara's mysterious history with him. "I'll tell you anything you want about Vara since she joined Sanctuary," the red-haired elf told him. "But don't ask me about anything before that, because I'll give you the same answer: it's a sensitive matter, one we don't talk about among outsiders."

As the days passed, the Mountains of Nartanis gave way to flat land on the edge of the Inculta desert: sparse, desolate terrain broken up by small villages at least a day's ride from each other. When they reached the village of Taymor at the far edge of the desert and on the shores of the Bay of Lost Souls, they stopped for the night.

The next day, Niamh transported them to a portal on the edge of the oasis, a lake in the middle of the desert. They spent the next five days traveling to seven villages that ringed the body of water. Each of the villages belonged to a different tribe of desert dwelling humans. Wild men and vicious fighters, the tribes of the south catered to travelers passing through as well as a few mining operations but were feuding with each other. The heat of the desert gave Cyrus a feeling of perpetual feverishness and even when they reached the end of their time in the desert and left, the feeling did not depart.

On their final day together, Niamh teleported them to a town in the Elven Kingdom, on the other side of Arkaria. They appeared at a portal not far from a village called Nalikh'akur close to the edge of the Great Dismal Swamp.

"Nalikh'akur," Niamh explained with the knowing voice of someone who had lived through more history than most humans had read about, "is an elven military outpost on the frontier of troll territory. During the war it was first to fall to their invasion but once they were defeated the Elven Kingdom rebuilt it, complete with a garrison to watch troll activity. Nalikh'akur means 'Last Bastion' in the human tongue."

"Hmh," Cyrus said, still feeling warm and flushed from their time in the desert.

"You don't look well," Niamh said. "I can't believe you've done this for the last five months."

"Neither can I," Cyrus said without energy. He pulled tighter on Windrider's reins. His arms felt heavy, as did his helm. "But 'time is of the essence'," he parroted Alaric for the umpteenth time.

"Getting close," she breathed. "We're meeting in the tavern." She guided her horse to a stop. Dismounting, she walked through the door.

Cyrus did not notice; he nearly fell off his horse in his dismount attempt. Struggling to put one foot in front of another, he made his way through the door to the elven tavern, and discovered a sight that under normal circumstances might have shocked him: Vara, sitting at a table with Niamh, drinking an ale and waiting with an air of impatience.

"Took you long enough," she harrumphed as he walked through the door.

"I made it as fast as I could," he said as forcefully as he could muster - which wasn't very forceful at all.

"We'll be leaving this town at midday tomorrow" Vara began, "after a meeting tomorrow morning. We'll ride south and west, to the Emerald Coast, and visit three villages there before we cross to the east and start meeting with some of the elves of the woods. From there we'll head south, wending our way toward the capital, Pharesia, where we'll conclude our business and teleport to Reikonos for a last meeting."

"I thought..." Cyrus said, fighting to squeeze every word out, "...Reikonos had already been picked clean by every other guild in Arkaria."

"They have. But Alaric believes that you may in fact be able to offer the last few unguilded souls in Reikonos something that no other guild can offer."

"What's that?" Cyrus said.

"A sense of honor and purpose," Vara answered in annoyance. "You know, these basic principles upon which we stand, that you are supposed to be emphasizing as you go across the land bringing word of our efforts?"

"He's telling everyone, trust me," Niamh said before Cyrus could try and formulate an answer. "He's doing a magnificent job of it. We managed to find another 165 potential recruits in the last four weeks."

Vara straightened. "Not bad. That's almost five hundred since you left, outside of our other efforts."

"Other efforts?" Cyrus's words sounded slow and distorted. Everything that was being said sounded as though he was listening to the conversation under water.

"Yes, we've not made you our only hope. Is there some reason," she nearly spat at him, "that your head is laying on the table?"

"I'm tired."

"Could you, for once in your time with Sanctuary, at least *try* to represent us with a spirit of dignity?" she snapped.

Cyrus was beyond caring. A moment after she spoke he slid from his chair and landed on the floor. There were interruptions in what he saw after that – Niamh and Vara, both looking concerned over him, talking quickly.

"He's burning up and my healing spells aren't doing anything," Niamh said, breathless.

"Some sort of natural fever then," Vara said from above him, looking down. "How long has he been ill?"

"I don't know; he hasn't complained about feeling ill – only about being tired."

"Can you hear us?" Vara asked, turning her attention back to him. Cyrus saw but did not feel her slap his face. He heard the impact echo in his brain. She was there, hair shining in the dim lamplight.

"I think... I should tell you," he said, focusing every last bit of his concentration on Vara, "I think you... need to know..." *Gods, she looks beautiful*, he thought. Even a bit concerned – a new expression to him.

"What?" came the elf's reply, distorted, slow.

Blackness claimed him.

Chapter 31

"I don't care!" Vara nearly shouted.

Cyrus awoke to the sound of an argument, still feverish. He clutched at the blankets that surrounded him, trying to pull them closer to his damp skin.

Niamh was standing in the corner, very near to a door, and Vara was facing her, back turned to Cyrus. The paladin was not wearing her armor. She was clad in a simple cotton shirt and pants, which was unusual for a woman – even an elf.

"Alaric wants it done now," Niamh said. "He sent me to tell you."

"If Alaric wants it done, then tell him to get off his etherial arse and do it himself!" Vara said, voice crackling with rage.

"I will tell him that," Niamh said with a trace of a smile. "If for no other reason than it will bring him a laugh." The druid brought her hands together and disappeared in a blast of wind.

Vara faced away for a moment, still looking at the spot where Niamh had teleported. He heard a sound come from her, something that sounded almost like a choked sob, and she turned to face him. His eyes were blurry as he stared at her.

"Ah," she said with a sniff. "There you are."

"Here I am," he whispered, straining to string words together.

"How are you feeling? I only ask," she said, "because Alaric is concerned that we are falling far behind on our mission."

"I've felt better."

"I should think so." Vara stepped to the foot of the bed and adjusted the blankets around his feet. "You are still feverish. Healing spells will not improve your condition, which means that if you die of whatever illness you seem to have contracted, we will be unable to resurrect you."

"Thanks," Cyrus said without emotion. "That's reassuring."

"I am merely trying to be honest," she said, eyes flaring in anger and – he might have been imagining it – fear?

"I see," he murmured and passed out again. When he woke, she was beside him in a chair. She had changed into something that looked like a nightgown, and she was sleeping. The only light in the room came from the lanterns and candles. He watched her for a while, then drifted off again.

When next he awoke, he felt something cool and damp on his forehead. His eyes opened to a vision of Vara, cloth in hand, dripping cold water onto his head. "I'm trying to bring down your fever," she said when her eyes met his.

He coughed and motioned for water, which she brought to his lips in a small dish.

"It's been very difficult to get you to take water," she said as he was drinking. "I'm glad you're awake, because trying to get you to drink when you're semi-conscious has been no mean feat. Niamh left a few days ago to let them know at Sanctuary that we wouldn't be making our scheduled appointments. I'm told they have managed to cover for our absence."

"It's a shame," Cyrus said. "I was looking forward to seeing the green elven country after the last weeks in the desert."

"Oh, really?" she said without turning back to him. "And here I thought you had decided upon seeing me that night in the tavern that you would rather collapse and lie in bed for the next four weeks instead of tour the Elven Kingdom with me as your companion."

"I'll admit," Cyrus said, shifting in the bed, "upon seeing you, I did have a momentary concern about working together. It felt as though as very big object was rushing at me, very quickly. But just moments later, it was replaced by the actual sensation of the tavern floor rushing up at me very quickly."

She laughed, a genuine, hearty laugh that turned into a somewhat girlish giggle partway through before she managed to choke it off. She turned her head; by the look in her eyes it was clear she hoped he hadn't heard her slip. A hand covered her mouth in semi-shock.

"Hah." Cyrus laughed at her. "You actually found humor in something I said – and we've exchanged a few sentences without bickering."

"I often find humor in what you say." She turned away from him again. "Unfortunately for you, it's rarely from things you intended to be humorous."

"Ah," Cyrus said with a little disappointment. "There you are again."

She frowned. "What do you mean?"

"Nothing," he said with a trace of sadness. "I'm tired. I think

I'm going to rest now..." He felt a sudden pressure from his head hitting the pillow as his neck muscles gave out, and he was unconscious again.

He awakened again at night, but something was different. The world around him was blurred, and lights seemed to streak in his vision. Urgent voices filled the air around him.

"My spells are still ineffective," came the voice of a man that seemed very familiar. "He's getting worse."

"No doubt," came Vara's reply. "The fever is going to kill him if we don't do something."

"I'm not sure what else we can do, here. If this were Sanctuary –" the man's voice came back.

"You're a healer, for gods' sakes!" Vara exploded. A moment passed with nothing said. "Fine," she continued, and Cyrus felt he might have imagined her gritting her teeth. "Help me get him out of bed."

"A walk would be nice," Cyrus said, but what came out was completely unintelligible. He felt strong hands grasp him under each arm and lift him out of the bed. The cloth nightshirt he wore was soaked, clinging to his skin and chest hair. He heard and felt the door to the room open as Vara and the man carried him between them, one arm on each of their shoulders and dragging his flailing legs behind him.

"Stop trying to help us," she snapped at him. "You're making this much more difficult."

"Okaaay," Cyrus said again, once more making a complete hash of his words. He turned his head to look back at what he could have sworn was Narstron, waving at him from the side of the street, but a flash of insight revealed that it was, in fact, a shrub.

"I had assumed," Vara said, voice strained, "that relieving him of his armor would make him considerably lighter but in fact I cannot tell a difference."

"Heh," came the man's voice next to him. Cyrus's head swung around, feeling a bit loose on his shoulders. He realized with a start from the carefully groomed hair that it was Curatio.

"Curatio!" he shouted, barely sensate.

"Sounds like he's at least conscious enough to recognize me," came a grunt from the elf.

"Marvelous," Vara said with sarcasm. "If only he were conscious enough to assist us in transporting his considerable bulk."

"I tried to help," Cyrus said, once again squeezing the words out, "but you told me to stop, and I did as you said."

"Why does it take being feverish to the point of near death and being dragged around to get you to listen and act on reasonable suggestions? All right, we're here. Curatio, wait on the shore; there's no reason for both of us to get completely soaked."

Cyrus felt water splashing around his feet, then ankles and knees, felt muddy dirt between his toes as their pace slowed and Vara took up more of his weight on her shoulder as Curatio relinquished his grip on the warrior. After a half dozen more watery paces, Cyrus could feel water up to his waist. Adjusting her grip on him with a hand across his chest and back, Vara kicked his legs from beneath him and dropped him onto his backside in the water, submerging him up to his neck. The water was cold and his teeth began to chatter immediately.

"Don't thrash about like a gutted fish," she said, voice stern.

"But it's really cold!"

"It's not cold. It is summer and this pond is warm. You are feverish." She clutched him tighter to her.

He felt her warmth – the only warmth he could feel in the freezing water and pulled nearer to her as well. His teeth knocked together and he hugged her so tightly that he feared for a moment he would crush her. When he went to loosen his grip, she pulled him closer. His face lingered over her shoulder, and he could feel her wet hair, hanging in tangles on the left side of his face. In spite of the chill, it felt good being this close.

"I always suspected you were trying to kill me," he said, "but I assumed it would be swordplay, not drowning, that you would do the deed with."

"If I were to truly try and kill you," she said with fake annoyance, "I would certainly use a sword, if for no other reason than it would not involve me having to carry your overmuscled arse across a village to 'do the deed', as you so eloquently put it."

"Overmuscled?" he said, drawing back to look at her eyes. They were such a bright blue, catching a glimmer of the lamps hanging on the streets of Nalikh'akur. "You noticed."

She flushed and her face softened. "It would be impossible not to notice, being pressed against you like... like..." He could tell, even in his weakened state that she was searching for an appropriately insulting analogy. "...like this."

He felt her hand slapping him on the face and realized his head had lolled back and disorientation had taken him. "Please...please...wake up!"

"You can stop slapping me now." His voice was a whisper. He lifted his head and steadied himself, looking once again into her eyes and found concern within them.

"Just... don't do that."

"I promise I'm not trying to."

Another giggle escaped her, then a slightly deeper laugh. She wrapped both arms around his neck to hold him upright and drew him close, keeping his head above water until dawn.

Chapter 32

After the sun came up, Curatio helped them out of the water. "Your fever is broken," the healer pronounced with a smile. Cyrus could barely stand under his own power. "You should be fine for now."

"I'm hungry," Cyrus said.

"Let's get back to the inn and I think we can settle that problem," Curatio said as he assumed a carrying position on Cyrus's left. Vara moved to his right and grabbed his arm, more gently this time. He looked at her, and she looked back at him, but there was no venom in her eyes. She blinked at his gaze and looked away first. They walked back to the inn in silence but for the groans of the two elves, who were still carrying most of the warrior's weight.

"You could at least help us!" Vara's tone was all irritation, the moment of calm gone.

"I'm trying," Cyrus said.

They deposited him in a chair at the tavern, where the owner proceeded to bring him platefuls of fresh eggs, beef, pork and chicken as he dripped on the floor.

Vara looked at him with a cocked eyebrow as he finished his fourth plate. "I don't wonder anymore why you were so heavy to lift," she said shortly after Curatio had left them to retire to his room upstairs.

The warrior looked back at her with a sly smile. "I bet you couldn't go five minutes without throwing a verbal barb my way."

"I could and I have, in fact, over the last few days – largely during times when you were sleeping." She smiled. "But I usually don't wish to defer such excellent ripostes to your often deserving statements."

"I rest my case – I don't think you could go a day without throwing some sort of jab my way." He grinned.

She feigned shock. "You assume because you lack the self-discipline to control your tongue that I do as well. I could easily go a year without verbally abusing you for being an incompetent oaf with poor habits in your swordsmanship and hygiene."

"Perhaps you could start with a week," he said with a raised eyebrow.

"I think..." she said, slowing the pace of her words, "a month would do nicely for a test, don't you?"

"A month it is. But if I win, I want something from you."

"What's that?" Her brow furrowed, curiosity in her eyes.

"I don't know yet. But traditionally, when you bet, there's something to wager." He sat back in his chair. "We'll have to agree on something later; I'm too tired to come up with something creatively punitive right now."

The next days passed in an agonizing mixture of quick moments and slow recovery. The fever lingered for two more days, hampering Cyrus's ability to move about. As soon as Curatio had pronounced him healthy, he jumped from the bed, eager to go anywhere else.

"You probably won't feel like yourself for a week or two," Curatio beamed at him. "Glad to see you're feeling better, brother."

"Thank you. It can't have been easy to leave Sanctuary right now, especially with everything that's going on." The warrior looked at Vara, who was reserved, but the ice normally present in her eyes had melted somewhat. Turning his gaze back to Curatio, he asked, "So, where do we go from here? I'd like to finish my mission in the Elven Kingdom."

Curatio raised an eyebrow. "For the last couple weeks J'anda and Niamh have been covering your absence. If you're feeling that much better, you could take over for them."

"I'm not opposed to you killing yourself in principle, but we just nursed you back to health." The fire was back in Vara's eyes now. "You could at least do us the courtesy of waiting a few weeks before undoing all the good we just did."

Cyrus laughed. "There's only two weeks left. I could handle two more weeks of that schedule, given what's at stake."

"You're mad," Vara said, pointing a finger at him. "Barking mad. Howling at the moon mad!"

"I need to finish this," Cyrus said, urgency permeating his voice.

"Why?" she asked.

"Because I feel this need to complete a task once I've started it. And before you answer," he said, interrupting her already forming reply, "remember that you just wagered me that you could go a full month without insulting me. Calling me crazy was close to the line." He wagged his finger at her.

She looked at him through half-lidded eyes, considering her response. She opened her mouth as if to speak, then shut it. Finally, she said, "Very well. But I want a lighter schedule that will allow you to take your time."

Curatio chuckled. "We can work something out. In any case, I'm needed back at Sanctuary to deal with the influx of new blood. Can I do anything for you before I go?"

"Yeah," Cyrus said. "What's the word on the weapons in Reikonos, Pharesia and Hewat?"

"No idea about Hewat." Curatio shrugged. "No one has contact with the dragons. We have a few people lingering outside the Citadel in Reikonos and the Museum of Arms in Pharesia."

"They keep the Scimitar of Air in a Museum?" Cyrus shook his head. "Elves are bizarre."

Curatio cast his return spell and disappeared into the burst of light that accompanied it, leaving Cyrus alone with Vara. "Back to bed with you," she said in a voice that left no doubt that it was not a suggestion.

"I've been in bed for days," he said, irritable.

"And you'll be in bed for a few more if you want to be able to travel in good order. Take a nap," she said, "and later we'll work on getting your strength back up by going for a walk. We leave the day after tomorrow, and we have a long ride ahead of us."

They left the inn two days later, setting out on horseback at a pace Cyrus would have found more appropriate for walking alongside an elderly grandmother. "We're not going to push you to your limit," Vara said. "I want you to be in good condition to talk to these potential recruits, else we might as well go back to Sanctuary."

"Fair enough," the warrior grumbled.

They settled into a silence that was only broken when Cyrus asked Vara a question. "I've heard about how busy things are back at Sanctuary but I haven't heard much about Alaric lately. How is he?"

"Alaric is fine," she said. "He was here, in Nalikh'akur. He came to check on you the day after Niamh left. We had..." her jaw tensed, "...a marvelous conversation, he and I." She did not elaborate further.

Three days journey south placed them in a town called

Traegon. Filled with exquisite elven architecture, the city had towers and minarets on almost every building. They ventured into a local inn and found Niamh sitting next to J'anda, who was wearing an elven illusion. After exchanging pleasantries over drinks ("Ale for us, water for him," Vara had told the innkeeper, pointing at Cyrus), J'anda and Niamh departed.

They met with many elves that day, and Cyrus could feel his vitality return as he spoke, telling them of the direction Sanctuary was headed, and of the opportunity they had to be a part of that movement. He shook a great many hands while Vara stood back with her arms crossed. A few looked as though they wanted to ask her something, but none ever said what was on their minds. They left Traegon the next morning, southbound once more, this time heading for a smaller village only a half day's ride away.

"When did you first start learning to cast spells?" Cyrus asked her in the midst of one of their increasingly common civil conversations.

"All holy warriors learn to use basic magics early in their training with the Holy Brethren," she answered. "I suppose it was somewhere in the first year or so after I began my studies."

"Holy Brethren?"

"It's the paladin's version of your 'Society of Arms'. They train us in the Crusader's path from an early age."

"Hm," Cyrus said aloud. "I wonder if I could learn any spellcasting ability. It'd certainly come in handy from time to time."

"You have all the magical talent of a silkworm. If you'd had any, it would have been identified by one of the magic-using Leagues and cultivated from childhood."

He regarded her with suspicion. "Sounded like an insult."

"No... ah..." she fumbled, "silkworms create a silk thread, you know. Spin it into fabric – it's really quite... magical."

He laughed at her, and she smiled at him. "You know," she changed the subject quickly, "I admire the effort you've put into this recruiting drive; especially how much fortitude it must have taken to do this." She shook her head in disbelief. "I doubt... no, I know that I could not have handled this as well as you have."

"It's not that bad; I haven't been in combat."

"No," she said with a grimace, "you've been dealing with rubes, which is infinitely worse." He shot her a look of confusion and she explained, "In combat, at least you get to strike down those who offend you. You can't kill a rube simply for being stupid, no matter how much you'd like to."

He laughed. "You're certainly not the patient sort."

"I would say that I have never been one," she said with an air of sweetness, "to suffer fools gladly."

"The problem with that approach is that you so loosely define 'fool' to encompass anyone whose name isn't Vara."

She feigned shock, mouth comically agape. "That's simply not true! It would also encompass Alaric and Curatio." The smile widened, mocking him.

"I see. Then I suppose there's no room in your heart for a certain human warrior to join that definition."

"My heart?" She stuttered, a bit caught off her guard.

He grimaced and cursed to himself. "Sorry, poor choice of words."

She seemed rattled by his comment, and they proceeded in silence to the next town, where they met with people throughout the day and at night retired to the inn, where they enjoyed a quiet meal next to the fire. Vara had removed her armor and was wearing her cotton pants and shirt. As she came down the stairs, the firelight glinted on her fair hair and a smile covered her lips, pushing up the edges of her mouth and making Cyrus realize for the first time that she in fact had very slight dimples in her cheeks. He rose to greet her, and kissed her hand in an oddly formal manner that brought a blush to the cheeks he had just been studying.

They chatted pleasantly through dinner, avoiding any serious subjects. He got her to laugh three times, aided by a very good wine suggested by the innkeeper that came from elven vineyards close to Amti in the southern lands. By the end of the evening, the blush on her cheeks was permanent, and in his somewhat weakened condition, he too felt the effects of the spirit.

"I think I've finally come up with an idea for our little wager," he said with a smile.

"Oh?" Her eyes bored in on his. "Do tell."

"I think that if I win, we do this," his hands moved in a sweeping gesture to encompass her and the room, "again. Except next time, you have to wear a dress."

She frowned. "I have never cared to wear a dress."

He grinned. "I'm sure it interferes with your ability to swing a sword."

A small laugh escaped her. "In point of fact, it does."

"And if you win...?"

"*When* I win, you mean? I haven't given it much thought. Perhaps I'll have you fetch my slippers in the morning and bring them to my bedside."

His grin grew wider. "So I'll be the first thing you think of when you wake up?"

Her eyes rolled. "Alas, Brevis could not have come up with a more pitiful response than yours."

"I am feeling a bit *short* on wit lately."

She snorted, almost spitting her wine back into the glass. "Terrible, that was."

"I have to know," he said after another sip of wine, "something that I've been wondering for months now..."

"What is it?"

"One of the other elves told me... that every elf knows your birthday and how old you are."

She pulled the glass to her lips, stalling. "Is that so?" she asked when she had returned the glass to its position on the table.

"Yes, that is so," he said, narrowly avoiding slurring his words. "So I asked... this elf, the one that told me that about you, and she said you're not royalty. What conclusion should I draw from that?" he asked with what he thought was an endearing smile.

She met his smile with one of her own that twisted her mouth as she considered his question. "I think you should presume that elves are very funny people with a culture unlike your own and that putting together the pieces of the puzzle you just described would be very difficult... without further information." Her smiled turned a bit wistful at the last.

Cyrus regarded her in seriousness. "Would Alaric know the answer to my question?"

She laughed. "Alaric might, but it would not be from me answering it. I suspect he and Curatio would have discussed that bit of elven trivia at some point."

"Elven trivia?" he said with undisguised curiosity, made all the worse by the heat of the wine. "Niamh said it was an internal matter, and you don't discuss it with..." he leaned across the table toward her, "...outsiders."

"Oh, Niamh said that, did she?" The hint of a smile graced her lips. "We're very private people, the elves. We keep a very intimate inner circle. What a human would call a friend, elves have a much deeper word for – *covekan*. It denotes an intimacy than humans can't experience because elven relationships can last millenia." She sipped from her cup once more. "Our closest *covekan* are with us throughout our lives, and the bond that entails means that once someone is part of your inner circle, you can truly share yourself with them. There are no barriers to communication, no withheld thoughts."

"The elven version of a circle of friends, but more intimate?" Cyrus asked.

"Yes. The fortunate human lives between eighty and one hundred years. In that hundred years you would meet literally thousands of people and have a few good friendships – but most of them would start in your twenties or so. A quarter of the way through your life – and they take at least a few years to build true depth." Her smile faded and her eyes became a bit lonely. "The average elf lives over five thousand years, some as many as six thousand. It takes over a hundred years for an elf to become *covekan* in the traditional sense of the word." The light in her eyes grew dimmer still. "Imagine how close you could grow to someone in a hundred years."

"You never did answer my question about you," he said.

"My point is, elves do not let people into their confidence all willy-nilly. I hope you don't take it as an offense, but I don't think it's something I'm ready to discuss with anyone."

"So there's no one yet that is *covekan* to you?" he asked.

She laughed. "No. As you pointed out, I am young by elven standards – at twenty-eight, I have not lived long enough to form that sort of attachment to anyone."

"By your very actions you seem to try very hard to discourage any sort of attachment at all."

"Yes," she said, voice filled with regret. "There is that too." She did not say anything for a few moments after that, but did not look away. She blinked a few times, then seemed to recover her newfound cheer. "So tell me," she said, eyes alight, "what's this I keep hearing about a sword you're working on?"

Cyrus was overtaken by a sudden coughing fit. "There are no secrets in Sanctuary, are there?" She shook her head. "It's just something I'm working on."

"You're blushing," she said with great amusement. "You're actually embarrassed!" She stopped, perplexed. "Why would you be embarrassed?"

"It's a grand quest, but it's ultimately fairly selfish for me to want a new sword so badly I'd try and drag our guildmates to some fairly dangerous locations," he explained with a shrug.

"I don't think it's selfish," she said. "We all want things."

"Even paladins?" Cyrus grinned.

Vara laughed. "Even the holiest of holy warriors wants something, although in most cases it's to complete their crusade." Her eyes refocused on his. "If you're providing service to the guild, I don't think it's selfish unless you don't tell anyone what you're doing. *Then* you'd be very selfish to drag your comrades at arms into danger unknowingly."

He chuckled. "And what is it that you want?"

She bristled for a moment and then relaxed. "That remains to be seen," she said, almost as though she were pondering whether she should tell him more. "I think I should retire for the evening. It's been a long day, and we have a longer one ahead of us tomorrow." She stood up and he joined her out of gentlemanly reflex. "Goodnight."

He leaned in close to her and felt the pressure of her hand as she deflected him gently to a kiss on the cheek. "Goodnight," he said with a whisper of sadness. As her back retreated up the stairs, he watched her go.

"What changed?" he called out. Blood hammered in his temples, filling him with a sudden recklessness. "A month ago you hated me. You would have danced on the day I left Sanctuary if you had heard I was never to return." He shrugged. "I'm the same man I was a month ago, so what changed?"

She froze in the middle of the stairs, pondering for a moment in silence before she turned to face him. She stared at him, eyes brimming with a silent sort of despair that he had never noticed in her before. "I think... that in seeing you vulnerable, I saw the real you. Not the blustering warrior who'd jump into the middle of a battle at the drop of a helm; not the dashing and confident – sometimes arrogant – human who was quick with an insult – I think I saw you," she said, words tumbling out. "And it was... different from what I had expected of you."

He closed the distance between them, finding himself on the stairs next to her. "What do you see now?"

She blinked and turned away from his intense gaze. "Something different." Looking back for just a moment, she added, "I see a good man, someone who won't lead us into foolish action or abandon us when things become difficult."

"Us?" he said, drawing closer.

"Yes. Us. Sanctuary."

"What about you?" His hand rested on her back, so close he could feel her breath.

"Me?" she whispered. She pressed her forehead to his for just a moment before he could feel the change in the air. "I'm not ready yet," she breathed, and pulled from his grasp, taking a few slow steps up the stairs, turning her back on him once more.

He stared at her receding back as she walked slowly up the stairs. "Just keep in mind, I don't live as long as you do – if you wait too long, I'll likely be dead." Though he meant it as a jest, to lighten the moment, she did not laugh or look back. Upon reaching her room she shut the door and he did not see her again until morning.

Chapter 33

The next day, they did not speak of their conversation and Vara's guardedness had returned. Although she admitted after a few hours that her head ached from the wine, she did not return to the more pleasant mood exhibited the night before. The next two weeks passed in much the same manner; Cyrus's repeated attempts to return to a more intimate and friendly conversational style failed. Although Vara remained pleasant, she also remained distant.

By the end of the week, Cyrus attempted to quicken their pace, striving to finish early. Every time he tried to get ahead of schedule, Vara would interfere with a demand that he take a rest, or that they stay an extra day in some out-of-the-way town. He did not argue, and they ate their meals in relative silence. Once, on the last night, he could have sworn he caught her looking forlorn.

They met Nyad outside the elven capital of Pharesia at the appointed time. The elf greeted them with silence and a stricken look.

"What happened?" Cyrus asked her while dismounting.

"I've just come from a meeting with my fa-" she looked flustered. "From meeting with the King of the Elven Empire."

Cyrus grinned. "Your father."

Nyad rolled her eyes. "He informed me that the Museum of Arms was broken into last night, and that Ventus, the Scimitar of Air, was stolen."

Vara's jaw dropped. "Did any of our detachment report seeing anything?"

Nyad shook her head. "There was no sign of anyone entering through any of the doors: the intruder appeared to have entered through a skylight from above."

Vara blinked. "Can we speak to our guild members from the detachment?"

"No." Nyad shook her head. "They are in the process of being released from the jail – it will be several hours."

"Jail?" Cyrus said with a start.

"They were all in proximity to the Museum at the time of the theft," Nyad said with a deep frown. "I've spoken with my father and he's agreed to release them on my request, but it will take time. Alaric ordered me to transport you to Reikonos. We've doubled the size of our detachment and he'd like the two of you to join him there."

"He's there?" Cyrus said. "Where can we find him? Around the Citadel?"

Nyad shook her head. "There's a contingent there, but they've set up a headquarters at your old guildhall in the slums." She looked at Cyrus as he blinked in surprise. "Andren is helping to lead the effort in Reikonos; he offered it."

"We need to go now," Vara said. "Who knows how much time there is before they strike Reikonos and takes the Spear?"

"Assuming they can. And assuming they're going for it," Cyrus said. "Who knows how many of these things they're really after?"

"They can," Nyad said grimly. "The Museum of Arms is one of the most well-defended buildings in the Elven Kingdom, complete with mystical barriers and a variety of other spells for defense, in addition to housing a large contingent of troops. If they can steal a weapon from here, they can take it from Reikonos."

"In any case, would you care to bet the survival of our world on the idea that this nameless, faceless enemy is going to stop before collecting 'the whole set'?" Vara glared at him.

"No." Cyrus shook his head. "All right, Nyad, take us to Reikonos Square."

Without a word, the wizard cast a spell that filled Cyrus's vision with light and landed him in Reikonos Square. He and Vara exchanged a quick goodbye with Nyad as she disappeared in a blast of energy. Cyrus looked to the north to see the massive Citadel filling his view.

"Ever been inside?" Vara asked, not looking at him.

"Never." Cyrus shook his head. "Let's find Alaric."

They made their way to the slums and Cyrus lashed Windrider at a hitching post outside the door of the old Kings of Reikonos guildhall.

"You actually lived here?" Vara said, voice high in disbelief.

"Yeah," Cyrus said without meeting her eyes.

There was a long pause. "I cannot believe I made that stupid wager," she said in a low tone. "The comedic possibilities here are endless."

"Hush."

Cyrus opened the door. Though the interior still contained the old bunk beds, they had been pushed against the walls and their old table had been set in the center of the room with a scale model of the Citadel sticking out from the middle. Clustered around it were Andren, Curatio, J'anda, Vaste and Alaric. Upon seeing them, the discussion halted.

Curatio greeted them with a smile. "Good to see you both – Cyrus, you're looking much better."

Alaric stood before him, helm placed on the table. The paladin's good eye surveyed the warrior, and a slight smile creased the lines on the Ghost's face. "It is good to see you, brother. I feared that I might have sent you to your death."

"It'll take more than a few months of hard work to kill me." Cyrus smiled as he strode in, Vara at his side, to join them at the table. "What's our plan?"

"As I was telling them, we have people here and here." Vaste pointed at two spots around the Citadel. "A few more are spread out in something of a roving patrol, and we'll increase our activity tonight."

"Do we have any idea how they penetrated the security at the Museum in Pharesia?" Cyrus asked as he looked around the table.

"Other than entering from the roof?" Vaste quipped.

"I mean the mystical security Nyad mentioned? Barriers and whatnot?" Cyrus said with a sigh.

"No." Curatio shook his head. "Although with their hands on the number of godly weapons they have, it would not be difficult for them to breach any mystical barrier, regardless of size." The elf looked sick. "I hadn't considered that."

"What do you mean?" Cyrus looked at him blankly.

Curatio steadied himself on the edge of the table, suddenly very pale. "All the magics of our world can be harnessed and used by spell casters to varying effects. Whether it's a druid, wizard, healer, dark knight or paladin, they all have different spells that harness the magics inherent in our world."

The elf looked around the table, pupils dilated, eyes wide. "The weapons that they've been capturing have an advantage because they're not from our world – they're from the gods. Those weapons can cut through any barrier put up by anyone on our planet. They were created by the gods transferring some of their own power – their own godhood – into the weapon. Our magic is no match," the healer finished with a sad finality.

"So why didn't they just cut their way through the front door if the weapons are so powerful?" Vaste asked.

"I doubt that whoever is gathering these weapons would dare to risk any of their acquisitions in a frontal assault when they now have the power to bypass the mystical barriers and the stealth to avoid a confrontation." Alaric leaned forward over the table, scouring the miniature streets.

"What's the point of having these weapons if you're not going to have a confrontation?" Andren mumbled.

"I'm sure they will," Alaric said with a rueful smile. "But at a time and place of their choosing, not ours."

"So the defenses for Reikonos are weaker than Pharesia's?" Cyrus looked at Alaric and Curatio in turn.

Curatio nodded, still pale. "Correct."

"So why take that one first?" Cyrus asked.

"No idea," Alaric shook his head.

"Should we consider sending an envoy to warn the dragons?" Vaste asked. "They may have the only other weapon still out there."

"They do not," came a familiar voice from the doorway. Cyrus turned to see a dark elf, axe slung behind him. The familiar smile was not present on the face of Terian Lepos as he crossed from the doorway to the table.

"I have asked for Terian's assistance in this matter," Alaric said, diffusing the surprise around the table. "He is well informed when it comes to the affairs of dragonkin; much more informed than anyone I have ever met."

"Yes, I'm still wondering how that is," Cyrus said with a smile.

"I'm friends with a few wurms – that's w-u-r-m," the dark elf said with a dazzling smile, aimed directly at Vara, who had already opened her mouth to say something and looked crestfallen. "The Scepter of Fire was stolen from them months ago, disappearing at roughly the same time as our old friend Kalam."

"What are the odds?" Cyrus said.

"Very good odds," Terian said, "when you consider that he was still highly placed in the dragon government, and would have had access to the weapon in question."

Andren looked around the table. "So did he have it when we killed him?"

Terian shrugged. "I don't know. When I checked his hoard

with the other Alliance officers, I didn't see anything that resembled it."

Cyrus froze. "Wait. The Hammer of Earth was traded during an Alliance invasion, the Staff of Death disappeared before or during one, and now possibly the Scepter of Fire? I'm not a big believer in coincidence."

Alaric folded his arms and deep creases knotted his forehead. "This does not bode well for the Alliance if someone from within is involved in this plot."

Terian snorted. "As though you trusted them to begin with."

Vara slammed her fist onto the table. "I have never seen clearer evidence of Goliath's treachery!"

"We don't know for certain that Goliath is involved – or even if any of their members are involved," Curatio said with alarm. "After all, the Warblade disappeared the night before our strike on Kortran. It could be someone from any of our guilds."

Vaste raised an eyebrow, and for the first time Cyrus looked close enough at the troll to realize he had a new scar running down his forehead, a little dash of angry green standing out from the rest of his skin. "Or the entirety of one of the guilds."

Alaric looked around the table, trying to meet the eyes of each of them in turn. "Or it could be none of them. I prefer to give them the benefit of the doubt on this occasion." The paladin cracked his knuckles. "Assigning blame would be pointless at this moment. We need to spend our time and energies on defending the last of the weapons."

Vara crossed her arms. "There is a limited amount we can do, is there not? Can we place sentries inside the Citadel?"

Alaric shook his head. "No. The Council of Twelve is unwilling to let us involve ourselves in their internal security matters. They will not bar us from placing our people outside the Citadel, but neither do they wish us to 'step on their toes'."

Vaste stared at the diorama on the table. "How many people can we place around the Citadel?"

Curatio answered. "We have about a hundred in Reikonos right now; another fifty from Pharesia once they're out of jail some time this afternoon," he added. "We've got about fifty or so still back at Sanctuary, trying to get our new prospects up to speed. Which is going slowly because we're spending so much time on these endeavors."

Alaric stared hard at the Citadel model in the middle of the table. "I think I can safely say that regardless of the outcome here we will need those new recruits soon." His eyes looked up to Curatio across the table. "Old friend, I need you to return to Sanctuary and speed up the training of our new adventurers. Don't bother to have our comrades that are leaving Pharesia join us here: I want them back at Sanctuary aiding you."

Curatio nodded. "I'll leave immediately." With a nod from Alaric, the healer cast the return spell and faded away.

"You're not giving up on protecting the spear, are you?" Vara asked the Ghost.

Alaric shook his head. "No, but we are unprepared for the next step and I doubt we'll need an army here."

"What is the next step if we fail to protect Amnis?" Cyrus asked.

Alaric's jaw tightened and he remained silent for a long moment. "The next step is facing whoever has these weapons when they make themselves known. And for that," the knight said with some reluctance, "we will require an army."

Chapter 34

They debated a course of action until sundown, when Alaric ordered everyone out of the old guildhall and to their stations around the Citadel. Cyrus knelt on a rooftop facing the towering spire. Vaste sat behind him a few feet, as did Andren and Niamh. Vara and J'anda were to either side of him. Cyrus surveyed the streets around the Citadel, his eyes seeing nothing but the city guards and members of Sanctuary. "Thanks for the frost stone," he said to J'anda. "I wish the moon would come out from behind the clouds."

The enchanter nodded. "All the better if it actually helps you see the thief."

Vara turned to glare at them. "Maintain silence," she hissed. "Our success is entirely predicated on the enemy not knowing we're here, so shut up!"

"You'd think someone in Pharesia would have thought to station someone on a roof watching their museum," Vaste said in a low rumble from behind them.

"High-born elves don't possess a great deal of what you would call 'common' sense," Andren said between swigs. "They rely on us lowborns to move their society forward while they watch. Amazing they're still in charge of anything, really."

Vara said nothing but Cyrus could see her roll her eyes.

Long moments passed in silence as the five of them scanned the nearby rooftops. Cyrus looked at the horizon, but the structures of Reikonos created an uneven skyline.

The Citadel was a spire that reached into the sky with a base as big around as any ten shops, perfectly rounded in structure. It stretched into the air to the height of thirty stories or more, the tallest building in Arkaria. At the top of the Citadel a bulbous expansion jutted out, wider than the tower that supported it, giving it the look of an exceptionally long neck with a rounded head at the top. Cyrus knew from rumor that within the top floors was contained the meeting room for Council of Twelve that ran Reikonos and the Human Confederation.

"How old is the Citadel?" Vaste said. "It's so unlike the other buildings in this city and so much taller."

"It's older than Reikonos," Andren said. "And older than me. The humans built the city around it."

"Am I right in thinking that the spear would have to be on the top floors?" Cyrus said, refocusing their attention on the matter at hand.

Vaste grunted, but Vara answered before the troll could. "Seems likeliest, doesn't it?"

Cyrus turned to face them. "If you were going to get someone into the top of that building, how would you do it?"

A moment of silence preceded the answers. "I'd take a flying mount, like a griffon," Vaste answered first.

"Falcon's Essence," Niamh said.

"Invisibility spell." Andren took the flask out of his mouth to answer.

"We can see through invisibility, you knucklehead," Vara shot back.

"Hopefully we can see someone flying toward the tower or a griffon if it approaches as well," Cyrus said. "Any other ideas?"

"An invisible person on an invisible griffon flying toward the tower?" suggested Andren half-seriously. Vara did not respond.

"If the Citadel were smaller," J'anda said, "perhaps a rope to climb." The enchanter looked at the structure. "But I think that even the strongest of warriors would have great difficulty ascending that height without falling."

Cyrus looked at the Citadel with skepticism. "I'd have to agree. Any elf, human, dark elf, gnome, dwarf or other race would have a hell of a time climbing a rope to the top."

They lapsed into silence. Something about that last exchange bothered Cyrus, tickling at the back of his mind. As he was considering it, the moon finally appeared from behind the clouds above them. A glint of something caught his eye in the moonlight. He looked closer. A strand was shining from one of the higher rooftops, leading up to the top floors of the tower and ending at one of the windows. Before he could say anything, a shadowed figure appeared from the window and began to descend in a line toward the rooftop below.

"There!" Cyrus hissed, finger extended to the rapidly descending shadow. An elongated rod was visible from the silhouette. "Whoever it is, they've got the Spear!" Changing his focus to Andren: "Get down to our troops on the street; get the rangers on their bows. Niamh, imbue him!" Without a word the healer ran toward the edge of the rooftop, running off just as Niamh's spell took hold. "J'anda, see if you can mesmerize –" Cyrus tossed over his shoulder as he and Vara charged over the edge of the rooftop, Vaste and Niamh following on their trail.

"ALARUM!" came a shout from the street below. "ALARUM!" Lamps were shining up toward them now, and other voices were taking up the cry of, "ALARUM!"

Cyrus sprinted as hard as he could, legs pumping and feet carrying him forward as he jumped from rooftop to rooftop. He kept his eyes fixed on the silhouette moving down the rope, much more quickly than he could have imagined. He jumped and his hands caught the edge of the last rooftop, pulling himself up as the silhouette reached the end of its crawl. Cyrus drew his sword and heard Vara behind him doing the same. The silhouette unfurled from the rope and a sudden realization filled the warrior's senses: it was not human-shaped at all. Eight legs set down upon the rooftop and two pincers clicked on the spear they grasped between them as the spider before him evaluated Cyrus. It was half his size and looked damnably familiar.

Cyrus charged and the spider bolted, crossing the rooftop in the opposite direction, spear clutched between its pincers, slung back over its torso. It slid across to the next rooftop on another thread of silk, and descended another after that, moving so quickly down the thread that Cyrus had difficulty keeping up, leaping from building to building. Vara was breathing heavily at his side, and considerably behind him the panting of Vaste was audible, as was the THUMP whenever the troll jumped to the next building. They crested another rooftop to find the spider descending from a one-story building into an alleyway.

Eight legs scampered along quickly, and Cyrus jumped to the street, bouncing off a wall and rolling to his feet. The spider turned a corner and dashed into the slums, but cut the corner a bit too short; Vara managed a slice that took off one of the furry legs at the second joint. The arachnid screeched in pain but did not slow.

"Seven legs to go," Vara said under her breath.

"ALARUM!" Cyrus heard shouted behind him as he pounded through the dark of the slums, dodging merchant carts that were closed for the night. The spider was desperate now, and skittered into one of the open plazas in the heart of the slums. A cloaked figure stood waiting, hand extended toward the spider, which raced toward it and threw the Spear of Water from its pincers toward the figure, who caught it deftly and swirled into the magical current of a return spell.

The spider turned to face them, hissing as he and Vara circled the arachnid. They both attacked at the same time and the spider turned to meet him, driving its large pincers into the joint of his armor as he slammed his sword into its exposed thorax. He let out a grunt as the pain hit him. Searing, it climbed up his side as he drove his blade deeper. His eyes locked on Vara, who was attacking the spider with her sword from behind, taking advantage of Cyrus keeping it pinned in place. Her eyes did not meet his, so focused was she on dismembering the arachnid one slice at a time.

Cyrus felt his legs buckle and he fell over from the weight of the spider and the pain in his side. He twisted his sword, trying to carve as much damage as he could. The pounding of plated boots to his left ended with an axe and a sword perforating the crawler. He barely felt it when the spider's pincers relinquished their hold on him and he fell to the ground. Vara was at his side, hand glowing. "It's all right," she said, eyes rimmed with concern. Alaric and Terian stood behind her, throwing the spider's remains off of him.

Vaste and Niamh rounded the corner then, walking on air, and the healer muttered a few words. The blood stopped flowing from Cyrus's side, but the pain did not disappear. Vara helped him to his feet and he looked at the dead arachnid with the others.

"Next time you're going to do a rooftop chase," Niamh said, eyes flaring, "wait until I give you Falcon's Essence first?"

"Unbelievable," Vaste said. "We actually catch the thief, in the act of the escape, and it turns out to be a spider." The troll frowned. "What's a spider going to do with a weapon forged by the gods?"

"Not a damned thing," Terian said, voice bitter. "They can't even use it."

"We saw the spider hand it off to some figure in a cloak," Vara said breathlessly.

"Did you get a look at them?" Vaste's eyes widened in hope.

"No." Vara shook her head.

"Doesn't matter," Cyrus said, his face a mask. "I know who's gathering them now." His head swiveled to Vara. "Go find our

people around the Citadel and get them out of there before we
have a repeat of Pharesia. Tell them to meet up with Niamh here
within the hour." He turned to Niamh. "I need you to get us back
to Sanctuary immediately: we have preparations to make." He bit
his lip. "It's going to be much worse than we thought."

Chapter 35

An hour later Cyrus and the rest of the officers of Sanctuary were seated around the Conference table. Alaric stared at the warrior, fingers steepled in front of him. "Are you finished being dramatic?"

Cyrus smiled. "You want to know who it is, don't you?"

The paladin's eyebrow raised in amusement. "I do."

Vara sat to Alaric's left, arms on the table. "I'm puzzled as to how you supposedly figured this out."

Cyrus looked at the elf, his eyes locked onto hers. "I'm surprised you haven't."

She spread her arms. "Enlighten me."

"Remember the day we met?" he asked with a smile.

She blew air from her lips. "I do. The sun was shining, the trees were swaying in the breeze, sulfur filled the air and I saved your arse from a dragon."

"And a horde of spiders," Niamh said with a note of surprise.

"Exactly. The Dragonlord was served by a horde of spiders like the one we killed in the slums." Cyrus leaned forward. "The day we faced Ashan'agar, he offered me whatever I wanted if I would become his servant. He showed me a vision of the Serpent's Bane, the hilt of my sword along with some of his other treasures. One of them was a flaming staff."

"Torris?" Terian said from the end of the table. "So he had it even then?"

"He did," Cyrus said. "Kalam gave it to him and was waiting around until Ashan'agar had the other pieces he needed."

"I still don't understand what a dragon is planning to do with all those weapons," Curatio said with a blank expression. "It's not as though he can use them, can he?"

"Not in the physical sense, no," Cyrus said. "But you were the one who gave me the reason for why Ashan'agar would be collecting them."

"I did?" Curatio said with a confused look.

"You did. Remember when you told us that the godly magic within the weapon could be used to breach the magical barriers that the elves had set up in the Museum of Arms?"

"Which they did so they could collect the Scimitar of Air." Curatio nodded. "I still don't understand."

"The barrier," Terian said in a choked voice. "The one that the dragons erected; the one that keeps Ashan'agar imprisoned."

"You got it," Cyrus said. "Dragon magic versus the essence of the gods – who wins?"

"That barrier is going down," the dark elf murmured.

"Why would he need more than one of the weapons?" Niamh looked around in confusion. "Wouldn't one be enough to drop the barrier?"

Terian shook his head. "Maybe not. Dragons are the longest lived creatures in Arkaria –"

"With the exception of the elvish old ones," Niamh teased.

Terian ignored her. "Their magic is ancient, and Ashan'agar was sealed in by not one but thirty of the wisest and most powerful dragons. Some of the spells they used included charms to warn the dragons should Ashan'agar attempt to breach the barrier. One of the dragons – Ehrgraz – is the chief of their army, and every dragon fears him."

"Because he's afraid one dragon might be warned he puts off his escape by six months until he can collect all the weapons?" Vara looked at Terian with undisguised skepticism.

Terian looked around the table. "He would have been the first to be warned if Ashan'agar was trying to escape and I promise you that the Dragonlord was trying to avoid confrontation with Ehrgraz. Six months is nothing to a dragon; he would have waited sixty years if it meant being able to escape without facing Ehrgraz."

"So the Dragonlord has plotted an escape," Alaric mused. "What will he do when he reaches the surface?"

"Without Kalam to act as his herald," Terian said, suddenly thoughtful, "he's going to have to go to the southern lands and marshal his loyalists." The dark knight shrugged. "After that, I would guess his followers will move north and create a new kingdom."

"Why wouldn't he fight for control of Hewat?" Vaste said. "I mean, he was in charge before, wasn't he?"

"He was," Terian said. "But he wasn't interested in starting a conflict with the other dragons. They don't war amongst themselves; it's anathema to them." He looked around the table.

"With a hundred dragons on his side, he could destroy the all the major northern cities and make his own kingdom here." Terian leaned back. "The only one keeping things in check in the dragon kingdom is their new leader. He's a moderate in that he's not totally focused on annihilating all life but dragons."

"All right." Alaric nodded. "I think we get the idea of what the threat is and where it will be coming from. Now what do we do?" He turned to Cyrus.

The warrior took a deep breath. "We need every single person in Sanctuary for this one."

Alaric raised an eyebrow. "You will have the support of every able body."

The warrior took another deep breath. "We also need our allies if they're willing."

A grimace lit the Ghost's face. "We will send messengers. I do not think we should wait for responses to move into action."

"Agreed," Vara said. "The northern lands could be in flames before Goliath decides to move."

"True." Cyrus nodded. "We move our entire force into the Mountains of Nartanis, now. All our veterans we bring down into the fire caves and leave the new inductees up top."

Curatio blinked. "You don't think we'll need them down below?"

Cyrus shook his head. "With the head start Ashan'agar has, I doubt we'll be down there for long – assuming he hasn't left already. We need to move now."

Alaric nodded. "So ordered. Niamh, get the word to our allies and meet us in the mountains."

They broke from Council and an alarm sounded, blowing horns and voices filled the corridors as the entire force of Sanctuary mobilized. Cyrus found himself next to Alaric on his way down the stairs.

"I would have you lead the force that is going into the caves," the paladin said, taking the steps three at a time.

"I assumed you would," Cyrus said, voice tight.

"I trust you to do your best," Alaric said. "You have my full confidence. Curatio and I will shepherd the inductees above ground until you return."

Cy blinked. "Thank you, Alaric. I'll do my best to make sure your confidence is well founded."

"It is," the Ghost muttered, so low Cyrus could only just hear it.

Within ten minutes nearly everyone was assembled in the foyer. Alaric stood before them on the balcony above the entryway and addressed them all.

"We face now the Dragonlord, a treacherous foe. Our time is short so I shall not belabor the point: our most experienced fighters will go into the depths of his den while the rest of our army remains above in case the battle should spill onto the surface. Cyrus?"

The warrior stepped forward. "Our worst case scenario involves the Dragonlord making it out of his den. If that should happen, we must keep him contained in the mountains and engaged in battle continuously. When the barrier goes down, the dragons of the south will receive a warning. Our objective is to kill him if possible but at least keep him occupied until they can arrive to deal with him. Should he escape..." The warrior's words drifted off. "Say goodbye to your homes and families."

A burst of alarm ran through the crowd. "Let us away, my friends." Alaric gestured toward the sky. Druid teleportation spells filled the room and the forces of Sanctuary disappeared in a hurricane of sound.

Chapter 36

The Mountains of Nartanis appeared and Cyrus felt the hot air around them. He looked to the army appearing at his back. "Veterans, this way. New folks, stay here." Without waiting for a reply, he headed west, boots crunching on the volcanic gravel.

"Not wasting any time, I see," came a voice from his right. He turned to see Vara, long legs straining to match his pace and jogging every few steps to keep up.

"We don't have any to waste," he replied. A look back confirmed that the force had split and part of it was following him. On the horizon was the cave entrance, nestled in the shadows of a cliff. "I need someone to help me see in the dark," he said and felt a flash of light enter his vision. "This way," he gestured and was on the move again.

"Short walk from the druid portal," Vaste said from behind him. "I'm surprised this cave doesn't get more visitors."

"Would you want to stumble into a dragon's den for entertainment?" Andren said.

"Of course I would. It's the reason I'm here." He paused. "Besides saving your sorry asses from imminent death. And possibly the world as well," he added.

"You seem a bit different since you got back from troll country," Andren said. "What happened?"

"You mean other than being beaten to the brink of death by my own people for trying to recruit some of them to come to Sanctuary?"

Cyrus could hear a momentary stutter in Andren's reply. "Yeah... other than that."

"I was saved by a shaman, one of the few magic users still among our tribe, and he taught me a few things."

"Such as?" J'anda's voice entered the conversation.

"I suspect you'll see very soon," the troll said.

"Love the suspense," Andren grunted.

Cyrus motioned for quiet behind him as they reached a fork in the path. He knelt as his eyes focused on each of the two tunnels before them.

"Do you remember which way to go?" Vara whispered in his

ear. Her hand rested on his shoulder, and her breath washed over him in a warm wave.

"I do." Cyrus frowned. "But where does the other path lead, and might it be faster?"

"Time is of the essence," she whispered back. "Perhaps explore some other time."

"Very well." He nodded. He charged down the passageway without further comment, bursting into a wide cavern with webbing in the corners of the chamber.

"All too familiar," Vara said from behind him.

"Yeah. Go stand in the shadows over there and it'll be just like the day we met – except this time I can actually see you."

"You couldn't see me that day?" she asked, surprised.

"Not until you jumped on the dragon," he said, watching for danger in the four corners of the cavern. He pointed at his eyes. "Human eyesight. Not as good as yours."

She nodded. "I didn't think about that."

"I'm surprised we haven't run into any resistance yet. But we didn't last time either." He frowned at the hole in the ceiling. "Better move quickly to the bridge ahead." They exited the room and found themselves on the bridge leading across the lava. "Where are the rock giants?" Cyrus chewed his lower lip. "Keep moving forward," he ordered with a shout over his shoulder.

"I hope our new recruits are all right," Nyad said from behind Cyrus.

"With Alaric and Curatio leading them, I'm sure they'll be fine," Andren said.

They crossed the final bridge into the chamber of Ashan'agar without incident. Nothing stood between them and the entrance to his platform. Cyrus stuck his head around the archway and breathed a short sigh of relief. The dragon stood beyond, along with the black-cloaked figure. Six weapons floated around the mysterious figure as chanting filled the air. There was a crackle of magic between the weapons, and Cyrus felt it before he saw it: a flash as a wave of energy filled the cavern, emanating from the cloaked figure. Cyrus dropped to a knee and grasped at the edge of the bridge to avoid being knocked off his feet.

"Unless I miss my guess," Vara said under her breath, "we were about ten seconds too late."

Cyrus gritted his teeth. "He's not out yet." Stepping out into the open of the Dragonlord's platform, Cyrus yelled at

Ashan'agar. "How far you have fallen – from Dragonlord of Hewat to a petty thief, stealing other people's treasures!"

The dragon's red scales stood out against the darkened cave walls around them. "I steal to garner my freedom," the Dragonlord bristled. "And I am far from petty in my thievery." The dragon's face turned toward Cyrus, as did the black-cloaked figure. "Petty thieves steal trinkets and purses; I have engineered the theft of priceless relics of the gods." The face of the dragon honed in on Cyrus, and the warrior could see the dragon's right eye was missing, an angry scar running between the scales toward the Dragonlord's snout.

"I see better than you do since last we met," Cyrus taunted. "You've become a low form of life, trying to warp the minds of others to your will so you can escape this well-deserved prison." Cyrus nodded to those behind him and the forces of Sanctuary began to spread out, encircling the platform.

"I have not needed to bend the will of my most recent servants," came the near-indignant reply. "They," he gestured to the figure in the black cloak, "have come to me willingly, offering their services for a price.

"You should have joined me." The Dragonlord looked back at Cyrus. "Today is the dawn of a new order, one which will see me as Dragonlord of the northern lands, and soon enough, all Arkaria. Dragonkin," Ashan'agar's eye narrowed, "are a superior race, and those of you who survive will be ruled by us."

"Where are your spiders and rock giants to defend you now?" he taunted the dragon.

"They are dealing with your rabble on the surface," the dragon said. A cold chill ran up Cyrus's spine and a cackle filled the cavern as the black-cloaked figure climbed onto the back of the dragon and the wings began to flap.

"Attack!" Cyrus shouted. The force of Sanctuary assaulted Ashan'agar from all sides. Vara leapt forward through the air as Cyrus experienced a moment of deja vu – brought to a halt when the dragon's wing extended, blunting her sword thrust and blocking her landing. She impaled the dragon's right wing, stabbing through the shallow tissue and out the other side. Her feet failed to find purchase, leaving the paladin hanging in mid-air, holding onto her sword.

Cyrus rushed forward, plunging his blade much more skillfully than he had a year prior, finding purchase between the scales of the dragon's foot. Spells crackled in the air around him and the dragon roared. A burst of flames shot past Cyrus and across the chamber. *I hope that didn't hit anyone,* he thought. He looked back to see people scurrying out of the way, a few narrowly dodging the fire.

He twisted his blade and pulled up, dislodging one of the scales as the dragon let out another shriek. Cyrus sheathed his sword and dug his gauntlets into the space between the scales of the dragon as he began to climb the Dragonlord's leg. A quick look over his shoulder confirmed Vara was still hanging from the wing.

The ground began to recede as the dragon flew toward the top of the cave. "Wizards! Evacuate to the portal!" Cyrus shouted to the army below. He scrambled, climbing up the dragon's shoulder. Upon reaching the wing, he wrapped his arms around it and clutched as hard as he could. "Vara!" he shouted over his shoulder. "Hang on!"

A jarring shook the warrior as the Dragonlord struck the ceiling of the cavern, claws digging in. Cyrus could hear the crumbling of the roof as the dragon smashed against solid rock at the ceiling of the cave. The sound of cracking stone filled his ears and boulders began to drop as the dragon hung upside down and clawed, throwing aside dirt and rock. Cyrus held onto the wing, protected from the falling rock by it.

A burst of sunlight filtered down and Ashan'agar's head snaked toward it. A roar of triumph filled the air as the Dragonlord wrenched himself through the hole he had created, widening it and dropping more and more rocks into the chamber below.

Cyrus could only bear to look down for a moment, but in that moment he saw the ceiling of the cavern beginning to collapse. The platform below was strewn with rubble. *Please, Bellarum, let them all have made it out,* Cyrus thought. The ground shook around him and Ashan'agar burst into the air, flapping his mighty wings and tasting the sky for the first time in years.

Cyrus climbed the shoulder of the Dragonlord, hoisting himself onto the back of Ashan'agar as Vara worked her way along the wing toward the back of the dragon. The black-cloaked figure was clutching the dragon's neck. Without much thought, Cyrus grabbed the edge of the cloak and tugged on it as he drew his sword. The dragon bucked and inverted, costing Cyrus the grip on his sword as he struggled to find something to hold onto. He saw Vara, hanging on the wing and a black cloak fluttering as he fell to the ground below.

There was a sickening crunch as Cyrus hit the rocks and bounced a few feet in the air, only to come down on his right arm. A snapping noise came beneath the armor, drawing a cry of pain. He rolled down a slope of magmatic rock and dust to come to rest at the bottom of a hill. He blinked and looked up. The Dragonlord was gone, having flown out of sight. The black cloak was fluttering through the air; the figure it was enshrouding nowhere to be seen.

"Hail," came a voice from above him. Orion was on the hilltop, looking down.

"Ah, there you are," Cyrus said. "Wondered when you'd turn up."

Orion grinned. "Knew I was coming, did you?"

"I did."

"Because of the call to the allies?"

"No," Cyrus grunted as he rolled over and used his good arm to boost himself to a sitting position. "Because you're a servant of the Dragonlord."

The smile disappeared from the ranger's face and his bow was out and raised. "How did you know?"

"Not so fast," Cyrus said with a grin, holding his bad arm with the good. "I'm not the only one that fell from your master. Selene fell with me, and I saw where she landed. If she died and you kill me you'll never find her in time to revive her."

The bow was drawn back, pointed at Cyrus's head. "Tell me where she fell." The ranger drew his bow back further.

"I can show you. Why don't we take a walk?" Cyrus grimaced from pain in his ankle as he forced himself to his feet. "I do have to ask... why?"

Orion scoffed. "You know why." The ranger kept the arrow pointed at Cyrus as the warrior began a slow shuffle up a nearby hill. "Because the Dragonlord can give me everything I've ever wanted. He will rule our world."

"He will wipe out every living being in order to make way for a new dragon kingdom," Cyrus said. "Ever heard of the Ashen Wastelands? Hundreds of miles of dust and fire? That's their home."

"He can't wipe out every living thing," Orion said. "But you're right: the major cities, like Reikonos, Pharesia, Saekaj – they'll burn. There will be nothing left of them as he builds his empire."

"I guess millions of dead don't matter as long as you have a new pair of chainmail pants." Cyrus shifted his weight from his left foot to the right to alleviate his pain. "The night I ran into you in the markets, that was from what he paid you – after you liberated Ferocis from Kortran for him?"

Orion raised an eyebrow in surprise. "You're good at guessing today. How did you know?"

Cyrus shrugged. "I've been with Sanctuary for a year now and I know what our stipend is. I also know that the only bonus you've seen from spoils of war was after I led the assault on Kalam. I've never seen the kind of money that would pay for chainmail like that. So after leaving me in Reikonos Square that first day, you caught a ride back to the square with a Sanctuary teleporter, paid someone for a lift to the mountains and strolled right into the lair of Ashan'agar and offered your services. He didn't even have to coerce you with magic like he tried to do to me."

Orion smiled. "What can I say? I'm motivated, and the price was right."

"And the price was?"

The ranger's smile widened. "The best equipment that money can't buy and all the gold I need for what it can."

Cyrus grunted. "Not enough. So why stick with Sanctuary after that? Why go to Goliath later?" The warrior shook his head, trying to brush out the cobwebs from the fall. He was having trouble seeing straight and he began to sway. "Why not just leave and follow your Dragonlord full time? You might have gotten him free even faster."

The ranger's eyes looked left to right. "And what if he didn't?" Orion shook his head. "No, I had to keep my options open until I knew we could deliver all the pieces. If we had failed, the reprisal would have been stiff and I'd have needed allies to help protect me."

"So how did you convince the goblins of Enterra to part with the Hammer?" Cy's eyes narrowed.

"I didn't." Orion looked around. "One of the Dragonlord's other servants struck a deal with them and also delivered the Staff of Death."

"Who was it?" Cy stopped as he felt his throat go dry.

"It's not my place to tell." Orion grimaced. "I didn't know about that servant until after Enterra."

"Would you have still led the expedition to Enterra if you had known the other servant would get the Hammer?" Cy eyed the ranger, measuring every word.

"Yes," Orion said, expression neutral. "The Dragonlord's other servant only acquired the Hammer because he betrayed us and gave the goblins..." His voice trailed off. "...what they were looking for."

"Which is?"

Orion's eyes narrowed. "Where's Selene?"

"This way," Cy resumed walking, pushing the thought of Narstron aside for a moment. "And in the Realm of Death? The Staff?"

"I told you, I didn't take it," Orion snapped. "Information was not forthcoming. The Dragonlord kept us in the dark."

"But you managed to steal Amnis and Ventus from two of the most guarded locations in Arkaria?"

Orion's eyes lit up. "Do you know how difficult those were to mastermind? Two of the most difficult sites in the world to break into, and we stole from both flawlessly.

"Reikonos was the toughest," the ranger said. "That's why we saved it until last. The elves, they're so arrogant and sure of their magics, they left their barriers as the only line of defense. And they should be proud – their barriers were much more powerful than the ones in Reikonos – not that it mattered." He chuckled. "Once Ashan'agar finally told us to use one of the weapons to breach the barrier, it was easy. Selene went in with the spider, broke the barrier and teleported herself out.

"In Reikonos, it was a different story," Orion said, relishing his superiority. "We both had to be there – I had to sound the alarm so you and the Reikonos soldiers would follow the spider, allowing Selene to escape and retrieve the spear from our eight-legged distraction." He chuckled. "It would have been a lot easier if I could have cast the return spell like Selene can." A grim look filled the ranger's eyes. "Where is she?"

"Close," Cyrus said. "I'm just trying to draw things out a bit, because once you find her, you have no reason to keep me alive."

Orion's face relaxed, and an expression of regret filled the human's features. "I wish you'd have joined us in Reikonos when I asked you to. You are the best warrior I've ever seen and with the power that Ashan'agar's gifts would grant you, we could have formed a guild that would be unstoppable. You would have had the best armor and weapons on Arkaria. The warriors of Amarath's Raiders and Endeavor would have begged at your feet for you to tell them how to be as great as you."

Light filled the ranger's eyes, and he lowered his voice. "These weapons, they could give us the power to slay the dragons – we could literally save the world, and no one from our guilds would have to know." Orion smiled. "We'd be heroes. We could write our own ticket – to Burnt Offerings, to Endeavor, Amarath's Raiders, our own guild, whatever. People would follow us. Those weapons grant power undreamed of in this age – enough to allow you to satisfy whatever ambitions you might have."

"You mean the weapons buried at the bottom of a hundred tons of rock and mountain?" Cyrus said with a hint of a smile.

Orion blinked. "No. You're kidding."

"The Dragonlord broke the barrier and charged out through the ceiling of his cavern, like some sort of crazed bird hatching out of the ground." Cyrus raised his hands in surrender. "He left them behind, buried."

The ranger's face contorted in seeming pain. "I guess the only way left is –"

"An eternity of service to the Dragonlord?" Cyrus said in a mocking voice, still trying to climb in spite of the pain in his extremities.

Orion's face hardened. "I didn't think you'd be wise enough to accept my bargain after refusing the Dragonlord once and me once, but now," a smile creased the tanned features of the ranger, "I cannot let you live. I warned you about falling into the trap of Alaric's nobility and where it would lead. You could have been the most powerful warrior in the world; instead your corpse will rot undiscovered in the mountains."

The crunching of gravel behind the warrior heralded the arrival of Selene. Pale and waxy, she looked like she had barely survived the fall.

Cyrus felt a sudden rush as his wounds healed. The blood that had been oozing out of the joints of his gauntlet stopped, his arm knitted together and his head cleared. Without a moment's hesitation he lunged forward, slapping aside the arrow pointed at his head as it flew from the bow and missed him by centimeters. Selene screamed at his side as Cyrus drove his head forward, knocking the ranger's helmet aside. A satisfying crunch told him he had broken Orion's nose.

He brought his head down again and again, both hands restraining the ranger's as he drove the edge of his helmet into the ranger's face. The crack of bones breaking, the sickening sound of flesh being hit by metal registered over and over again in his ears. Orion's arms went limp in his grasp.

Cyrus stood, blood dripping down his face and locked his gaze on Selene, who charged him, arms flailing in mute rage. He dropped his shoulder, catching her in her breastbone. Another cracking sound filled his ears, then the wheezing sound of Selene struggling for a breath. He flipped her easily over his back and she hit the ground with a satisfying *THUMP!*

"You could have put Orion down a little faster," came a voice from behind him. He turned, wary. Vaste's hands came up in surrender. "Or you could have lied to him and told him you wanted to join him. That would have been smart; maybe even saved your life." The troll frowned. "Why didn't you tell him what he wanted to hear?"

Cyrus smiled blankly. "I'm just a warrior. I don't have much use for lying. Thanks for the mending spell. It was well timed." A sound from behind him drew his attention back to Orion and Selene. The healer had crawled to her husband and they both disappeared in the light of her return spell. "Damn..."

Vaste shrugged. "We have a dragon and an army of his cronies to deal with. Settle personal scores later."

"They're responsible for letting that dragon out!" Cyrus said. "They set this whole mess in motion!"

"Focus on the threat to the world, man!" the troll shouted. "Vara's still riding the Dragonlord. I saw them fly over a few minutes ago –"

A whooshing sound overhead surprised Cyrus. "Good timing." The scales of the dragon flew low over his head. "HEY!" he shouted at top volume. "HEY, ONE-EYE!"

Ashan'agar tilted his head back to peer at the warrior. Vara was holding onto her sword, which was plunged between scales in the dragon's side, her legs wrapped around the dragon's wing. The Dragonlord swept down, coming to a dramatic landing in front of Cyrus, forcing he and Vaste to dodge to the side to avoid being trampled.

"You again." The Dragonlord flung his wings up and down,

finally dislodging Vara. She flew to the side, ricocheted off a nearby boulder and came to rest, unmoving.

"Me again," Cyrus said. "I'm like a bad case of the dragon pox; you just can't get rid of me." His eyes fixated on Vara's sword, still stuck between the scales of the dragon. He dodged forward, rolling under the dragon's wing before Ashan'agar could strike. With a quick reverse, he climbed the back leg and hopped up to grab hold of Ashan'agar's back. "Let's go for a ride."

A frightening laugh filled the air around him. "As you wish," the Dragonlord said as he lifted off from the ground. "I must ask," Ashan'agar said with a quick flick of his head to look at the warrior, now climbing his back. "How did you resist my charm magic? It has been a long time since it has failed to dominate one of your kind..."

"I'll let you know when I figure it out," Cyrus said, pulling Vara's sword from the Dragonlord's back and thrusting it into his belt. Ashan'agar had shifted direction and was flying almost straight up.

"Disappointing," the dragon fired back over the howling wind. "I had assumed you had powers unknown, but perhaps you were just lucky."

"I'm a lucky guy," Cyrus said. "Where are we going?" He was only a few feet from the neck now, but was forced to climb using entirely his upper body strength. One arm length at a time, he scaled the dragon until he reached the neck and wrapped his legs around it, taking some of the weight off his hands. He climbed faster now, hand over hand, up the dragon's long neck, Vara's sword hanging from his belt.

"To your death," the dragon answered with another unsettling cackle. "I will take you where there is no air to breathe. Worry not," he said, soothing. "We'll be there soon enough." The dragon turned his head around to glare at the warrior, who had almost reached his head. The red eye glared at Cyrus. "Where do you think you're going?"

"Getting a closer look at my death," Cyrus said, pulling Vara's sword from his belt and stabbing forward as the dragon dodged out of the first strike and wheeled to the left. *Now you see me*, he thought, a grim smile covering his lips. Cy's fingers dug between the scales and his second thrust penetrated the dragon's single remaining eye. A scream rent the air around him, drowning out the howling wind. *And now you don't.*

Sliding Vara's sword back into his belt, Cyrus grabbed both sides of the dragon's writhing neck and turned him – just a bit – to the right. Unintelligible howls flew from the dragon, along with staccato bursts of flame and curses in the dragon language. The ground whirled beneath them as Cyrus tightened his grasp around the dragon's neck.

Ashan'agar entered a desperate end over end spin toward the ground below. The Dragonlord's wings flapped to little effect; they were going down. "You fool! You will die too and no one will ever find your body!"

"Small price to pay to defend the world." Cy braced himself against the neck of the Dragonlord.

During the descent, Ashan'agar did not cease screaming. The mountains below them were spinning. Cyrus could see masses of people, an army, moving in the hills. It was like he was watching ants. They kept getting bigger and bigger – the Dragonlord flapped his wings – and then they hit the ground –

Chapter 37

The Dragonlord roared somewhere in his mind. Curses rained from Ashan'agar's mouth as Cyrus drew back to consciousness. The warrior blinked, sick to his stomach. He rolled over and surrendered to the nausea, throwing up violently.

"How charming to see you again," came Vara's voice from above him.

Cyrus buried his face in the volcanic ash. "I don't feel well." He rolled to his back. "Resurrection aftereffects, I presume?"

"I assumed you were greeting me in the traditional manner of your people," came Vara's voice once more, laced with equal parts sarcasm and relief, unmistakable even in Cyrus's diminished condition.

"You do make me rather sick sometimes." Cyrus pulled himself to a sitting position. "Alaric," he said in surprise.

"What about him?" Vara replied with irritation.

"He is here," came the deep voice of the Ghost of Sanctuary. The crunching of his feet upon the rocks behind them had been drowned out by the thrashing and cursing of Ashan'agar.

On the ridge above them a ragged cheer could be heard; the Army of Sanctuary began flowing down the hillside en masse. Cyrus picked Elisabeth, Erith, Cass and Tolada out of the crowd of them; the allies had arrived. Curatio was a few steps behind Alaric, as were the rest of the officers of Sanctuary and Andren.

Alaric extended his hand to Cyrus, who took it. The paladin pulled the warrior to his feet with power that the Ghost's wiry frame did not indicate. "I am pleased to see you have survived, my brother."

Cyrus blinked, a bit unsteady. "Not half as pleased as I am." The warrior stared into the army massing behind him. "How did we do?"

Alaric smiled. "We did very well. The forces of the Dragonlord were no match for the reforged Army of Sanctuary and its allies."

Malpravus glided to them from behind Vara. "Most impressive," the necromancer whispered, eyes fixated on the writhing dragon. "Bringing down the Dragonlord by yourself – I did tell you I expected great things from you."

Alaric cleared his throat but Cyrus met the necromancer's gaze. "Two of your guildmates were aiding the Dragonlord in his endeavors. Selene and Orion assisted him in stealing the weapons of the gods and Selene cast the spells that allowed him to break his barrier."

"That is... disconcerting," Malpravus said, so low that Cyrus had to concentrate to hear him. "I will look into these allegations immediately."

"While you're doing that," Cyrus said, "you might look into who stole Letum during our attack on the Realm of Death."

"All in good time. We have a more pressing problem to deal with," Malpravus whispered again. "The Dragonlord yet lives."

"Ah, yes," Alaric breathed. The Ghost strode to the downed dragon, rasping. "Any more venom to spew, Ashan'agar, before the end of your days?"

The dragon stiffened. "Whose voice is that? I know you..."

"I doubt that," Alaric said with a tight smile. "Have you any last words, Dragonlord?"

The mountains were silent for a long moment, and only the rasping of Ashan'agar could be heard. Cyrus stood a few paces behind Alaric, and watched the Dragonlord's side; ribs shattered. In every breath the scaly flesh heaved up and down only with monumental effort.

"Yes," came the rasp of Ashan'agar's voice. The dragon's head turned and Cyrus found himself looking into the pits where the dragon's eyes had been. "I offered you all; you would have been my Sovereign and ruled all the lesser races of Arkaria." A tinge of sadness entered the dragon's voice as he gasped for breath. "I would have given you purpose."

The weakness in Cyrus's knees faded. His jaw set and his spine straightened. "I have a purpose," the warrior intoned.

Without warning, Alaric leapt forward, sword drawn so quickly it was almost imperceptible, and thrust it through the scales of the Dragonlord's head. Cyrus blinked in surprise; the strike had been perfect, sliding between the scales and strong enough to break through the dragon's thick skull. One final scream tore through the Mountains of Nartanis, and then Ashan'agar, the Lord of the Dragons, was finally silent.

Chapter 38

The day after the final battle had dawned especially bright at Sanctuary. Cyrus saw it through the window in the Halls of Healing, where Curatio had urged him to stay overnight. At sunrise, having had his fill of rest, he had argued with the healer until the elf had finally given in and let him leave.

He entered the Great Hall before the usual breakfast time to find a cluster of members sitting around a table in the corner, new faces by far outnumbering the old. Andren waved him over. Amidst handshakes and congratulatory slaps to his back, the warrior made his way over to his oldest friend. "Did we just save the world yesterday?" Andren asked him with a smile.

"I believe we did," Cyrus said with one of his own. "I think we're still wanted in Reikonos, though."

"Bah." Andren waved him off. "We're heroes now; they'll drop the charges."

Cyrus's smile turned sardonic. "I'm sure that's been said a time or two."

Andren's expression turned downward. "I heard Ashan'agar's den got buried – treasure trove and all." The corners of the healer's mouth drew tight, giving him a pained expression. "I guess you lost your sword hilt."

Cyrus sat back and adopted a pensive expression. "The Serpent's Bane?" He frowned. "I didn't even think about it until now, I was so focused on stopping the Dragonlord." A roiling torrent of emotion poured through him; hot regret tempered by a cool realization. "I'll be all right," he said and meant it.

"Did you hear?" Andren looked at him with an expression of wonder. "We captured one of Ashan'agar's rock giants! It talks and everything. They're keeping it in the dungeons below until you Council lot," he waved in Cyrus's direction, "work out what to do with it."

The warrior's eyebrow raised. "A rock giant? Why don't we just kill it and be done?"

Andren shrugged. "Alaric said no. Not sure why."

Cyrus shook his head. "Damn, I am hungry."

"Killing a dragon works up an appetite, eh?"

The two of them laughed their way through breakfast, their first together in months.

"I almost forgot," Cy said as their meal drew to a close. "Orion told me that someone betrayed us to the goblins in order to get the Earth Hammer. I guess the goblins wanted something from our expedition." His jaw tightened. "The same person stole the Staff of Death when we were in Mortus's Realm. They're in the Alliance."

Andren blinked several times. "Do you know who it is?"

"No," Cy exhaled, expression grave. "But I will find out. We owe them – for Narstron."

"For Narstron," Andren said. "And for us."

With a nod, Andren strode out the doors of the Great Hall. Cyrus was congratulated over and over again by mostly familiar faces; people he'd recruited in the last six months who had proven themselves in the crucible of the battle the day before. Their excitement was palpable, their hope for the future buoyed by the realization that they had played a part in saving the world.

Seeking solitude, Cyrus exited through the front door, wandering the still quiet grounds in the light of early morning. He found himself near the gardens and saw a familiar figure on the bridge. Today, her shining armor was once again missing, as was the ponytail. Vara stared at the waterfall across the pond. She was clad in something remarkably close to her attire on the night they had dined together in the elven realms. Her hair shone in the sunrise and a slight smile graced her face – which evaporated to neutrality upon notice of his approach.

"I am pleased to see you are up and moving again," she said with a nod. "I was concerned," she coughed, "that you might not have survived your encounter with the Dragonlord."

His eyes met hers, and she looked away first. "I was more concerned with you. I'd have gotten back to Ashan'agar sooner if I hadn't gotten bushwhacked by Orion." He scowled at the memory.

Vara's brow knit with concern. "I didn't get a chance to ask you, but you and Selene fell quite a distance when the Dragonlord threw you off his back. How did you manage to beat both Orion and Selene? I assume you were," she coughed again, "badly injured," she finished with downcast eyes. "And I know you lost your sword."

"I was injured." Cyrus nodded. "And unarmed. I bought some time by telling Orion that Selene was either injured or dying and telling him that I knew where she was. It bought me enough time for Vaste to find me, right about the time Selene came wandering up. Vaste healed me and I jumped Orion." The warrior paused in thought. "I beat Orion pretty badly. I think I killed him – I'm not sure."

"You held Selene's whereabouts hostage," Vara said, voice neutral.

"You don't approve."

"No, it's not that. My code would prevent me from doing such a thing – deceptive means and all that – but it was quite brilliant. I give you credit for thinking on your feet, injured and unarmed as you were." She frowned. "One thing I don't understand: how did Orion and Vaste find you, in the midst of the mountains?" She thought about it for a moment. "And again, after you fell from Ashan'agar, Vaste found your body."

Cyrus shrugged. "Orion must have seen me fall; he was lurking in the area for some reason." The warrior blinked. "Odd that he would see me fall and not see Selene." Cyrus shrugged again. "Don't reckon I'll get a chance to ask him anytime soon."

Vara still frowned. "But what about Vaste? He was in the middle of the battle with the rest of the army. How did he know where to find you?"

"I don't know." Cy smiled. "I appreciate how hard you must be trying to discuss my actions over the last few days and not come up with something critical and insulting to say."

"I don't mind not insulting you," she said with a deep breath. Her hair hung loose around her shoulders. "It seems to be the sort of habit that grows on you after a while."

"The wager ended yesterday."

"You're aggravatingly daft. I can't believe the best stratagem you could come up with to defeat the Dragonlord involved running him into the ground at terminal velocity." She exhaled, fury spent.

He cocked his eyebrow in deep amusement. "Actually, I lied: the bet ends tomorrow. I win."

"You bastard," she hissed. She glared at him for a moment before a laugh escaped her lips. Her expression softened. "Don't change the subject. You took a very great risk in bringing the Dragonlord crashing to the ground with you on his back."

"First of all," Cyrus said, "he told me he was going to take me up to where there was no air to breathe and kill me – so I really didn't have much of a choice. Second," he said with a tremendous and self-satisfied grin, "I didn't know you cared. You are so up and down – first you seem like you hate me, then you tell me you don't, and that I'm 'a man Sanctuary can rely on' and then you go cold again. Could you find some stability in your reaction to me?"

"I will... try," she said with a thin smile.

"That will do for now." He returned her smile and felt a flush color his cheeks. "I'm still feeling a bit weak..."

"I'm not surprised," she returned, blue eyes locked on his. "You did plummet to your death yesterday. Perhaps you should rest for a while."

He did not break her gaze. It was pleasant, looking into her eyes. "Before I go," he said, and reached into his belt, drawing her sword with a flourish. "I couldn't have done it without this." He turned the sword so that he gripped the blade, pointing the hilt toward her.

She flushed. "Thank you for returning it to me. Could you leave it outside my quarters? I think I'll be out here for a bit longer and I don't want to carry it up when I go."

"Sure." He nodded, waving it in the air to the side of them. "Heavy, but perfectly balanced." He peered at the elaborate carvings on the blade. "It looks old."

She smiled. "It is. You really should rest."

"I think perhaps you're right. I'm going to go sleep for a bit longer." With a sweeping bow that made her giggle behind her hand, he walked away. He looked back once to find her still watching him. Her cheeks blushed and she looked away, back toward the waterfall.

When he reached his chambers, he opened the door to find the lamps already lit. He shut the door and unstrapped his armor, fitting it piece by piece onto the shelves and bust set aside for it. "Where's my helm?" he wondered, then saw it on the bed next to a small parcel. Eyes narrowed in curiosity, he picked it up and unwrapped the small silk ribbon that encircled the box. He pulled the top off of it to find –

– the Serpent's Bane. His eyes widened, and he turned it over and over in his hands, scarcely believing it to be the real thing. He looked into the box once more to find a small note in unfamiliar handwriting that was neat but nondescript.

Just because you give your all
doesn't mean you have to lose it all.

One hand stroked his chin as he stared down at the unsigned note. A smile crept across his face; deep, sincere and spreading from the corners of his mouth as he contemplated the possibilities in front of him.

NOW

Epilogue

Sanctuary stood before him, massive and foreboding. A fog had crept over the plains, blown by the wind. He looked at the ancient gates as he walked through them, feeling like a man stepping into his past, something he'd left far behind. Crumbling stones greeted him on the path to the entrance and the tall wooden doors had been torn from their hinges in the last attack.

The hallowed halls were silent when he walked through them. The foyer was abandoned, dark and filled with shadow. Each footstep was measured, every sensation was catalogued. Remembering the happier times, he cast his eyes to the lounge; scorch marks were all that was to be found there. He strode past the grand doors to the Great Hall. Massive tables overturned, the stained glass windows broken. He felt a pain deep inside and knew it was not physical.

Walking to the staircase, he climbed to nearly the top. Stepping out in front of the Council chamber, the ghost of a smile flitted across his features as he shouldered his way into the room.

It was more damaged than he could have imagined. The table, the rectangular one that had replaced the round one of old, was splinters. Chairs were completely upended or destroyed entirely. Tapestries had been torn from the walls, and the few remaining were not without damage. The windows were completely destroyed, flooding the room with fog and a brilliant view of the shrouded Plains of Perdamun.

Quelling his emotions, the warrior picked his way through the wreckage to far side of the room. He opened the door to the Council Archives, and beheld the smell of old parchment. This was the most intact room he had seen thus far. "Maybe the gods are with me," he said, mocking voice echoing in the empty room.

He rifled through the books until he found one that interested him. Dragging one of the surviving comfortable chairs from the Council Chamber into the Archive, he sat down, opening the book to the first page.

The Journal of Vara – An Account of My Days With Sanctuary

Cyrus browsed the book, skipping through large parts of it, eventually finding what he was looking for.

Today I attended a dragon expedition gone horribly wrong. I was approached while in the markets of Reikonos by one of the most annoying disgraces to the title of paladin that I have ever observed. This bejeweled buffoon observed me in close attendance to Niamh and Orion, as well as Selene and asked if we would assist in mounting a strike upon a dragon in the Mountains of Nartanis.

"I don't think so," I sniffed. I confess, this highborn piece of flotsam irked me, as all do who measure themselves by class. One of the benefits of being born and raised in Termina is a healthy disrespect for the accoutrements of the elven caste system beloved by the rest of our dying kingdom.

There was a flicker in her eyes as she recognized me. "Vara?" she said. "You're Vara!"

"I'll thank you to keep your voice down," I ordered. Funny image: me, a Terminan ordering a highborn elf to shut her mouth. She did. I looked around, a bit embarrassed at being recognized. I could tell by Orion's reaction that Selene had told him about me; he was utterly unsurprised.

"Where are you planning to attack?" Niamh intervened.

The elf's chin jutted out. "We're planning an assault on the den of Ashan'agar, the former dragon king. There will be much in the way of treasure..." She prattled on and on for several more minutes, but when Orion offered her counsel on defeating the Dragonlord, her ears were suddenly deaf to even my entreaties.

I eyed her army as she walked away after we had told her we were uninterested. There were a large number of them, many fresh faced and innocent looking. As an emotion, I find pity most annoying; you cannot feel pity for someone who is at the same level as you. It requires you to look down on someone and consider yourself their superior in some way. I felt a great swell of pity for that army of hers. The odds were against them in their experience, in their leader – they seemed destined to die.

I caught a glimpse of a warrior, clad in black armor, across the mass of people. I hate human warriors. I find their arrogance to be nearly unmatched – in fact, only by my own. This human, however... there was something so familiar about him. He reminded me so of... you know who. I tried to look closer, but I couldn't. Not without stalking up to him in the middle of Reikonos Square and grabbing his face so I could examine it.

It was for he I felt the greatest pity. I am young, but as an elf, I will look young when that warrior turns one hundred. He was young in appearance and fact. He was familiar to me in a way I can't describe. Call it elven intution but I knew that I had to save his life.

"I cannot abide such a waste," I said under my breath.

"It's a shame," Niamh said. "They'll all be dead soon enough."

"We have things to accomplish today," Orion said.

"We should go along and save all we can when things go awry," I said. It was not one of my better ideas. If you had asked me in that moment why I was suggesting this, I could not have defined it for you. If you had picked that warrior out of his group of friends, dragged him over to me and forced me to explain exactly, precisely, what it was about him that was causing me to (somewhat uncharacteristically, even for a crusader) lead my party into gravest danger against such odds, I could not have told you in that moment why.

"Are you mad?" Orion said, amazed. "This is certain death! Even a noble paladin must recognize such a hopeless cause."

"I recognize no cause as hopeless," I said, surprised to find it true. Perhaps I was not as cynical as I believed.

"They will die and they will take us with them," Orion said. Selene stood at his shoulder, expression neutral. "That interferes with my other plans for today."

"Niamh can stand ready to teleport us out when things go wrong." I exhaled, annoyed at having to convince this tree herding so-called officer of Sanctuary to behave with honor. "We can save at least some of them."

"No." Orion shook his head. "We're a group and I say we vote – and I vote nay."

Niamh looked at him. "I vote we go. This is our purpose in Sanctuary, remember? We help those who can't help themselves, and I don't think I've seen a more obvious group in that department."

"I think it's obvious I vote yes," I said. All of us turned to Selene, who had frozen in place. Her expression was peaceful, but her eyes were closed in deep contemplation. After a moment, she spoke.

"We follow shelas'akur," Selene whispered. Orion's face fell, but he gritted his teeth and came along.

When we reached the depths of the cave, Orion introduced himself to several people, trying to make inroads to save us time when the moment came that we had to take over to save their lives. When he began a conversation with the warrior, I was in a position to look at him, observe him. I fear I might have stared a bit too much, however.

He really did look a bit like... you know.

In battle, he was brave. I'm not reticent about fighting, but the warrior killed a rock giant singlehandedly through brilliant positioning. He's a bit more action than brains, and I let him know that, but in truth... he is strong and skilled. He fought the Dragonlord from underneath with me and survived. More than that, he somehow resisted the Dragonlord's coercion spell, his hypnosis. I had been told that it never failed against our races, that if you looked into the eyes of Ashan'agar, he would own you down to your very soul, forever.

The warrior not only shrugged off the coercion – he struck the Dragonlord's eye from his body. Impressive. I have no idea how he managed to avoid becoming a slave to Ashan'agar's will.

Naturally, I did not let the warrior know I found any of this impressive in the least. When it comes to a warrior such as this, too much reckless confidence can lead to quick death. Orion began to fawn over this warrior, Cyrus, begging him to join Sanctuary. I, on the other, was much more reserved in my reaction. I suspect he may even have found me to be a bit cold.

If only he knew.

Cyrus looked up from the journal. The script was beautiful, flowing. He flipped ahead, finding a passage of great interest, and stopped to read.

Alaric gauged my reaction carefully. "If you say there is something... special about this warrior, I believe you."

"There is," I said. "He is... he reminds me of... but he's not the same as..." My voice trailed off. My thoughts were chaotic, annoying. My mind was so firmly under my control until he showed up on that damned dragon expedition. "He somehow broke through Ashan'agar's mind control."

Alaric's reaction was immediate. "How?" the Ghost demanded.

My eyes fell in embarrassment. "I don't know."

He leaned forward, hands crossed in front of him on the table in the Council Chambers. "Very interesting. I confess, I had met one other with that particular strength, but that was..." a smile crossed his face, "...long ago." He stood. "Very well. This warrior bears watching, then."

Cyrus frowned and looked up from the journal. The skies had begun to darken, lengthening the shadows in the room. The fireplace sprung to light, followed by the mystical torches, one by one around the room. With a smile of appreciation, Cyrus continued his reading by the firelight. He skimmed until another passage caught his eye.

"He's going to die!" I shouted at Alaric. The innkeeper in Nalikh'akur was a man of great discretion, and had shown me the utmost respect since our arrival, having known I was shelas'akur on sight. I heard the back door open and shut as he left me to my conflict with my Guildmaster. "He's going to die right here in this inn, and there's not a damn thing any of us can do about it!"

"This one has great strength: I doubt a simple fever will claim him." Alaric studied me, his eye fixed on mine.

"While I will agree he is easily as stubborn as twelve mules, that does not make him immune to the laws of nature, Alaric."

Alaric eyed me carefully. "Your conduct toward this warrior is most bizarre, my friend. You spar, you attack, you remonstrate and verbally eviscerate the man, yet in private you defend his conduct, his character and praise him with words that, were they to come out in public, would make you blush." He folded his arms. "I am quite used to defending you for your verbal tirades but I am quite unused to you being less than candid with someone in this way."

I looked down, unable to meet his gaze. "I... my history, as you know, is somewhat complicated."

A nod. "I know."

"I cannot... explain what it is about him," I said, searching for the words.

A twinkle filled the old paladin's eye. "I believe I could find a word, if pressed into choosing one."

"Oh, shut up," I told him, a bit cross.

"You will continue to attend him?" Alaric gazed at me with that eye that bored into my very soul.

"Until he's fully recovered," I agreed without hesitation.

The Ghost pursed his lips as he pondered his next words. "I will send Curatio to aid you as soon as I can spare him." His hand came up to forestall the protest already making its way to my lips. "He is a healer. He can help. Cyrus's life is at stake."

I nodded in surrender.

Alaric turned to leave, placing his helm back on his head. As he turned to go, he paused and looked back at me. "I offer you this final piece of advice in the spirit of our longstanding friendship. Since the day we have met, I have had nothing but the utmost respect and affection for you..."

I blinked, not quite sure what to say.

"I tell you this now: however you feel about this man, know that the *way you are treating him is driving him down the road of hating you." I bit my lip. "You cannot spew the venom that you do and then be sweet and kind behind his back and expect to have any sort of relationship – friendship or otherwise." The Ghost's eye narrowed. "If you ever mean to be closer to him than you are, you must stop," he sighed, "or at least try to cut back – on the biting repartee." He left without another word.*

I hate crying. And yet, after he left, I sat in the chair next to Cyrus and wept for the next three hours, staring at the warrior the whole time.

Cyrus blinked in astonishment as he pictured Alaric and Vara sparring at the inn in Nalikh'akur. Flipping a few more pages he found an entry that looked as though it had water spilled on it, then dried. Streaks had caused the ink to run.

I am actually crying as I write this. Damn the man. Damn him for scaring the hell out of me. When he vanished out of sight on the back of the Dragonlord, Vaste and I scanned the sky continuously. I confess, with great difficulty, that I was worried.

A small speck caught my eye first. "Over there!" I shouted as it grew in size. I realized it was the Dragonlord spiraling to the ground. "My gods, he's actually done it," I breathed.

"It would appear there's more to our warrior friend than meets the eye," Vaste said.

"Or less," I said without any conviction. "It could be less," I said in reaction to Vaste's look. He didn't believe me. Hell, I didn't believe me. I took off toward the nearest peak, crossing hills for a closer look as the dragon continued to plummet. The descent slowed at the end but a tremendous crash could be heard throughout the mountains.

As soon as the impact was assured, I began an immediate descent of the slope in the direction of the sound, panic filling my senses. It took long minutes over the uneven ground of the Mountains of Nartanis, as well as much grumbling from Vaste ("Couldn't we have just fought the dragon on the Plains of Perdamun?") before we reached the site of the Dragonlord's landing.

When I crested the last hill, my breath caught in my chest. Ashan'agar was stretched on his belly across the small valley, one wing ripped from his body and the other twisted at a sickening angle. The Dragonlord was breathing, a sad, rattling sound, and both his eyes were now missing. Without thought to my own safety, I ran down the hill, tripping several times and cutting my hand on one boulder.

I reached the dragon, who had moved only slightly since I had started my descent. Forgetting myself and that I had no weapon, I ran to the

Dragonlord's neck. "Where is he?" I asked, only then remembering I had no sword.

"Dead," came a rattling pronouncement from the blinded Dragonlord. "I am triumphant."

"Triumphant? You are blinded and dying!" I spat at him. Rage filled me. "Know this, Dragonlord: you were bested by a human warrior who fought you without assistance from any other. If that is your version of triumph then I would hate to be defeated under your definition."

"I am not dead yet," Ashan'agar rumbled. "And I am free. I have tasted the sky once more."

"If I had my sword, I would kill you now," I said, fury shaking my hands.

"For him?" the dragon needled.

"I would kill you for my own account."

The dragon's jaws snapped together and his head twisted toward me. Bones cracked as he moved. "Step closer; I will reunite you with your lover."

"He's not my..." My voice trailed off. "...lover," I finished, inflection flat.

"He's over here," Vaste said from behind me.

I abandoned my conversation with the dragon and ran toward the troll, who stood above Cyrus's shattered body.

"No no no no no." I hit my knees by his side, grasping at him. I tore the helmet from his head and flung it aside, lifting his face to mine. I pressed my forehead to his, clutching him tightly, praying that the breath of life would be on his lips. He hung limp in my arms, tears falling from my eyes and splattering on the fallen warrior's face.

"Would you like to compose yourself first or should I revive him now?" Vaste asked with a slight smile crooking his green face. I must confess, in my anguish I had quite forgotten about the resurrection spell. Seeing him lying there, I had only the thought that he might never speak again, that I might never argue with him... or tell him... I can't even say it. I can't even write it.

I sniffed and ran my hand across my eyes, dislodging the tears resting there. "Yes," I said. "Please, do revive him." I stood and dusted the ash and dirt from my greaves as the magical effect touched him and his pale skin flushed with the breath of life.

Cyrus blinked. He had known Vara for a long time, and to read her innermost thoughts was almost disconcerting. It did not fit well with his memories of the events in question; he had always ascribed her motives to hating him somewhere deep inside. To find it might not be true... he stroked the paper and closed the book, listening to the quiet shuffle of the pages brushing against each other. He set it aside and stood up, walking to the window.

Recalling the certainty he'd felt in that first year in Sanctuary, that strength of purpose, gave him pause. The feeling of confidence reached across the years and touched him where he stood, in the wreckage of this place he had called home, although it no longer had the power it once did. A tear ran down the warrior's cheek at the memory of all that had been lost in the interceding years.

Out on the plains, the wind continued to whip under the gray skies and that same feeling came once more, the uncertain mixture of fear and regret, and the warrior in black looked across the horizon in hopes that soon – very soon – that feeling would be gone.

A Note to the Reader

I wanted to take a moment to thank you for reading this story. As an independent author, getting my name out to build an audience is one of the biggest priorities on any given day. If you enjoyed this story and are looking forward to reading more, let someone know - post it on Amazon, on your blog, if you have one, on Goodreads.com, place it in a quick Facebook status or Tweet with a link to the page of whatever outlet you purchased it from (Amazon, Barnes & Noble, Apple, etc). Good reviews inspire people to take a chance on a new author – like me. And we new authors can use all the help we can get.

Thanks again for your time.

Robert J. Crane

About the Author

Robert J. Crane was born and raised on Florida's Space Coast before moving to the upper midwest in search of cooler climates and more palatable beer. He graduated from the University of Central Florida with a degree in English Creative Writing. He worked for a year as a substitute teacher and worked in the financial services field for seven years while writing in his spare time. He makes his home in the Twin Cities area of Minnesota.

He can be contacted in several ways:

Via email at cyrusdavidon@gmail.com
Follow him on Twitter - **@robertJcrane**
Connect on Facebook **– robertJcrane (Author)**
Website **– robertJcrane.com**
Blog – robertJcrane.blogspot.com
Become a fan on Goodreads –
http://www.goodreads.com/RobertJCrane

The Sanctuary Series
Epic Fantasy by Robert J. Crane

The world of Arkaria is a dangerous place, filled with dragons, titans, goblins and other dangers. Those who live in this world are faced with two choices: live an ordinary life or become an adventurer and seek the extraordinary.

Avenger
The Sanctuary Series, Volume Two

When a series of attacks on convoys draws suspicion that Sanctuary is involved, Cyrus Davidon must put aside his personal struggles and try to find the raiders. As the attacks worsen, Cyrus and his comrades find themselves abandoned by their allies, surrounded by enemies, facing the end of Sanctuary and a war that will consume their world.

Available Now!

Champion
The Sanctuary Series, Volume Three

As the war heats up in Arkaria, Vara is forced to flee after an ancient order of skilled assassins infiltrates Sanctuary and targets her. Cyrus Davidon accompanies her home to the elven city of Termina and the two of them become embroiled in a mystery that will shake the very foundations of the Elven Kingdom – and Arkaria.

Available Now!

Crusader
The Sanctuary Series, Volume Four

Cyrus Davidon finds himself far from his home in Sanctuary, in the land of Luukessia, a place divided and deep in turmoil. With his allies at his side, Cyrus finds himself facing off against an implacable foe in a war that will challenge all his convictions - and one he may not be able to win.

Coming Fall 2012!

Savages
A Sanctuary Short Story

Twenty years before Cyrus Davidon joined Sanctuary, his father was killed in a war with the trolls and he has never forgiven them. Enter Vaste, a troll unlike most; courageous, loyal and an outcast. When Cyrus and Vaste become trapped in a far distant land, they are forced to overcome their suspicions and work together to get home.

Available Now!

A Familiar Face
A Sanctuary Short Story

Cyrus Davidon gets more than he bargained for when he takes a day away from Sanctuary to visit the busy markets of his hometown, Reikonos. While there, he meets a woman who seems very familiar, and appears to know him, but that he can't place.

Available Now!

Alone
The Girl in the Box, Book 1

Sienna Nealon was a 17-year-old girl who had been held prisoner in her own house by her mother for twelve years. Then one day her mother vanished, and Sienna woke up to find two strange men in her home. On the run, unsure of who to turn to and discovering she possesses mysterious powers, Sienna finds herself pursued by a shadowy agency known as the Directorate and hunted by a vicious, bloodthirsty psychopath named Wolfe, each of which is determined to capture her for their own purposes...

Available Now!

Untouched
The Girl in the Box, Book 2

Still haunted by her last encounter with Wolfe and searching for her mother, Sienna Nealon must put aside her personal struggles when a new threat emerges – Aleksandr Gavrikov, a metahuman so powerful, he could destroy entire cities – and he's focused on bringing the Directorate to its knees.

Coming Summer 2012!

Soulless
The Girl in the Box, Book 3

Coming Summer 2012!

Printed in Great Britain
by Amazon.co.uk, Ltd.,
Marston Gate.